THE SPECIAL MAGIC OF
VALENTINE
FIVE HIGH
AUTHORS OF LOVE

MARY BALOGH won the *Romantic Times* award for Best New Regency Writer and its Reviewers' Choice award for Best Regency Author in 1985 and 1989. She lives in Kipling, Saskatchewan, Canada. Her latest book is *A Christmas Promise*.

SANDRA HEATH, author of *A Country Cotillion*, is one of Signet's most talented writers and the author of the highly popular *A Christmas Courtship*. She lives with her husband and daughter in Gloucester, England.

CAROL PROCTOR was nominated for the *Romantic Times* Best New Regency Author award in 1990. She resides in Fort Worth, Texas. Carol's most recent book is *Theodora's Dreadful Mistake*.

SHEILA WALSH, whose latest novel is *The Arrogant Lord Alistair*, lives with her husband in Southport, Lancashire, England, and is the mother of two daughters. After experimenting with short stories and plays, she completed her first Regency novel, *The Golden Songbird*, which won her an award from the Romantic Novelists' Association in 1974.

MARGARET WESTHAVEN is the author of fourteen Regency novels. She lives in Oregon with her husband and young son. Her most recent novel is *Four in Hand*.

New from the bestselling, award-winning author of
Silk and Secrets and *Silk and Shadows*

VEILS OF SILK
Mary Jo Putney

Golden-eyed Laura offers hope for a new life to Ian after years of captivity in Central Asia have shattered this army major's dreams. Ian, in turn, offers Laura a marriage proposal she dares to say yes to.

From India's lush plains to its wild mountain passes, they struggle to build a marriage unlike any other. Yet the danger and intrigue that surround them are less perilous than the veiled secrets of their own hearts—for only indomitable courage and unshakable love will free them to claim the fiery passion they both fear . . . and desire.

TOKENS OF LOVE

Five Regency Love Stories

by

Mary Balogh

Sandra Heath

Carol Proctor

Sheila Walsh

Margaret Westhaven

Ø

A SIGNET BOOK

SIGNET
Published by the Penguin Group
Penguin Books USA Inc., 375 Hudson Street,
New York, New York 10014, U.S.A.
Penguin Books Ltd, 27 Wrights Lane,
London W8 5TZ, England
Penguin Books Australia Ltd, Ringwood,
Victoria, Australia
Penguin Books Canada Ltd, 10 Alcorn Avenue,
Toronto, Ontario, Canada M4V 3B2
Penguin Books (N.Z.) Ltd, 182–190 Wairau Road,
Auckland 10, New Zealand

Penguin Books Ltd, Registered Offices:
Harmondsworth, Middlesex, England

First published by Signet, an imprint of New American Library,
a division of Penguin Books USA Inc.

First Printing, January, 1993
10　9　8　7　6　5　4　3　2　1

Contents

The Substitute Guest

by Mary Balogh

LADY FLORENCE CARVER set the letter down beside her plate and frowned at the toast rack, which was standing inoffensively in the middle of the breakfast table. If she could just get her hands about Hetty's neck at this precise moment, she thought, she would happily squeeze. Drat the woman! Though she herself was most to blame, she supposed. She might have guessed that Hetty would develop one of her frequent ailments at the last moment and cry off from the house party she had agreed to attend.

Hetty's defection meant that only ten guests would arrive on the morrow, six gentlemen and four ladies, five counting Lady Florence—a disgusting and quite impossible imbalance of numbers.

Tomorrow! There was no point in frantically scouring her mind for another lady to invite, Lady Florence thought, though she found herself doing just that. It was far too late. Everyone was arriving the next day. St. Valentine's Day was only four days off. Even if someone could be invited in a hurry and could arrive in time for the day of the festival, it would be too late. For St. Valentine's Day was to be merely the culmination of the events she had planned.

Lady Florence picked up the letter and crumpled it viciously in her right hand, winning for herself a nervous glance from her butler. Damn Hetty! She hoped the woman really had the migraines this time and was not merely imagining them as she usually did.

What could she do? Lady Florence drew a deep breath and forced her mind to calmness. This was no time to give in to the vapors. Stop one of the gentlemen from coming? Tell him that she had been forced to cancel the party for some reason? Percy Mullins lived only twelve miles away. But of course he would find out soon enough that she had lied to him. And Percy had a nasty gossiping tongue and would spread the word far and wide. No, she could not do that.

What about ladies within ten or twelve miles? Were there any worthy of the rest of the company she had invited? Any that would accept an invitation from her on such short notice? Any of suitable age and character? She immediately thought of Susan Dover, elder daughter of Sir Hector Dover. But Sir Hector and his wife would never allow it. Besides, the girl was probably no more than twenty.

There was Claire Ward, of course. She was the right age—she must be very much closer to thirty than to twenty, and her eldest brother, though a commoner, had a considerable estate and fortune. She lived with him and his family no more than eight miles away. But Miss Ward was a confirmed spinster and a prude. She would not do at all.

And then there was . . . There had to be someone, Lady Florence thought, her mind a blank. Ah, there was Edna Johnson, a widow like herself and amiable enough. But Mrs. Johnson, she remembered now as she thought about it, was in the north of England visiting relatives of her late husband.

Well, she thought ten minutes later, having wandered through to the morning room from the breakfast room and stared out on a damp and gloomy morning, there was no one. No one at all. And everything was going to be ruined. Everything that she had so carefully planned in order to bring herself some amusement after a winter of nothing but dullness. London had been dull without the crowds that the spring Season would bring, and Christmas at the Byngs had been insipid.

It was going to be worse than ruined, in fact. It was going to be a total disaster. How did one entertain six gentlemen and five ladies—including oneself—for a Valentine's party? Assign two gentlemen to one of the ladies? The idea had interesting possibilities, but would probably be far more appealing to the fortunate lady than to either of the two gentlemen.

She rapped her fingernails impatiently on the windowsill. She was going to have to try Miss Ward. The woman would stick out in the company rather like a sore thumb, and some poor gentleman would doubtless return home less than satisfied after the party was over. And the chances were strong that Miss Ward would refuse the invitation. Very strong. But there really was no alternative. She must be tried.

Lady Florence crossed the room to the escritoire and looked down at the blank sheets of paper and the quill pen and inkwell set out there fresh that morning as they were each day. It was going to have to be a very carefully worded invitation if it was to be accepted. How did one persuade a prudish spinster to attend a house party at the home of a wealthy widow who had acquired something of a reputation for wildness since the demise of her husband two years before?

She seated herself and tested the nib of the pen with one finger. Well, the words would have to be found somehow. She dipped the pen in the inkwell with more confidence than she felt.

She might have decided differently, Claire Ward thought later that evening as she puzzled over what clothes and other belongings should be packed inside the empty trunk open on the floor of her dressing room, if only the Reverend Clarkwell had not been visiting when the invitation arrived. In fact, without a doubt she would have decided differently. But he had been and she had not and there was an end of the matter.

Should she pack any of her lace caps? she wondered, and she glanced into the looking glass at the one she wore on her smooth brown hair. She looked like a plain and placid spinster—which was exactly what she was. No, she thought, caps would doubtless be inappropriate at a house party. She would leave them at home. Truth to tell, she did not know what was appropriate for a house party, the only ones she had attended having been family affairs, for Christmas or birthdays or christenings. This was to be a party of strangers—"a select group of the most prominent and respected members of society," as Lady Florence Carver had phrased it in her letter.

Why had she been invited? Claire wondered as she had wondered when the invitation arrived soon after luncheon. But the answer was as obvious now as it had been then. Someone had let Lady Florence down and she had had to make up numbers at a moment's notice. There could be no other possible reason.

She really ought not to have accepted the invitation. She had had no inclination to do so even at the start. Had she been alone when it had arrived, there would have been no decision to make. She would simply have penned a polite refusal and sent Lady Florence's messenger on his way. But she had not been alone. And when Myrtle, her sister-in-law, had asked her what the unexpected letter was all about, she had answered truthfully.

"Lady Florence Carver?" Myrtle had said, her usual breathless little-girl voice sounding shocked. "Oh, Claire, love, she is very fast." And she had colored up as if she had just used one of the worst obscenities one of the stablehands might have uttered.

"Her guests are to be a select group," Claire had said. "The most prominent and respected members of society." But neither Myrtle nor the Reverend Clarkwell had recognized the gleam of amusement in her eyes as Roderick, her brother, would have done.

"I do believe, my dear Miss Ward," the vicar had said, "if you will excuse me for voicing my opinion, which I make bold to do only because I am your pastor and you one of my flock, my dear ma'am. I do believe that for the sake of propriety and your reputation you should return the most formal of refusals. I only lament the fact that Lady Florence is one of the lost sheep of my flock and that any kindly words to point out the error of her ways would only fall on dry ground."

"They cannot be respectable, Claire, if they are to be Lady Florence's guests," Myrtle had said. "Indeed, I do believe it is an insult that she has invited you, and I am sure that Roderick will agree. I wonder why she did so. But of course, you will take the Reverend Clarkwell's advice. Indeed, love, we will excuse you now so that you may write your reply immediately. I believe you may mention that Roderick disapproves of such country parties."

"May I?" Claire had asked. "Without his permission, Myrtle?"

"It is quite seemly, my dear Miss Ward," the vicar had said, "for a dutiful sister and wife to use the name of the gentleman of the house in his absence under such circumstances, especially when they have the advice of a sincere man of the cloth such as myself, if I may so call myself without losing my humility."

"It is settled, then," Myrtle had said, looking and sounding relieved.

"Is it?" Claire had tapped the invitation against one palm. "I am rather inclined to accept. I am curious to know what such a party will be like and who the select and respected members of society are."

Myrtle had had to ask the Reverend Clarkwell to ring for her maid so that her vinaigrette might be

brought to revive her. And that gentleman had
launched into a speech that almost rivaled one of his
Sunday sermons for length and moral rectitude and
dullness.

And so she had accepted her invitation, Claire
thought with a sigh, drawing her best blue silk out of
the wardrobe and trying to remember when was the
last time she had worn it. How could she have re-
sisted? And if the truth were known, she had really
felt that twinge of curiosity she had pretended to.
What *did* happen at such parties? What were such
people like? What sort of people associated with the
widow of a baron and daughter of an earl, a woman
who was known as "fast"?

Her life had been so bounded by respectability and
duty, Claire thought. And it was not an exciting life,
she had to admit. Those people who had assured her
during the years she had devoted to her ailing father
when she might have been getting married and starting
a family that she would one day receive her reward
had been merely mouthing platitudes. The truth was
that she had been left on the shelf and that being
forced to live with a brother and sister-in-law and their
two children, however kind and affectionate they were
to her, was nothing like any reward she might have
imagined.

She was twenty-eight years old and had never done
anything remotely out of the ordinary or exciting. Perhaps after all it was a good thing that the pomposity
of the vicar and the timidity of her sister-in-law had
tempted her into being rash for once in her life.

She was to spend four nights at Carver Hall and
three and a half days. With total strangers. Even with
Lady Florence herself she had only a nodding
acquaintance. Oh, dear, Claire thought, her hand still-
ing on her russet velvet riding habit, what had she
done? Twenty-eight seemed a very advanced age at
which to decide to be impetuous and adventurous.

But there was nothing much she could do about it now. She dragged the habit from its hanger. She had already weathered the vicar's lengthy sermon and Myrtle's vapors and Roderick's frowns. It would be just too anticlimactic if she were to change her mind now. Besides, she had written an acceptance of the invitation.

"An adult party," the Duke of Langford said, following his hostess upstairs to the room that had been allotted as his bedchamber. Lady Florence Carver would not do anything as formal and proper as having one of her servants show him there. "The emphasis you put on the word *adult*, Florence, would suggest that you mean more than that we need not expect nursery infants to be chasing between our legs."

"There is not a guest below the age of six-and-twenty," she said, leading the way into a large, square chamber and crossing the room to throw back the heavy curtains a little wider. "And not one who does not know a thing or two about life, Gerard."

"Interesting," he said, his hand toying with the ribbon of his quizzing glass, though he did not raise it to his eye. Lady Florence had crossed to the bed and was fussing with the bedhangings, though they were already looped back quite firmly.

"I can recall your saying just this past winter," she said, "that you were bored with all the sweet young things fresh every year on the marriage market. Your very words, I believe, Gerard."

"Oh, very probably," he agreed. "Not that I have any quarrel with sweet young things as such, Florence, but only with their eagerness despite everything—or more accurately, the eagerness of their mamas—to believe that I am shopping."

"Then I believe that this will be just your kind of party," Lady Florence said, sitting on the edge of the bed and smiling at him. "And it is a Valentine's party,

Gerard. Did I mention that? It is a party for love and merriment and—love." She smiled archly at him.

"Intriguing," he said. "Depending, I suppose, on the guest list?" He lifted his eyebrows and ignored the invitation of her hand, which was patting the bed beside her as if unconsciously.

"Lady Pollard is coming," she said. "Mildred always livens any party. And Frances Tate. Her husband is busy as always at the Foreign Office. She finds life in town quite tedious. And Lucy Sterns and Olga Garnett. Oh, and Claire Ward."

The duke pursed his lips. "And yourself, Florence," he said. "An interesting guest list. Who is Claire Ward?"

"A neighbor," she said. "Hetty let me down at the very last minute, the tiresome woman. The migraines again. I invited Miss Ward to take her place."

"Ah," he said, strolling to the window and glancing out at the park that stretched to the front of the house, "your tone is dismissive, Florence. I gather Miss Ward is the weak link in this chain of delight that you have forged for yourself and your guests."

"No matter," she said. "Tomorrow I will have everyone paired, Gerard. An old Valentine's game, you know. I shall see that she is paired with Percy Mullins. I was obliged to invite him because he considers himself a neighbor and would have pouted for a year if I had omitted him from my guest list and would have gossiped viciously about me at the gentlemen's clubs for five." She got up from the bed and strolled toward him. "I shall leave you to freshen up if you do not need me," she said, setting a hand on his arm.

"Everything seems to be in perfect readiness," the duke said, turning from the window and surveying the room through his quizzing glass. "No, I think I have no further need of you for the present, Florence. And doubtless your other guests are beginning to spill downstairs. I was not the first arrival, you said?"

Left alone a short time later, he lowered his glass and looked about the room again. An adult party. A guest list that included two widows, a married lady whose infidelities to her husband were an open secret, and two unmarried ladies who had one foot each in the demimonde and one in the world of respectability. He had not asked about the other male guests.

And a Valentine's party. One intended for love and—love, according to Florence. He did not doubt that she would ensure that it was just that, though perhaps love was a euphemism for what she really had in mind.

Well. He shrugged. It might be interesting. All five of the ladies with whom he was acquainted would make amusing companions for three days. Probably a good deal more than amusing too. As for Miss Claire Ward . . . He shrugged again. Florence seemed to have everything organized so that he would not have to concern himself with the substitute guest.

He wandered through to the adjoining dressing room, where his valet had already laid out a change of clothes for him. Steam was rising from the water in the basin on the washstand.

Let the party begin, the duke thought.

One thing at least she could feel relieved about, Claire thought at dinner that evening. She was not to be the grandmother of the gathering, as she had rather feared—though, of course, she had known that Lady Florence was older than she. Indeed, it was quite possible, Claire thought, that she was the youngest guest present. It was good to know that she was not going to feel uncomfortably elderly.

There was little else to be relieved about. Everyone else was acquainted. Only she knew no one. And though Lady Florence was graciously condescending and a few of the other guests courteous, she felt uncomfortable. They all talked about London and common acquaintances and appeared to derive a great deal of amusement out of being nasty about the latter.

She wondered if the three remaining days would creep past at snail's pace and if she would soon regret more than she already did that the Reverend Clarkwell's visit had coincided with the arrival of Lady Florence's invitation.

"Ladies," Lady Florence said, rising from her place and smiling about the table, "shall we leave the gentlemen to their port? Make the most of it, gentlemen. This will be the only evening we will allow you such an indulgence."

While the other ladies laughed and some of the gentlemen protested, Claire got hastily to her feet and followed her hostess from the room. She should have worn her best blue silk, she thought, looking at the very fashionable gowns worn by the other ladies and aware that her own must look almost shabby in contrast. But then if she had worn it tonight, she would have had nothing suitable to wear for the Valentine's party Lady Florence had planned for the final evening.

"Do let us have some music," Lady Florence said, wafting a careless hand in the direction of the pianoforte in a far corner of the drawing room. "Who plays? Lucy?"

"Not since my come-out year when it was obligatory to play and sing in order to impress the gentlemen," Miss Sterns said with a laugh. "Not me, Florence."

It seemed that the other ladies had similar objections to playing.

"Miss Ward," Lady Florence said, "you play. I am quite sure you do, being a lady who has cultivated all the country virtues. Do play for us."

"Yes, do, Miss Ward," Lady Pollard said, smiling charmingly.

And yet when Claire obliged and seated herself at the pianoforte, no one paid either her or her music the slightest heed until she finished her piece and rose to her feet. Then the ladies interrupted their gossiping about the fire.

"That was quite divine, Miss Ward," Miss Garnett said.

"Oh, do play on, Miss Ward," Lady Florence urged her. "You have a quite superior touch."

Claire played on, smiling inwardly as the ladies resumed their conversation. She did not mind playing or being ignored. Indeed, she felt far more comfortable where she was, especially after the gentlemen came in from the dining room. And safer. She was a little overawed by the presence of so many strangers and despised herself for being so. One of the gentlemen was even a duke—the Duke of Langford.

Why she should feel suddenly fearful of playing a wrong note just because she had remembered that there was a duke present in the room she did not know. He was no more human than she, she told herself firmly. Besides, no one was listening to her music and so there was no reason for nervousness.

And yet when she glanced up and across the room to assure herself that in truth she was being ignored, it was to find herself looking straight across into the dark, hooded eyes of his grace. Claire looked down hastily and indeed played a wrong note. She grimaced and played on.

She rather thought that the man might make her nervous even without the exalted title. But then perhaps it was the title that gave him his remote, haughty air. His dark good looks merely enhanced it—though the silver hair at his temples proclaimed him to be a man well past the first flush of youth. He regarded the world from lazy dark eyes and occasionally from a quizzing glass. Claire suddenly had a panicked feeling and looked up to find the quizzing glass trained on her. She played on, unaware of whether her fingers had faltered again or not.

He had not spoken a great deal either at tea or at

dinner. And yet he was clearly a favorite with all the ladies. And they made no secret of the fact, something that had rather shocked Claire. She had lived such a sheltered life, she realized. She knew nothing about the manners of polite society.

"Miss Ward." Lady Florence's voice stopped Claire's hands on the keyboard. "Of course you must join us before I tell everyone what is planned for this Valentine's party. I was so enjoying your music that I almost forgot to call you over until Gerard reminded me."

Claire was not sure which of the gentlemen was Gerard. But she felt instant regret after all that she had been persuaded to play the pianoforte. All eyes watched her as she rose from the stool and crossed the room to take an empty chair close to the fire. She felt like a gauche girl, she thought in some annoyance, her movements jerky and self-conscious.

Lady Florence stood before the fire, looking as if she was thoroughly enjoying herself. Her red silk evening gown complemented the color in her cheeks. Claire looked at the latter in some fascination. Was the color natural?

"Tomorrow morning," their hostess said, "we are going to observe the custom of the gentlemen drawing lots for valentines."

"Two days early, Florence?" Lord Mingay asked.

"Why wait?" she said. "I have six identical valentines ready. Tomorrow each lady will write her name on the front of one and place it facedown on a table. Each gentleman will pick one, add his name to the lady's, pin it to her bosom, and take her for his valentine for what remains of the party."

Claire's cheeks felt as if they were on fire. She must be sitting too close to the heat.

"I say," Mr. Tucker said, looking about him. "A random choice, Florence? The whole thing is to be left to chance? No cheating?"

"Now, why do you ask, Rufus?" Lady Pollard

asked, rapping him sharply on the knuckles with her fan. "Are there any of us ladies whom you would hope to avoid?"

"Or anyone you particularly favor, Rufus?" Miss Garnett asked.

Rufus Tucker looked about slowly at the ladies. "Not I," he said. "No to both questions. So after tomorrow morning, Florence, we are to be in couples?"

"What a splendid idea, Florence," Mrs. Tate said. "For three whole days we will each have the undivided attention of a gentleman? What a treat that will be."

"I have plenty of activities planned to keep everyone entertained for three days," Lady Florence said.

"Oh, bother," Lucy Sterns said with a laugh.

Lady Florence held up one hand. "With plenty of opportunity for private tête-à-têtes," she added.

"Ah, this is better," Lucy Sterns said.

Sir Charles Horsefield seated himself on the arm of Lady Pollard's chair. "Your servants are like to benefit too, Florence," he said. "Six fewer beds to make up each morning after tonight."

"Charles, you naughty man," Lady Pollard said, slapping him on the knee while there was general laughter from the rest of the company. "You are quite putting me to the blush."

"Then I am doing something no one else has accomplished these ten years past, Mildred," he said, and there was another general burst of laughter while she shrieked again.

In addition to being too close to the heat, Claire thought, she was too far away from the door. Too far away from air. She was having difficulty breathing. Could she possibly be misunderstanding what she was hearing? But of course she must be. Everyone was laughing and in the best of good humor. They were joking. The jokes were in the poorest of taste by her standards, but she knew nothing of London standards. The truth was that Lady Florence had tried to orga-

nize a party that would be romantic in the true spirit
of St. Valentine's Day, and her friends were making
lighthearted fun of her plans.

And yet, Claire thought, it would be unutterably
embarrassing. Tomorrow morning she would be chosen to be one of these gentlemen's valentine for three
whole days. One of the gentlemen was going to find
himself with a dreadfully dull companion. She was
quite out of her depth in this company. She did not
know how to laugh and talk wittily as these people
did. Which gentleman would it be? she wondered. Her
heart was racing and she felt more breathless than
ever. And she did not know if the cause was panic or
excitement.

She glanced up at the Duke of Langford, who was
still standing and lounging against one corner of the
mantel. He was looking back at her from those heavy-
lidded eyes and idly swinging his quizzing glass on its
ribbon. Claire licked her lips and looked back down
again.

"But how annoying of you to make us wait until
tomorrow morning, Florence," Mrs. Tate was saying.
"How are we to sleep tonight? This is almost like
being a child at Christmastime again."

"Ah, but, Frances," Mr. Shrimpton said, winking,
"Florence is kindly giving us the chance to have one
last good night's sleep."

There was that general laughter again, but Claire
found herself as unable to join in as she had before.
There could be no mistaking Mr. Shrimpton's meaning. But surely he must be merely joking. Oh, surely.
Lady Florence Carver had a reputation for fastness.
Claire knew that. But surely being fast did not mean
being quite so unprincipled. Surely it meant just this—
talking in rather a vulgar and suggestive manner.

Claire wondered as everyone stirred when the door
opened to admit two servants with the tea tray
whether it would be possible to return home the fol-

lowing morning. It would mean sending for Roderick's carriage, which was not supposed to come for her until the fifteenth. It would not arrive until the afternoon even if she sent early.

But she would not go, she knew. She would not be able to bear having Roderick and Myrtle—and doubtless the Reverend Clarkwell too—tell her that they had told her so. Besides, she was curious. More curious now than she had been before she came. Curious about this totally different world that she seemed to have landed in at the grand age of twenty-eight. And a little excited too. Yes, she had to admit it, however reluctantly.

She had never been anyone's valentine. Certainly not for three whole days.

The Duke of Langford had had the advantage of the other guests, if advantage it were. Lady Florence had divulged a part of her plan to him on his arrival. He had known that on the morrow she and her guests were to be paired. It would be interesting, he had thought at the time. A companion and a bed partner for a few days without any effort on his part either to entice or to hold at bay. February was a dull month of the year—not quite winter, not quite spring, Christmas festivities well in the past, the Season still in the future. Valentine's Day had been a brilliant invention of someone who had known something about boredom.

He had spent the latter part of the afternoon and dinner surveying the possibilities—not that the choice would be his. It was to be by lottery. He was not actually averse to any of the ladies except Miss Claire Ward, of course. She was the country mouse Florence had led him to expect. Florence herself would be a voluptuous armful and had much experience with the art of love, if gossip had the right of it. Mildred, Lady Pollard, had an earthy sort of humor and a certain beauty of her own. Lucy Sterns was on the loose after a stint as Lord Hendrickson's mistress. Olga Garnett was without a doubt the most beautiful of the ladies with her blond tresses and creamy complexion. Frances Tate—well, he hoped he would not pick up her valentine. He had always avoided bedding other men's wives, however desirable they might be.

The duke found himself mildly interested in the possibilities of the following days without in any way being excited by them. The trouble with any of the four unattached ladies, he could almost predict, was that they would assume that a short liaison in the country would blossom into a longer liaison in town. It would mean his having to be absent from London just at a time when events were leading up to the Season.

Perhaps, he thought idly during dinner, there would after all be more to look forward to if he were landed with Hetty's substitute. It might be amusing—it would certainly be a new experience—to try seducing a country mouse. And for the first time he really looked at Miss Claire Ward.

Slim, straight-backed—her spine did not once touch the back of her chair—disciplined: she was the picture of an aging spinster. Which she was except that she must be seven or eight years younger than his own thirty-four years and except that she would be pretty if she once relaxed and smiled and if she wore her hair in a less severe style.

She scarcely spoke except when spoken to. He did not once hear her voice. And yet she appeared calm and unflustered. His look became especially keen when twice he thought he detected a gleam of amusement in her eyes as someone made particularly spiteful remarks about "friends." Miss Ward might be a prude, he thought—indeed, he did not doubt that she was—but he suspected that she might be an intelligent one.

He watched her again in the drawing room after

dinner, at first sitting apart playing the pianoforte, which she had been asked to do, according to Florence, though no one was listening to her. She looked unabashed by the fact. She actually looked as if she was enjoying herself—and she played extremely well—until she looked up and caught his eye and looked down in confusion.

A virgin if ever he had seen one, he thought. And he watched her a little later contain her shock and dismay as Florence explained her plan for their Valentine's entertainment and everyone added comments, several of them risqué. It was all enough to give a virgin spinster a fit of the vapors severe enough to last a month, he thought. And yet Miss Ward sat straight-backed and silent and calm—and scarlet-cheeked. Even without the relaxation and the smile and the more becoming style of hair she looked pretty.

The Duke of Langford swung his quizzing glass pendulum-fashion from its ribbon and declined tea. He had an idea, one that might bring more amusement than any of the five experienced flirts and respectable courtesans would bring.

He walked upstairs later with Lady Florence. It was not difficult to arrange since both of them seemed intent on maneuvering it. "Er," he said, "your lottery is to be a random thing tomorrow, Florence? And yet you are to arrange it that Mullins gets Miss Ward?"

She flashed him a brilliant smile. "It is fitting, don't you think, Gerard?" she asked. "He is dreadfully dull. I should hate to feel that he might draw my valentine. And she, of course, is impossible. I would not have dreamed of inviting her if the alternative had not been having uneven numbers."

"Then it is wise to pair them together," he said. "But how, pray, is it to be done if there is to be no cheating?"

Her smile deepened. "Perhaps just a little manipulation, Gerard," she said. "I shall see to it that Miss

Ward's valentine is at the bottom left of the table—
as far from mine as it can possibly be, in fact. And I
shall warn each of the gentlemen except Percy that
that is where it will be."

"I see," he said. "And I take it that Mullins is to
be the last to choose?"

"But of course," she said, widening her eyes at him.
"And you are to be first, a tribute to your superior
rank."

"Ah," he said.

She smiled. They had passed his room and had
come to a stop outside hers. "Three days and three
nights," she said. "Of course, for one couple it could
be three days and four nights."

"Ah," he said again, "but that would be unfair to
the other participants in this party, Florence. Don't
you agree?" He took her hand in his and raised it to
his lips.

She pulled a face. "What does fairness have to say
to anything?" she asked him.

"Everything." He bowed over her hand before re-
leasing it. "To a man of honor, that is."

She smiled as he turned away. He heard her bedchamber door open and close again before he reached
his own room.

The valentines were red silk hearts trimmed with a
double layer of white lace. They were exquisite, all
the ladies agreed. There was a heightened air of excitement in the morning room as each in turn wrote
her name carefully on one heart, leaving room below
for a gentleman's name. The gentlemen were still in
the breakfast room.

Claire wished more than ever that she had sent for
the carriage. A night of restless tossing and turning
and bizarre dreams had not convinced her that innocent romance was the object of Lady Florence's party.
And think as she would of the six gentlemen, any one

of whom might be her valentine, she could not imagine one with whom she might be comfortable—or one who would be pleased to draw her name.

Lady Florence gathered up the six hearts when they had all finished and the ink had dried. "Now, over to the fire all of you," she said, laughing, "and no peeping. I shall arrange the hearts on the table so that none of you will know which is your own. That way there can be no cheating, no secret signals to a favored gentleman."

The ladies laughed merrily and moved obediently to the fireplace.

"But indeed," Mrs. Tate confided to Claire, "I have no favorite. Well, perhaps one, but then who would not favor him in any company? But Florence has chosen her gentlemen guests well, would you not agree, Miss Ward? They are all personable."

"Yes," Claire said.

"One can only hope," Miss Garnett said with a titter, "that the gentlemen feel the same way about us, Frances."

"I have no doubt of it," Mrs. Tate said, looking about at the group. "I do believe Florence has chosen us carefully too, if I may be pardoned for the vanity."

"Poor Hetty," Lady Pollard said. "It is a shame she had to cry off at the last moment. She would have enjoyed nothing better than Florence's little entertainment." Then she glanced at Claire and looked uncomfortable. She spread her heavily ringed hands to the blaze. "There is nothing as cozy as a large fire in a morning room, is there?"

Claire smiled to herself. So she was poor Hetty's substitute, was she? Well, she had known it, or all but the name of the absent guest anyway. But Lady Florence had sent a servant to summon the gentlemen. There was no time to dwell on the fact. Claire's heart began to thump, just as if she were fresh out of the schoolroom and meeting gentlemen for the first time in her life, she thought in disgust.

"You are each in turn to choose a valentine from the table," Lady Florence told the gentlemen after they had arrived. Her cheeks were glowing and she had her hands clasped to her bosom. She was throughly enjoying herself. "You must not turn it over until everyone has chosen. Then you will all turn over the valentines together, add your own name beneath the lady's, and pin the valentine to her bosom, as I explained last night. There are pins on the table. Are there any questions?"

There were not. Claire seated herself on the chair just vacated by Lady Pollard. She wished heartily that she could fade out of sight altogether.

"Very well, then," Lady Florence said. "Gerard, will you make the first choice?"

"Me first?" he said in the rather bored drawl Claire had noticed the night before during the few occasions when he had spoken. "Ah, the choice is overwhelming, Florence. And all quite identical?"

"But not the ladies whose names are written beneath, Gerard," Lady Pollard said.

He stood at one corner of the table for a long time—all the gentlemen did when their turn came except Mr. Mullins, who was last and had no choice at all—before finally picking up the heart closest to him. It must have taken ten minutes for all the hearts to be chosen, though why it took so long Claire did not know. Since the hearts were identical and there was no knowing which belonged to whom, there seemed little point in pondering the choice. She could only conclude that the gentlemen were enjoying and savoring the game as the ladies clearly were. Her own heart was beating in her chest like a hammer.

"Now," Lady Florence said, her voice so bereft of the gay excitement with which she had set the game in motion ten minutes before that Claire looked at her in some surprise, "you may turn your hearts over, gentlemen, and discover the identity of your valentine. Add your own names, please."

Not one of the gentlemen as he read the name of his valentine either looked at her or spoke her name. Another five minutes passed—or it seemed like five to Claire, though perhaps it was not quite so long— before Percival Mullins, the first to use the pen, picked up a pin and crossed the room to Lady Florence.

"Ah, Percy," she said, her smile not quite reaching her eyes, "how charming."

"My pleasure, Florence," he said. "I hope I do not prick you with the pin." Lady Florence had an ample bosom.

And then Sir Charles Horsefield was bowing before Olga Garnett and Lord Mingay was approaching Frances Tate. Rufus Tucker had some difficulty writing on silk with the quill pen. There was a delay before he turned to locate Lady Pollard with a smile.

Claire felt quite sick. She and Lucy Sterns were left. The Duke of Langford was bent over the table, the pen in his hand. Maurice Shrimpton waited behind him.

"The suspense is killing," Miss Sterns murmured, leaning toward Claire. Claire could only swallow.

And then the Duke of Langford straightened up, handed the pen to the remaining gentleman, took what seemed like half a minute to pick up a pin, and turned to walk toward the fireplace. Lucy Sterns smiled. But his eyes were directed downward to the chair when he came up to them and he reached out a hand to Claire.

No, there is some mistake, she almost said foolishly. *Miss Sterns is standing beside me.* But she did not say it. Instead she set her hand in his—she did not realize until his closed about it how cold her own was—and raised her eyes to his. He was looking at her steadily from beneath lazy eyelids. She got to her feet.

"Ah, Maurice," Miss Sterns was saying beside her with warm enthusiasm. "How wonderful."

In fact, the whole room was buzzing with exclamations and laughter. And yet it all seemed to Claire to come from a long distance away. She was wearing a high-necked wool dress. She watched as he pinned the heart just above her left breast, felt the heat of his fingers burn through to her flesh—they were long, well-manicured fingers—and read his name upside down as it had been scrawled in bold strokes beneath the small neatness of her own name. "Langford," he had written.

She looked up when he had finished to find his eyes gazing directly into hers—keen dark eyes despite the sleepy eyelids. She was too close to the fire again, too far from air, she thought. His eyes were not smiling or his close-pressed lips either. He was displeased, she thought. Of course he was displeased. She fought back the impulse to apologize to him.

And then someone took her right hand in a warm clasp—but of course, she thought in some confusion as her hand was raised between them, who else would have taken it? He touched his lips to the backs of her fingers, and Claire felt the sensation of their touch all along her arm and down into her breasts and all the way down to her toes.

"Well," someone said heartily—it was Mr. Tucker, Claire realized with a start—and laughed, "may the party now begin, Florence?"

The party was to begin with a ride to Chelmsford Castle, six miles away.

"We will all ride together," Lady Florence said. "There is a remarkably well-preserved castle to explore and a river before and a forest behind. I am sure that we will find six separate ways to go." She smiled about at the company.

But not at him, the Duke of Langford noticed. Flor-

ence was displeased. Furiously angry if he was not
mistaken. He would be willing to wager that in the
private word she had had with the other gentlemen,
Mullins excepted, she had mentioned only the fact
that the valentine at the bottom left of the table belonged to Miss Ward. He did not doubt that only he
had been favored with the seemingly unconscious remark that Miss Ward's valentine was as far from her
own as it was possible to be.

He would have to think of something to say to her
to smooth her ruffled feathers. Especially since by
some chance her own valentine had been the last to
be chosen—by the last gentleman to choose.

He was still wondering by what folly he had chosen
Miss Ward as his valentine and how soon he would
actively regret his decision. Tonight, perhaps, when
everyone else retired to bed in couples? He doubted
that he and Miss Ward would be retiring to a shared
bed quite that soon. Perhaps the next night. More
probably the next. Perhaps not at all. He had no experience whatsoever in seducing virtuous spinsters. Indeed, he had no experience in seducing any female,
having found seduction quite unnecessary since his
eighteenth year. After succeeding to his title at the
age of twenty-four he had found himself more often
than not having to ward off unwelcome advances,
rather as he had done with Florence. Not that hers
should have been unwelcome exactly. She was attractive enough. Perhaps it was just that he had a perverse
preference for choosing rather than being chosen.

Miss Ward was dressed in a russet-colored velvet
habit for the ride, a matching hat with a black feather
on her smooth brown hair. She looked slim and lithe,
the duke thought, his eyes moving over her critically
as he drew closer to her to help her into the saddle.
She looked as if she probably spent more time outdoors than in. Lucy Sterns, on the other hand, was
having to be lifted into the saddle by Shrimpton and

was nervously expressing the hope that Florence had chosen her a quiet mount.

"You ride frequently, Miss Ward?" the duke asked her as they rode out of the stableyard into the freshness of a bright springlike day.

"I live in the country, your grace," she said.

"And not many miles from here," he said. "You must know Chelmsford Castle. Is it worth a visit?"

"Oh, yes," she said. "It is a favorite picnic spot in the summer. It should be lovely now. There will probably be primroses and snowdrops on the bank of the river."

She spoke softly, seriously, unsmilingly. It was a long time, he realized suddenly in some surprise, since he had spoken with a lady—with a true lady, that was, not just one whose birth gave her the right to call herself so. Noisy flirting and raucous laughter were going on all about them.

"Then we must pick some," he said.

"I would prefer to leave them to live out their natural span, your grace," she said. "And in their natural surroundings."

"Ah," he said. "Yes, you really are a country dweller, are you not? But if we are to be in each other's company for three days and if we are to be valentines, I really do not want to be 'your graced' every time you address me. My name is Gerard."

She said nothing.

"And yours is Claire," he said.

"Yes, your gr—," she said. "Yes."

He found it easier after that to ride in near silence, merely commenting on the scenery now and then. She rode well, her back very straight, her hands light on the reins, her body relaxed and graceful. How, he wondered, was he to flirt with such a woman? How was he to seduce her? He should already have been regretting his actions of that morning, he thought, since she was clearly not comfortable when he spoke to her. And yet strangely enough he felt somewhat exhilarated by the near-impossible challenge he seemed to have set himself. There had been so few challenges in life of late.

They dismounted and tethered their horses when they reached the foot of the hill on which the castle was built.

"Unfortunately," Lady Florence said gaily, "there are only four compass directions and six couples. But I believe we can find six different directions to take, after all. Who wants to take the castle?"

"Claire is going to give me a guided tour," the duke said. "Are you not, Claire?"

"If you wish," she said.

They were to have the castle to themselves, it appeared, everyone else having found some other satisfactory destination with Florence's help. They would all meet in an hour or so's time and adjourn to a nearby inn for refreshments.

"Have fun!" Lady Florence called gaily, linking her arm through Percival Mullins's and smiling dazzlingly up at him. "The forest is delightful at this time of the year, Percy. And quite deserted and secluded, of course."

The duke offered his arm to Claire. "It seems we are to be lord and lady of the castle," he said. "Is it in as good repair as it looks from here?"

"Not quite," she said. "The outer walls of castles were always the strongest part. Much of the inside has crumbled away. But there are still two towers that are quite safe to climb, and the battlements are in good repair and give a wonderful view of the surrounding country."

"Ah, then," he said, "we must climb. I would guess that you are not one of those ladies who have to pause for breath every ten steps on a staircase, are you, Claire?"

"No," she said.

They entered the arched gateway into the grassy courtyard and could see the ruined walls of what must have been the kitchen and living quarters.

"The tallest tower is safe?" he asked, pointing to the one opposite them.

"Yes," she said.

Spiraling stone stairs led steeply upward from the courtyard, the only light provided by the narrow slits of the arrow windows. The climb seemed interminable. The duke amused himself with the sight of Claire's shapely derriere and neat ankles as she climbed ahead of him. And then they came out onto the open top of the tower, surrounded by a reassuringly high crenellated wall. The clouds scudding by on the blue sky made it appear as if the tower were moving.

"Well, at least," he said, "we are having our exercise for the day."

"Yes," she said.

"I have the feeling," he said, "that I am to be totally nameless for the next three days. You can no longer call me 'your grace' since I have specifically asked you not to, but you find it quite impossible to call me Gerard. Am I right, Claire?"

"I am sorry," she said. "I am afraid I have always moved in less exalted circles."

"If you pinch me, you know," he said, "I say *ouch*. If you cut me, I bleed. Say Gerard."

"Gerard."

"Good," he said. "That point is settled. Do you like Florence's Valentine's idea?"

"It is suited to the occasion," she said. "She thought to bring some sense of romance to the festival."

"Hmm," he said. "Romance." The wind was blowing the feather of her hat across her chin. He reached out one hand to move it aside and looked down at her mouth. It was a rather wide mouth that was made to smile, he believed, though he had never seen it do so. "Do you really believe that is her purpose, Claire?"

She licked her lips in a gesture that he guessed was not meant to be provocative. "Yes," she said. "Valentines chosen by lottery, rides to places of beauty like this." She gestured at the miles and miles of country visible from the top of the tower.

"I wonder if you believe your own words," he said, moving his hand to beneath her chin and rubbing his thumb across her lips. "Can you be that naive?"

"It is meant to be more, then?" she asked.

"More, yes," he said, and he leaned forward and laid his lips against hers for a brief moment. Her own lips remained still. He found her passivity strangely arousing. Perhaps because he was unaccustomed to it, he thought.

"Please," she said. "Don't."

"Why not?" he asked her. "Is a kiss not appropriate between valentines?"

"We are not—" she began.

"Oh, yes, we are," he reminded her. "You have a lacy heart pinned to your wool dress with both our names on it. I won you by lottery."

She said nothing but merely looked at him. Her eyes were a mixture of blue and gray, he thought. Rather lovely eyes. He touched the pad of his thumb to the center of her lips.

"Is a kiss sinful between willing adults?" he asked. "I do not insult you by assuming that you have passed your majority, do I?"

"Of course not," she said. "I have—several years ago."

"Well, then," he said. "Are you repulsed by me, Claire?"

"Repulsed?" she said. "Of course not."

"And neither am I repulsed by you," he said. "And we are valentines, after all. For three whole days,

Claire." He was going to add *and for three whole nights too,* but he stopped himself in time.

"Yes," she said.

"And there is nothing improper about valentines exchanging kisses," he said. "Not when they are both adults and in no way repulsed by each other."

"No," she said.

"Then we have no quarrel," he said, setting both his hands on her shoulders and drawing her upper body loosely against his before kissing her again, parting his lips in order to do so. Her own stayed closed, though they trembled as her shoulders trembled beneath his hands. He licked her lips from one corner to the other before raising his head and setting her back away from him.

"It is my guess, Miss Claire Ward," he said, "that you considered flight both last evening and this morning. And I right?"

"Yes," she said.

"But you had a little too much courage to give in to the urge," he said.

"A little too much stubbornness, I think," she said. "And a little too much curiosity, too." There was the suggestion of a smile about her lips for a moment.

"Ah," he said, "stubbornness and curiosity. Qualities I like. Going down the steps of these old towers is far more intimidating than going up, is it not? Would you like me to go first?"

"Yes, please," she said.

He would have had the vapors from any other female, he thought as he started down into the steep darkness. Or at least shrieks and shrinking pleas for assistance. Claire Ward came steadily and quietly after him. He could see her trim ankles in their black riding boots whenever he turned his head.

He thought of what was probably happening between five other couples down by the river and in the woods and fields about the castle and thought ruefully of his two chaste kisses. And yet he would not, he thought with a wry smile, change places with any of the other five gentlemen. No, not for a thousand pounds.

Claire looked at her mirrored image and wished again that she had more gowns as attractive as her blue silk. She had always liked the yellow one she now wore, but she knew that it was unfashionable by London standards, the neckline conservatively high, the sleeves too narrow, the hem unadorned. She spread her hand for a moment over the valentine heart, which she had removed from her wool dress and pinned to her evening gown. His signature, she saw when she removed her hand and looked at it reversed in the mirror, quite overshadowed her own.

It was time to go down to dinner. But there would be none of the awkwardness and self-consciousness of the evening before when she had known no one. Tonight it was all arranged. The Duke of Langford—Gerard—would be leading her in to the dining room and seating himself beside her.

She was almost ashamed to admit that she was beginning to enjoy herself. There had been the ride, an activity she always liked, and the hour spent exploring Chelmsford Castle and the refreshments at the inn afterward. And the ride home. She was twenty-eight years old. All her adult life she had been alone. Oh, not quite solitary, it was true. But whenever she went anywhere with Roderick and Myrtle, it was always they who were the couple and she who was the single. There was great pleasure, she had discovered that day, in being part of a couple. And a great sense of security.

And he seemed not to be too displeased at having drawn her as his valentine. That was what had worried her most that morning. She had fully expected to be treated with haughty disdain. Instead he had behaved with courtesy—and something more. Her cheeks grew warm and her mirrored image flushed as she remembered that he had kissed her on top of the tower. And had done more than kiss her, too. He had touched her lips with his tongue and sent sensation sizzling through her.

At least now, she thought with a wry smile for her blushing image, she would not have to go through life with the regret that she had never been kissed. She had been and by a duke no less. Now that would be a memory with which to soothe her old age. Her smile became more amused.

Yet she really ought not to be enjoying herself, she thought as she left her room and descended to the drawing room, where she could hear that some people were already assembled prior to dinner. It was not a proper party she was attending. If she had had any doubts, the duke had dispelled them that afternoon. And if any had lingered, they would have disappeared at the inn, where Miss Sterns had sat all through tea with her shoulder pressed to Mr. Shrimpton's and where Lady Pollard had turned to Mr. Tucker at one point and they had kissed each other. Claire had been very glad at the time that she was not given to the vapors.

But she was enjoying herself. As soon as she stepped into the drawing room he came toward her, his hand stretched out for hers. And he looked quite magnificent in a brown velvet coat and buff-colored knee breeches, with a waistcoat of dull gold and white linen. Oh, yes, she thought, almost smiling at him but holding back in case after all he was less than pleased with the situation—oh, yes, it was all very romantic, whatever the rest of Lady Florence's guests made of it. To have a valentine for three whole days—and such a very handsome and distinguished valentine—was quite the pinnacle of romance to an aging spinster.

They would play forfeits that evening, Lady Flor-

ence announced gaily during dinner and the announcement drew titters and exclamations.

"Really, Florence?" Sir Charles said. "Forfeits?"

"Forfeits?" Mrs. Tate said. "Spare my blushes,
Florence."

Yet they all seemed pleased, Claire thought. She
played forfeits with her nephews and nieces on occasion, sometimes with small coins, more often with an
imposed task to be performed as a forfeit, like a song
to be sung. The children always enjoyed it when the
adults joined in and showed themselves willing to
make themselves look rather foolish.

But it seemed that she was not to have a chance to
play that evening. After they had adjourned to the
drawing room and drunk their tea—the gentlemen did
not remain in the dining room after the ladies left—
the Duke of Langford laid a hand on her shoulder and
spoke to Lady Florence.

"You will excuse Claire and me for the next hour
or two, Florence?" he said in his most bored-sounding
drawl. "We feel a pressing need to, ah, view the por-
traits of your husband's ancestors and the other paintings in the gallery. Don't we, Claire?"

Did they? Claire looked up at him, startled. But
she did not want to go. She did not want to be alone
with him. He could have only one reason for suggesting such a thing. And everyone else must have
thought the same thing. There were knowing smiles
from the ladies and winks from the gentlemen.

"You naughty man, Gerard," Lady Pollard said.
"Why did we not think of that, Rufus?"

"Well, there is still the conservatory, Mildred," he
said.

"Ah," she said, "but we would have to miss the
forfeits. Are you sure you wish to do so, Gerard?"

Claire looked at him hopefully. She should speak
up, she knew. But such people always tongue-tied her.

She never knew the right thing to say or when it should be said.

"We have better things to do," he said, and he lifted his hand away from her shoulder and brushed the backs of his fingers against her cheek before extending the hand to help her to her feet.

"Then go," Lady Florence said with what sounded almost like impatience. "The rest of us are ready to proceed with the fun."

Carver House had been a Tudor manor before centuries of rebuilding had transformed it. But the long gallery was still on the top floor, running the whole width of the house. They were on their way up the stairs, the duke carrying a branch of candles in one hand, before Claire spoke. By that time she was angry—perhaps more with herself than with him. Was she going to allow herself to be awed into behaving against her nature?

"I don't think this is a good idea, your grace," she said. "I don't think I wish to be so alone with you. It is not proper."

"Far more proper than being in the drawing room for the next couple of hours is likely to be," he said.

She looked at him. They had paused on the second landing. "Playing a game in the company of the others?" she said.

"Forfeits," he said. "Do you have any idea what that means, Claire?"

"I have played it all my life," she said.

"With articles of your own clothing as the forfeits?" he asked.

She stared back at him, the implications of what he had said dawning on her. She felt heat mount into her cheeks. "No," she said almost in a whisper. "But surely . . ."

"So, my dear Claire," he said, offering her his arm again, "you and I will go and admire art in the gallery. Shall we?"

She took his arm hesitantly. Had he spoken the truth? Surely even these guests would not behave with such utter—impropriety. Was it all an elaborate ruse to get her alone? Alone in an upper gallery for more than an hour? Surely she should resist. She should plead a headache and retire to her room. Or better still, she should just tell the truth and retire to her room.

But she remembered the titters and the comments at dinner when the game had first been mentioned. Besides, she thought, placing her arm on the duke's and allowing him to lead her up the final flight of stairs, she wanted to go. And no, she would not feel guilty about it either. Good heavens, she was a woman, not a girl. And she was a woman with feelings and needs—and a longing to be part of the romance of St. Valentine's Day for once in her life.

They wandered down one side of the gallery and back along the other, looking dutifully at the paintings while he held the candles aloft. They scarcely spoke a word. But Claire deliberately reveled in having her hand on a man's firm arm, in being alone with him, part of a couple. Whatever might be happening downstairs, and whatever he might be thinking or feeling, she thought, she was going to enjoy this hour. She was going to pretend that they belonged together, that they were more than just valentines for three days.

"Unless we can convince ourselves that we are great devotees of art, Claire," he said as they stood before the last picture—a painting of a single horse and rider and a crowd of hunting dogs, "we are going to have to find some other way to amuse ourselves for what remains of the evening."

She stiffened.

"Shall we sit down on the bench beneath the window and exchange life stories?" he asked.

She seated herself obediently and he sat beside her, his knee brushing against hers.

"How old are you?" he asked.

"Eight-and-twenty," she said, looking at him, startled.

"And why are you twenty-eight years old and un-married, Claire?" he asked her.

Because no one had asked her, she thought. But she could not say that out loud.

"I have observed no defects of either person or character in you during the past day and a half," he said. "Indeed, I would have to say that you possess some beauty."

It was no lavish compliment, but it warmed her to her toes. "My father was an invalid," she said. "He needed me. He died a year and a half ago."

"Did he?" he said, and his dark eyes wandered over her face and hair. "So you are one of those too-numer-ous females whose personal happiness is sacrificed at the family altar, are you?"

She said nothing.

"And as a reward you have been taken into the home of relatives, where you will live out your life making yourself useful and always feeling that you do not belong."

Her hands clenched in her lap. "My brother and my sister-in-law have always been good to me," she said.

"Of course." He took one of her hands, unclenched her fingers, and curled them over his. "And so, Claire, you have not been allowed to learn anything of life."

"I believe my life has been useful," she said. All the joy of fantasy had gone out of her day. She was back to reality again. There was no romance after all.

"I am sure it has," he said. "Useful to others. But to yourself?"

"There is satisfaction to be gained from serving oth-ers, your grace," she said, lifting her chin and looking him in the eye. "Probably a great deal more than would be gained from wasting one's youth in the ballrooms and drawing rooms of polite society in London."

He set his other hand over the back of hers. "Is that how you have consoled yourself, Claire?" he asked.

It was. But in one sentence, with one question, he had shattered even that illusion, exposing to her view all the yearnings of years that she had ruthlessly reasoned away.

"You should not be here, you know," he said. "You are about as at home here as I would be at the bottom of the ocean."

"I know," she said, her voice unable to hide her bitterness. "Naive spinsters of eight-and-twenty do not belong at a house party with people who know a thing or two about life and the world. I should be at home with my brother and sister-in-law."

"That was not my meaning," he said. "You should be in your own home, Claire, with your husband, your children abovestairs in the nursery."

She pulled her hand free and got to her feet. She took a few steps along the gallery. No. She had closed that yawning empty pit years before. It was not to be, and that was all there was to it.

She had not heard him coming up behind her. She tensed when she felt his hands on her shoulders.

"I am sure even you know what a rake is, Claire," he said. "Florence has six of them as her guests. I include myself, you see. You have no business being here with me."

"I can look after myself," she said. "I am not a helpless innocent."

"You must know what I have set myself to do since this morning," he said. "Don't you?"

She dropped her chin to her chest. Yes, she had known, she supposed. She was not quite as naive as she sometimes pretended even to herself to be.

"Yes." Her voice was a whisper.

"I am not the sort of man to be satisfied with kisses for three days," he said. "And three nights."

She covered her face with her hands for a moment before turning to look up at him. He had set the candlestick down beside the bench when they sat down earlier. His face was in shadows.

"Perhaps I am not the sort of woman to be satisfied with a few kisses for a lifetime," she said, hearing the words almost as if someone else were speaking them, but amazing herself with the truth of what she was saying.

She heard him draw breath and expel it slowly.

"I am not used to situations like this, Claire," he said.

"Neither am I—Gerard."

He touched the backs of his fingers to her cheek as he had done downstairs earlier. "You are offering yourself to me for two days and three nights," he said. "You are worth more, Claire. Far more."

"Life has always been bleakest on Valentine's Day," she said. And she wondered somewhere far back in her mind when she would feel horror and embarrassment at having so bared her lonely soul.

"Has it?" His hands framed her face gently, his fingers stroking back the hair from her face. "Has it, Claire?"

And then his arms were about her and drawing her against his body and her own were up about his shoulders and neck, and his mouth was on hers, warm, light, open. Without conscious thought she arched herself against him, feeling hard masculine muscles pressed to her thighs, her stomach, her breasts. She sighed with contentment and parted her lips beneath his so that she could taste him too.

He had been wrong. He had been quite certain that it could not be accomplished this first night. Perhaps tomorrow night, he had thought. More probably the last night. Possibly not at all. But he had been wrong.

She was his. His for the taking. He knew it the moment her arms came up about his neck and her body arched to his and her mouth opened beneath his. He knew it as he slid his tongue into her mouth and fondled one of her breasts and felt the taut nipple with his thumb. He knew it as both hands moved down her sides to her small waist and down to her shapely hips and behind to spread themselves over firm buttocks and she neither cringed nor pulled back. She was his.

He returned his hands to her waist and lifted his head. She opened her eyes and looked into his. She was utterly beautiful, he noticed for the first time. Oh, perhaps not in the most obvious of ways. In many ways she was not as lovely as any of the other five ladies belowstairs. But then their beauty was all of the surface. Hers shone from within. Her whole soul looked at him through her eyes.

And he saw Claire. Not just a woman from whom to take his pleasure, a woman on whom to use the sexual expertise of years. He saw a woman whose family and whose own sense of duty had taken her past the usual age of marriage and motherhood. A woman who had compensated outwardly with a quiet dignity. A woman who had allowed him to cut a chink in her armor so that he had glimpsed all the longing and all the loneliness within. A woman who, as he had told her, should have been in her own home at that moment with her own family. But who instead was with him.

She was his, he thought again, with a pang of regret for conscience and for years of life wasted on pleasure and the constant restless search for more pleasure.

"Then we will have to make sure that this is a Valentine's to remember, will we not?" he said.

"Yes." She searched his eyes with her soul.

"Romance," he said. "That is the word, is it not?" It was a word he knew nothing about. "We will avoid the more sordid of Florence's plans together, you and I, Claire, and seek out romance for two days instead. Shall we?"

She nodded, but she was still looking deeply into his eyes. "Will I be ruining your party?" she asked. "Do you wish to be with the others?" She hesitated. "Do you regret that you picked up my valentine?"

"No," he said, bending his head to kiss her softly beneath one ear. "No to all of the above."

"Thank you," she said, and a smile hovered about her lips for a few moments, so that he found himself inexplicably holding his breath. But she did not allow it to develop.

"It is far too early to go back downstairs," he said. "We did not get very far in the telling of our life stories, did we? Shall I tell you something of mine? I was my parents' sole darling for six years before my brother arrived—he is just your age, Claire—and then four sisters in quick succession. I do not believe I have ever recovered my temper."

He sat down with her again on the bench and took her hand in his, setting it palm down on his thigh and playing with her fingers while he talked. He did not spend much time with his family. He resented their disappointment with his way of life and their occasional reproaches. He hated his eldest sister's matchmaking schemes, though she had given up her efforts of late. He felt uncomfortable with the fact that they were all married and all parents, even Sarah, the youngest.

However, it was not of his adult estrangement from his family that he talked, but of earlier years when he had been the adored and pestered eldest brother and when he had loved and hated and played and fought with his brother and sisters and felt all the unconscious security of belonging to a large and close family.

"My father died quite unexpectedly," he said, "when I was only twenty-four. He was the sort of man one would expect to live to a hundred. It was a nasty age to be suddenly saddled with all the responsibilities of a dukedom, Claire, and all those of being head of a family. My mother collapsed emotionally and my brother and sisters resented my authority. And I rebelled."

"And I suppose," she said, "that there are those who believe you must be happy because you apparently have everything."

"Oh, legions of such people," he said. "You have only the one brother, Claire?"

"Oh, no," she said. "I have two other brothers and two sisters. All married, like yours. And all parents. I have eleven nieces and nephews to romp with at Christmas and other family gatherings."

"And you are the youngest," he said. "The sacrificial lamb."

"I loved my father," she said.

"I am sure you did." He squeezed her hand.

It seemed strange, he thought as she told him some memories of her childhood, to be having such a conversation with a woman. His conversations with women usually consisted of light repartee and sexual innuendo. His more usual dealings with them were entirely physical. He could not remember ever telling any woman—or man either—about his family and childhood. He could never remember any woman wasting time telling him about hers.

He felt strangely honored to have won the confidence of Claire Ward. She looked relaxed and unselfconscious beside him. And then she shivered. There was no fire in the gallery and it was only February.

"You are cold," he asked.

"Not really," she said.

But her arm was cool, he could feel when he set an arm about her and drew her against him. "It is time to go back downstairs," he said regretfully.

"Yes," she said.

"I imagine the game will be finished now," he said as they got to their feet and he picked up the branch of candles and offered her his arm.

They descended the stairs in silence. But she paused at the top of the flight leading down to the drawing room. "I don't want to go back there tonight," she said. "Will it be ill-mannered if I do not?"

"Not at all," he said. "And neither do I, Claire. Let us go straight to bed instead."

She looked calmly into his eyes as he set down the candles on a small table. She did not quite know his meaning, he thought, any more than he did. But there was acceptance in her eyes. She had made a decision up in the gallery, and she was not going to go back on it. He took her arm through his and led her to the door of her bedchamber.

"Claire," he said, smoothing back her hair from her face with one hand, cupping her cheek with the other, "it has been a lovely day. Romantic."

"Yes," she said.

He kissed her softly on the lips and felt her arms come about his waist.

"Let us keep it that way, at least for tonight and tomorrow. Shall we?" he said, looking down into her eyes.

There was a moment's silence. He watched her swallow. "Yes," she said.

"Good night, Claire." He kissed her softly again. "Good night, my valentine."

"Good night, your gr—" she said. "Good night, Gerard."

And he opened her door for her and closed it behind her after she had stepped inside. He stood where he was for a while, staring down ruefully at his hand on the doorknob. He could be on the other side of the door with her, he thought. She had been his. That had been very obvious both upstairs and here a few moments ago. And he wanted her badly enough, God knew.

He must be getting soft in the head, he decided, turning away in the direction of his own room. Or perhaps it had just been a fear of the unknown. He had never had a virgin. And he was a total stranger to the sort of tenderness he would need to exercise when bedding Claire. Well, perhaps tomorrow night. Undoubtedly tomorrow night.

Claire came awake with a surge. The sun was shining through the window with all the promise of a beautiful day. But it was not newly risen, she thought, sitting up in some surprise and stretching her arms above her head. She must have slept deeply right through the night when she had expected to lie awake.

She got out of bed and crossed to the window on bare feet, heedless of the coolness of the room. She felt wonderful, and indeed it was going to be a glorious day. There was not a cloud in the sky.

She stretched again. There was not a trace left of the sadness she had felt at first the night before when the door of her bedchamber had closed behind her. She had felt bereft and instantly lonely as she had leaned back against the door with closed eyes. And rejected. He did not want her after all. She was perhaps acceptable to talk with and even to kiss. But not for anything else.

But the moment had passed almost instantly. *Good night, my valentine,* he had said. He had said no when she had asked if he regretted drawing her name. He had said it had been a lovely day. Romantic, he had said. And he had suggested that they keep it that way.

Oh, yes, she thought now, resting her hands on the windowsill and leaning forward to look through the window, yesterday had been wonderfully romantic. And there was the whole of today to look forward to and the whole of tomorrow. And perhaps tonight. She

felt her cheeks flushing. But she wanted it, she realized, as much as the romance. Perhaps more so. She
wanted it, brazen and immoral as the wanting was.
She had been kissed for the first time the day before
and it had been far more wonderful than she could
possibly have imagined. She wanted the rest of it too.
Oh, yes, she did. She wanted to be able to hug to
herself for the rest of her life the secret knowledge
that once—at Valentine's—she had been wanted and
had herself wanted and that that desire had been
satisfied.

Claire determinedly blocked images of the Reverend Clarkwell and of a lifetime of moral training from
her mind. She was in love, she thought as she turned
away from the window and considered what to wear.
But that was irrelevant to anything. Of course she
was in love. Was it surprising that a romance-starved
spinster should fall in love with the first man to kiss
her? She would suffer from her feelings. She knew
that too. Life would be almost unbearable for a while
after she went home again. But it did not matter. The
suffering would be worthwhile. And there were two
whole days to be lived through before the suffering
began.

She would wear her favorite pink wool day dress,
she decided, shrugging off the wish that she had
clothes as fashionable as those of the other ladies. She
did not, and that was that. Nothing was going to spoil
this day for her.

Although she had feared that she was late for breakfast, Claire found that there were only five people in
the breakfast room—Lady Florence and Mr. Mullins,
Miss Garnett and Sir Charles Horsefield, and the
Duke of Langford. She felt suddenly shy as all heads
turned her way and not nearly as confident as she had
felt since waking. He looked again the very remote
aristocrat. Surely it could not have been about him
that she had been weaving such dreams?

But he got to his feet immediately and came across the room to her, his hand outstretched for hers. And his eyes looked far less haughtily lazy than usual as he smiled.

"Claire," he said, taking her hand. "Good morning. Come and have some breakfast."

He looked almost like an eager boy, she thought in some wonder, and all her happiness came back in a flood. She smiled radiantly at him. "Good morning, Gerard," she said, and she looked about the table to include everyone in her greeting. "Is it not a beautiful morning? I do believe spring is here to stay."

Sir Charles groaned. "Morning, did someone say?" he asked. "Would you not know that I would pick up the valentine of a morning person?" He shook his head at Olga and raised her hand to his lips.

"My dear Miss Ward," Lady Florence said, "you are looking quite radiant this morning. I wonder why."

"Ah," Mr. Mullins said. "Probably because it is Valentine's Day tomorrow, Florence."

"And so it is," she said. "If the weather holds, we will have a drive this afternoon. Everyone is free this morning since we do not seem to have a large number up yet anyway."

"Ah, freedom," Sir Charles said. "I do not suppose I can interest you in a little more, ah, relaxation, can I, Olga?"

The Duke of Langford seated Claire beside him after she had filled a plate at the sideboard. "Would you care for a ride?" he asked.

She smiled at him again. She could think of nothing she would love more even if she had had to do it alone. But with him? "More than anything in the world," she said.

Sir Charles groaned again.

He fell in love with her when she smiled. His stomach felt as if it performed some sort of somersault, which was rather a shameful thing for a man of thirty-four to admit to himself. But the smile utterly transformed her and made nonsense out of all the barriers he had tried to build up about his heart during a largely sleepless night. He had never been in love before. But he was in now—deeply.

With a totally unsuitable woman. He was a rake and had lived a worthless adulthood. He could not think of one worthwhile thing he had done in the past ten years or more—unless it was allowing her to go to bed alone the night before. She had lived a selfless adulthood and was very definitely—despite her behavior of the evening before—a virtuous woman.

Marriage and the raising of a family did not enter his plans at all. Years ago he had decided that his brother and his brother's sons were quite worthy of taking his place when he died. More worthy than he, in fact. He would take no personal responsibility for the succession. The only use he had for women was that they cater to his pleasure.

Claire Ward was not the type of woman with whom he normally associated. One could think of Claire only in terms of virtue—of spinsterhood or marriage. And marriage seemed to have passed her by. She was not the type of woman with whom he would have chosen to fall in love, if he could have chosen. But then if he could have chosen, he would not have fallen in love at all. He had never either wanted or expected to do so.

But in love he was, he thought, watching her as she ate a hearty breakfast, watching that brightness and radiance that he knew the other occupants of the room were interpreting quite wrongly as having come from a night of sexual activity. He did not care what they thought. All he cared for was that there were two full days left before he would have to face reality and say good-bye to her, knowing that the total difference in their lives necessitated such an ending to their Valentine's romance.

Romance! He had always laughed at the word and thought it for women only.

She had finished eating. Horsefield and Olga had left the room already, evidently on their way back to bed. Florence and Mullins were impatient to be gone from the table too, perhaps with the same destination in mind.

"How long will you need to change into your riding habit?" he asked Claire, laying a hand over hers on the table.

"Ten minutes." She smiled into his eyes. There was light in them and color in her cheeks, and he found himself smiling back.

"I shall meet you in the hall," he said. "In ten minutes' time." He rose as she got to her feet and left the room. Any other woman would have demanded at least half an hour, he thought.

"Oh, Gerard," Lady Florence said. "Do have a care. You will be having Mr. Roderick Ward and the Reverend Hosea Clarkwell paying you a call in town within the week demanding to know your intentions and waving gloves in your face."

"Will I?" he asked, fingering the handle of his quizzing glass. "That might be an interesting experience." He strolled from the room.

It was like the middle of spring, they both agreed, but with the added attraction of freshness in the air and pale green grass dotted with primroses and snowdrops. The trees were still bare, but there was all the promise of the coming season in the warmth that radiated through their branches.

They rode and rode for what must have been hours but might as easily have been minutes. They rode the length of the park to the south of the house and through pastures and around hills and even over a low one, along country lanes and through lightly wooded groves. They rode without conscious purpose or direction.

And they smiled and laughed and talked on topics that they would not afterward remember. It did not matter what they talked about. They were together and happy and in love—though that was certainly not one of their topics of conversation—and the next day was St. Valentine's Day and it was spring and the sun was shining. Was there any reason—any whatsoever—*not* to be happy?

They came to open pasture after riding slowly through one grove of trees and nudged their horses into a canter by unspoken consent. And then into a gallop. And then into a race. Claire laughed as her mount nosed ahead of the duke's.

"What a slug!" she called and laughed again. And would have won the race to the gate at the other side of the pasture, she was sure, if she could have stopped herself from laughing. As it was, he beat her by almost a length, and leaned across to take the reins of her horse as she drew level.

"*What* did you say?" he asked. "Were you referring to my horse or to me, ma'am?"

She laughed.

"I will assume it was my horse," he said. "But if he is a slug, pray, what does that make yours?"

"Lame in four feet?" she asked, and they both dissolved into fits of laughter far in excess of the humor of the joke.

They passed through the gate and walked their horses through the trees beyond it until they came unexpectedly to an ornamental lake, half covered with lily pads.

"Oh," she said. "Beautiful."

"Oh," he said. "Opportune. I think our horses could use a rest, Claire. I certainly could." He slid from his horse's back and lifted her from hers before tethering the animals to a tree under which there was grass for them to graze on.

He took her hand and laced his fingers with hers. They strolled together about the small lake, not talking, enjoying the utter peace of the scene. Only the chirping of birds and the occasional snorting of one of the horses broke the silence.

"Well, Claire," he said when they had completed the walk, "even nature is on our side. Pure romance, is it not?" He smiled at her in some amusement.

She nodded. "I should have known this was here," she said. "But we have never had many dealings with the Carvers."

They sat down on the grass facing the lake and lifted their faces to the warmth of the sun.

"Did you sleep well?" he asked her.

"Yes." She turned her head to look at him. "Yes, I did. I knew I had today and tomorrow to look forward to." She flushed. "Did you?"

"Sleep well?" he said. "Well enough. You asked me if I was sorry I had picked up your valentine. Are you sorry I picked it up? Do you wish it had been someone else? Or do you wish that after all you had gone home?"

She shook her head. "No," she said.

He smiled slowly at her. "Ah, Claire," he said, "you should be sorry. But now is not the time for that, is it? Today and tomorrow are for romance."

"Yes," she said.

He *was* regretting it, she thought. He was wishing he was back at the house with one of the other ladies. Or perhaps wishing he had not come at all. But he was still smiling, and his hand was stroking gently over one of her cheeks, and his head was lowering to hers. And she knew that he was not feeling regret but that he was enjoying the day as much as she. She closed her eyes and parted her lips.

He had agreed to romance, he thought as his mouth

met hers and he felt heat flare instantly despite his
intention to make it a light and warm embrace. But
how could he give her romance when he knew only
about physical passion? And how could he toy with
her body and her feelings when she was not like those
women back at Florence's house, eager and able to
change lovers as they would change their frocks? And
for the same reason—that keeping the same one bored
them.

And yet the choice, the control over the moment,
was not his for long. He lowered her to the grass and
kissed her eyes, her temples, her cheeks, her throat,
and her mouth again. His hand found its way beneath
her velvet jacket to the warm silk of the blouse covering her breasts. Her arms reached up for him and
circled his back, drawing him down half on top of her.
And she moaned into his mouth.

She was aching, and throbbing with the ache from
head to foot. And yet she had never known a pain
that was pleasurable, a pain that she wanted to perpet-
uate. She searched for his mouth when it moved from
hers for a moment and sucked inward on his tongue
when it slid between her teeth. Thought, rationality,
were gone and only feeling was left. Only the pleasure
and the pain.

His hand was on her knee. She could feel the cool
air against her lower leg, where he had pushed up the
velvet skirt of her riding habit. And then his fingers
were feathering their way along her upper thigh before
stopping and lying still and warm there.

"Oh, please, Gerard," she said, turning in to his
body when his hand did not resume its movement.
"Please. Oh, please."

His mouth found hers again and kissed it warmly
while his hand lifted from her leg and lowered her
skirt again. She heard herself moaning and did not
care.

"Claire," he murmured against her ear, wrapping

both arms around her and drawing her snugly against him. "It is too public a place. We dare not."

Yet it was not public at all, he knew. He doubted that anyone had been there since the previous summer. There was an overgrown, neglected air to the place despite its beauty. And he knew that if she had been any other woman he would have had her skirt to her waist by now and the buttons of his breeches dispensed with. He would be inside her by now, taking his pleasure of her, bringing her pleasure as payment.

If she were any other woman. Her face was against his neckcloth. She was trembling. He was unsure whether she was crying or not but did not have the courage to shrug her face away from him so that he could see for himself. He settled his cheek against the top of her head and held her tightly until she relaxed. And then for five, perhaps ten minutes longer.

She was warm and comfortable and sorry it had not happened. And perhaps a little relieved as well. To be taken on the hard ground in the outdoors—would there not have been something a little sordid about it? No, there would not have been, she decided. But it did not matter. She was comfortable and he felt wonderful and smelled wonderful. Why was it, she wondered drowsily, that masculine colognes smelled so much more desirable than feminine perfumes? Perhaps because she was female, she thought with an inward smile. This was what it must feel like to sleep in a man's arms at night, she thought. But the thought threatened to make her sad. She drew back her head.

And they looked deeply into each other's eyes and smiled slowly.

"I have very little experience with romance, I'm afraid, Claire," he said.

"And I have none at all," she said. "We make a fine pair."

He chuckled. "Does luncheon sound tempting?"

It did not. She did not want to go near civilization

for at least the next ten years. "I suppose so," she said.

He laughed again. "Marvelous enthusiasm," he said, laying one finger along the length of her nose. "We had better get back and fall in with Florence's plans for this afternoon, Claire, or we will incur her undying wrath."

Claire really did not care about Lady Florence's wrath, undying or otherwise. But she merely smiled.

"Naughty," he said. "Very naughty. She is our hostess, my dear valentine. On your feet immediately."

But he was laughing and making no move to get up himself. Another five minutes passed before they rose and mounted their horses again. Five minutes of kissing and smiling and talking nonsense.

But finally they were on their way back—to civilization and a Valentine's house party.

After luncheon Lady Florence and all her guests drove in three closed carriages all the way to the seashore, almost ten miles distant. Not that there was anything to be seen there, she said, except a few fishermen's cottages, but there were miles of headland to be walked along and miles of beach for those adventurous enough to descend the precipitous cliff path. And there was a small inn for those who did not enjoy being buffeted by sea breezes, however sunny the day.

"Just a short walk to look down at the sea before coming back here, Gordon," Mrs. Tate said firmly to Lord Mingay as they all descended from the carriages outside the Crown and Anchor Inn.

"If we are not blown off the cliff, Frances," he said. "It is considerably more windy here than at Carver Hall."

"I have seen enough lovely scenery from the carriage windows," Lady Pollard said. "Do you not agree, Rufus?"

Mr. Tucker put up no argument, and the two of

them disappeared inside the inn in search of warmth and refreshments.

Olga Garnett thought that a brisk walk along the clifftop would nicely blow away the morning cobwebs. Sir Charles grimaced and pulled his beaver hat more firmly down over his brow. "Not only a morning person," he muttered, "but an outdoors one too."

Lucy Sterns was already strolling away from the inn on the arm of Mr. Shrimpton.

"The beach, Florence?" Mr. Mullins asked. "Do you know the way down? I have never been on this particular stretch of the coastline before, I must confess."

"There is a perfectly safe path," she said, "even though it is rather steep."

The Duke of Langford looked at Claire with raised eyebrows.

"Oh, yes, the beach," she said. "This is another place where we used to come for picnics in summer. We even used to bathe as children."

"Perhaps," he said, "you will have to carry me up this precipitous path afterward. But by all means let us give it a try."

She laughed and took his arm, and they strode on ahead of the other couple. He let her precede him down the winding dirt path from the clifftop to the large rocks and smaller stones at the top of the sandy beach. She half ran down, tripping along the path rather like a fawn, he thought. If he did not know her and had never seen her face, he would have thought during the descent that she was a mere girl. He smiled and remembered his first impression of the prim Miss Ward just two days before.

"This could be ruinous on Hessian boots, you know," he said when they were at the bottom and scrambling over the rocks toward the beach. "And I shudder to think what the sand is going to do to them. My valet's wrath will be a terror to behold, Claire."

She laughed gaily and he looked up into sparkling eyes and at rosy cheeks and untidy wisps of windblown hair beneath her bonnet. "Then you must set them outside your door and hide from him," she said.

"Now that would be a fine ducal thing to do," he said, laughing and catching at her hand to run—actually to run—down the beach with her toward the incoming tide. If she looked like a girl, he thought, then he felt remarkably like a boy.

"We used to stand at the water's edge," she said, "seeing how close we could come without getting our shoes wet. Oh, dear, that led to much scolding when we returned to our parents."

"And I suppose," he said, "you intend to do it again, Claire. My valet will be handing in his notice. And then what am I to do?"

"Well," she said, "you might try cleaning your boots yourself."

He looked at her in mock horror. "What?" he said. "Or more to the point—how?"

Love nonsense—sex nonsense—he was used to murmuring in the beds of courtesans and his mistresses. He was not used to talking nonsense for the mere sake of lightheartedness. But he talked it for a whole hour while he got his boots wet—she stayed back a safe distance, giggling; not laughing, but giggling—and then walked with her along the water's edge, the wind in their faces, their arms about each other's waist.

They stopped when they reached the ancient wreck of a boat, almost disappeared into the wet sand.

"It was there even when I was a child," she said. "I believe it was something as unromantic as a fisherman's boat that had outlived its seaworthiness, but we used to weave tales of pirates and treasure about it. We used to hunt for that treasure at the foot of the cliffs. We were convinced that there must be a cave there that had always escaped our notice."

"And I suppose," he said, "you want to take me cave hunting and treasure hunting?"

"No." She laughed and turned to him and set her arms up about his neck as if it were the most natural thing in the world. "We found it centuries ago and spent every penny of it. It was the treasure of childhood."

"Ah, yes," he said, and he had a strange and fleeting image of the small children—her own—to whom she should be telling this story. He could almost see them scampering off to find the treasure for themselves. Her children and h— *Her* children.

"Gerard." Her smile softened. "It is beautiful here, is it not? I always feel most the wonder of creation when I am close to the sea. A little fear and a whole lot of awe."

"It is beautiful," he agreed, and he circled her waist with his arms and kissed her. And smiled at her. And that was another thing he could not remember doing before, he thought. He could not remember kissing a woman purely for the pleasure of her company, her friendship. But their kiss was no more than that. And no less.

It was a good thing, he thought as she lowered her arms and they turned to stroll back the way they had come, their arms about each other's waist again, that Florence's party was not to be a week-long affair or a two-week-long one. Three days of this intense, unreal type of romance were quite long enough. Even now it was going to be difficult . . . But he would not think of that yet. There was the rest of the day to enjoy and all of tomorrow.

"Florence and Mullins were walking off in the opposite direction," he said. "But there is no sign of them. Do you suppose they have gone back up to the inn already, Claire? What poor-spirited creatures our fellow guests are, are they not?"

"Yes," she said. "Inside a stuffy inn when they might be out here."

"Getting cold and windblown," he said, "and having their complexions and their boots ruined."

"Very poor-spirited," she said.

And they were off again, talking nonsense and laughing and finally puffing their way up the cliff path and to the inn, which they would not for worlds have admitted was warm and cozy and welcome.

All ten of the others looked at them, when they came inside still laughing over some nonsense, rather as if they had two heads apiece, the duke thought. Claire's cheeks, he saw at a glance, were apple-red, as was her nose. Her hair beneath the bonnet looked as if it had not seen a comb for a month. He looked down at his boots and grimaced. At least, that was what he would normally have done. Actually he did not—he grinned instead. And Claire had never looked more adorable.

The evening passed quickly. Indeed, it was not a long evening after the return to Carver Hall, several of the ladies pleading weariness after the afternoon's excursion and Sir Charles Horsefield declaring quite candidly that he was not averse to going to bed before midnight, though not necessarily to sleep, of course.

But they were not allowed to escape too early. They must all provide some entertainment to set the mood for St. Valentine's Day on the morrow, Lady Florence insisted. And so there was singing and reciting, one very short story, two off-color jokes, and one solo dance—by Olga Garnett.

Claire played Beethoven and closed her eyes and thought of the sea, not as she had seen it that afternoon, but at nighttime with moonlight across the ripples and a strong arm about her waist and a broad shoulder against which to rest her head. And the Duke of Langford sang one of Robert Burns' songs— to Claire's accompaniment. He had an unexpectedly fine tenor voice, she thought, listening to him even as she concentrated on her own part. And Burns had never sounded so romantic.

"Why, Gerard," Lady Florence said after the applause, "I had no idea you were hiding away such a talent."

"A relic of boyhood evenings spent *en famille,* Florence," he said, his eyes hooded, his hand straying to the ribbon of his quizzing glass. To Claire he sounded a little sheepish. "It was either sing or play the violin. The only time I tried that, my father offered to bring up the cat from the kitchen so that we might play a duet." He spoke in the languid voice that Claire had not heard all day.

Sir Charles Horsefield yawned loudly. "Well," he said, "now that we are all in the mood for tomorrow's festival, Florence, may we retire to sleep on the expectation?"

"You may, Charles," she said. She tittered. "And so may you, Olga."

Claire felt uncomfortable again as all about her guests rose in couples and stretched and seemed to feel it necessary to pretend to tiredness, although it must still be earlier than eleven. She did not know if she should rise with them or stay quietly at the pianoforte. It was the first time all day that she had felt awkward, except briefly that morning when she had entered the breakfast room.

"Claire." The duke was bending over her. "Shall we stroll into the conservatory?"

She smiled up at him gratefully and got to her feet.

But the awkwardness remained even after they had reached the conservatory and wandered among the plants there and looked out into starlit darkness beyond the windows. The day was over—the day of romance—and it was nighttime again.

He set an arm about her waist and turned her against his body. "Claire," he said, kissing her briefly on the lips, his voice low. "You know what this party is all about. Last night you were willing."

"Yes." She closed her eyes. But she was glad it was

out in the open again. The tension had been too great to bear.

"And tonight?" he asked. "You are still willing?"

The silence lasted only a moment. And yet it was the most fateful moment of her life, Claire felt. "Yes."

"You know what it will mean to you, do you not?" he said. "For you it is a far more momentous decision than it is for me."

"Yes." She opened her eyes again and looked up into his. "It is something I want, Gerard. A Valentine's Day to remember. I want to know what it is to be fully a woman."

His eyes searched hers in the dim light. Gone were all the gaiety and laughter and teasing of the day. In their place was a hunger almost frightening in its intensity. But Claire did not look away. And her own heart was beating so fast that she could hear it hammering against her eardrums.

He framed her face with his hands, ran one thumb across her lips and circled her cheeks with both. And he kissed her softly on the throat, on the chin, on the mouth.

"Come on then, my valentine," he said, and his voice was almost unrecognizable in its huskiness. "Let me find somewhere comfortable to lay you down."

"Yes," she said.

She hardly knew how she set one foot ahead of the other to walk back into the hall and up the stairs and along the corridor to her bedchamber. Every breath she took, it seemed, was a conscious effort. All the way up the stairs she told herself that she would turn him away at the door, that she would find some excuse, that somehow before it was too late she would shake herself free of the dreadful immorality that she had allowed to rule her for the past two days. But when they reached her room and he opened the door, she stepped inside with his arm about her waist and not one word or gesture of protest. She turned as he closed the door and raised her face for his kiss.

And having passed the point of no return, she abandoned conscience and the moral training of a lifetime and molded her body to his as his hands came to rest on her waist, and opened her mouth to his seeking tongue. She would not allow guilt to spoil her night. Doubtless it would have its way with her in the coming days. But not tonight.

"Claire." His voice was a murmur against her mouth. His hands were in her hair, withdrawing the pins one by one, sending them tinkling to the floor. And then his fingers were pushing through her hair and it fell in a heavy cloud over her shoulders and down her back. "Claire."

"Make love to me," she whispered back into his mouth as his hands came beneath the fabric of her dress to mold her shoulders. Her own hands found their way inside his coat to the satin of his waistcoat. "Please, Gerard. Make love to me."

And then both his arms came about her and hugged her to him like iron bands. Her face came to rest against the folds of his neckcloth. She could hear him inhaling deeply and exhaling raggedly through his mouth.

"I can't," he said at last. "My God, I can't, Claire."

She felt frozen. Every muscle in her body tensed. Her eyes were tightly closed.

"I can't," he said, his voice against her ear softer, more normal in tone. "Do you not realize what you are doing, Claire? You are becoming part of a Valentine's orgy arranged for the amusement of twelve bored members of the *ton* with not a moral principle amongst the lot of them. You are merely a substitute guest to take the place of the twelfth. As soon as you lie down on that bed and allow me the use of your body, you will be catering to the pleasure of perhaps the most bored and the most depraved rake of a select six in this house."

"No," she said, but she did not lift her face away from his neckcloth. "It is not like that, Gerard. Not with us. There is romance. Not for long, it is true. But for a short while. There is beauty in it. And you are not like that. I have seen beneath the mask you put on for the benefit of the world. Don't make this seem sordid."

"It *is* sordid," he said, and he took her arms in an ungentle clasp and put her from him. His face was harsh, his eyes hooded. "We were strangers two days ago, Claire. After tomorrow we will be strangers again for the rest of our lives. But for tonight and tomorrow night we are to lie naked on that bed taking pleasure of each other's body—in the name of romance? In the name of St. Valentine, whoever he might have been? It is sex, my dear. Sex pure and simple."

"You don't want me," she said, and she could hear petulance in her voice and could seem to do nothing either to change her tone or her words. "I am undesirable. You have been kind and you have tried to make the best of a bad situation. But when it comes to the point I am undesirable."

She turned sharply away from him as his figure blurred before her eyes. She hated herself. For being undesirable. And for whining about it. She seemed to have left her pride at home with everything else.

She heard him draw breath and release it again. "If you believe that, Claire," he said, "you are indeed inexperienced. Let's keep to the romance, shall we? It has been a lovely day, has it not? Let's not spoil it by doing what we will both regret afterward. You *would* regret it, Claire, much as you think you would not. Let's try to make tomorrow as good as today has been, perhaps even better. Shall we?"

She set her hands over her face and could find no words with which to answer him.

"Good night, then," he said softly at last from behind her.

Her misery was too deep to allow her to return the words. If she opened her mouth she would begin to beg again, she knew. And somehow pride was beginning to return already.

She thought the silence would never be broken. But finally it was. The door of her bedchamber opened quietly and then closed again as softly.

And then at last she allowed the tears to flow between her fingers.

The morning of February the fourteenth was as bright as the morning before had been and the sky was as blue and cloudless. But this time the brightness hurt the eyes as sleep was reluctantly relinquished—it had come only a few hours before. And this time there was nothing to stretch for, nothing to make her want to bound from the bed and over to the window to see what type of day was facing her.

It was St. Valentine's Day, she thought, her eyes still closed, and she swallowed against the lump in her throat. The day for love and lovers. But she felt alone—more achingly alone than she had ever felt. And she felt dull and unattractive and knew even without having to look in a mirror that she would not look her best. She had controlled last night's tears after just a few minutes of self-indulgence. She could not be seen belowstairs with red and puffy eyes. But sleeplessness always made her pale and her eyes dark-shadowed. And she was no beauty even when she did look her best.

She wanted to go home, she thought. More than anything she wanted to climb into Roderick's carriage, draw the curtains across the windows, and know that she was being taken away from it all, away to forgetfulness and the familiar dull routine of her life. She was tempted. It would be so easy to ring for a maid and send the message, to remain in her room until the carriage came. She could plead a headache.

But there was one day left. They would try to make today as good as yesterday had been, he had said. Perhaps better. Claire grimaced and opened her eyes at last and swung her legs determinedly over the side of the bed. At least she must not add cowardice to everything else. She had not behaved in a very admirable manner since her arrival. At least let her face this final day with her chin up. In one month's time, one year's time, she knew she would be willing to give all she possessed for just one hour with him. Yet now she had a whole day.

She dressed herself and did her hair without the services of a maid, as she usually did. And she went resolutely downstairs to breakfast. Everyone was there except Mrs. Tate and Lord Mingay. And except him.

"Ah, Miss Ward," Mr. Shrimpton said. "Looking, ah, as if you could do with another few hours of sleep."

It was not an insult. Everyone laughed and someone commented on the fact that they all felt that way this morning even if they did not all look it.

"But Gerard could not stay abed so long," Lady Florence said, a gleam of something like malice in her eyes. "He went galloping off for a ride more than an hour ago. But he will be back, Miss Ward. How could he not be? This is St. Valentine's Day, after all."

Lady Florence had wanted the duke for herself, Claire thought. Indeed, it was surprising that she had not found some way of ensuring that it was her own valentine he had picked up. Claire half filled a plate and sat down at the table and felt awkward and self-conscious again. And somewhat relieved too. She did not know how she would face him today, how she would look him in the eye.

He did not return until luncheon was almost over. He strode into the dining room in his riding clothes and apologized to Lady Florence. Claire kept her eyes on her plate, even when he took the empty chair beside her. She had hidden away in the library all morning, looking resolutely at page one hundred and twenty of a book whose title she could not now even remember. She had not wanted to intrude on a houseful of amorous couples. And she had sat through luncheon, eating food that tasted like paper and wishing the floor would open up and swallow her.

"Goodness," Lady Pollard had said. "Did you and Gerard have a lovers' quarrel, Miss Ward?"

Claire set her spoon down as soon as he sat down at the table. Her hand was trembling and she would not have anyone else notice. He did not speak to her but conversed with everyone else. He had been so absorbed with the beauties of nature around him, he explained, that he had lost all track of time.

Claire rose from the table with everyone else and hurried from the dining room. She half ran toward the library, as if it were the only haven in the whole wide world. Or as if she had the hounds of hell at her heels. She grabbed a book from a shelf and threw herself down into a deep leather chair, wishing she could be swallowed up by it. The library door opened behind her.

There was a lengthy silence before a pair of Hessian boots and buff-colored pantaloons above them appeared before her and he sat down on a low table.

"Forgive me for being late to wish you a happy Valentine's Day?" he asked her quietly.

"Of course," she said, looking up quickly. "There is nothing to forgive." She had forgotten just how handsome he was, she thought with great absurdity.

"Come walking with me outside?" he asked.

"There is to be a picnic," she said.

"Hang Florence and her picnic too," he said uncharitably. "Come walking with me to our lake. Will you, Claire?"

She looked at him and shrugged slightly.

"It is warmer even than yesterday," he said. He got to his feet and held out a hand for hers. He looked down at the book closed on her lap and smiled. "Do you enjoy reading Greek philosophy?"

She bit her lip as she set the book aside and placed her hand in his.

The ornamental lily pond was not far from the house, they had discovered the day before. They set out for it now on foot, and he took her hand and laced his fingers with hers just as if he had not slapped her in the face, figuratively speaking, the night before. And just as if she had not humiliated herself by begging him to take her. Just as if the romance of the day before could be recaptured. And perhaps it could be. She closed her eyes briefly and willed herself to live for the moment, to enjoy everything that she would remember in the coming days with an ache of longing.

"My valentine is not smiling today," he said softly.

She shrugged.

He untwined his fingers from hers to set an arm about her shoulders and draw her against him as they walked. "I hurt you, Claire?" he asked her. "I did, didn't I?"

"It does not matter," she said.

"It does." He squeezed her shoulder. "Did you not realize that I could not do it because I like and respect you too much?"

"Respect is a cold lover," she said.

"And because I love you too much," he said as they came through the trees to the small lake. The sun was sparkling off the water that was not covered with lily pads.

She laughed, though the sound was not one of amusement.

"I have never before loved a woman," he said. "And it is many years—far too many—since I have liked and respected one. I could not take you to bed last night, Claire, in a parody of love. Sex is not love. At least, it never yet has been with me."

"It does not matter," she said. "You do not need to explain. Today is the last day. Tomorrow we will both be able to return to the lives with which we are familiar."

"Do you want to?" he asked.

She laughed again and hesitated before seating herself on the cloak he had spread on the grass. He sat down beside her and rested his elbows on his knees and stared out over the water.

"I don't think I do," he said. "In fact I know I do not, though of course launching out into the unknown is a little frightening too."

"Men can do something different with their lives anytime they wish to," she said. "Women cannot."

He looked over his shoulder at her. "You can if you wish, Claire," he said. "If you wish, we can share the terror—and the exhilaration. You can be a duchess if you wish. *My* duchess. You can discover all you have missed in the last ten years, good and bad. You can have children if you wish and nature cooperates— my children. You can be my valentine for a lifetime if you choose. Will you?"

She merely stared at him. Somehow reality and fantasy had got all mixed up in her head and she was paralyzed with the confusion of it all.

"It is not quite the fairytale situation that many might imagine it to be, Claire," he said. "I have not lived a good life. I have a deservedly bad reputation and would not be received in any reputable home if it were not for my exalted title. I am almost estranged from the family that sustained me and loved me through my formative years. And I draw revenue from my estates without putting anything into them in exchange. I rarely even visit them. I know nothing about love and tenderness. I know nothing about making

myself worthy of a gentle and virtuous woman. When
I talk about wanting to step out into the unknown,
you see, I speak nothing but the stark truth. For I
want to change everything, Claire. But only if you are
with me. I am not sure I would have the courage or
the sense of purpose otherwise. Will you stoop to my
level to raise me up to yours?"

Fantasy had the agonizing ring of truth. She bit her
lip and felt pain. "Gerard," she said. "I am twenty-
eight years old. I know nothing. I have been nowhere.
I am dreadfully dull."

"You are beautiful and sweet and wonderful," he
said. "If you are dull, Claire, then it is dullness that
I crave. Will you marry me? Please?"

"Oh," she said.

"Now does that mean yes?" he asked. "May I smile
and relax—and kiss you, Claire? I have the blessing
of your brother and sister-in-law, you know. More
than a blessing from your sister-in-law, in fact. I would
not have been surprised to see her eyes pop right out
of their sockets. Both she and your brother were very
ready to poker up when they knew I had come from
Florence's. I made haste to explain who I was. Your
brother, to give him his due, was not satisfied with
that alone. He seemed to feel it necessary to have me
assure him that I could make you happy or that at
least I was eager to try. I believe he is very fond of
you, Claire. And rightly so."

Her eyes had widened. "You have been to see Roderick and Myrtle?"

"This morning," he said. "Did you think I had
abandoned you, my valentine, on the very day when
we should most be together?"

She hesitated. "Yes," she said. "I thought you had
taken me in disgust last night."

"If you only knew how I wanted you last night," he
said, his eyes kindling. "But it has to be in a marriage
bed with you, Claire. Please don't try seducing me

again tonight. Promise? We will be together for the first time in our marriage bed, my love. If there is to be a marriage bed, that is. Is there?"

She felt herself flushing and bit her lip again. And then he moved resolutely closer, set one arm about her shoulders, tipped up her chin with his other hand, and kissed her soundly on the mouth.

"Will you marry me?" he asked. "Say yes, Claire. I shall keep on kissing you until you do. I have decided after all not to play fair. Say yes, my valentine. My love."

"Yes," she said.

He drew back his head and grinned at her. "Are you as terrified as I am?" he asked her.

"Yes."

"Well," he said, "I think perhaps we had better go in search of Florence's picnic, don't you, Claire? For two particular reasons. If we do not, I may be trying to seduce you here or you may be trying to seduce me within the next few minutes. And I am quite determined to hold out until our wedding night, which I insist will be not a moment longer than it takes for the banns to be read and our considerable families to be gathered. And secondly, I have an overwhelming urge to shout out our news to the world. The world not being available at the moment, Florence and the others will have to do."

"Oh," she said as he drew her to her feet and kissed her soundly again, "think of the strange chance that has led us to this, Gerard. If that other guest had not become sick, I would not have been invited. And if you had not picked up my valentine by the merest chance, I would be with someone else and so would you."

"I'll grant you the first," he said. "But not the second, Claire. I chose you quite deliberately, my love. I knew your valentine would be at the left-hand corner of the table. Florence had arranged it that way. There was no chance for me in that lottery. No chance at all, in fact, to take the pun to its conclusion."

"You chose me deliberately?" she asked, amazed. "You did, Gerard? Over all the other ladies? Before you even knew me? But why?"

"I am really not sure," he said, circling her waist loosely with his arms and gazing down into her eyes, his smile gone. "I rather suspect, Claire, that without anyone's having noticed it, there must have been a fat and naked little cherub hiding up on the chandelier, a bow and arrow in his hands. And his arrow must have pierced my heart right through the center. He was taking quite a chance. Rumor has had it for several years past that I have no heart at all."

She smiled slowly at him and he smiled back until for no apparent reason they were touching foreheads and both laughing. And hugging. And kissing. And assuring each other that yes, in just a minute's time they really would go in search of Lady Florence's picnic.

Saint Valentine's Eve

by Margaret Westhaven

HE SAW HER first from the back.

She was standing in the midst of a crowd of gentlemen of varying ages and degrees of distinction. Colonel John Fairburn noticed at once the regal tilt of the head, the elegance of the upswept hair—pretty golden hair with undertones of light brown, the sort of hair that reminds one pleasantly of days spent in the sun.

When she turned around, John's first sensation was of surprise. Despite her hair, Lady Ashburnham's delicate skin showed no signs of the sun's ravaging. How had she kept the one feature so guarded while allowing the bright climate of India full liberties with the other?

And as for the face itself, it did not disappoint. No woman who carried herself so could be less than striking, and Lady Ashburnham was beautiful, with large, liquid brown eyes, high cheekbones, and a sweet expression. Though he knew her to be a widow of several years' standing, John doubted she could be as old as thirty. Why, he wondered, did there seem to be something familiar about her? He would certainly remember having met such a sophisticated beauty, and her name was new to him; he was sure of that. He had the rare talent of remembering names.

She gave him a startled glance from those beautiful eyes, then schooled them into impersonality so quickly that John thought he might have been mistaken about their first expression. Why indeed should she be sur-

prised to meet another officer just arrived in Calcutta?
There were enough of them.

He did rue that fact. He was common as dust in this
place, whereas she, a lovely and evidently aristocratic
Englishwoman, was a pearl of great price. She would
never single him out.

Startled, he realized that he wanted her to. And
at first sight! Was the climate affecting his brain-box
already? He had never had much time to spare for
the ladies, preferring to find his pleasures among those
females who would not expect more than the most
perfunctory of gallantries.

He would definitely make an exception in this lady's
case.

"Well, Rosamund," croaked old Lady Tidbury, who
had undertaken to introduce him, "here is another
one for you to charm. At least this specimen's tall and
handsome."

There was a disgruntled murmur from Lady Ashburnham's hangers-on, some of whom *were* good-
looking.

Lady Tidbury looked satisfied to have taken those
vain males down a peg. "Lady Ashburnham, may I
present Colonel Fairburn. Of the Hampshire Fairburns, you know. Distant cousins of mine."

"Hampshire," Lady Ashburnham said. John could
have sworn she turned two shades paler and wondered
uneasily why this should be so. "Yes, I know."

He bowed over her hand. "Do you mean to dance,
madam? And if you do, may I have the pleasure?"

Lady Ashburnham hesitated for the merest instant,
then nodded. The crowd of gentlemen fell away, forming a sort of chorus as they vainly protested a newcom-
er's luck. Colonel Fairburn led the lady to the floor.

She was his hostess, and this Twelfth Night ball of
hers was the event of the season in Calcutta. He was
drawn to her more with each passing moment, still
wondering why he should feel this intense admiration.

He had met his share of beauties, after all. Was Lady Ashburnham that special?

He had already admired her house. Its refreshing air of oriental coolness was something distinct from the usual British residence in Bengal. Most of the Europeans tried simply to duplicate the buildings of home. The Ashburnham house showed that someone— likely this lady—had been thoughtful enough to borrow from the native culture. Perhaps this was her unique quality: an air of understanding. He observed her more carefully.

"You are quiet, Lady Ashburnham," John said when their hands met for the second time in the figures of a country dance. He had addressed several innocuous comments to her already, trying to draw out the alluring beauty who so intrigued him. But she was silent and appeared to be thinking furiously.

"Forgive me," she said at last with a sad smile. For some reason, John fancied she looked defeated. "I'm a little surprised, I suppose, to see you again."

"Again?" John stared into her face. "Do you mean we've met before? Surely I would remember." So she *was* familiar. Desperately he searched his memory, but it would not do. He couldn't recall her name.

"Ah, no, you wouldn't remember." She shook her head. "That is only in books." She drifted away then, gold and ivory skirts lifting on a welcome breeze, to the next gentleman, the next steps.

When they met again, John's curiosity was at its peak. "Do forgive my wretched memory, dear lady, and end my suspense. Where was it? London? Did I dance with you in your come-out year and fail to recognize you? Have you grown so much lovelier with time? Although you can't have been out long, at that."

"Flattery," said the lady. "You were always too good at that. Now it doesn't ring true, sir. I shouldn't bother with any more of it."

The dance ended, forcing her into a deep curtsy. John remained speechless with surprise at her bitter words. When she rose and took his offered arm, she was still smiling in that peculiar, pained way, which had gone beyond fascinating him. It was becoming maddening.

"Perhaps if I quoted Shakespeare, sir, it would jog that dismal memory of yours," she said in a musing tone, not looking at him as they paced across the ballroom to one of the open French windows, she leading the way.

"Shakespeare?" Truly mystified, John faced her. They were on a terrace now, looking out upon a dark garden full of scents and trees and rare flowers which were all new to him. Supper having just been announced, they were the next thing to alone.

She studied him carefully. " 'Tomorrow is Saint Valentine's Day, all in the morning betime, And I a maid at your window, to be your Valentine . . .' Mind you, I would rather not recite poor Ophelia's mad scene, but I can think of nothing more appropriate." Her tone was light, sophisticated, but with an undernote of something else.

What this might be, Colonel Fairburn could not imagine. "I don't understand you, my lady." He had never been a student of Shakespeare and didn't know the rest of the words to that particular speech.

She shrugged her beautiful shoulders.

John had the sudden urge to kiss her, or to strangle her. Saint Valentine's Day indeed! And what did she mean by quoting Shakespeare at him? Had the London party he had jokingly suggested taken place upon that date on the calendar? Women were fanatics for remembering dates, a talent he had never possessed.

Lady Ashburnham sighed, causing her bosom to rise and fall in a manner most distracting to a man who, though by now unwilling, was falling ever deeper into her sensual spell.

"I've spent years blaming you, yet not blaming you," she said. "I convinced myself that I was worthless, wicked, stupid for believing your lies. I told myself I was so common a creature in your life that you wouldn't even remember who I was after a little time had passed. But when I saw you tonight, Colonel Fairburn, and knew I'd been right about it all, such a rush of anger came over me that I determined to reveal myself." She laughed. "But it didn't work even then, did it? Foiled again by the same male indifference which once broke my heart. How I hate you."

The last words were casual, more matter-of-fact than such a statement usually warranted. "Please tell me," Fairburn said, catching her arm. "If I've earned your hatred, you must allow me to try and make amends."

"Oh, must I?" She jerked her arm away and stroked it as though he had held it too tightly—which he had not, he thought in resentment. "No, Colonel, I don't think I'm obliged to do so much."

Again he caught her, this time by the shoulders. "Who the devil are you?" He whispered the words, mindful of a small group of people who ambled out at that moment, supper plates in hand, and passed by them down the terrace steps, laughing and chattering too loudly to notice one contentious couple. "Who can you be?"

"Nobody," she said, but this time she did not wrench herself away. "To you, nobody at all."

She reached up to touch his face; the touch burned him. Then she kissed him, hard. Taken by surprise, John forgot their mysterious quarrel and focused only on his strange attraction to her, clutching her to him like a madman.

After an enthralling few minutes, she disengaged herself from his arms and gave him a cold, assessing look. "I rather like kissing people I hate. Did this help your memory along?"

"My God." He was gazing down at her in astonishment. The years fell away and he saw another face—no, it was the same face, fined down and with a different look, but the same face! Why, though, did she profess to hate him? It was his right to hate *her* for the hell she'd put him through—sweet Jesus, it must be ten years ago! "So changed—your hair, your face, your figure, even your name, yet it is you. It is *you,* Elizabeth. Elizabeth Rosamund Manton, as I believe you told me once."

"Welcome to India, John," said Lady Ashburnham with a demure lowering of lashes and a small, secret smile. She turned her back and left him.

"Did you meet anyone last night, my dear?" Rosamund, Lady Ashburnham, asked her guest at the breakfast table.

"Oh, quantities of people, ma'am," the young lady responded. Brown-haired and blue-eyed, of the type that is usually referred to as "a sweet creature," Minna Peabody was sensibly clad in flowing muslin, a welcome contrast to the severe and slightly stiff morning gowns she had brought with her from England. As a clergyman's daughter from Yorkshire, she had owned clothing that was practical to the point of absurdity and not very cool. Rosamund had immediately ordered some new dresses.

After a few weeks in residence with Lady Ashburnham, Minna was not only looking more the thing, she was finally beginning to lose that perpetually startled expression. Perhaps, her hostess considered, the girl was coming to realize that there was not a poisonous snake or a snarling heathen behind every chair in the house even though she was in fabled India. Or perhaps not. Rosamund watched Minna catch sight of a passing servant and jump as though the salver he carried bore a knife with which to cut her throat.

"You know what I mean, Minna." Rosamund was

weary already of giving the young lady hints on kindly behavior to servants, and she determined to stick to the subject at hand without digressing into a lecture. "Did you meet anyone in particular?"

"I don't think so," replied the girl, frowning. Her blue eyes took on a scared look, and she burst out, "Oh, Lady Ashburnham, please don't quiz me anymore. Can it really be true that you won't force me into marriage with the first old nabob who looks twice at my ankles?"

Rosamund's laughter trilled out. "It is true indeed. My home is yours for as long as you wish. But you are a lady who attended her first ball last night, and I'm naturally curious to know if anyone intrigued you."

"I don't think so," Minna repeated, shrugging.

Rosamund sighed. Until John Fairburn's arrival had distracted her, she had observed with a keen eye Miss Minna Peabody's maiden assault upon society. The girl's manner was that of a rabbit in a crowd of poachers. One would have to trust to time to convince Minna that no, she was not to be sold off into marriage to the first interested party.

The last thing Rosamund remembered was watching Minna scurry behind a pillar as some young officer approached her, or seemed to do so. Then that old busybody Lady Tidbury had reached out her claw and spun Rosamund around to face John Fairburn.

John Fairburn. Thoughts of him easily crowded out any worry over Minna. Rosamund put her head in her hands and sighed again deeply.

"Oh, ma'am." Minna started out of her chair, tipping the delicate carved piece to the carpet in her rush to reach her friend's side. "Is it the headache? Let me go and make you a tisane. I made sure to pack a good supply of every remedy, for Aunt told me I was not to trust foreign potions, and I was packing for a lifetime, you know."

"No tisane, thank you, dear." Rosamund raised her head and managed to smile. "Packing for a lifetime. My poor girl, you didn't wish to leave England, did you?"

"You must know I did not." Minna hung her head.

"No more did I, once upon a time." Rosamund looked away, into the distance. "Yet India can wrap round you with its magic, Minna. You must give it a chance."

The girl shivered, as though India were a cobra and she a helpless small animal. A rabbit, Rosamund thought again, wishing she had the wit to think of some other comparison.

If only Minna would meet somebody worthy of her! By which Rosamund supposed she meant somebody who had not yet reached old age, somebody fine, somebody understanding who would not demand too much in the way of intellect from a bride. For though Rosamund had been honest when she had agreed to shelter Minna forever, if need be, she was already convinced the girl was not companion material for her.

Moreover, Rosamund knew in her heart that the young woman's best chance for happiness lay in a home of her own. And children. Minna was an angel with little Sam and talked incessantly of the crowd of younger siblings she had left behind in England.

Hers was an old story. Minna's parents had been gently bred, the father a clergyman. After his death and the subsequent impoverishment of the family, well-meaning relations took over as they were obliged to do. A clergyman's fine family of children was an encumbrance to all and sundry once the clergyman was gone. The mother found a position as housekeeper in a great house. The children were deposited wherever there were spare corners. The eldest girl, deemed too silly for governessing, was sent to India.

The tale was indeed familiar, too familiar to Rosamund. Yet aside from a similarity of background—she

too was a vicar's daughter—she did not see much of
herself in Minna. She did wish the girl the same happiness she herself had found in India, a place she had
approached with as much loathing as Minna's when
she had been a young miss of eighteen.

"I'm so grateful to you, ma'am," Minna was saying
earnestly. "I do hope you're not worrying over my
prospects. I'll come about, perhaps find some post,
and meantime I'm so lucky that someone like you has
taken an interest in me. Why, you've already taught
me so many things I never would have guessed about
this awful—about this place. Fancy whalebone stays
rotting in the heat! I was never more distressed than
to hear that, though to be sure these metal things are
scarcely more uncomfortable than my old ones . . ."

Minna chattered on, not asking for a response. This
was a talent of the child's that Rosamund sometimes
regretted. Now the prattle was most welcome as a
distraction, for Rosamund was suddenly in no mood
to take a real interest in her young guest's prospects
or problems. Her own were at issue.

Would he call? Would he dare to call? Once breakfast was over, Rosamund deposited Minna in the
morning room and helped her over the hard place in
her needle-work, then roved about the lower floor of
her house, remembering too many things—and too
few. A shame how memory faded in ten years' time.

Why, pray tell, had she been daft enough to kiss
him? That experience had not brought back her buried
memories as she expected; it had merely set her on
the road to imagining blissful new encounters.

The kiss had restored *his* memory, though, and
serve him right. She had hoped kissing him would jar
him into recognition; she had done it for that reason
and no other. Certainly she'd had no wish to be in his
arms for the activity's own sake.

Rosamund caught herself on that thought and admitted she was being less than honest. Yes, she hated him. At one time she had thought he had ruined her life. Yet no matter how she·felt about him, she had to admit he was a fine specimen. He was handsomer than ever, drat the man. The dark hair, the deep blue eyes that had once so entranced her, were the same, and added to the old attractions was a something that had been missing in the lad of twenty: a new air of maturity, the vigor of a man who knew what he wanted and how to get it.. Yes, she had wanted to be in his arms.

Her attraction was madness, of course. She had loved her husband Sam and would be true to his memory. She would not profane it by thinking of John.

Even as she had these pure thoughts, she realized Sam would not wish such fidelity from her. He would be the first to tell her she was alive and must *live;* she could nearly hear the emphasis in his weak voice, insisting just that as he lay on his deathbed. She was even certain that he would urge her to claim her first love if she could.

She smiled, and a glance into a convenient mirror told her it was a poor excuse for a smile. If not for John, she would never have known half of Sam's perfections. Her husband's kindness, his angelic tolerance, had earned her gratitude at first, then her love.

Sam had been gone four years, and sometimes, to her shame, she couldn't even recall his face.

She sank down upon an ottoman and started to cry.

"Forgive me, ma'am," said a familiar voice. "I don't believe your servant knew you were in here. He told me I was to wait while he ascertained whether you were receiving."

Rosamund looked up into Colonel John Fairburn's face. "Come now, I know my banyan better than that. He doubtless said, 'You wait. I see,' for that's Hari's answer to any domestic problem."

"I'm a domestic problem, am I?" Fairburn said with

a crooked smile. "Sorry to have disturbed you, ma'am. I'll leave quietly." He turned on his heel.

"Wait!" Rosamund stretched out one hand, furiously wiping the tears from her face with the back of the other.

He turned to look at her, a quizzical look. His gaze lingered on the outstretched hand, and she jerked it back to her lap.

"Why did you come?" she asked quietly.

"Why were you crying?" he countered.

She lifted her chin. "I was thinking of my late husband."

"Was he so precious to you, then?"

"Yes!" she snapped, turning from his cold eyes. "He was the best man in the world, and I loved him dearly. Not the least of his virtues was his gallantry. Would you—would any man but the most chivalrous one in the world take a soiled bride?"

"Soiled." He repeated the word softly. "Is that what you call it? Is that how you remember our night together? The night we pledged to marry?"

She shivered. "It is none of your business how I remember something you couldn't even recall until—until you were beaten over the head."

"I think it is my business, Rosamund. The name suits you, you know. You never seemed an Elizabeth to me."

"I undoubtedly seemed a Magdalen," she muttered, half to herself.

He caught the words and had the gall to laugh. "You know better than that, I hope. My night with you was magic; a turning point, or so I thought. The quiet young girl I had been dreaming of became my lover, my bride-to-be. When I awoke to find you gone I was broken-hearted. I searched for you, you blasted stubborn female. But I never found you, and so I acted in self-defense. I put you out of my mind and actually succeeded in forgetting your face." Another laugh, a harsh one.

"Broken-hearted." She repeated his words, shaking her head. "I was nothing to you. I could have been nothing, so poor and plain as I was."

"You think little of yourself, Lady Ashburnham."

"You mistake, sir." She set her shoulders proudly. "I was naive ten years ago, John, naive enough to believe your convenient professions of love, but I'm not so green now. I told you where I was going; you knew I was to leave that day. So you searched, did you? Not very hard."

"I went directly to Portsmouth and combed every vessel," Fairburn said stiffly. "There was no sign of you. Only one deuced ship in the whole harbor was en route to the East and you were not on board."

"Portsmouth? I didn't sail out of Portsmouth," Rosamund said in surprise. "What made you think so?"

"Good God! I assumed when I didn't find you that you had been lying to me about your plans."

"Lying to you?" She repeated the words in disbelief. "But why?"

"Because you didn't mean for me to find you. Because you didn't really want to marry me, a poor younger son."

She stared at him incredulously, nearly shrinking at the hard expression in the blue eyes.

"Where was your ship?" He crossed the room and knelt by her couch. "Tell me, damn you."

"London," she said, still staring into his eyes. His profanity didn't disturb her in the least. She welcomed the freedom it gave her. "London, damn *you*. As you must have known."

"Elizabeth—Rosamund, I give you my word I did not," he said. His rugged face softened; he looked, for a moment, exactly like the boy she had fallen in love with so many years ago. The boy she had made love to in defiance of every rule of conduct.

She had been married to him already in her mind,
as he had sworn they would be by law as soon as he
could manage all the details. She had felt no guilt,
only a blessed rightness, the same sense of peace that
stole over her now as she looked at his face. . . .

Then the spell was broken, and he was only the
man who hadn't recognized her the night before. The
man who by his own admission had done quite well
for ten years without a thought of her.

"Please leave me now," she said in a wooden voice.

He did. "This isn't finished," he said, pausing at
the door but not turning his head. Then he was gone.

Rosamund sank back down upon the ottoman and
gave way to gloom. Had he really tried to find her?
Had she been wrong to hate him all these years?

In the end, it mattered little. Fate had taken its own
turn, and it was too late for her and John. Ten years
too late.

She had known him for so short a time—only a few
days at the country-house gathering in February, her
last month in England.

She, like Minna so many years later, was being sent
to India because she was orphaned, poor, and had no
prospects at home. The very thought of being shipped
abroad to make a match with a stranger had revolted
her. After she met John, her desperation grew along
with her love.

She had thought carefully and finally made up her
mind. John was dependent and as poor as she was.
He couldn't marry her if he wanted to. But she did
love him so, with the fierceness of one who has not
loved before and expects never to love again.

She did the unthinkable. On the night before Saint
Valentine's Day, on her last night at the house, she
went to his room after all was quiet and offered herself
to him.

"Are you out of your mind?" she remembered him

whispering as he drew her into his room from the corridor.

"No, John. I'm going away forever, and I'll be forced to marry some old nabob, and submit to being touched by him, and you simply *must* be the first, I love you so." Her sentences ran together in her nervousness, but she never faltered.

She remembered the joy dawning in his eyes. "You love me? But I love you, my darling. I was afraid to speak, afraid to hurry you."

"Hurry me? When I'm to be bundled off out of the country tomorrow?" And, dizzy with relief, she threw herself into his arms. He loved her. She would carry the knowledge with her always.

When they paused for breath, he murmured, "I don't know how, but we'll find a way to marry. No money on either side, but someone will help us. Someone must. I'll take up a profession—I'll contrive something."

More kisses, and he was gently urging her to go back to her room. "Come. If anyone sees you, you'll be ruined."

Then came the worst mistake of her life—or was it? Even from a distance of ten years, Rosamund didn't know.

"No, John. I can't leave you. What if they won't let us marry? I'll have nothing to take with me. Please, I'm so afraid something will go wrong. Make me yours now. Tonight."

They were both so young. His chivalry held out a little longer, but his desire and hers won out in the end.

She had not meant to disappear that Saint Valentine's morning. But Mrs. Fallow, her chaperon, surprised her in the act of sneaking back into her room. And for what? Only some silly feminine vanity. As a young girl, Rosamund had not been very pretty; she had known it despite John's flattery. When she had awakened, rumpled, by his side, every instinct insisted she go at once to her dressing table. It was not yet morning. She could be back before he awoke.

"So, miss! You've been up to no good," Mrs. Fallow had said with her grimmest frown. And she matter-of-factly locked her charge into her room. Rosamund hadn't had the courage to cry out and bring the whole house running. She would wait for morning and John's support.

She had waited in desperation for John to appear at breakfast; and when he did not come down—too tired, she supposed, from the exertions of the night that had so enchanted her—she had trusted he would find her before her gruesome keeper could bundle her away to India. It was Valentine's Day, for heaven's sake, and they were true lovers. He had to find her.

He didn't. She had to face the facts that his promise of marriage had been a clever ploy. She had seemed to be the one to insist on her own ruin, but he had probably led her on somehow.

She soon found out she had no stomach for the sea. She became sick before the ship was out of the harbor. The most vivid memory of the seven-month voyage into a life of gloom had occurred when her monthly courses arrived, a couple of weeks late and unusually painful, in the wake of a particularly severe storm.

Mrs. Fallow took in the situation with one of her condemning glances and told Miss Manton that she was lucky to be going out to India, where gentlemen couldn't be as choosy as they were in England.

And Rosamund—she had decided sometime on the voyage to be called from now on by her second name—didn't ask too many questions. She knew scarcely anything of female functions, but she suspected she had miscarried a child. Knowing she should be relieved, she felt a little more alone, a little sadder.

By the time she arrived in Calcutta she was a pale shadow, and she had never been blessed with a high color. Along with the other girls Mrs. Fallow was shepherding, she was paraded at church, taken to parties and on outings of every kind. She truly couldn't believe it when handsome, if middle-aged, Sir Samuel Ashburnham looked twice at her. The circles under her eyes were surely disgusting, and she was thin as a wraith—a change from her former plumpness that was nowhere near as flattering as she had always expected it would be.

"Sir Samuel knows he can't expect the best," Mrs. Fallow said through tight lips. Rosamund was not her favorite, and Ashburnham was fabulously rich. "There is Levantine blood there, my dear. You might as well know."

Rosamund listened quietly to Sir Samuel's proposal and followed it, not with an answer, but with the story of her night with John. She felt she had to tell him.

"Did you love him?" her husband-to-be had asked gently.

She nodded, too embarrassed to look at him.

"Then I hope to be so fortunate one day," he answered, and took her hand.

They had been happy. They were married on Twelfth Night of 1804, and each year thereafter gave a ball to commemorate the occasion. They became parents after a few years of marriage, and little Sam was their greatest joy.

Sir Samuel caught the fever one rainy season. It carried him off within a fortnight, and Rosamund became as quietly sad as she had been quietly happy.

After four years she had adjusted to widowhood. She could not imagine being unfaithful to Sam; she felt, almost, that what was living in her had been burned on his funeral pyre in a mental version of the infamous Hindustani custom of *sati*—though naturally Sir Samuel had not had a pyre, but an ordinary coffin like any Englishman.

Rosamund went back into society after a year of

mourning, but she had not exerted herself to entertain until last night. She had decided on a whim to revive the Twelfth Night ball. And what was her reward? Her past had walked up to her and demanded a dance.

John's claim to have been mistaken about her whereabouts, that long-ago February, was troubling. Even if he was telling the truth, she repeated to herself in desperation, it was too late for her and John.

Yet he had said he was not finished with her.

"And now what am I to do?"

"Ma'am?"

Rosamund whirled about. She had not realized she had spoken aloud. Minna was standing in the doorway, hesitant, a work bag dangling from her wrist.

"Oh, nothing, child. I was merely thinking of the housekeeping." Not altogether untrue. How to keep John out of her house? That was the question. The servants would be of help, if need be, but John would certainly see reason after only a few hints. She could not have him in her house again, would not have him.

"I've come to another odd place in the embroidery, Lady Ashburnham, and if you could . . . you do such fine work . . ."

"Do sit down by me," Rosamund said, summoning a welcoming smile as she patted the ottoman. "Then we must go out. I'm determined to introduce you to the Burleighs today. Did you see young Mr. Burleigh last night?"

"Red hair and a clubfoot?"

Rosamund winced at Minna's offhand tone. The girl was meek and mild most of the time, but she had a certain heartlessness one would not have expected in a vicar's daughter—if one were not a vicar's daughter oneself, and perfectly cognizant that the breed was as full of human failings as any other. Minna would have to learn that people's characters couldn't be determined by their surface qualities.

But what a teacher fate had sent poor little Miss

Peabody! Rosamund smiled in spite of herself. A wealth of surface qualities had once convinced her, a silly eighteen-year-old, that she loved John Fairburn to distraction. She was sure, from the vantage point of twenty-eight, that her infatuation and subsequent ruin had been the result of an inane calf love based on John's handsome face. Yes, he had been kind as well as handsome, but he was probably kind to every young lady; the sympathy they had seemed to share, the understanding on all important points, was doubtless also a ploy to seduce unwary maidens.

She had been so stupid, so naive. So vulnerable.

She would try to see that no such tragedy befell Minna.

"Blast the woman, and double blast!" raged Colonel Fairburn, throwing his hat across the room.

His young nephew deftly caught it and grinned. "Any woman in particular, sir?"

"Get out of here, Percy, if you value your life," Fairburn said with what was very like to a snarl.

Uncle John was never the most even-tempered sort, and today was only a particularly vivid illustration of that truth. Percy Fairburn left quickly but peeked his head of butter-colored curls back in at the door to say, with a proper meekness, "A book you asked for arrived while you were out."

"Book? Oh, yes." Fairburn's scowl was eloquent. "I suppose I'd better see it."

Within moments the colonel's batman had delivered a mildewed copy of Shakespeare's plays.

John looked through the book, which had several missing pages, until he encountered *The Tragic History of Hamlet, Prince of Denmark.* Then he began to examine each leaf more closely; he had never seen the play performed, barely remembered reading it, and he didn't know where the speech in question occurred. His nephew stayed in the room, doing what he had

been doing on John's entrance: making serious inroads
into his uncle's stock of Madeira.

Finally John came upon the song in question.

> *Tomorrow is Saint Valentine's day,*
> *All in the morning betime,*
> *And I a maid at your window,*
> *To be your Valentine.*
> *Then up he rose, and donn'd his clo'es,*
> *And dupp'd the chamber door;*
> *Let in the maid, that out a maid*
> *Never departed more.*

Reading the words, he had to smile, a rueful smile.
They fit so well. So that had been the eve of Saint
Valentine's Day, that night so long ago; if he had
known the date at the time, it hadn't stuck in his
mind.

It had certainly stuck in Rosamund's.

"I say, Uncle," spoke up Percy. "Have you found
what you wanted?"

"You'd better go," the colonel responded. "I'm not
fit company."

"Well, who is, sir? It's devilish hot today for January, and you aren't used to the climate," Percy said
with the wisdom of one who had been several years
resident in India.

John sighed. To read the Shakespeare he had flung
himself into the nearest chair, and now he stretched
out his long legs. Rattan creaked as he tipped the
chair back.

Percy was perched on the handiest hard surface, an
inlaid teakwood chest. "Perhaps if you told me what
the trouble is? In the strictest confidence, of course.
Women can drive one mad."

"Let me have one thing understood," Fairburn said,

his dark brows forming a forbidding shelf. "There is no woman in particular. Do you understand?"

"Perfectly, Uncle."

"Good fellow. Well, given that circumstance, let me tell you a story."

Percy kept quiet, but straightened his shoulders to an almost military erectness as an expression of his interest.

Fairburn took this as encouragement—not that he needed any. "Imagine yourself in this situation, my boy. As an idle youth, while making a forced visit to a pack of dull relations, you meet a girl."

Since Percy was a youth, though not so idle as he had been before he shipped out to India, he had a ready answer. "I'd say I was a lucky devil. Relations, you know. Helps to have them off one's mind, what?"

Fairburn's frown deepened, and Percy made no further attempt at levity.

Looking away, Fairburn continued, "You meet a girl, and she's *the* girl, Percy. You have only a few days together, a few precious days, for she's about to depart for a distant place. Then, on the night before she goes, you—you confess your love and decide to marry." Young Percy did not have to be told what would interest him most—that the girl had not only confessed her love but had insisted—pleaded—that the young man take her to his bed. She wanted to be his at once, she said, and he was not hard to convince. They were only anticipating marriage vows; they had already made those in spirit.

John had his youth to contend with as well as his passion and hers. In the event he hadn't been able to play the gentleman and insist that she return to her room. He had taken her, knowing that in the morning they would announce their imminent marriage to the assembled company, a gathering that included the most stringently disapproving of his relations and her witch of a chaperon.

They were both underage. He was a second son and had no future laid out for him, no profession. He had been wavering between the church and the law, liking neither prospect. As for her, she was being shipped off to India precisely because she too was poor; orphaned besides. She was considered to be quite lucky that some friends of her late parents were buying her outfit and her passage for the great eastern marriage mart. They were depending on her to marry well. All this she had told him in confidence; to the others at the gathering she was simply Mrs. Fallow's charge.

Later he was to wonder if her whole tale about India was a lie, told for some unknown reason.

Nobody would approve such a match, but in the morning it would be too late to forbid it. After ten years, Fairburn could still remember the serene sense of rightness that had accompanied their lovemaking. She had been innocent; she had been loveliness itself. A secret, quiet beauty all the more precious because it was known only to him, for nobody else considered her anything but a plain dab of a girl.

He awakened late in the morning; several times during the night he had reached out to pull her close. But when he reached out again, she was gone.

She would be gone, of course. He hadn't worried. Naturally, since she had awakened before he had, she had returned to her own quarters to avoid an open scandal.

He hurried down to the breakfast room, but he had been a true slugabed, and breakfast was over. Not only that, she was gone, she and her hatchet-faced duenna, and nobody cared where.

Nobody but John Fairburn. He started on his fruitless search within a half hour of rising.

When he found the ship at Portsmouth, and no Miss Manton or Mrs. Fallow listed among the passengers, John had been forced to conclude that his love had sneaked away from him. He further concluded that she must have used him to satisfy her curiosity; that she hadn't loved him at all, hadn't meant to marry him. Not only that, she obviously wasn't going to India; then where on earth was she?

He couldn't find out. He forced himself not to care. And now, so many years later, she had the nerve, the absolute insolence, to chastise him for not finding her. Women!

Once all hope of finding her was gone John charged home, full of new determination to forget the fair sex. He begged his father to buy him a pair of colors. For once his eloquence overrode his sire's objections to such a dangerous and precarious occupation, and John began, at last, on a career that demanded all his energies.

He had been careful to steer clear of females' snares in the years since Elizabeth—since Rosamund. Women were nothing to him; they existed only to give momentary pleasure, and then they were most welcome to disappear.

Percy was clearing his throat in the uncomfortable silence, and his uncle realized that he had wandered off by himself into the past and forgotten such a person as his nephew existed.

"In the morning she was gone, lad," Fairburn said softly. "Gone without a trace! Devil take her. Years later she met the man again and accused him of trifling with her. Accused *him*! Unbelievable."

"Maddening, sir," offered Percy.

"Shall we go out?" John asked suddenly, rising to his feet. "Maybe I can walk it off."

Not inquiring what "it" was, Percy declined the honor. "I never walk at this time of day. You'll soon learn, Uncle John."

"The hot season hasn't started yet."

"You'd do much better to stay and have a drink, sir."

"That would be too easy. But feel free to help yourself," John said, starting out the door.

Percy shook his head at his uncle's stubbornness, then filled his glass complacently. Dashed comfortable to have a relation in this part of the world.

John set out for Maidan Park across from Government House, not because he had a wish to join in any fashionable promenade, but because he was new to the place and had no idea where else to walk. The gardens were quiet; the only Europeans Fairburn spied were nursemaids and their charges. He was quite at liberty to stalk about giving full play to thoughts both romantic and vindictive.

They had been victims, Rosamund and he, of circumstances. If he were to believe her version of events—and he did not see why he should not—and if she were to believe his in return, they must eventually arrive at the conclusion that neither had been at fault. She had not stayed by him, but he had not found her. The score was even in an odd, sad way.

She was an intelligent woman and must realize this; yet she had told him it was too late. She had warned him off.

As a confirmed bachelor, he ought to be relieved. He was not obliged to offer again for the girl he had ruined, in popular parlance, so long ago. They had evidently each been haunted by the episode. Now she was giving them both leave to put it behind them.

There was only one problem. When John had belatedly recognized his Elizabeth—no, he would always call her Rosamund now, a much better name for her—when he had recognized her it had simply not occurred to him that they would not pick up where they had left off. At the moment she had left him standing alone on her ballroom terrace, he had sworn to win her. A hasty oath, perhaps, formed by the magic of the soft tropical night and the lady's intoxicating presence, but one that he still believed made perfect sense.

As he marched across a stretch of green, wondering what in God's name he was to do next, a small child careened into his knees and fell backward onto the grass.

"Oh, Sammy!" A young lady came shrieking toward them; definitely not a servant, but she seemed too young to be the lad's mother. She pulled the boy to his feet while Fairburn was still blinking from the sudden jolt back to reality. "Now bow to the gentleman, dear, and ask his pardon," the girl addressed the child, giving his narrow shoulders a squeeze. She smiled nervously up at Fairburn.

He touched his hat to her. A pleasant-looking little thing, no more; a face just this side of plain, with brown curls peeping from the muslin bonnet and a passable form under the white muslin dress. He found himself smiling at the frightened look on the girl's face. When he glanced at the boy, who was also staring at him with wide, scared eyes, he smiled wider.

"I hope you weren't injured, my lad."

"No, sir," a little voice piped. The child executed an acceptable bow for one so young. He was a bit over waist-high measured against John, who had no idea what age such a stature would betoken. Clearing his throat, the child continued, "Your pardon, sir."

"Thank you. I do not regard it in the least."

"You won't be demanding satisfaction, then?" the boy burst out.

"No," Fairburn said in a serious tone, exchanging a merry glance with the lad's keeper.

The boy sighed in evident relief. "I've heard that officers pick quarrels a lot, and as this was my fault, you've every right to ask me to name your friends, but—thank you, sir."

Fairburn's lips twitched. "I believe the expression you are looking for is slightly different. That is, I

would ask you to name *your* friends. I could hardly
expect you to know mine."

The child nodded studiously and replied, "I did
wonder how that worked. Thank you." Holding out
his small hand, he added, "I'm Samuel Ashburnham."

So the brown eyes, first fear-struck, now trusting,
were familiar indeed; John had not just imagined it.
He saw the young lady and the boy looking at him
curiously and realized that an ominous silence must
have followed young Ashburnham's words. Worse,
John had not yet taken the offered hand.

Managing with great difficulty to keep his countenance, he shook the boy's hand and replied, "John
Fairburn. I'm delighted to meet you, Sir Samuel."

"Not a 'sir,' " the little lad admitted with a hint of
regret. "Papa was only a knight, and Mama says I
can't be a 'sir' unless I earn it for myself. Like Papa,"
he added, squaring his shoulders in obvious pride. He
eyed Fairburn's regimentals wistfully. "Are you a
general?"

"Colonel." John was absurdly gratified by the admiring glances sent his way by both child and young
lady. He was still endeavoring to hide his shock. Of
course Rosamund had a child. Married women were
supposed to, weren't they? And this boy was much
too young to be the result of that one night . . . besides, he didn't look in the least like a Fairburn. Dark
as John himself, young Samuel was yet made in a
different mold, reed-slender instead of sturdy, with a
face that might well turn scholarly in a few years' time.

He must look like the husband. Rage rose in John's
breast. Was there no end to the woman's audacity?
By her own admission she had loved her husband;
John, for all his vagaries, had not loved again, and
the notion that Rosamund had was bad enough. But
now! She had shared a child with the late Sir Samuel,
had she, and without a by-your-leave. This boy should
have been a Fairburn.

John tore his mind from such idiotic wanderings and addressed the young female. "I apologize, ma'am, for any lack of formality in my manners. But might I beg an introduction from you, too? It seems odd, somehow, for you to remain incognita when your young man has betrayed his identity." If this girl were a relation of Rosamund's, or a friend, she might be useful to him in some way as yet unfathomed.

The young lady dimpled and curtsied. "Miss Peabody," she said softly.

"Her name's Minna," put in young Samuel. "Fancy her forgetting to tell you that. She's looking for a husband."

"Sammy! I am not," Miss Peabody protested with a weak smile in Fairburn's direction. "That is precisely why I'm staying with your mama; because I'm not looking for a husband."

"Oh." Samuel frowned as he considered this explanation. "But all ladies are looking for husbands, Minna. Everyone knows that."

"Everyone in India, I make no doubt," Miss Peabody returned with a sniff.

Fairburn scented some interesting mystery here. Had Rosamund gone into the business of sheltering runaways? Young Master Ashburnham had hit the mark with his ingenuous statement. All young ladies were indeed seeking husbands, especially in India. They were usually sent here for no other purpose. If Miss Peabody was not on the catch, she must have an independent fortune stowed away.

Yet she didn't look rich by any means, an impression he got not from her wardrobe but from her manner. She looked capable and useful, if a bit officious. Not one's image of an heiress.

All these thoughts went through John's mind quickly, causing him to wonder in the next second why he was engaged in such speculations. He realized that he was matchmaking for his nephew, Percy. The lad's only way out of India was to make his fortune or to marry it, and how much easier for him if he could do the latter.

John realized further that Miss Peabody's existence would indeed be useful in the coming days. Rosamund had indicated she had no wish to see him. He could bring his nephew to meet her young guest, though. That was surely most proper. Whatever Miss Peabody's personal feelings on the subject of matrimony, he was willing to wager that Rosamund would wish this young woman to meet all the personable young men Calcutta had to offer on the off-chance that true love might blossom. And Percy was well-looking and of good family.

As for a real attachment developing between the youngsters, John didn't have any insight. The important thing was to use them as a blind for his own purposes. He must hope they would be able to stand the sight of each other.

"The day grows warm," he said with his most charming bow. "May I see you home, ma'am?"

Miss Peabody eyed the ground. "Why, I suppose so, sir. Thank you." She looked up.

John did not miss the flirtatious glance flashed to him from a pair of china-blue eyes. It rather shocked him. He would have to nip that notion in the bud. A dose of his stiff military manner would quash any symptoms of calf love.

Not looking for a husband indeed! He supposed he could acquit the demure Miss Peabody of looking for a lover. What, then, did she mean by such behavior? Rosamund ought to be warned of the girl's boldness with strangers.

He smiled. He was becoming adept at turning everything that happened to him into another excuse to seek the company of Rosamund.

Sammy Ashburnham slipped a confiding little hand into John's as the party set out. He would have to compliment Rosamund on her fine son. He had never had any use for children, but this little fellow was special. Was it only because one knew who his mother was? John wondered as he led his charges out of the Maidan and in the direction of the Chowringhee Road.

"Oh, my lady," Minna said with a sigh of rapture, bursting into the library where her friend sat. "I've met him."

"Have you indeed?" Rosamund looked up from the book she had been perusing; not that she had been seeing the words. Reading simply seemed the thing to do in a library, and Persian poetry, so difficult to decipher, a practical answer to the problem of wayward thoughts. Not to mention that the vaulted, book-filled room was the coolest spot in the house at this time of day. "I knew you would meet someone," Rosamund said with a fond look at her young charge.

"There's only one problem," the girl continued. "I told him I wasn't looking for a husband."

"Heavens! If you've only just met the man, your friendship has certainly taken an intimate turn."

With a giggle, Minna sat down next to Rosamund and explained. "I was with Sammy in the park. He bumped right into this gentleman, and in the bustle of bringing Sammy to rights—he has grass stains on his trouser knees, I fear—and having him apologize, the little dev—dear said I was looking for a husband. Naturally I had to contradict him."

"Naturally," murmured Rosamund, beginning to be diverted. A charming meeting in the park, chaperoned by Sammy. Most promising. Perhaps she would find Minna that perfect match after all. "What is this gentleman's name?"

"Fairburn. And he's so very handsome." Again Minna sighed. She had a full bosom, and it rose and fell dramatically.

"Oh, how delightful." Rosamund was satisfied. She was acquainted with Percy Fairburn, a sweet young man who could by a stretch of the imagination be called handsome, though Rosamund had never thought much of fair-haired men. He had a promising career with the East India Company. She remembered that Minna hadn't been at home when the young Fairburn had called upon her earlier in the week, the day she had invited him to bring his "old uncle" along to the ball.

If Percy Fairburn started coming to the house to court Minna, it was to be hoped he would leave his uncle out of the project. The man had military duties, for heaven's sake. Surely he couldn't spend his days paying morning calls.

"Sammy thought he was wonderful," Minna went on.

Rosamund recognized the irresistible urge to talk of the beloved object and admired the blush staining her young friend's cheeks.

"A colonel, after all."

"What?" Rosamund let out a gasp before she could stop herself. "You mean *Colonel* Fairburn is your new swain? Colonel John Fairburn?"

"I would hardly call him a swain," Minna said shyly. "Would you? He saw us home and was most polite. He was telling me something about his family, I think. I don't remember his exact words, but I thought it most promising that he should wish to talk to me about his family . . ."

Minna's voice went on. And on. Rosamund had never before wanted to shake the girl, but now she was seized by just such an ill-tempered notion. She managed only with difficulty to listen to Minna's effusions.

She told herself more than once during the recital that she would be glad if John's attentions were directed elsewhere. Minna could be called a pretty girl, and John probably didn't need money. Such a match wasn't impossible, and a flirtation in that direction would be quite in his style. Rosamund could vouch for his effect upon naive vicars' daughters.

"So, Uncle." Percy Fairburn, at liberty yet again from Company business, swirled the brandy in his glass as he and John sat at their ease beneath the punkah fans at Fort William. Turbanned servants were energetically working the cords that made the fans swing and rendered the large room breezy. "I didn't think you believed I should entangle myself with females until I made my fortune."

John shrugged. The lad was sounding unexpectedly shrewd. "I don't say you should entangle yourself by any means. You're the one who's been running about the town meeting every female you can. My dear nephew, anyone who would accompany Lady Tidbury on a visit to her physician because he heard the physician had a pretty daughter should not balk at being introduced to Lady Ashburnham's house guest."

"Use me if you will, sir," Percy said cheerfully. "This girl ain't old and ugly, I trust?"

"Not a bit of it," the colonel nearly growled, not at all liking his nephew's astuteness. He did mean to use the boy—and the girl—and was already feeling guilty. "Miss Peabody is a sweet young thing with the usual number of eyes, a shy manner, everything that makes a young lady desirable, I daresay. And according to my calculations, she could well be an heiress. But you're right. Though I think you'll like her, I have no reason to wish her on you except my own desire to have another excuse besides myself to visit Lady Ashburnham."

"Why?"

John took a draft of his own brandy. "Call it the art of subtlety, my dear fellow."

"I'll be pleased to call it anything you wish, Uncle,"

Percy responded. "At your service in this as in all things."

"Family loyalty," muttered John, sensing an edge of satire in the boy's words. "There's nothing like it."

The ladies of the Ashburnham household were having a quiet morning at their work; it was not Rosamund's ordinary day for receiving, and they expected no callers.

As Minna struggled with some straight hems, Rosamund, whose artistic yearnings were partially filled by the intricate embroidery her young guest so admired, was poking her needle listlessly in and out of a piece of silk, wondering if she would go mad.

Her night had been an unproductive and wakeful march of hours. She would give anything not to have seen John again.

Had she already been disloyal to Samuel's memory? The thought made her uneasy. She had kissed John deliberately that night at the ball; worse, she had enjoyed it. Worse yet, she wished that his visit of yesterday had ended in another embrace.

One was only human, after all, Rosamund excused herself, trying for philosophy. Lust was a human failing. She had succumbed to it once, though she had believed it to be love, and it was no great surprise that the same man could provoke such feelings in her again. At least she was not promiscuous in her ill-bred longings.

She was just beginning to meditate, for the hundredth time, on John's story of searching for her, that long-ago St. Valentine's Day, when her banyan Hari entered.

Minna jumped and emitted a small "Oh!" She had not yet got used to the large and burly Indian, made even taller by the massive turban in the Ashburnham colors.

Hari ignored the young lady's jitters and, speaking

only to his mistress, announced that the Fairburns, uncle and nephew, were waiting to be admitted.

Rosamund pulled herself resolutely back from her unproductive dreaming and managed a nod of acquiescence.

Hari disappeared on soft feet; soon he was back to fling the doors wide, and John entered the room.

Rosamund watched Minna stab herself with a needle and blush to a fiery hue. What a blessing indeed to be beyond that terrible age.

She herself, with ten more years than Minna's to her credit, greeted her old love with what she hoped was a serene air. Minna stammered and blushed even redder.

Then the ladies turned their attention to the colonel's nephew, who had come in on his heels. One had to admit that Percy Fairburn did not look like much next to his uncle. There was a sort of vapid lightness about the boy, who couldn't be much more than twenty. Yet Rosamund would be willing to swear that looks were deceiving and that he was solid, that he possessed what her mother used to call "bottom."

Absurd, though, to believe that Minna would look twice at such a youth when John Fairburn was in the world. Nor should she. Percy Fairburn had no establishment as yet, nothing but his cheery manner to recommend him to any young lady.

Nevertheless, Rosamund performed the necessary introduction, wishing against all logic that Minna would develop a *tendre* for Percy; it would make life so much easier.

"Miss Peabody!" Percy was his typical enthusiastic self and sat down right next to Minna, perhaps thinking the place she quickly made by her side was on his account. "Didn't I see you at the ball the other night? You were in white, I believe. Couldn't get next or nigh you to beg a dance."

Rosamund hid a smile. She suspected Percy was

indulging in a polite fiction. He probably hadn't seen Minna. Since all young misses were likely to wear white, his statement was safe enough. Minna had spent most of her time at the ball in hiding from the gentlemen. Perhaps he meant he hadn't been able to get near her because she was so often in the ladies' retiring room.

Minna was directing a pleading look at John, as though to beg his pardon for conversing with another. Colonel Fairburn did not have his attention on the young lady, nor did his eyes rest on his hostess. He had not yet taken a seat, and he seemed to be enthralled by Babur, the parrot, who was perched as usual on his stand in one corner of the room.

The late Sir Samuel had doted upon Babur, as did his son. Rosamund had never been able to see much personality in the brightly hued bird, named for a Moghul emperor; yet, while less than demonstrative in her affection, she valued Babur for her husband's sake and Sammy's.

"He doesn't talk," she informed John.

"Doesn't he? Unusual. But then, everything about you is most unusual, Lady Ashburnham." His manner was all politeness, as though he hadn't found her crying the last time he had visited this house; as though angry words hadn't passed between them. Rosamund had to admire his poise—and her own.

John crossed to her side. "Will you take a turn around the room with me, ma'am?" He held out his arm. "Let us examine this recalcitrant bird more closely."

Rosamund rose and took his arm, wondering what he planned to say to her that couldn't be spoken before the young people. As she and John walked away, she could feel Minna's eyes boring into their backs. Percy's bright chatter continued.

"Tell me," John said in a lowered voice, reaching out his hand to stroke the parrot's feathers, "can you

give me some information on Miss Peabody? Your
ward, I understand?"

"No, she is not exactly a ward." Rosamund hesitated, uncomfortable with the flare of feeling that rose
up in her. Was it jealousy? Absurd! Could he really
be interested in Minna? And why, if so, should she
gratify such an interest?

She could not think why not. She looked full at
John and was disconcerted to find his eyes as blue as
ever, and as keen. "Miss Peabody is a friend of mine.
Her father died leaving nothing, and so she was sent
to Bengal by her relations to make a match. Any
match. And the girl was repelled by such a necessity."
She paused. "Minna is in worse case than many young
ladies who find themselves in her situation. Can you
feature it, her people were so clutch-fisted they didn't
even outfit her for the journey. She came out in nothing but her Yorkshire wardrobe, which you may imagine is of little use to her here."

"Indeed," John was nodding seriously and motioned her to continue.

There was little more to tell. "We met not long
ago—I try to meet all the girls who come here—and
I took a fancy to her. And so I got permission from
her guardians for Minna to stay with me for a time.
To look about her without being forced into the first
objectionable match that comes along."

"She told me she is not looking to marry. And now
I find she's not an heiress, either. What future is left
for her, Rosamund?"

"Perhaps she is the best judge of that," she returned. "I've told her my home is hers for as long as
she desires it. But I believe better times may be coming to her. She has met someone."

"Ah! The perfect man?" John glanced across the
room to where Minna and Percy were making conversation—animated on the boy's side, monosyllabic on
the girl's.

"A man, at any rate."

"You don't approve of this gentleman?" he asked.

"If she is to be fascinated by him, I can only hope she has better luck than I had in a similar situation," Rosamund said evenly. She was almost enjoying this. She had always admired people who could speak well. So she too could say what was on her mind, yet pepper her speech with double meanings. Perhaps this only meant she was growing old; Lady Tidbury was a great one for speaking her mind.

Rosamund fought down the unaccountable urge to laugh as another thought came to her, a thought she did not voice. The ladies of her household were certainly practicing economy: they had hit upon the same gentleman to figure in their adolescent dreams.

"I do wish Miss Peabody luck," John said.

Rosamund wondered if he were so blind he did not know that Minna was smitten with him.

"Love at first sight is a difficult course," he continued. He looked long at Rosamund.

She studied her hands in embarrassment, remembering too well his youthful declaration of love so long ago. Did he remember hers?

He spoke again just as the silence was growing unbearable. "I admire you, Rosamund, for your kindness."

She looked up. "My kindness? Have I missed something? What are you talking about?"

Fairburn smiled. "I've been asking others in Calcutta about you and your activities, you see. I happen to know, ma'am, that Miss Peabody is not the first girl you've taken under your wing. In fact, ever since your marriage your house has been constantly open to at least one poor Bengal Bride. You shelter them, befriend them, see that they marry or find employment as governesses or companions. You even give them dowries. And then you find others to take their places in your home."

"That is nothing," she protested. "The very least I

can do is be a sort of substitute aunt to these girls. I, who was so lucky. I do remember the fear, the absolute disgust I felt at the indelicacy of the whole project. Being sent out to marry the first comer, in effect! How lowering to a female of pride, and many of these girls are strong-minded, of independent spirits. They are crushed by this fate. Even for a female of no pride at all, it was harrowing."

"Had you no pride?"

"None at all," she said, looking him in the face. "You must know that better than anyone. By the time I arrived in India I was thoroughly broken in spirit."

He appeared to be struck by her words. "My dear . . ." he began softly.

She couldn't let him comfort her; not now, when she was recalling her first days in Calcutta, when she had been so miserable, and all on his account. Shuddering, she remembered that first trip to the major showcase for young ladies, St. John's Church; the two elderly men who had offered their arms to escort her to the pew, and her disbelief at the naked lust in their eyes. What if she hadn't chanced to meet Sam soon after? Yes, she would keep thinking of Sam. "I had nothing fine and noble to offer a husband, and yet I was chosen by the best man in Bengal. I found that marriage could be a beautiful thing, not simply an embarrassment."

"I'm glad for you, Rosamund," John said, still speaking low, with a glance across the room at the other two.

"Are you?" He didn't look glad. His expression was strongly reminiscent of jealousy, in fact; she wondered if he could really be jealous of her memory of Sam, and felt an unworthy stab of gratification.

"I knew every girl couldn't be so fortunate," she went on, "and so I decided to help others like me. I have great wealth, you know, and it has never set easily on my shoulders. And I don't do so very much, at that."

"You do more than you know. All Calcutta sings

your praises," John declared, smiling a kinder smile than she had yet seen from him.

"And is Calcutta so very large a place?" She tried for a bantering tone, annoyed to find her voice on the verge of trembling.

"For us, my lady, Calcutta is the world." Suddenly John reached out and grasped her hand, carrying it to his lips, then turning it over to kiss the palm with such easy intimacy that Rosamund gasped.

He had done it to her on purpose, turned her into young Elizabeth with a mere touch of skin on skin. Rosamund had no happy memories of young Elizabeth; she was accordingly annoyed that he had been so heartless as to bring her back in all her contemptible weakness.

Her sentiments must have shown in her face. "Ah, my lady," John said, squeezing her hand, "I believe my nephew and I have outlasted the proper time for a morning call. We must leave you to your thoughts."

"I have no intention of being left to anything as unproductive as my thoughts," she said in an angry undertone.

She was most disconcerted when he laughed at her. And surprisingly sad to see him go away, he and his nephew, in the wake of Minna's unusually eloquent protests that they must stay to take tea.

"What did the colonel say to you, ma'am?" Minna asked in breathless accents once the gentlemen had gone.

Rosamund hesitated, then spoke a version of the truth. "We were talking of young ladies sent out to India."

"Oh!" Minna turned a most becoming shade of scarlet.

Rosamund wished she could administer a swift kick to her own backside for raising the girl's hopes.

While Minna tangled her thread, Rosamund returned to her embroidery with a ferocity not often brought to such a peaceful project.

A few more calls from Colonel Fairburn and his pleasant nephew, a few not-quite-accidental meetings in parade ground and park, sorted out to Rosamund's satisfaction the players in this new comedy.

Percy Fairburn, if not in love with Minna, was disposed to think of her as a good-natured girl and to flirt with her when he should have been putting his mind to his business with the Company. Rosamund had the instinctive feeling that Percy singled Minna out only so his uncle might have reason to call at the Ashburnham house.

Minna betrayed no inkling of this. Her attention was for no one but Colonel Fairburn. Rosamund would swear that, if asked to describe Percy's hair and eyes, Minna would not only have been inaccurate but unable to remember if the young man possessed those features. She seemed to take Percy's admiration as her due; take it, and leave it without a thought.

As for John Fairburn, he parried Minna's shy advances and did his best to push her into his nephew's arms. He looked at Rosamund with undisguised longing but did not bring up the subject of their past. Significantly, he made no further attempts to touch her except in the most formal of situations. That unnerving kiss on her bare palm was not repeated.

And Rosamund could only hope that she herself was behaving with the dignity and impersonality the world demanded of a woman in her position. She knew nothing beyond the most animal of admiration for John's looks, his manner, his astuteness on all points. Sometimes she was certain he was avoiding any renewal of intimacy on purpose to drive her mad.

But she couldn't let him know that she returned his evident desires. It would be folly to plunge into an *affaire* with her former love, and she was not prepared to admit the possibility of anything else.

"Mama," said little Sammy, leaning at her side as she played and sang to him on one dreamy golden evening, "shall I ever have a new papa?"

Rosamund's hands came crashing down on the keys. "What are you talking about? You have a father; he is gone from us, but he will always be your papa."

"I know that," the child replied with a wave of his plump hand. "But a second papa would be most convenient. He would be *here*."

Rosamund couldn't dispute that logic. She hugged her son to her. He needed his own father, whom he could not recall despite her stories. And lacking a father, he needed male discipline when he left the nursery.

How she would miss him when he went away! Soon he would be old enough for school, and he would be better off in England. Her clergyman assured her that Sammy needed a strict environment; her friends agreed that a mother's tender heart was no guide for bringing up a boy. Rosamund knew she was overly sentimental in wishing to keep him by her. Send him to England she would, though Sammy, with his mixed heritage, would not have the world's easiest time in that land.

But her son was a strong little fellow. He would survive, and so would she without him. She had long ago made up her mind to staying in India, in her home, while her child was at school.

Now, though, she began to wonder if she shouldn't travel with him when he went. She might rent a house near Eton, or whatever school she settled on, and see him every holiday. She had not considered this path before; as the widow of a rich man, she must be admitted to some society, though there would be the inevitable whispers about the Ashburnham blood. Would she like to go back to England?

For ten years she had thought that land still held John Fairburn, and she would not have hesitated to say no. Now, though, she might escape him by returning to the country of her birth.

Perhaps they should leave for England now, though

Sammy was much too young for school. Minna could go along as a sort of companion and be found a position or a husband on British shores as easily as here.

The parrot squawked from his place in the corner, and Sammy stirred against her. "Mama, you're holding me too tight. Babur is scolding you."

"Sorry." She released her son and patted his shoulder. "I was thinking."

"About a new papa for me?"

So he hadn't quit that topic. Children did tend to stick to a thing. "What has put such an idea into your head, Sammy?"

He shrugged expressively. "I don't know. Somebody was asking me the other day."

"Who?" Rosamund spoke sharply.

The child apparently noticed. He looked a touch uncomfortable as he answered, "I don't remember, Mama."

Male dissimulation, Rosamund suspected as she eyed him keenly. But she could read nothing sly on her boy's little face and chose not to insist on his searching his memory. Some dowager had probably been teasing him about his mama's likelihood of remarriage. More than one old lady incessantly harped on such a possibility, to Rosamund's perpetual distress. One could expect nothing better, she knew, in the restricted society of Calcutta.

"People like women to be married," Rosamund said, half to herself. Sammy gave her a startled look, but made no remark.

Babur squawked again.

"Did you hear that, Mama? He almost said a word."

"What word?" Rosamund scrutinized the untalented parrot for signs of new intelligence.

"I couldn't quite tell. Will you sing to us?"

Another, louder squawk escaped Babur's beak,

something that Rosamund could not understand. It did sound close to a word, but which word?

"Who has he been talking to?" Rosamund asked, eyeing the bird suspiciously. She hoped he would not come out with some Hindustani curse.

To forestall any such indelicacy, she immediately began to play and sing Sammy's—and Babur's—favorite song.

Colonel Fairburn, meanwhile, was spending what free time he had in musing over what might have been. This he did despite his conviction that such idiocy was ruinous to his peace and of no practical use to his future.

Still, he found himself doing it at the oddest moments, especially when he should have been about his military duties: sometimes actually in the middle of a meeting to plan strategy! Once he had passed an entire interview with no less a personage than the new governor-general, hearing nothing of his lordship's talk, merely counting the hours until he could once more present himself, dragging his nephew, at Lady Ashburnham's.

Being a man of sanguine temperament, he soon passed from musing to a definite wish for action.

"Babur," he informed Rosamund's parrot one day, "love is a snare. As a bird, you must be especially wary of snares." The parrot was his only companion, for Percy was entertaining Miss Peabody across the room. Rosamund was out. Colonel John Fairburn was talking to parrots. Nothing was as it should be on this ill-arranged morning.

John scowled right at the insipid Minna, who was looking at him and started violently. He had the grace to glance away. He had not meant to frighten the chit, he had merely been thinking murderous thoughts of Lady Ashburnham's banyan. Why hadn't the fellow said his mistress was out? John would swear that Hari had had a sly look in his eye as he ushered the gentlemen in to—of all the deadly dull things!—the sole presence of Miss Peabody.

"Sir," piped a small voice at John's side, "why are you talking to my parrot?"

John was surprised to see young Sammy Ashburnham standing by his chair. "Don't you talk to him?" he asked with a smile.

"Why, yes," Sammy replied. "But grown people don't. Not often. And I've never seen a gentleman speak to him."

"Do you meet many gentlemen here?" Contemptible though the tactic was, John couldn't resist trying to find out something more about Rosamund's life. Perhaps he had a more serious rival than her husband's ghost.

"Oh, yes, a quantity, though I'm usually in the nursery," the boy was answering. "They like Mama, you see. She's so pretty."

"She is," John agreed, smiling again. This was quite a winning little fellow. "And does she like any gentleman in particular?"

"A new papa, you mean? I've been trying to find out. I don't think so," Sammy said with a sigh. "Babur could tell me if only he'd learn to talk. He's down here often when I'm not."

"Babur is a gentleman. He doesn't repeat gossip," said John. "Now tell me, little friend. I see there is a ball in your hand. Do you have a cricket bat in the house?"

"Oh, yes, sir, a new one. I'm not quite big enough to play, but I'm going to be ready."

"I propose you fetch your new cricket bat, take me to a likely spot in the garden, and I'll show you some tricks of the game. Do you suppose Miss Peabody and her suitor would like to join us?" With these words he indicated Percy, who appeared to be telling the young lady a long story. John would wager his nephew would be glad to give his prattle-box a rest in favor of some exercise.

"Oh, yes," repeated the boy, brown eyes nearly brimming over with joy. "Minna, Minna!" He crossed the room at a run.

Words tumbling over one another, Sammy explained the colonel's plan to the others. Minna looked at John with sparkling eyes; she appeared to be taking the compliment to herself. Percy winked at his uncle, rose and bowed to Miss Peabody, and offered to escort her to the garden. Sammy dashed away for the cricket bat.

John was about to follow the young couple when he felt a tug at his coat.

"She don't like him, you know; she likes you," Sammy whispered in a confiding tone. "Better watch yourself, sir."

"Thank you for the warning, my boy." John was more than ever convinced that Rosamund's little son was a most knowing young man who would go far.

The cricket game was precisely what was needed, as it turned out, for the ideas to flow from John's brain regarding his situation with Rosamund. They were so close; only a little push on his part should suffice to make them love again.

As soon as he was free, he called upon Lady Tidbury in her opulent garden house upriver from the city and set his plan in motion.

"A dinner," Lady Tidbury muttered, looking narrowly at the colonel. "You want me to give a dinner?"

"Not just any dinner," he said. "A Saint Valentine's Eve dinner. With perhaps a little dancing in the evening—informal, by all means."

"Why not a ball the next day?" demanded the lady. "A Valentine ball? Since Sir Magnus has provided me this splendid house, with an adequate ballroom, I wish to show it off as much as possible, and to as many people as I can collect. A dinner for ten or twenty will be positively dull."

"No, the exact date is important. And it wasn't a ball." John shook his head.

"What wasn't? I thought we were discussing the future, young man," snapped the general's lady.

"May I speak plainly to you, Lady Tidbury?"

"I wish you would, sirrah."

John hesitated the merest instant while he surveyed her ladyship's stern profile. Could he trust her? More important, did he have a choice?

He plunged into speech. "I find that I can only be happy if I win a certain lady. She and I parted ways through an unfortunate accident, some years ago in England. Our last evening together was Saint Valentine's Eve, and at the house where we were both staying, there was a small dinner. She had to leave the next morning—pressing engagements, you understand—and so the little gathering meant a great deal to us. It was our last chance to be together, you see."

"Charming," Lady Tidbury muttered. "A man who remembers dates! Never thought I'd see the day." She looked as though she didn't believe a word of his story.

John inclined his head in modesty, pretending not to notice the touch of satire in the lady's words; far be if from him to confess that it had taken the hints of his lady to recall the date to his mind—if it had ever been there at all.

"So tell me, Fairburn: why exactly did you jilt Rosamund Ashburnham?"

John's jaw dropped, and he found himself at a complete loss for words.

His elderly companion continued quite as if he'd made some rejoinder. "Oh, it's obvious to anyone with an eye. You're mad for her, and there's something about the two of you together—one can tell you've met before."

This was an uncomfortable notion. Were the secrets of one's heart indeed laid open for the amusement of the idle multitudes? Upon reflection, he supposed they were. He had never been good at hiding his feelings. "Why do you assume I jilted her?"

"I know her ladyship came out to India a Bengal Bride," Lady Tidbury said flatly. "Impossible to suppose she would have done the jilting, a girl in her position. She'd have been glad to marry the devil himself to stay in England. So why didn't she marry you?"

"Misunderstandings," said John. "Partings which did not have to be. The usual thing, I believe."

"The world would run a lot smoother if everyone, not just myself, would speak plainly at all times."

"I agree. Yet we had no lack of plain speaking." A smile played about John's lips. Oh, he and Rosamund had spoken very plainly. "Our problem had more to do with erroneous information; assumptions, if you will."

"Sounds to me as though five minutes telling each other what's what would have done the world of good, and not left you ten years older, begging a sharp-tongued harridan to help further your suit."

"You do yourself too little credit, madam," John said with a bow. "I don't consider you sharp-tongued at all."

"You're a fool," cried the lady, but her eyes were twinkling, and she ended the interview by agreeing to give a dinner on the date in question.

ᴛohn resolved to make good use of the time remaining to him before that day arrived. He had not been making much headway with Rosamund; indeed, he hardly knew what to say to her beyond the commonest of civilities. He still had inconvenient spells of wishing to wring her pretty neck for leaving him on

that night so long ago. If she had only stayed by him
. . . Still, even such a dullard as he ought to be able
to manage to pave the way to a charming rapproche-
ment by Saint Valentine's Eve.

"Do you know, Rosamund, that Fairburn fellow is
determined to bed you," Lady Tidbury said the next
time she called at the Ashburnham house—which was,
not incidentally, the very morning after John Fairburn's visit to her.

"Oh, dear." Rosamund tried for a bored air. Lady
Tidbury had surprised her in her favorite garden retreat. Wearing a wide-brimmed hat with a hole cut
out of the crown, Rosamund was letting her hair take
the sun while her face did not, a necessity if she was
to maintain her blondness.

The first and only time she had been taken ill from
too much sun, shortly after her marriage, Rosamund
had noticed with approval what the sun had done to
her hair even as she bemoaned the temporary disfig-
urement of her skin. Since that accident, she always
took care to bathe her hair in sun as she had since
read the Italian ladies of the Renaissance used to do
long ago. She had been thrilled to escape, even in so
superficial a manner, from her young self.

She had done quite well in that project. A change of
name; hair altered by a few shades; and a figure and
face vastly improved. She was nothing like that stupid,
naive Elizabeth she remembered with shudders. If it had
been possible, she would have changed the color of her
eyes . . . but she couldn't escape John, she thought
drowsily. Neither she nor Elizabeth could resist John.

The sun always made her sleepy. Perhaps she was
dreaming now; had only imagined that Lady Tidbury
had come storming in to see her over the protests of
Hari, who knew that Rosamund's time in the garden
was private time, and was now plumping her robust
self down in a handy garden seat after delivering that

blunt statement about John. Rosamund focused her attention on her visitor and saw that it was indeed so.

"You're in love with him," Lady Tidbury accused, peering through an eyeglass. "Silly chit! Your pride is at stake, girl. He cast you aside like an old boot. You can't let him charm you now."

"How do you know all this?" Rosamund asked in appalled curiosity.

"Guessed," muttered the other. "The dignity of womanhood is at issue here, my dear. Don't let him play with you again."

Rosamund knew her face must be red and was thankful for the sheltering hat. "This is dreadful," she said, meaning her ladyship's uncanny guesses as well as John's supposed designs on her virtue. "What does he plan to do?"

Before she would answer the question, Lady Tidbury snapped her fingers. At once her hookahburdar was at her side. A pause in the conversation ensued as that servant busied himself with the water pipe, placing it on a suitable small table, readying it for his lady's pleasure. Rosamund looked on fascinated at the spectacle, which was becoming increasingly rare in society. The gentlemen really preferred cheroots these days, and few ladies smoked hookahs—only the elderly and opinionated ones clung to the habit.

Lady Tidbury qualified on both counts. She took up the agate mouthpiece and puffed, then, having built up enough suspense, finally returned to the conversation. "Fairburn has got me to promise to give a party in a couple of weeks. The day before Saint Valentine's Day, for some odd notion. I gather he wants to sweep you off your feet by re-creating your first meeting, or your last—forget which. Either way, it's not worthy of you, my dear. You won't be taken in."

Rosamund agreed that she would not. Burrowing even deeper under the hat, she wondered what on earth John was trying to do.

"Colonel Fairburn must be put in his place," Lady Tidbury said firmly, fingering the black tube of the hookah. "They say widows are easy game, but you must prove them wrong, child. I'm counting on you to be strong. For the—"

"Yes, for the dignity of womanhood," Rosamund interrupted with a sigh. She wished that Lady Tidbury were not quite so emphatic on this issue. Rosamund felt bent under the weight of becoming a symbol for all females.

A squawk pierced the air. Rosamund looked past her hat brim to see Minna, Babur the parrot perched upon her shoulder, standing quite close to the two women, right beside the mango tree that shaded Lady Tidbury. The girl was staring at Rosamund in horror.

Rosamund remembered that Minna often liked to take Babur for a constitutional around the garden, but she had never known the girl was in the habit of eavesdropping.

"I suppose you've been standing there for a long time," Rosamund said, feeling tired.

"You never told me a thing about you and—him," lashed out Minna, and then she was gone, Babur fluttering a bit, but clinging to her shoulder. A particularly loud squawk drifted back on the air where they had just been.

Rosamund frowned in perplexity. "What did that parrot just say?"

" 'Love.' " Lady Tidbury shrugged. "Rubbish. I taught mine to call me the queen of the world in Persian. Sets one up a great deal, especially early in the morning."

Domestic harmony in the Ashburnham house did not improve markedly after the incident in the garden. That very afternoon, Rosamund found Minna packing her modest traps.

"You have betrayed me," the girl cried into an al-

ready sodden handkerchief, turning from Rosamund
in distress as soon as her hostess entered the room.

"My dear girl, I once knew your Colonel Fairburn.
That is all. Would you have me pretend I did not?"

"Did he really jilt you?" Minna demanded, drying
her eyes.

"I don't know," Rosamund said quietly, remembering John's story of a fruitless search of ships. "I simply
don't know."

"There! You see? We are bitter rivals."

"You sound pleased, Minna. I've been thinking our
relations with the Fairburn gentlemen are very like a
play. Is this to be the dramatic climax?"

Minna looked scornful, then insulted. Both these
expressions softened into mere uncertainty.

Rosamund took this as a good sign and decided to
try an authoritative tone. "Now do tell me where you
plan to go in this wild state."

"To Lady Pratt. She was most kind when we met
at the parade ground."

As Rosamund remembered, her ladyship had civilly
greeted Minna and promenaded on. The woman might
be disconcerted to find a renegade Bengal Bride on
her doorstep.

"I wish you'd reconsider, my dear. We aren't really
rivals, you know. I don't mean to remarry."

"I suppose you think I don't know what's what,"
Minna cried, her blushes causing odd blotches to appear on her sensitive skin. More tears tumbled on her
lashes. "You mean to keep him as your lover even
when I marry him."

"Oh, is that how you see it?"

"Of course. I know you don't want to marry. And
why should you? You've everything you need without
doing anything of the kind. You—" Minna hesitated,
and her chin trembled—"you're the luckiest woman
in the world."

"Why, you little—sit down and listen to something

besides your romantical ravings." Rosamund reached
out for Minna's shoulders and pushed the young
woman down upon the bed. "Lucky, am I? I buried
my husband four years ago, when I was only four-
and-twenty. I've been raising my little boy on my own,
without a father for him to look up to. Samuel didn't
even have a portrait taken, drat the man's modesty. I
can't remember, sometimes, what he looked like. And
I was happy with him, Minna. Can you even feature
what it is like not to remember the face of the one
you loved?"

Minna said nothing and turned her head away.

Rosamund was wound up too tightly to stop speaking. She had never wallowed in self-pity, especially in
front of a virtual stranger, but she could not help herself. "Yes, I have more worldly goods than when I
came out to India, but there are so many other things
I've lost forever."

"Money softens suffering quite well, I daresay."

Rosamund barely caught the sarcastic words, but
she felt them like a slap in the face. "Money does
nothing of the kind. But you may have it if it's your
only desire. You know I've promised to dower you
when the time comes. How would you like me to settle a sum on you now instead? Then you might be
quite independent, go back to England, set up house
with your family if you wish."

"Don't insult me, please, Lady Ashburnham," Minna
said with dignity. "I won't let you pay me to get out
of the country."

"Very well, *I'll* get out of the country," Rosamund
all but shouted. "I can't last another minute in this
bedlam. Go where you will, you silly girl."

So saying, she slammed out of the room and made
her way to her own, where she sank onto the sofa and
shook. A few angry tears ran down her face. What
was happening to her? How had she so lost her composure with a young woman who depended on her not

only for bed and board but for common sense, for security?

"I must be going mad," she said aloud.

Speaking the words seemed to make the possibility recede, and Rosamund soon found herself back in Minna's room, comforting the weeping girl and begging her forgiveness. In return, Minna begged Lady Ashburnham's pardon quite sweetly. She hadn't done any further packing; in fact, a few things had already been returned to their places in the room. Rosamund suspected that neither she nor her guest was thinking quite clearly.

"Do you plan to attend this Valentine dinner?" Minna asked in a tone of offhand curiosity.

"I suppose so. You will, too, won't you?"

"Of course. I'll go anywhere to see him. You know that." Minna frowned. "Perhaps old Lady Tidbury is wrong. She makes up stories, they say, and she can't always remember where she gets her information. Perhaps Colonel Fairburn never spoke to her at all; the dinner could be all her own idea."

"Likely so," Rosamund murmured. Might as well let the girl draw comfort where she could.

But even Minna could not let her fancy take her that far. "Then why did she speak so to you? As though she knew something private about your past? You did know Colonel Fairburn once, didn't you? When you were young? She was right about that, wasn't she?"

"So I've told you," Rosamund replied, feeling a hundred years old. *When you were young.* Heavens, she was not yet thirty and until recently would never have called herself ready for the boneyard.

"And there was something to it," Minna stated. "I can tell by the way you are looking, ma'am. But I warn you, I shan't be set aside from my purpose."

"You've changed your opinion of marriage very quickly, child. Well, what can I say? I wish you luck, and I assure you I don't want to dally with your favorite."

This was the truth. The desires of her body didn't count; her mind, the part she respected, had not the slightest wish for a liaison with Fairburn or any man.

Minna looked a little embarrassed, and a sort of truce was declared.

If Rosamund felt, in the days to follow, that Minna's pose of tragedy queen bordered on the ridiculous, she had the good form not to tell the world she thought so.

Others were not quite so reticent. "I say, ma'am," Percy Fairburn commented one morning, when he had paid a call without his uncle (Colonel Fairburn, for once, having business at Fort William with the governor), "what's wrong with Miss Peabody? She's drooping about like a deuced ghost. Has she a head? I know she don't normally take too much wine."

Rosamund's lips twitched. Did all young men assume that females' headaches were the result of being jug-bitten?

The room was full of visitors, and Minna had drifted away from all of them and was standing languidly at a window. The pose was most attractive, Rosamund thought critically: despite the heavy rain, wind stirred the light curtains around the girl's figure. Her brown curls were not really dressed, just bound back with a ribbon. Minna looked ripe for romance, in fact; she was standing at the window looking exactly like a beleaguered heroine in a gothic novel.

"Why are we females so preoccupied by love, Mr. Fairburn?" Rosamund asked.

Percy started at the odd question, which made no pretense of answering his own a few minutes before. "Why, I suppose for the same reason we males are," he finally said with a grin.

Rosamund was pleased at his gallantry. The young man had the makings of a drawing-room favorite.

"Ah, you gentlemen don't spend half the time we do worrying over that particular emotion. I'm afraid Miss Peabody is preoccupied by thoughts of one who doesn't think of her. Why don't you help her out? I don't mean court her, if such isn't your desire, but try to bring her out of herself, if you would. She looks positively depressed."

"Perhaps 'cause Uncle isn't here. It's Uncle she's acting a gudgeon over, you know."

"Oh, dear. Do you think so?" Rosamund was concerned for Minna's dignity. If such an untried youth as Percy Fairburn had noticed the source of the young lady's preoccupation, she might well be the laughing-stock of the British community, and Minna didn't deserve such a fate.

"Don't worry," Percy replied, as though he read her thoughts. "All girls act silly over Uncle."

"Oh." Rosamund laughed. "Then you won't feel you're stealing a march on the colonel."

"Ma'am?"

"By distracting Miss Peabody. You do remember that I asked you to do so?"

Having a rapidly moving mind which rarely lit anywhere, young Fairburn remembered no such thing, but he readily promised and was soon approaching Minna's side under Rosamund's careful eye. She was happy when Minna smiled at one of Percy's sallies, or perhaps it was some compliment. Rosamund wasn't near enough to the window to hear the exchange.

So all the girls were "silly" over Colonel Fairburn, were they? Rosamund was not surprised. She looked around at her chattering guests, none of whom appeared disposed to go out into the rain. She knew she ought to be relieved at John's absence, but somehow she quite wished he were here. She felt the need to spar with someone, and who better than he? Ah, well,

there would be other days. She rang for Hari and
ordered a cold collation for the company. If they
wouldn't leave, they might as well be fed.

"The lady *sahib* does honor to her house," Hari
said in approval, moving importantly away. Soon he
returned at the head of a long line of servants bearing
meat, fruit, and cakes, and directed the placing of
long tables and chairs that other retainers carried in.
Hari was in his element when there were guests in the
house.

Percy Fairburn stayed by Minna during tiffin; and
he was not alone. The girl had by this time collected
a small circle of admirers, young men with the Company or sons of British residents, and though she took
no notice of any of them, they clustered around her
loyally. Perhaps, thought Rosamund as she busied
herself with her own regiment of suitors—an older
group, this, with as many would-be lovers as would-
be husbands—Minna's allure was helped, not hin-
dered, by her uncaring attitude toward any man who
was not Colonel Fairburn. People always did want
what did not come easily.

The rain was over, and some of the guests were at
long last calling for their palanquins, when the double
doors of the grand salon opened to admit Colonel
Fairburn. Rosamund instantly came out of the torpor
the wet day and dull company had induced. She forgot
what she had been doing or saying. Absently, she
placed an empty wineglass in the hand of one Mr.
Lutis, a new swain of hers, and advanced to meet
John with a welcoming smile and an outstretched
hand.

He lifted the hand to his lips. "Your servant,
madam. I come to collect my rapscallion nephew; he
and I are due at Lady Tidbury's within the half hour."

Rosamund tingled strangely; he had not kissed her
hand like that in a long time. She nodded and was
about to speak when Minna rushed up, hand held out

quite as expectantly as Lady Ashburnham's had been, and said in a high, clear voice, "We are so glad to see you, Colonel. You mustn't run away at once."

Fairburn couldn't ignore the little hand; he shook it firmly, which was evidently not what Minna had expected. She was frowning in puzzlement as Rosamund added, "We'll hope to see you for a longer visit soon, Colonel Fairburn. But you mustn't disappoint Lady Tidbury." After a pause, she added, "I hear that she is planning a party soon, on your orders."

His eyebrows shot up. "You don't say? How news does travel, to be sure."

"Lady Tidbury told me," Rosamund said. "Told us." With a smile she indicated Minna, who had grown tense at the awful reference to the Valentine's Eve dinner. "Her ladyship can be fanciful. She would have it you're planning to play a trick of some sort on a certain woman."

"Good Lord!" Fairburn gave Rosamund a searching look. "The old—the dear lady has gone and spilled the story. I wouldn't have thought it of her."

Rosamund shrugged. "Her loyalty to womanhood, as she sees it, supersedes any arrangements she may have made with you."

"Ah! So she warned you off."

"I must say I was surprised to hear her story, John. Surprised and displeased. But now that you know I know, you may call off whatever you had planned." Rosamund paused, then added, "I'm sure we understand each other."

Fairburn cast a questioning look at Minna, who was evidently listening with all her ears.

"Oh, Miss Peabody knows that you and I were once acquainted," Rosamund assured him.

Minna caught her breath at this and turned pleading eyes to Lady Ashburnham.

Rosamund understood that she must not, for the sake of domestic peace, continue her frankness by in-

forming Colonel Fairburn that Miss Peabody was
dying of love for him and had actually fought with her
hostess over him.

Naturally she had no such plan. "That's all I have
to say," Rosamund said with a reassuring look at the
girl. "I do hate to see you go to all the trouble of
some complex prank, sir, and have it all for naught.
It will be for naught, you know."

"Your consideration, ma'am, is most gratifying."
Fairburn was still regarding her in that unbelieving
way. "I can see my call on Lady Tidbury is doubly
necessary now. I'll have to scold her."

"Please don't do that, John."

He laughed. "I won't, and well you know it. Tell
me, did you accept her invitation for the dinner?"

"I did."

"Then we are no worse off than we were before.
Your servant, ma'am." As his nephew approached, he
added, "We'll be off, then. I hope to see you soon."

Rosamund inclined her head in a noncommittal
fashion while Minna babbled that she did indeed hope
she would see the colonel soon.

When the girl's words died away, John looked at
Rosamund. "I forgot, my lady, to congratulate you on
your friend Babur's new talent. I find he's learned his
first word. And a most important one."

Rosamund flushed. *Love*. The parrot had been
squawking it incessantly.

"Why, Colonel Fairburn, I've been trying and trying
to understand Babur's new word. What is it?" Minna
gushed into the silence.

"Ah, my dear young lady, you'll have to find that
out for yourself," John said with a slow smile. Then,
with another significant look at Rosamund, he went
on his way, followed by an amused Percy.

Rosamund watched them leave, wondering why the
setdown she had planned had not quite come off.

"That was so strange, ma'am," Minna murmured at her side. "I—I was afraid you'd tell him about me."

"No, dear, I wouldn't embarrass you so. Did you think the conversation strange? Let us simply say that I'm tired of men having the upper hand because of dishonesty."

"Whose dishonesty, my lady?" Minna turned a fiery hue.

"Why, anyone's," Rosamund replied, wondering if she ought to suspect her young protégée of some dire doings. What sort of doings, she could not imagine, and so she forgot the fleeting impression that Minna was hiding something.

Contrary to his word to Rosamund, Colonel John Fairburn had something resembling a scold to read Sir Magnus Tidbury's lady for her perfidy. "Well, ma'am, it's all up with me. So you told Lady Ashburnham to beware my stealthy plans. To hear her talk, she expects to meet with some hackneyed joke at your dinner table."

"I couldn't let the girl walk blindly into your trap, could I, boy?" countered Lady Tidbury. They were riding through a green field near the river and the Tidbury's villa, on ground that still steamed from a recent rain, and Percy had just galloped ahead on the lady's strong hint that he was not wanted.

"It's worse than an old ballad," John muttered. "Tragedy for no reason. Tell me, ma'am, what is to stop me from winning the woman I love? She loved me too, once, and I'd wager she could learn again."

"Love? What has love to do with this, you rake? Ah, I know very well you gentlemen cloak everything in that word. Gets you where you would else never tread. Lady Ashburnham has the wit to know it too. Love, my foot. If you had loved her you would never have cast her aside."

"I didn't—oh, what's the use." John understood

completely, or thought he did. This old meddler had been prating on to Rosamund about male lust. Little did the Tidbury know that Rosamund already thought he was a creature driven by no other feelings, a heartless seducer who would promise anything in the heat of the moment. "So you told her I was plotting her seduction."

"Well, I hinted as much," Lady Tidbury admitted. "You're a fiend to try to bed that virtuous young woman. Why, she's never looked at another man since her husband's death, and there's been droves of you fellows swarming round her. Just because she has a weakness for you doesn't give you leave to toy with her affections. Good God, man, she has her son to think of! She can't become a notorious woman. It wouldn't do the boy any good at all. They have enough trouble as it is, Sir Samuel having had Jewish blood."

"Do you really think she has a weakness for me?" John asked with interest, ignoring the bit about Rosamund's late husband. He had heard it before.

"Oh, no, you'll get no encouragement from me," snapped the old lady, wheeling her horse about. "Percy!" she bellowed across the plain. "We're going back."

In the distance, Percy took off his hat and waved it, then galloped toward them.

"I don't know, ma'am," John said, shaking his head. "I had understood that one's female friends were supposed to help young men with affairs of the heart."

"Leave the heart out of this," Lady Tidbury said with a snort. "You're possessed by quite another organ—"

"Ahem!" John cleared his throat loudly as Percy rode up. "Shall we race back to the compound, ma'am, nephew? I'll give you both a start, of course."

The change of subject worked as expected. Lady

Tidbury and Percy crashed off into the distance while John let his own mount amble behind, not intending for a moment to take part in any race.

So Lady Tidbury's delicate sensibilities had been offended by what she assumed was a fury of male lust. John didn't know where she could have got such an idea. He imagined she would be glad to tell him, and that her answer would involve some of the many men she had known in her colorful past.

He was growing ever more certain, as the days passed, that Rosamund was necessary to his happiness, and that he was the only one who could assure hers. They must find a way out of their confusion.

Perhaps Lady Tidbury would turn out to be, after all, the gruff yet warmhearted old crone of song and story. Perhaps she only liked having everybody dance to her particular tune and was annoyed that John had called this one. Despite warning Rosamund of Colonel Fairburn's vile intent, the old lady was still holding the dinner party. She could well be plotting to push Lady Ashburnham and Fairburn into each other's arms—by some method of her own contriving—on that very night.

John hoped so. He could use all the help he could get.

Rosamund had no wish to turn back the clock when she dressed for the Tidburys' dinner party, though she could not help remembering how she had been ten years before.

Her teenaged self, that poor Elizabeth, had been plain and mousy, flat-chested yet plump, with too-round cheeks and a dismal eye for color. Color? She had worn nothing but white muslin, the cheapest respectable fabric. The Rosamund of the present day, from fined-down face to sun-lightened hair, was a much more desirable article.

Rosamund remembered how she had known even

before going down to dinner on that fateful night that
the following morning would see the end of her maid-
enhood. She and John had had some peculiar electric-
ity between them. Innocent though she had been, she
had been absolutely certain that he wanted her, that
she could have him for the asking, and that she would
indeed ask. She would experience his love, cost her
what it would . . .

Oh, it had cost. She wondered, in sudden shakiness,
if anything had changed in that regard. The way he
looked at her—could she be looking at him in the
same fashion? No, surely not. She was a mature
woman and could govern herself better than that.

Rosamund put on her favorite rose-colored silk
gauze, trimmed with intricately worked silver thread,
for the tenth anniversary of her madness—a gown as
unlike white muslin as anything she owned. She put
on her diamond necklace, too, her wedding gift from
Sam. When she looked into the mirror, she met a pair
of brown eyes that were surely not the unknowing
eyes of a poor, besotted girl.

"Mama!" Sammy burst into her room, pursued by
his English nursemaid and the ayah. "They told me I
can't see you all dressed up. I say, you look fine."

"Child, you ought to be in bed. I know you always
look at me in my evening clothes, but you see, Lady
Tidbury is holding her dinner at such a late hour that
it's already past your bedtime."

"Well, I've seen you, so that's all right," said the
little boy with a stubborn setting of his chin that reminded Rosamund of his father. "Now they can do
what they will."

Nurse and Ayah both objected to Sammy's grim
tones, protesting that they had no intention of tortur-
ing the young master for his enthusiasm.

"I know the two of you are as soft as I am," Rosamund agreed, smiling at both attendants. "We can
overlook it this once."

As though any of the females in the house would do anything else! Even Rosamund's dresser had an affectionate smile for the young master as she bustled away on some errand having to do with the new silver slippers. Rosamund shook her head as Sammy and his keepers left the room. The child would soon be spoiled; was spoiled even now. She thanked heaven for his sound and unassuming nature.

When the maid came back, slippers in hand, Rosamund completed her toilette quickly and went down the hall to Minna's room, where she knocked.

A nervous, birdlike sound came in answer. Rosamund took this as permission to enter and turned the handle.

Minna was ready, in a new gown of yellow silk gauze. She was standing before a long glass, staring into her own eyes quite as Rosamund had done a few moments before.

"You look lovely my dear," said Rosamund. "Shall we go?"

Minna whirled about and surveyed Rosamund, from coiffure to slippers, in evident dismay. "Oh, no. This will never come off as I wish."

"What won't?"

Minna sighed. "As you tell me you don't want Colonel Fairburn, my plan is to attach him myself tonight. He's bound to be off his guard, if he's thinking of you, and I wish to make good my time. But if you *will* go about looking so beautiful, I shan't have a chance."

"Thank you for the compliment; I'm sure I don't deserve it," Rosamund said. So this was what Minna had been hiding. How lucky that she confessed her little plot; how much better than if Minna had decided to proceed with her project in secret. This way Rosamund could safeguard the girl from the worst consequences of folly. "So you're going to make a push tonight? Do you mean to trap him?"

Minna cast down her eyes, and Rosamund knew she had guessed correctly. What was it to be? A staged compromise scene in some antechamber?

"You promised not to interfere," Minna said in the direction of the floor.

"So I did, and I keep my promises. Still, he won't be caught that easily," Rosamund predicted. "I pray he doesn't hurt you."

"As he hurt you once?" Minna's words had enough of a malicious undertone to kill Rosamund's sympathy.

"I would hope he wouldn't get that far," she murmured. She didn't gratify her young friend's evident curiosity on this point, but turned and led the way downstairs.

Lady Tidbury's ornate Chinese drawing room was filled with people, or so it seemed to Rosamund as she presented a cheek to the spry Sir Magnus and endured a half-dozen of his compliments with a good grace. But John didn't seem to be present.

Lady Tidbury swept up, nearly bumping aside her husband. "Rosamund! A fine entrance. You and little what's-her-name are the last to arrive."

"But . . ."

"Oh, you're looking for Colonel Fairburn. Didn't I tell you? No, I couldn't have; just happened. He sent his regrets to me earlier today. I'll have his hide! Not only did I arrange this whole party at his behest, I've had to resort to Mr. Phineas Appleton to avoid thirteen at table." Her ladyship indicated a heavyset gentleman decked out in high shirt-points and skintight pantaloons. "He's the veriest bore, and so I was sure he would be free."

Rosamund nodded politely, wondering at the cloud of gloom she could feel enveloping her.

"Appleton is your dinner partner," Lady Tidbury said with a certain malicious glee which Rosamund did not miss. She supposed she deserved it; the party was in some measure her fault.

"Did you hear?" Minna sidled up with an anguished look once Lady Tidbury and Sir Magnus had passed to some other guests. "Colonel Fairburn couldn't come tonight. Percy just told me."

"What was his excuse?" Rosamund asked vaguely.

"Something military, I assume. He would never miss the party he had arranged if he could help it," was Minna's opinion. "I shall simply have to set forward my plans some other time."

Rosamund couldn't help wondering if John hadn't staged all this—the party, the build-up of suspense, the final disappointment—to drive her mad. If Minna were foiled in the process, it was no more than the girl deserved for setting out to trap him. How could she think one such as John Fairburn would be satisfied with such a plain little thing?

Rosamund caught herself. His taste ran to plain little things; at least it had ten years ago.

The evening began to resemble a thousand other evenings in Calcutta. Dinner-table talk was of the approaching hot season, the brewing trouble in Nepal, the unusual rain the other day. Mr. Appleton decided to enumerate for Lady Ashburnham the number of bolts of silk in his warehouse, or so it seemed to Rosamund.

She could see that Percy Fairburn was entertaining Minna, kind lad that he was. Would this night never end? No, for this was only the first course, and surely the company had been dining for an eternity. Rosamund tried to take a forkful of curry and returned it to her plate untasted. She managed a small sip of Persian wine.

"Now, now, Lady Ashburnham, you'll never grow stout if you don't eat more," Appleton said. "Stout women are my passion."

Rosamund had no response to make to this, and Appleton finally gave up and turned to Minna, the lady on his other side. The girl happened to be sighing over her plate during a break in Percy's chatter. Rosamund was gratified to see Minna's eyes light up on being addressed by Appleton. She seemed to like the man better than Percy! Well, there was no accounting for tastes.

More platters of food were set out on the table: a turkey, a very British saddle of mutton, more curries, and enough exotic fruits and nuts to prove this was India. The process was repeated with joints, jellies, and a spicy Burdwan stew which Appleton exclaimed over. Rosamund couldn't eat a thing. She amused herself as best she could by observing Minna's shining eyes. Appleton devoted himself to Miss Peabody, and the devotion seemed to be mutual. Curious . . . was John to be forgotten so suddenly?

Lady Tidbury eventually led the ladies out of the dining room, ending up in the cavernous ballroom rather than the Chinese salon.

"Since we are to have an impromptu dance," Lady Tidbury said with a certain look at Rosamund, "we may as well be handy to everything. I've had chairs drawn up over here near the pianoforte. Perhaps, Lady Ashburnham, you would consent to play to us while we wait for the gentlemen?"

"Certainly, ma'am," Rosamund answered. "I'd be delighted to play for the dancing, too."

With a start, she realized she had done just that ten years ago, on that other Saint Valentine's Eve. Her chaperon Mrs. Fallow had volunteered her services, as she recalled.

Lady Tidbury agreed with a nod. One of the other ladies protested that she would play, too, though of course her talent was nothing compared to Lady Ashburnham's.

Feeling almost disoriented, Rosamund sat down at the instrument and began softly an arrangement of an old folk tune. Minna offered to turn the pages, which, as Rosamund wasn't using music, brought a smile to her lips. She assumed that Minna was simply feeling shy and not equal to socializing with the other ladies.

She hardly noticed when the gentlemen came in; wouldn't have noticed at all, had not Mr. Appleton come lumbering up to the piano.

"May I rescue you from this drudgery, dear lady?"

Rosamund hadn't yet phrased an answer when she heard Minna voicing some coy rejoinder and realized that Appleton had been addressing Miss Peabody, not herself.

She watched Minna walk away on the gentlemen's arm. Well! The girl looked elated by this development. Would Appleton, of all the unlikely people, succeed in replacing John Fairburn in her affections?

"He ain't that bad a catch." Suddenly Lady Tidbury was whispering in Rosamund's ear. "Came out here at the age of fifteen, as so many of 'em do, and immediately began to dig his grave with his fork. Rich devil, and they say he's finally begun to hang out for a wife. He needs someone to pull him back from the table before he grows stout as a barrel, and your little friend looks capable."

"But Minna is nowhere near large enough for his taste," Rosamund replied with a notable lack of seriousness. If the two did fall in love, she would be too relieved for words; the mere idea put her in a good mood. "He's been telling me how much he adores stout women."

"She could grow into it," suggested Lady Tidbury. "Well, don't give up hope, child. That girl will be off your hands one day soon. Unrequited love makes the best of us long for an establishment."

"I don't wish only that for her. I want her to be happy," Rosamund protested. She had been irritated with Minna, true, but she would never cast the girl into an objectionable marriage. Mr. Phineas Appleton, indeed! When Minna might have her pick of a dozen young and personable men.

Who weren't as rich. The nasty suspicion crossed Rosamund's mind that maybe her young charge would not find a large supply of money amiss. Minna had accused Rosamund of being—what had she said?— the luckiest woman in the world, purely on financial grounds.

They must await events. Rosamund would see to it that Minna only married Appleton if her heart was in it.

Lady Tidbury clapped her hands. Rosamund stopped her dreamy playing and listened along with the rest of the company.

"Now for the dancing," her ladyship stated, not evincing much enthusiasm. An impromptu dance carried with it little in the way of status for the hostess involved. "Lady Ashburnham has consented to play. If she will start with a country dance, the general and I will be top couple. Sir Magnus?"

Her husband stepped up and swung her ladyship away by the waist before Rosamund could think of a suitable tune. She was glad of the ensuing confusion, for she was perilously near laughter. Finally she struck up "Sir Roger de Coverley," knowing she ought to be more original, yet unable to think of anything better.

The dancers bounced away as Rosamund played, quite enjoying the view she had, over the top of the instrument, of all the proceedings. Minna was dancing with Percy while Mr. Appleton stood by looking romantically jealous. The other guests, paired mostly with their mates, were laughing and joking. Perhaps an impromptu dance was the best kind.

Rosamund had never expected to find diversion this evening. She would have to thank John after all for arranging the party.

She played another country dance, another, then a daring waltz. The couples swam before her eyes as she let her fingers roam. She feared she was growing sentimental and resolved to make the next set a spirited reel. And wasn't it time for someone else to play? She might find pleasure in a dance herself, even if it was only a hop with Sir Magnus.

"There were no waltzes on that other February night," said a voice in her ear.

Only the greatest self-possession kept Rosamund from stumbling through the next passage.

"John," she whispered, not looking over her shoulder. She had the tune by heart, and it was almost over. Then she could ask him what he meant by arranging this stupid party which he hadn't even thought fit to attend. . . . "You're here. Didn't you send your regrets?"

He waited to answer until she had brought the tune to its end. It being the first waltz, the dancers spent some time laughing and complimenting each other. They didn't seem to notice that the music was not recommencing at once.

"Don't you remember?" John smiled. "I wasn't there for dinner. I wandered in sometime during the evening and rescued you from your servitude at the pianoforte. As I'm about to do now." He offered his arm.

As if on cue, the lady who had offered to play, a Mrs. Seldon, approached the instrument looking quite contrite. "I've left you to play on and on, my lady. Can you ever forgive me?"

"I enjoyed it, and I only noticed this moment that I'm growing a little tired," Rosamund said. She walked off on John's arm.

She supposed they were about to have it out. It was time. She was weary of the game, and he must be too.

As they walked out of the ballroom and down a corridor, she looked up at him. His face was cheerful, youthful, as though the last ten years had not hardened it. He had never come so close to resembling his nephew.

"It's not so easy as this, John," said Rosamund.

"What do you mean, my dear?" He kept walking, drawing her along. They came to the door that lay open to the dark grounds. He led her outside.

"You are so lovely," he began, reaching out to touch her face. "You've become such a stunner. There is a little heartbreak in that face of yours, something that wasn't there before. You're more beautiful because of it. Tell me, is the grief all for your husband?"

"You know better, or you should," Rosamund said. "If I have done something to my face from grief, it was doubtless complete before I arrived in India. Let's not mince words, John. Why did you arrange this evening? What strange trick are you about to play?"

"None at all."

"Then I must go back to the ballroom. Not that I'll save the situation by doing so. Everyone saw us leave together."

"Precisely." John motioned to a nearby bench. "Why not stay a little longer? Your reputation will be in shreds already."

Rosamund followed and sat next to him, but she couldn't keep back her greatest fear for this evening— at least she thought it was a fear. "You aren't planning to ravish me in some lonely room of this gigantic house, are you? Your mania for recreating the past can't reach that far."

"Don't tell me I ravished you ten years ago. I can't remember that at all, but then, they say men are notorious for forgetting things."

She sighed in vexation but made no answer.

He took her hand in almost an absent gesture. She was absurdly glad she hadn't put her gloves back on after leaving the pianoforte. His hand was bare too, and it felt so warm, so good.

Touch was confusing. Rosamund knew it would be best to draw her hand away. After one feeble tug got her nowhere, she gave up what had been at most a halfhearted desire.

"Tell me one thing," John said. "Why did you leave me that night?"

"I meant to return." Rosamund saw no reason to dissemble. She told him the whole embarrassing little story of wishing to primp for him, to be pretty for once in her life. And of being caught out by her chaperon, who had retaliated by locking her in her room, then dragging her away as early the next morning as possible.

"Good Lord, such an explanation never crossed my mind." He stared at her. A torch nearby made his expression clear. He looked truly astounded. "How could you be so silly as to leave me?"

"Vanity runs strong in a young female," she returned, shrugging. "I might as well ask why you didn't come down to breakfast that morning, when I so needed to see you again, to know that I hadn't dreamed our promises to each other. There, also, life is made up of little mistakes, not great drama. I'm sure you were simply tired."

"I was." He said nothing further, but their palms suddenly felt too close together to Rosamund. She was remembering why he would have been tired, and she suspected he was doing the same. Again she tried to withdraw her hand. It wouldn't come.

"Do you know, Rosamund, I never stopped loving you. Not really."

"You simply forgot me."

"I did try. And, my dear, if you change so very much, you must forgive an old friend for not recognizing you, for seeing you in his mind as you were when he fell in love."

The wind rustled a nearby palm. Some small animal cried out far away. Finally Rosamund spoke. "You sound so reasonable. What am I to do now? Forget my family responsibilities and take you to my bed? Do you really think I'm that weak? Yes, I know there is some attraction between us, but it won't vanquish me. I promise you that."

"Rosamund, you can't think I only want to bed you. I want you to be my wife," John exclaimed. A note of irritation was clear in his voice. The change was so great from his former loving manner that Rosamund was startled. Startled, and comforted in a way. She was much more used to argument these days than she was to soft words.

"Many men in Calcutta want to marry me," she replied with a toss of her head. "I'm quite the catch."

He sighed deeply. "Oh, the devil take you for being rich and beautiful. I want you anyhow. Grow ugly if you wish, and as soon as possible. Give all your money away to the orphan asylum or the Asiatic Society. I have enough now for both of us."

Rosamund felt herself flushing at the angry words. He was hurting her hand, and this time when she tugged it, he abruptly let it go.

"The devil take *you*," she said softly, "for being a young girl's dream. Now Miss Peabody is starry-eyed over you, and while you don't seem to care, you don't reject her outright. Who knows what you plan for some future dark night when she's feeling particularly desperate? You haven't changed at all, have you?"

John looked amazed at her words. "Can we leave other people out of this? If that girl has some infatuation for me, I can do no better than to let her grow out of it."

Rosamund was silent. From her observations tonight, she believed Minna was well on her way to a cure. So John had been wise, not cruel. She had nothing now to reproach him for.

"Now can we stop cursing each other?" he asked.

Rosamund's shoulders sank as she let out a struggling breath. "I hope so."

He reached out to touch her cheek again. "I haven't changed; you're perfectly right. Ten years ago I fell in love with you. I came downstairs that Valentine's morning to announce our marriage plans, and you were gone. Though I didn't know it, I've been searching for you ever since."

"Hardly. You knew where I was."

"I wasn't sure. And I came as soon as I could, didn't I? A soldier isn't at liberty in some things."

Rosamund was mightily confused. He said he loved her and wanted to marry her; she believed him. Her resolve was slipping fast, but she had to be honest with him. "John, you're good enough to say you haven't changed. Well, I have."

"What do you mean?"

"It isn't only that I married and grew to love my husband. I went beyond you, beyond my girlish dreams into adulthood. I can't go back. Not now, when I've come so far."

Her words died away.

"Are you saying that you don't love me? That you never really did?" John said.

"I loved you to distraction," cried Rosamund. "To my own great unhappiness. The only thing which could have made leaving England worse was leaving my heart there. And so I did, like the silly fool I am. Was."

"And my heart sailed with you."

"With hearts on separate sides of the world, perhaps it was inevitable that we should grow apart," Rosamund said. "I didn't lose myself pining for you. I found great happiness without you."

"Why do you say that as though it's some dire confession? I've told you before that I'm glad for you. You were happily married, and you have a delightful child. Do you think I wished years of suffering on your head?"

She remembered his blazing eyes when she first told him she had cared about her husband. "Well, yes."

"At one time I suppose I did," John admitted, smiling. "But I got over that selfish notion."

Once more there was a silence, broken only by the dark garden sounds. At last John spoke into Rosamund's ear. "Is there room in your heart for only one love, then?"

She knew the answer to this; had always known it since she married Sam. "There is always enough room for love. The fond memory, the present feeling. It's all love."

"You have a present feeling of love, do you? For anyone in particular?"

She could only nod; her heart was too full for speech.

"May I kiss you now?"

"You're asking? Why don't you simply kiss me, as I did you at the Twelfth Night ball?"

"Perhaps because this is Saint Valentine's Eve, and I'm waiting for you to give the first kiss as you did on that night in Hampshire. I was so delighted by your boldness."

Feeling shy, Rosamund turned to face him and put her arms around him with trusting affection, as she had been longing to do for weeks. For years, really.

"I liked kissing you when I thought I hated you," she said after a while. "This is much better."

"And it's only the beginning." John grinned. "We can't have this night, though. I insist upon being sure of you before I lose my virtue again."

"I don't think a loss of virtue can happen twice," Rosamund considered, eyes twinkling. "Though I'm not quite certain. Shall we test out the theory?"

"Rosamund, you are a shameless creature."

"So Lady Tidbury has been fearing. I hate to tell her I've indeed succumbed to your blandishments." Rosamund stroked John's face, wondering how she could have held out against him for even a moment.

She should have admitted on Twelfth Night that he was still the man for her.

"Let her ladyship bury her disappointment in arranging a magnificent quick wedding breakfast for us. With a grand ball, if she so desires. We'll be married as soon as I can arrange the license."

"Do you know, my son has been teasing me for a new papa. What if he thinks this is all for him?"

"We'll take that chance, my dear. Along with my nephew's levity and any other little problems which may arise. We're of an age not to let others direct our actions."

He gathered her closer into his arms for more kisses, more caresses. The night surrounded them like velvet.

"Happy Valentine's Day, John. I heard Lady Tidbury's clock strike midnight."

"Is that what it was? I thought it was my heart talking to me again."

"And what was your heart saying?" Rosamund decided she was quite comfortable with lovers' talk after all. Indeed, she couldn't get enough of it.

John held her even closer. "I'm afraid my heart sounds remarkably like your parrot, my own."

"Like Babur? What do you mean?"

"My poor heart knows only one word. *Love.* And it's been shouting at me incessantly." He kissed her softly at the base of her throat. "Happy Valentine's Day, Rosamund. My love at last."

"And at first," she whispered as she drew his face to hers.

The London Swell

by Carol Proctor

REALLY, it was deuced odd, the fuss that was made about the business of courtship and marriage. One would think it was a terribly complicated sort of thing, when in actuality there could be nothing easier. Once you had decided that you needed a wife (or your parents had informed you that you did), all you had to do was to visit the London assemblies and routs and balls where young, unattached ladies literally flocked during the Season.

Having done so, what could be simpler than to fix upon the loveliest and most charming of these young ladies and ask for her hand? And yet, from all the pother the subject seemed to stir up, you would think it was the most arduous and complicated task in the world. So ran the thoughts of Charles Henry Fitzhugh, the Viscount Hunsdon, on this chill day as he rather dreamily urged the big bay hunter over a wall.

The truth of the matter was that Lord Hunsdon had rarely encountered any difficulties in his two-and-twenty years of life. As the only son of the second Earl of Wittenham, and blessed with a fortune as well as a title, he had found every path smoothed for him, every obstacle overcome. Well-meaning friends tried to explain to him how unusual it was for a gentleman to secure the affections of one of London's reigning beauties with a single dance. He listened patiently, but their words were meaningless to him.

"Stands to reason. You'll never make him comprehend you," had unsympathetically commented Lord Brandville, three years senior to Hunsdon and one of his closest friends. "How should he? When Hunsdon threatens to catch a cold, I daresay Wittenham pays one of his tenants to have it for him."

It was a tribute to the extent of Hunsdon's charm that Brandville spoke without undue bitterness. Inheriting little but a title and debt himself, Brandville was continually, as he himself put it, "in danger of being blown up at point nonplus." Indeed, perhaps Hunsdon's greatest gift was his disarming friendliness. Even those with most cause to resent him found it difficult to do so, at least in person. Miss Mariabella Fostwick's disappointed suitors might have suggested duels at dawn to another rival who had cut them out with such efficiency. Instead, they accepted their loss more or less philosophically, relieving their feelings only by uttering imprecations against Hunsdon's "usual plaguy good luck."

As Lord Brandville had suggested, though, the object of their curses could have no real idea of the singularity of his achievement, nor was he one to dwell overlong on such matters. His thoughts at the moment centered on Mariabella herself. What a handsome and distinguished girl she was. How well she would become the title, a point that had concerned his mother greatly. A brook presented itself and the hunter cleared it with ease, fortunately for its preoccupied rider.

Of course, he was a little ahead of himself. Mariabella had not actually accepted his hand yet, though he had no doubt that she would. She had made that clear enough to him. It was a great pity that family illness had forced her to leave London while the Season was at its height. Still, it had given him time to tend to affairs and to consult his parents on the matter. And his friends Roger and Anne had assured him that Mariabella's father was completely recovered by now.

In one way the timing was fortunate. Since he had come here to Leicestershire in the month of January, a scheme had suggested itself to his mind. He would give himself and Mariabella a few weeks to become reacquainted, then on St. Valentine's Day ask her to be his wife. Hunsdon was an incurable romantic at heart.

It was almost more than he could bear, to be so near to achieving his goal after all these months. Upon his arrival at Blakemore House, he had been tempted to change out of his driving clothes and to go call upon Mariabella immediately. The project had been abandoned when his hostess, Anne, had gently reminded him that he had arrived a day early and that Mariabella would not expect to see him before Thursday. He had attempted to argue with her, pointing out that he and Mariabella were soon to be affianced. He ventured to remark that in the same situation she herself would have welcomed Roger.

"Yes, I would, but then I am not Mariabella." She glanced up from her sewing for a moment and intercepted her husband's gaze. A look passed between them and she bent her head to her task once more.

Hunsdon waited for her to elaborate. She struggled for words for a moment.

"She is . . . she is not given to impulse. I have often heard you say that it is one of her virtues."

It was true. His mother had explained to him what an undesirable quality impulsiveness would be in his future countess. He had prided himself on selecting a future mate so free from this lamentable trait. He tried not to look as dejected as he felt, but apparently he did not succeed, for now Roger laughed. He crossed the room to clap Hunsdon on the back.

"Come, come. You've been patient all these months. Surely you can wait another two days."

Hunsdon smiled, though it was not without effort. "You're right, of course."

Anne was smiling too, with some inexplicable relief. "It's not as if you must remain inside. I have some pressing business to which I must attend, but you are welcome to take a horse out. There's a chill wind, but the sun is shining and the ground's not soft. Come to think of it, my hunter could use some exercise. You would be doing me a favor."

Anne laughed. "Yes, you would. Roger doesn't trust any of the grooms with him. I daresay poor Aghadoe hasn't been ridden all week."

It was an inspired suggestion. A punishing ride was just what he needed to relieve his pent-up emotions. And as Anne had prophesied, the horse seemed just as eager for the exercise as he. They set off at a gallop and he did not particularly notice which direction he took or how far he was riding. His mind was totally occupied by his concerns. Perhaps if he sent a note today, Mariabella might prepare herself to receive him tomorrow. After all, he had been expected to arrive then. Part of the reason he had decided to reach Blakemore early, before the rest of the house party, was so that he might have an opportunity to call upon Mariabella by himself. Anne was probably just being overcautious. Nothing should prevent him from seeing Mariabella tomorrow.

He reached this happy conclusion just as the horse approached a blackthorn fence with a coppice a short distance beyond it. He heard a dog barking somewhere but thought nothing of it. He put the horse's head at the fence and the animal responded with its usual eagerness. It wasn't until its front hooves were leaving the ground that he realized that he had made a grave error. Something or someone was on the other side of that fence. There was a flash of fire and a startled cry and movement and he yanked the horse's

head to the right desperately, trying to avoid landing
on the person beneath them. He was successful in
changing the trajectory of their flight to some extent,
but in so doing he had assured disaster for himself.
Clearing the fence, he and his horse parted company
in midair, each tumbling to his separate destination in
the ditch on the other side.

When he hit the ground, Hunsdon's first thought
was that Roger had been proved correct. It was not
soft. He lay in a heap for a moment before his body
decided to respond to the commands of his brain once
more. He sat up in a cautious manner, and noticed
that the horse was rising shakily on its legs. Good.
Neither of them was dead. He rubbed his head gin-
gerly. He had taken quite a knock. At least his arms
seemed to be working. Now for his legs.

He gathered them underneath him and was attempting to rise when a small, great-coated figure
rushed over to him. Taking his arm, it helped to raise
him to his feet.

"It's a rasper, isn't it? What a fall you took! It's
lucky I saw you when I did or you might have landed
on top of me. Spoiled my shot, too, but mum for
that," the husky little voice assured him magnanimously.

He hardly knew how to reply to such a speech and
instead regarded the youngster in some surprise. He
had taken the urchin for a boy, but now he saw that
from under the hem of the overlarge and well-worn
coat emerged skirts over a scuffed pair of boots. He
surveyed this apparition in some shock. Reposing at
an awkward angle upon her head, a tired bonnet no
longer contained an unruly mop of reddish-brown
curls. The face underneath it was small, pale, and generous as to nose and mouth. The only attractive features were the large, wide-set blue eyes. A rather
elegant fowling piece rested casually in the crook of
one arm. It was impossible to draw any conclusions
about the child or her situation. Her voice, despite

her incoherent manner of speaking, had a well-bred tone, ruling out his first idea, that she was some sort of parish waif.

She released his arm and began brushing herself off. "Had the wind knocked out of you?" she asked cheerfully, misinterpreting the reason for his silence. "I know that sensation. You'll be better in a moment or two. *Rob Roy!*" she abruptly added with a bellow, for no apparent reason. He glanced about nervously. Did she really expect a tartan-clad figure to come leaping out of the woods?

She seemed not at all dismayed by the lack of response to her call, but attempted to straighten her bonnet, only succeeding in making it tilt at a different angle upon her head. Seeing that he remained unmoving, she added brightly. "I'll catch your horse for you." She turned to where the animal, making the best of a bad situation, was cropping some dead grass. Of course, if she were of a good family, the child would hardly be ranging about unaccompanied, that is, she wouldn't unless they were unaware of it, unless she had escaped. . . . He blinked with the force of it as the idea hit him. Good Lord, that would explain why she dressed and behaved in such an eccentric manner. He wondered how long she had been thus. What a pity, and it was just a child, too.

Finally coming out of his reverie, he would have stopped her, but taking his first step forward, he instead let out an exclamation of pain. It didn't matter, however, for in a moment she had grasped the trailing rein and led the horse over to him. She glanced first at the horse, then back at him. Her eyes narrowed in caution. "This horse looks rather like Sir Roger's bay hunter."

"It is. He lent it to me." He held out his hands for the reins, but she still did not proffer them.

"So you *can* speak. Sir Roger does not allow *anyone* to ride his bay hunter. *Rob Roy!*" She appended her

remarks with another unexpected yell, causing Aghadoe to dance nervously backward.

He should have been more ready this time, but he
could not help giving a start. "So Lady Blakemore
said. I suppose that since I am both his friend and his
houseguest, he knew that the horse would be safe with
me." He tried to keep his tone of voice even and
calm, and now he ventured a gentle smile which he
hoped might reassure her.

She made a sound suspiciously like a snort. "*Safe!*
You are fortunate it didn't break a leg. Galloping
along in that heedless way, when you don't even know
the country hereabouts—you might easily both have
been killed."

Hunsdon was unused to receiving such scathing crit-
icism and he would not stand for it, even though she
was mad. All his previously unexpressed anger returned to him in a rush. "Yes, we both might have
been killed, thanks to you! What did you mean by
crouching under the furze like that, where no one
could see you? If I hadn't acted quickly, you might
have been the one who died!" It was perhaps bad
policy to ask a deranged person to account for her
actions, but Hunsdon was too angry to consider it.

She grew pale with anger. "So I am not to be allowed to hunt upon my own land, for fear that some
oafish stranger might attempt to put a period to my
existence. Sir, I must inform you that you are on the
grounds of Sherbrook and that I am Lady De Neresford!"

Poor, poor child. His anger evaporated suddenly.
Truly, he was an oaf to overlook her condition. Well,
he must do his best to make amends now. He had
better humor her. "I beg your pardon, your ladyship.
I had no idea that I was trespassing upon your
grounds. You are right. I was not paying attention to
where I was going."

She softened visibly, and held the reins out to him
in a gesture of forgiveness. "That is all right . . . since

you are a friend of the Blakemores. Truly, I did not mean to lose my temper. It was an accident, after all. You could have no idea that it had taken me all afternoon to find a pheasant."

It was fortunate that his wits had reassembled themselves in time for him to realize that hers were scrambled. "All afternoon?" he remarked sympathetically. He hoped he could make her trust him. She would have to tell him where she lived if he were to take her home, and he did not want to use force on the rather fragile-looking child.

"*Rob Roy!*" Better prepared, he managed not to leap as she yelled once more. He was clever enough not to betray himself by glancing around them again.

She gave a rueful smile. "I know. You will say that I would have done better to go out in the morning, but Mama wanted me to repair the torn fringe on the drawing-room curtain, although I think it was unjust of her to blame me for it. I am sure that I never let Rob Roy inside the house and . . . but that is beside the point. Ah, Rob Roy, there you are!"

A small, rough-coated terrier of the Scottish type had trotted soundlessly up to her side. Now he flopped down beside her, tongue lolling from his exertions. He lifted his face to survey the startled Hunsdon and wagged his tail once or twice by way of an introduction.

"My gun dog. Most people would use a spaniel, *I* know, but Mama has ruined the spaniels, which makes it all the more unjust of her to blame poor Rob Roy for everything, as if those little wretches weren't willing to cause some mischief, but actually it is fortunate since he's much better at flushing birds than any of them ever were, and goodness knows it is hard enough to find even one for him to flush since we had to let the gamekeeper go after Papa died." She paused to draw breath. The horse gave an impatient tug at the reins.

Hunsdon was relieved to know that at least she had

not been expecting a fictional character to appear in
their midst. He tried to make his expression convey
that he thought there was nothing unusual in keeping
a terrier for a bird dog and that he was able to follow
everything that she had to say. Her mention of a
mama confirmed his supposition. The family preferred
keeping her at home to admitting the child to a public
hospital. She probably was usually confined in the
attics. At least there was nothing about her to suggest
that she was dangerous. He hoped that both barrels
of her firearm had already been discharged. "Hadn't
you better be returning home?" he inquired kindly.

She looked doubtfully at her dog. "Perhaps you are
right. I am certain that we shan't see another bird
today, though I hate to think of what Mama will say
when I don't return with a pheasant. I myself thought
that a brace or two of woodcocks would do nicely,
but she insists that it will take at least a pair of pheasants to impress the London swell, though if he is so
used to grand dinners I would think he'd not notice
them." She grimaced without interrupting the flow of
her words. "I can just hear her, too, 'Barbara, *all* my
dependence was upon *you!*' "

He had been about to say in a soothing tone of
voice that he was certain that her mama would be
relieved to have her back, with or without the pheasant, but the cant phrase caught his attention. "The
London swell?" he asked. The horse tugged again,
more emphatically this time.

"Mama says I must not call him that, but that is
what Alfred calls him, and Alfred is Mariabella's
brother, after all." She saw his puzzlement and continued by way of explanation, "I am speaking of the
London lord who is arriving tomorrow to stay with
the Blakemores. He is coming here to ask Mariabella
Fostwick for her hand, but Mama means to have him
marry me instead."

The reins fell from his nerveless hands, which the

horse took as permission to partake of more refreshment and so proceeded, but Hunsdon hardly noticed. His mouth dropped open in astonishment, which Barbara apparently took as a request for further elucidation.

"That is what the pheasant's for, you see. It is part of Mama's grand strategy. She means to have a dinner for him here so that he may meet me without Mariabella around." Her eyebrows drew together in a frown. "Mariabella is a beauty, as you may know. Mama thinks that she would prove too great a distraction."

The first of many objections that had come to mind now escaped his lips. "But you're a child!"

She drew herself up haughtily. "I am seventeen, and will be eighteen in August!"

He had thought her fourteen at most. He stopped himself just in time from raising another obstacle, that of her mental condition. She misunderstood his silence. Her tone was troubled.

"I know it might seem somewhat underhanded to you, but Mama says that since Mariabella has so many suitors she will not miss just one. And since we cannot afford to hire a house in London, or servants, or gowns, or any of the rest, I will not be presented, so there is no other way for me to meet an eligible gentleman." She sighed unconsciously. "Sometimes it is hard to be a baroness, for Alfred told me that he would marry me when he became twenty-one—not that I should want to really, but if I must marry someone I suppose it would be easier to marry someone that I know—but Mama says that none of the young gentlemen hereabouts are my equals in station."

Was this another fantasy of a deranged mind? Somehow it had the ring of truth instead. Could he have been wrong about her mental condition? He had heard that there were occasional examples among ancient families where the barony was not entailed away from the female line, but it was quite rare. Was it possible that this eccentric little waif was one? And even given that *she* was the sane member of her family, could it be true that anyone would honestly wish to marry her?

Barbara suddenly brightened. "There is always that other London lord, after all. Alfred told me that she was about to be engaged to him, but he lacked a fortune. This swell is said to be as rich as Golden Ball, so naturally when he appeared, she rid herself of the first suitor."

It was an unattractive picture of his soon-to-be-fiancée. He had never heard of a serious rival for her hand, and for a moment he wondered if there were any truth in it. In another moment he came to himself. Barbara was undoubtedly mistaken. He was still not certain that her wits were entirely intact, after all. His duty was clear. He must disabuse this child of her chimeric notions as gently as possible.

"My dear," he said quietly, as she paused for air again, "had it occurred to you that this London lord would not . . . might not wish to . . ."

She was regarding him with a frank, wide-eyed gaze that made it even harder for him to speak.

"I mean . . . that you might not suit?" he finally finished.

She gave an unhappy little laugh. "Might not suit? Yes, I am certain that we won't, if what Mariabella says of him is true."

"What Mariabella says . . . ?"

"Yes, well, I know that he's tall and handsome and distinguished-looking—"

Hunsdon blinked. Although powerfully built, he was only of medium height. His features were too marked to be considered handsome, though it was considered that his disarming lack of pretentiousness, as well as his amiability, rendered him attractive.

"And from everything she has said, he must be the greatest dandy on earth. She's always swooning over his exquisite manners and dress. I expect that he wears four pocket watches and has a ring on every finger and uses a walking stick and probably wears pomade in his hair and drenches himself in scent." She had closed her eyes in distaste at the picture. "And I cannot doubt that he has never gone hunting, and probably rides a slug and refuses to live anywhere but London. Yes, I am quite certain that we will not suit. Fortunately, I am not romantic."

He wasn't certain whether to be insulted or amused. He had never formed one of the dandy set. With all modesty, he knew himself to be a sportsman of some renown. It was irritating. Mariabella might have boasted of his proficiencies as a shot, or a whip, or a rider to hounds, but then, such abilities might seem less impressive in Leicestershire, after all. They were scarce twenty miles from Melton Mowbray.

In the end, amusement won out, as much from Barbara's dramatic manner of speaking as from the picture of the idle fop she imagined him to be. He was tired and ready to go home. First he meant to confess the whole truth to her, but he had no chance for she misinterpreted the reason for his laughter and quickly took offense.

"So, you find all this diverting, do you? Is it just that my problems seem so trivial, or is it"—her eyes narrowed once again—"that you think that this London lord would not be interested in marrying me?"

It was exactly what he thought, actually what he knew, and he supposed that his answer must have shown in his face, for now she gave a sniff of outrage. "That shows your ignorance. I have told you already that *I* am a De Neresford. I am also the last of my line!"

He tried to look suitably impressed, but apparently failed, for now she sniffed again even more forcefully. "Well, I suppose I have to explain such things to an outsider. Our title was created in 1312, making it one of the oldest in the country."

It was an ancient family, then. He did not know what that had to do with the matter at hand.

She looked at him for his reaction, then shook her head pityingly. "You still do not understand. Very well, this London swell does not come from an old family. Mama made inquiries, and his title, even the oldest of his *inferior* ones, is but fifty years old."

He must have looked blank, for she shook her head again. "Mama explained it all to me, you see. *My* great-grandfather was an earl. *His* was probably a cheesemonger or some such thing. By his marriage to me, his child some day would inherit one of the oldest baronies in the country. Mama said that he would leap at the chance to marry me." She looked a little uncertain. "Of course, Mariabella *is* a great beauty, and wealthy, which I am not, but Mama says that is not of the slightest consideration beside the fact that I am a De Neresford." She pressed her lips together, then glanced at him from under an unusually thick pair of reddish-brown lashes. "Do . . . do you think that Mama is wrong?"

"My dear Hunsdon, you had us quite worried." Roger's tone was light, but there was sincerity in his words. "Anne was ready to send the servants to look for you." Hunsdon had lost all track of the time and now his conscience smote him as he realized that the two were dressed for dinner and had likely been waiting for him this past half hour or more.

Anne pinkened, but retorted, "I was simply afraid for your life if you had let anything happen to Aghadoe."

"We took a fall, but fortunately we're both unharmed."

"A fall! You? I have known love to have an adverse effect before, but this is certainly—"

"Roger," said Anne seriously, "it is hardly the time to be teasing Lord Hunsdon." She turned to address him. "You are limping! Are you quite sure that you have suffered no ill effects from your accident? Would you care to take dinner in your room tonight?"

"Thank you, no to each of your questions. I am sorry for being so deucedly late. If you will permit me, I will go and change out of my leathers and return in a trice." His leg was still smarting, but not as grievously as before.

It was devilish odd. He had been meaning to regale them with an amusing account of the eccentric little chit who was setting her cap for "the London swell." He was certain that Roger would find the situation as exquisitely entertaining as he himself did. Somehow, when he had entered the room, the humor of the situation had vanished. As he tied his starched white cravat with only a modicum of care, he frowned in thought. He would have to inform them of the meeting, of course, but there was no need to discuss her pretensions. She was only a child, after all. It would be sheer cruelty to make sport of her.

At dinner, he apologized for causing them any anxiety and mentioned that he had been detained in conversation with their neighbor, young Lady De Neresford. Neither Roger nor Anne seemed particularly surprised. The former gave a snort and said, "That explains it. I've no doubt she was happy to bend your ear for hours. It's your own fault, Hunsdon, for having such a confounded sympathetic face."

It was all too true. Handsome he might not be, but there was something about him that inspired others to pour out their confidences to him. He had no time to make any sort of reply, for now Anne commented, "Poor little thing. I suppose I should not speak of her ladyship so, but truly, I cannot help but feel for her, as alone and friendless as she is. It is little wonder that she unburdened herself at the sight of an amicable face."

"Nonsense," said Roger roughly. "She has her

mother and the friendship of all the families in the neighborhood."

"I know, but . . ." Anne sighed. "Of course, I should not wish to criticize her mother or the late baron, but it has often seemed to me that Barbara's education was sadly neglected, particularly for a young lady of title. Even given their regrettable circumstances, something more might have been managed."

"Balderdash. I daresay you would have to chain her to a pianoforte in order to make her learn the notes, and as for painting screens, or netting, or . . ." He shook his head. "I've heard her mother despair over her a thousand times. Barbara would rather be out shooting, or riding, or engaged in deviltry with Alfred Fostwick or some other buffle-headed clod."

"Sir Roger!" Anne looked unusually stern. "You will give Lord Hunsdon a false impression of our neighbor." She shook her head. "I was not speaking of feminine accomplishments, but rather of her conduct. She cannot fail to please with her openness and her sincerity, but if she had been permitted to go about more in society, she might find herself more at ease—"

"A hoyden. You might as well say it." Roger met his wife's glare and sighed. "Well, I pity the chit myself, my dear. I don't know how they manage with scarcely two farthings to rub together, particularly since they are as proud as the day is long. Why, do you remember how insulted they were when I brought them that haunch of venison last fall—as if it weren't a thing I might have given to any of my neighbors? There's not an ounce of harm in Barbara, that I will say, and I do not envy anyone with that mother. I misdoubt whether she is worth your concern, however, and I am certain that she would not thank you for it, so let us find a more agreeable topic of conversation."

Obediently, Anne began a discussion of the guests

they expected on the morrow. Hunsdon's crony, Lord Brandville, was one, and there were a few other acquaintances, but the rest were strangers to him. That seemed odd, as did the fact that Brandville was the only other bachelor. Well, it was all for the best, as far as his courtship of Mariabella went.

He had intended at least to confess his deception to them, that when Barbara had shyly (and most improperly) asked his name, he had replied without mentioning his title. He still was puzzled by the question of why he had done it. It would have been the perfect opportunity to put a period to her misconceptions. He was not a naturally dishonest person.

Of course, since Roger had closed the topic of the baroness, it would seem rude to reopen it. Perhaps, upon consideration, it was not necessary for them to know. He could easily visit her tomorrow and explain matters to her. With such a resolution, he banished Barbara from his mind and entered into his hostess's discussion of entertainments that might amuse the company. It did not occur to him that he had forgotten to send a missive to Mariabella, nor did he remember that she was the one he had intended to call upon that day.

He suffered some indecision upon awakening, for he shrank from calling upon Barbara in formal morning attire, given that they had not even been properly introduced, and yet he feared that to call upon her in his leathers might seem an insult. Remembering her own eccentricity of costume, it seemed preferable not to dazzle her with the elegance of town dress, and so he dressed simply in his driving clothes and called for his curricle to be harnessed.

Roger might have suffered under a misapprehension about his destination, for he murmured something about the "impatience of young love" as Hunsdon departed, but the latter chose not to enlighten him. In-

stead, he inquired the direction to Sherbrook of the
young groom who held his horses. The groom appeared surprised, but after recovering, gave him con-
cise and clear directions.

It was an easy distance, but as Hunsdon prepared
to turn his curricle down the drive, he wondered if he
had not made a mistake. The drive was sadly overgrown, barely permitting the passage of his curricle,
and he nervously hoped that the paint might not be
scraped from it. As bad as it was, the way must be
almost impassable in the summer. If this indeed was
the drive to Sherbrook, it did not appear that even
tradesmen's carts were in the habit of visiting it
regularly.

When he reached the grounds of the house, however, he was certain that he had hit upon the correct
destination. Sherbrook obviously had originally consisted of an ancient manor house, strongly constructed
of clunch and rubble. It had been added to in a hap-
hazard fashion in the centuries since its erection. Here
was the half-timbered Tudor wing, there a red brick
Jacobean one, and at one end an uncompleted project
in the Palladian mode.

Glancing about the grounds, he surmised that some
ancestor of Barbara's had undertaken a great land-
scaping plan, perhaps a century before. Whether he
had accomplished what he had intended was an unan-
swerable question, for neglect had ruled during the
intervening years. The De Neresford family might be
one of the oldest in England, but apparently it had
not been prosperous for some time.

Perhaps he *had* been wrong to bring his curricle,
and to leave his groom at home. He had not wished
to arouse Ned's curiosity. The stables here looked di-
lapidated, but they must house animals of some sort.
He prayed that there was a groom.

He needn't have worried, for as he approached the
house a lad burst from the stables and ran to the car-

riage with an alacrity that might have been admired in a ducal household. By the time Hunsdon had pulled the carriage in front of the house, the groom was already at the horses' heads. The youth took hold of the near horse by the reins, his eyes shining with awed admiration for the animals. He was obviously unused to being in such proximity to blood cattle, and Hunsdon suspected it might have been the reason for his haste. The lad nodded respectfully, clearly awaiting further orders.

"Walk them." Hunsdon tied up the reins and leaped down from the carriage. Now that he was here, his crime seemed even more heinous. To this proud, impoverished, country-bred young girl, it would probably seem that he had been making cruel sport of her. He resolved to make his confession quickly. It would not be easy to do.

The ancient manservant who opened the door to his knock, blinked at him in surprise. It would have been easy to have the servant announce his title to Barbara, but Hunsdon considered it the coward's way out, and merely gave his name instead. In another minute he was ushered into the drawing-room, where Barbara sat sewing on the fringe of a curtain that lay across her lap. The contrast to her appearance yesterday gave him a considerable shock.

The green-sprigged muslin gown she wore was well-worn and somewhat behind the mode, but it revealed enough to make him wonder how he ever could have thought her a child. When she saw him she smiled, and he thought to himself that he had underrated her attractions.

"Mr. Fitzhugh! I did not expect to see you this morning, but it is a pleasure. I am so glad you are not limping now. I would rise, but this blasted thing is so heavy."

The word shattered today's impression of a well-bred young lady, but he hoped he did not let it show.

He took the seat she indicated and assented when she asked if he cared for tea. Most young ladies would never be left alone in a room with a gentleman, particularly a strange one, but he had already guessed that this was an unusual household. Barbara rattled on as if there were nothing out of the ordinary.

"Rob Roy is quite in disgrace today, but I *told* Mama that it was the sort of thing that would happen if persons insisted upon leaving the doors open." Her voice dropped to a whisper. "He's torn the fringe again, you see." She resumed her normal tone of voice. "Mama was ready to have him *shot,* but I reminded her that there would be no chance of my getting a pheasant without him—and, of course, she could say nothing, for she knows as well as I do that it is her fault that the spaniels are useless."

He was studying her as she spoke. Really, he had been much too hard on her. Her appearance and her manners were both rather rough, but it was as Anne had said. If her hair were fashionably arranged and if she wore a gown that was up to snuff, there was no doubt that she would attract male attention. With only a little polish to her manners, she might easily find an eligible husband, except of course that her family could not afford a Season. He looked at the long fingers unskillfully plying the needle, just as she stabbed herself with it.

"Blast!" She unconsciously put her finger in her mouth, looking endearingly childish once more.

He had risen. "May I be of assistance?" He took the wounded digit and extracting his handkerchief, wrapped it about it. The monogrammed "H" might have puzzled her, but Barbara did not notice it.

"Thank you." The tears had sprung to her eyes, but she made no complaint. "Please be seated again. I should have a handkerchief with me. I am sorry to be so foolish. I dread what Mama would have to say if I dripped any blood on the curtain."

He scowled and would have spoken, but they were interrupted by the arrival of the elderly manservant with the tea. He had just set down the tray on the ancient gate-leg table in the corner, when a tall, handsome, and imperious lady swept into the room.

"Barbara. What is the meaning of this? It is most improper of you to be entertaining a stranger without telling me of it." Trailing her, three overfed spaniels wandered in and sniffed interestedly at the tea tray.

Hunsdon had risen and now he bowed as Barbara introduced him.

"Mama, this is Charles Fitzhugh, who is a friend of Sir Roger Blakemore's and is a guest in their house. We met yesterday when I was out and he was kind enough to call upon us today. Mr. Fitzhugh, this is my mother, Lady De Neresford."

Somehow, by her tone of voice and by introducing Roger's name, she managed to imply that he had also been present and had introduced them in a proper manner. There was an anxious expression in her eyes, and Hunsdon guessed that her mother would undoubtedly ring a peal over her head if he betrayed her. Poor lonely girl! She had been only too eager to talk at length to a sympathetic stranger. He resolved to preserve her secret.

"I am charmed, Lady De Neresford. Sir Roger had not informed me that he had such lovely neighbors." Discerning what was required, he let his gaze rest upon her admiringly as he straightened himself.

Even though her hair was graying, she was still a remarkably beautiful woman, dark-eyed and regal, and she softened visibly at his words. "It is a pleasure to meet you also, Mr. Fitzhugh. Barbara! Why haven't you poured tea for our guest already? Oh, I suppose I must."

She seated herself in front of the table on a scrolled-back sofa, its green plush covering worn thin in spots. She then waved Hunsdon into an elaborately carved,

caned-back chair in the Flemish style. "For heaven's
sake, Barbara, put that curtain down and find yourself
a chair near us. Mr. Fitzhugh will think you have no
manners at all!"

The girl said nothing, but laid aside the heavy curtain and crossed the room.

"Only see how you have let it crush your dress. You
must learn to be less careless. Nan will have to press
it again. I vow I do not know why you must persist in
being so unthinking. Milk and sugar, Mr. Fitzhugh?"

He pressed his lips together to stifle a protest and
managed a civil response instead. It was likely to be
even harder on Barbara if he defended her.

He remained only as long as politeness dictated.
There would be no further opportunity for private
conversation with Barbara, it was clear. He did not
wish to make his confession to her in front of her
mother, particularly given the circumstances. At the
same time, he felt increasingly uncomfortable about
having let his innocently begun deception extend to
another person. Lady De Neresford would probably
be furious when she learned the truth. It was no more
than she deserved for her officiousness, but now he
realized that her wrath would vent itself upon Barbara. Perhaps if he bent his mind to it, he could hit
upon some scheme to help her. He must think about
it.

When he arrived at Blakemore House, Hunsdon realized that his visit must have taken longer than he
thought, for it seemed that most of the other guests
had already arrived. He met Roger outside, busy giving directions to the head groom.

"And how is Miss Fostwick today? Lovelier than
ever, I suppose?"

"I went . . . for a drive instead," replied Hunsdon,
more or less truthfully, to Roger's teasing query.

"Ah, showing excellent restraint, my dear fellow."

Roger clapped him on the back absentmindedly before signaling to the groom once more. "And Simms, remember—Lord Brandville's gray is to be kept anywhere but in the box next to Aghadoe's—they'll be kicking and biting at each other all the time otherwise."

"Brandville's here? I'll have to go and greet him."

Roger had not even heard him, for now the groom was shouting about a problem with one of the mares.

"In season? Good Lord! She'll have to be put out to pasture."

It was a fortunate thing that he had arrived when he did, for none of the other guests had reason to wonder where he had been and Roger and Anne were too busy to give the matter thought.

He was half afraid that the question might surface at dinner, but his host and hostess were occupied with seeing that none of their guests was neglected. He would have liked an opportunity to talk to Brandville, but the latter was courteously devoting his time to Miss Eldridge, a quietly pretty girl who had been designated as his dinner partner. Neither could Hunsdon manage to single his friend out after dinner, for as soon as the ladies had departed, talk turned to the Congress of Aix-la-Chapelle and the conversation became general. Wasn't it an absurd suggestion on Czar Alexander's part? That an international military force be maintained to protect countries from violence? It was all well and good to say that the Barbary pirates must be stopped, but could the Russian ruler really expect Britain to donate its ships and crews to an international naval pool? If they truly wanted the pirates stopped, they and the rest of the countries would permit the Royal Navy to stop and search their vessels. If they had nothing to hide, why shouldn't they cooperate?

Perhaps it was the port, but Hunsdon could not keep his mind on their discussion. Bonaparte was safely imprisoned on St. Helena. The details of peace

could not matter beside that fact. Instead, his thoughts
turned to Mariabella. She would be expecting him tomorrow; he must go to see her. Perhaps he might ask
Anne for a posy from their hothouse. Such an offering
would certainly be in order. It was, after all, almost
February. Provided her affections had not altered (and
he doubted that they had), he was prepared to make
a declaration in form on St. Valentine's Day. But first
he meant to woo her with all the sorts of romantic
trifles in which she might delight. In spite of its interruption last summer, she should not be cheated out
of a complete courtship. She was entitled to it, after
all.

He did not awaken from his reverie until he heard
the squeaking and scraping of chairs and realized that
they must be ready to join the ladies.

Mariabella looked beautiful, lovelier even than his
memory had painted her. The dark curls, the porce-
lain complexion, the large eyes of that unusual shade
of grayish-blue—he had remembered them, but not
the sheer perfection of her features, the graceful curve
of her neck, the elegance of her bearing. She was most
fashionably attired in a gown of fine jaconet muslin
with a Henrietta ruff, epaulettes on the sleeves, and
a frilled double flounce about the hem of the gown.
It was quite short, as the current mode dictated,
allowing him a full view of slender ankles. Her appearance was in keeping with the rest of the house—elegant, wealthy, and modish.

She seemed to have anticipated his arrival this
morning and had received his flowers with practiced
ease. For a wild moment he had thought to take her
in his arms, but he recovered instantly. Of course he
could not do such a mad thing. It would probably
utterly disconcert her.

Her mother had seen them to the parlor and tactfully disappeared for "a moment" to see that tea was brought to them.

"I have missed you, Mariabella," he said.

She accepted the compliment with a smile.

He inquired about her father's health, her own, and that of the rest of her family, receiving positive responses to each of his questions. He mentioned the weather (so pleasant for February), his drive here (just a short distance from Blakemore House) and the charming dress she was wearing. He asked if she missed London, how she had been occupying herself, and whether she thought they might yet have another snow.

It was odd how difficult conversation could be without company about them to discuss or the music of a concert or the refreshments at an assembly to occupy their time.

In desperation, he mentioned the only other thought that occurred to him. As he reclined upon the damask-covered French sofa, ornamented with tassels, cord and fringe, he could not help comparing his opulent surroundings to those of yesterday. Seeing Mariabella dressed so strikingly had brought to his mind's eye a picture of Barbara, wearing her much simpler and less fashionable gown.

"I met one of your neighbors, young Lady De Neresford, the day before yesterday." He realized it was a tactical error. Mariabella would undoubtedly wonder why he had not called upon *her* yesterday.

She did look very surprised, but apparently that was not the thought that occurred to her. "You met Barbara? But how . . . ?"

"I was out riding and only narrowly avoided landing on her when we took a hedge."

Her hand flew in front of her face, but it was impossible not to discern her mirth. "I am afraid that she is our local quiz."

"She was out hunting a pheasant."

She lowered her hand, and though she did not laugh out loud, her smile danced about her eyes and mouth. "Then I can just imagine how she was dressed. No"— she held up a hand to prevent his words—"you may tell me if I am wrong. Let me see. Probably a great-coat of her father's, a bonnet which looked as if a horse *had* landed upon it, a pair of boots with the toes curling up, and in general she looked as if she wished to convince you that she was the village idiot."

He flushed. She had come much nearer the mark than she could imagine. He suddenly felt irritated with her for her amusement, and angry at himself for re-acting to Barbara in the same way. He spoke more heatedly than he intended.

"I felt sorry for the girl."

"So do we all." He must also have spoken more loudly than he should, for as Mariabella's mother glided into the room, she joined the conversation. "I am sorry that it took me so long, my dears. There was a crisis in the kitchen which required my attention."

She crossed over to her daughter and kissed the top of her head affectionately. "Don't let Mariabella deceive you into thinking that she feels no sympathy for Barbara. There *are* some young ladies hereabouts that delight in ridiculing the poor child, but Mariabella has always remained her friend."

She gave her daughter a gentle hug and then settled herself in a mahogany-and-gilt chair with red silk cushions. "If she seems to jest about Barbara, it is only because she is far too familiar with her unhappy situation. Is that not right, my dear?"

"Of course, Mama." She returned her mother's gaze with equal affection. "Who could help but pity her?"

Hunsdon smiled warmly. "I could not believe otherwise."

What a contrast this visit was to that of yesterday, this mother and daughter both amiable, exhibiting polished manners, clearly enjoying his company and each other's. No casual observer might have guessed from their demeanor that either of the two women looked upon Hunsdon as Mariabella's marital prospect, even though all of them knew it was his sole purpose in visiting there. A younger sister of Mariabella's appeared and was introduced, as well as her brother, Alfred. Hunsdon found himself scrutinizing Alfred rather closely. A skinny and unlovely lad of about seventeen, with a prominent Adam's apple and an unruly dark shock of hair, he did not favor his sister at all. It was easy to see why Barbara did not regard him highly as a possible spouse. Still, Barbara might fare worse, Hunsdon supposed. He might consider doing what he could to promote the match, after he and Mariabella were married, of course.

It was most difficult to tear himself away, but the moment was made somewhat easier by Mrs. Fostwick's invitation that he join them for dinner the following evening. He accepted with alacrity. Roger and Anne would surely forgive his absence since they knew his motive.

He should have been a completely happy man, but a troubling thought occurred to him as he drove away, still considering the differences between the two families. The Fostwicks, though far inferior to the De Neresfords in birth, were markedly superior to them in fortune. Wasn't it probable that if their financial situations had been reversed Barbara might be the reigning local belle and Mariabella, beautiful as she was, the object of neighborhood scorn? If Barbara had the money for governesses, and trips to town and proper gowns and such . . . It was a new and disturbing train of thought, and as he recognized, an unproductive one. He was relieved to spot a tall and elegant figure in front of him. It was Lord Brandville, walking in the direction of Blakemore. When Hunsdon's curricle had reached his friend's side, he pulled up his horses and inquired whether he wished for a ride. Brandville accepted, taking the seat beside him.

"Why were you out on foot?"

His friend gave a sardonic smile. "Since *I* cannot afford to keep a carriage, it is unlikely that *I* should have one here to drive about, isn't it?"

Hunsdon rarely allowed himself to be pricked by Brandville's barbs. "What blether you speak! As if Roger mightn't be happy for you to take one of his carriages out. Besides, I overheard Roger say that you brought that devilish beast of yours here yesterday. You might be riding."

"True, but . . ." Brandville heaved a sigh. "Sometimes walking is a more effective way of purchasing solitude. But tell me, how fares Miss Fostwick? As lovely as ever, I assume?"

His dark visage was inscrutable. There was never any sense in asking Brandville what he meant when he determined to be enigmatic. Hunsdon therefore wisely ignored the first part of his remarks, instead answering Brandville's question. "Quite well, thank you." Really, it was a trifle irritating to have every person within thirty miles or so cognizant of his affairs. Perhaps he was too romantic, but he wished there might be at least a *little* pleasurable anticipation involved in the process of becoming engaged.

"Well, if anyone is to fall into the parson's mousetrap, better you than I, I say," remarked Brandville cynically. "I am certain that her family must be delighted."

"Her family is charming and I wish you would drop that odious sneering manner," replied Hunsdon stiffly. "I also wish you would refrain from discussing the matter as if it were settled. I have not asked Miss Fostwick for her hand yet, you know."

"Oh, but you will, my dear fellow, you will. It is what you were born for—to fulfill some family's grandest hopes. I cannot help it if I wished better things for you." He saw that Hunsdon had set his mouth and was looking quite offended, so he reached over to tap his friend gently on the chin. "Come now, don't be angry with me. It is all base envy, you know. I am sure that I will wish you and Miss Fostwick most happy . . . when the matter is settled, of course."

It was impossible to tell whether or not Brandville were secretly laughing at him; it was equally impossible to resist him. Hunsdon gave a reluctant smile. "Very well, but I will expect you to refrain from discussing the matter until I have good news for you— and I mean that you will refrain from discussing it with anyone."

"My dear fellow, mum's the word." He settled back in his seat with his arms crossed and his legs stretched out in front of him. He regarded the bleak countryside about them indifferently. "D'you know, I happen to detest the country. I wonder why I torture myself by coming here?"

"Because Roger and Anne are two of your dearest friends and you are quite as fond of them as they are of you," replied Hunsdon stoutly. He did not add that Brandville's circumstances frequently made him more or less dependent on his friends' hospitality.

"Hmm. I suppose you are right. Just at the moment, though, I wish that Roger and Anne were slightly less fond of me, or less concerned for my welfare, anyway."

There was no opportunity to ask him what he meant, even if Hunsdon had wished to do so, for they had reached the grounds of Blakemore House and now encountered a party of riders returning from an expedition. Chief among them was Miss Eldridge, Brandville's dinner partner of the previous night. She presented a charming picture in a riding habit of soft gray, and she colored prettily at their greetings and compliments. Hunsdon observed that her gaze did not leave his friend's face, but that was hardly surprising.

Brandville was handsome in a saturnine way. Despite his financial ineligibility he always attracted female attention.

The unforeseen problem with the Fostwicks' invitation to dinner was that it left Hunsdon to cool his heels for the entire day. He had been the first to quit the whist table, at half-past one that morning, and in consequence, he was up and about before most of the other guests. He encountered his hostess downstairs; she looked somewhat fatigued and, in response to a question, replied that Roger and Brandville had gone out riding this morning.

"They intend to have a race. I hope they do not break their foolish necks."

"I am certain that there is no danger."

"I suppose not—I am just a trifle irritated with Roger for leaving me to deal with all these guests alone, and particularly since he took Lord Brandville with him." She looked conscious at this last remark and added hastily, "I thought that all the gentlemen might wish to form a shooting party, and one cannot tell how long this favorable weather may hold. The gamekeeper assured me that the pheasants are prolific this year."

The word "pheasants" made Hunsdon start guiltily. It really was past time for him to be telling Barbara the truth about himself. Of course, he did not know how he could contrive to meet her without her mother about. The obstacle seemed insurmountable.

"Is anything the matter?" Anne asked.

"No, nothing at all."

"I imagine you are wanting to see Miss Fostwick— it is a pity—but perhaps it is wise not to spend too much time together when you are just becoming reacquainted." She looked up from her sewing with a little smile. "I wish there were anything I could do to help, but of course there is not." She bent her head to her work again, then added shyly, "Perhaps you might care to relieve your feelings with a brisk walk, or a ride, or a drive."

"Thank you." He might as well drive out and see if he might not happen to encounter Barbara without her mother. He would be better this time about coming to the point. It would give him something to do this morning anyway.

He had just slowed the curricle to turn it down the drive to Sherbrook when he heard it. Even above the sound of the horse's hooves, the jingle of the harness and the rattle of the wheels, he could hear a female shrieking. As they approached the source of the sound, he could make out the words.

"Blast! *Blast!* Blast you . . . you . . . you *jackass!*"

The tone was too patrician to admit the possibility of the voice's belonging to a servant. Hunsdon thought he recognized those particular curses. He would have liked to urge the horses, but the overgrown lane was too narrow to permit it.

As they came around a bend, his suspicions were confirmed. A donkey stood in the drive, its hooves planted stubbornly and its ears pinned back. Barbara, mounted upon it, was doing her best to urge it forward with reprimands, and with the use of a light riding crop, but the donkey was having none of it. As Hunsdon pulled up his horses, the donkey seemed to come to a final decision and the animal abruptly sat, causing Barbara to tumble backward over his hindquarters.

It was fortunate that Hunsdon had brought Ned. With a call, the groom was at the horses' heads and Hunsdon was able to leap down from the carriage to help Barbara to her feet. Although now somewhat dirty, there was nothing eccentric about her clothing today. She wore a drab brown wool pelisse over an unremarkable, if outmoded, riding habit in a dark green. On her head perched a chip bonnet garnished

with ribbons in a matching shade. Her face was red
from her exertions and her anger.

"Blast! Blast the animal! It took me all morning just
to get him this far and then a rabbit dashed across the
road and he refused to go another step." The animal,
having dislodged himself of his burden, had risen and
now stood with deceptive meekness in the road.

"Hmm." To his surprise, Hunsdon saw that Barbara's eyes were overbright, suggesting the possibility
that she was close to tears. "May I be of service? I
should be happy to convey you wherever you wish to
go."

"W-would you? Oh, but . . . but I should not wish
to disrupt your plans. . . ."

"You would not be doing so at all. As a matter of
fact, I was on my way to pay you a visit today."

Her face brightened. "If that is so—well then, it is
the most fortunate circumstance—I was going into the
village, but I had something that I wished to tell you,
also."

"Shall I have my groom return the animal to your
stables?"

"Oh, that won't be necessary. *Hah!*" She took a
step, slapped the animal sharply across the rump, and
with a bray of protest it turned on its heels and with
surprising alacrity fled in the direction of Sherbrook.

He gave the groom his orders. Fortunately, they
were in a clearing, which gave Ned enough room to
turn the horses around.

Hunsdon offered Barbara his arm, which she accepted with a sudden diffidence, then helped her into
the carriage before climbing into it himself. He took
the reins while the groom scrambled back to his own
seat. Ned's face was expressionless, but Hunsdon
dreaded to imagine what he was thinking. He must
see that the groom kept his mouth shut. Neither
Mariabella nor his parents would be happy to hear of
this episode.

Barbara's eyes were on his horses. "What a pair of prime 'uns," she exclaimed admiringly in her boyish way as they started off. "Joe—the stable lad—told me, but I had no opportunity to see them myself. How I should like to drive animals such as these." Her face assumed a droll expression. "Our horses have to be used for farm work, so although they are strong, you can't coax them into a trot."

There was no chance to make his confession with the groom seated just behind them, so Hunsdon instead asked Barbara if she had shot her pheasants yet.

"No, I had no luck yesterday, and Mama has decided to wait before inviting anyone to dinner. The London swell is here now, you see," she added in a low voice. "Alfred told me that he had been to visit his sister yesterday."

Word certainly traveled fast here, thought Hunsdon. Odd that she still should have no suspicions concerning his identity. A simple description from Alfred would have shown her the truth. She answered his unspoken question with her next words.

"Of course, Alfred is useless when it comes to telling you anything of import. All he could say was that the gentleman was dressed very fine—which of course we already knew he would be." Her voice had risen unconsciously, but now she dropped it to a whisper again. "I saw him myself yesterday."

Hunsdon could not help starting. "You did?"

"Yes, while I was out hunting—at least, I am sure it must be he, for he was dressed very fine—imagine, he was wearing his top hat just to go out walking—and he had a most arrogant expression—and gloomy, too, as if he detested being in the country. I knew it must be he from Mariabella's description, 'tall, and handsome, and distinguished'—he had a walking stick— just as I thought he would—and you have never seen a cravat like that in your life. But you must have met him by now yourself."

By now Hunsdon had recognized this description of
Brandville and was hard put to keep from laughing
aloud at it. Brandville would be deflated if he knew
how signally he had failed to impress a female observer. As entertaining as it was, though, his conscience reminded him that he should not allow this
misapprehension to continue. "But my dear—" Why
had he called her his "dear"? "How can you be sure
it was Lord Hunsdon? There is a large party at Blakemore House, after all."

"Oh, but I am sure." She giggled. "He had on a
pair of Wellingtons, and a pebble must have landed
in one, for he had to stop and remove it and shake it
out. He had a great deal of trouble removing the boot,
and I could hear him cursing the countryside and
swearing that he would never leave London again."

It did sound like Brandville. No wonder he had
been in such a sour mood. The thought of the impeccably groomed peer hopping up and down on one foot
on a country road, cursing at the top of his lungs, was
an amusing one. Hunsdon just managed to keep from
smiling himself. "I am afraid that it sounds suspiciously as if you have been spying, your ladyship."

"Well, I cannot help that he did not see me," she
said mischievously. "The timing would not have been
fortunate for a meeting. But that puts me in mind of
something that I must tell you . . . when we have
opportunity, of course."

She would not elaborate and he did not press her.
Instead, the conversation easily turned to sport, and
to Hunsdon's surprise, he discovered that Barbara was
knowledgeable about horses, dogs, guns, and all sorts
of hunting. Her father, at least, had not neglected her
education. It was an unusual acquisition for a young
lady, but it did not take Hunsdon long to discern, in
spite of her disclaimers to the contrary, that she often
provided meat for the family table. After meeting her

mother, he had begun to suspect that whatever small income they had was badly mismanaged.

They had reached the outskirts of the village, and now she directed him to the store. Lady De Neresford had belatedly realized the necessity for amaranth ribbon to match her new gown, and Barbara had been commissioned to fetch it.

"Though I doubt Mrs. Gray is likely to have any, since it is a new color. Still, Mama would not be content until I asked and I would rather go outside on this sort of day than remain cooped in the house."

Hunsdon's first thought was that she was right and that the weather had been glorious and unseasonably fair for January and February. He was also quick, however, to catch the wistful note in her voice. It would be misery to be entrapped in a house all day with her mother. The poor child! He must think of some way to improve her situation. With all the resources at his command, there must be something he could do for her. Perhaps Mariabella would have an idea. He would have to mention it to her.

As she had predicted the amaranth ribbon, since it was a new shade, was not available in Mrs. Gray's modest shop. The proprietress assured her that she would be certain to have her assistant, Miss Tinsley, obtain some for Lady De Neresford when she next went to London.

Barbara shook her head resignedly. "I am afraid that it may be too late by then. Mama never can find the colors she wants until a new color has already become the fashion instead."

The neighborhood might look upon Barbara with scorn, but it was clear that in this domain, she was regarded as an august personage. Hunsdon was aware that there had been a flutter of interest when he had entered the shop with her, and several speculative looks had passed from him to Barbara and back again.

It was rather ridiculous. She was, after all, only an infant.

They were ready to leave when inspiration seized him. With all this ribbon and lace about, why shouldn't he buy the materials to make Mariabella a valentine? It was a childish thing, it was true, but secretly he hoped she might find it romantic, also.

"I'll take an ell of that red ribbon," he announced abruptly, startling Barbara and the shopkeepers.

"An ell?"

"Yes, and some of that pink ribbon over there, too. And show me some of your lace also, please."

"What in heaven's name?" The muttered exclamation had come from Barbara, who was quite unused to such extravagance.

"I am purchasing materials for a valentine. Do you think that one ell is not enough? Perhaps I should make it two. I wonder how one ties a love knot?"

Barbara's face was suffused with color. She responded to his inquiries about which lace she thought was prettiest with barely audible murmurs. When his purchase was concluded and they had left the shop, she said in an urgent whisper, "I . . . that is, Mr. Fitzhugh . . . I must have speech with you immediately."

He had been thinking much the same thing. There could be no reason to delay his confession any longer. He must acquaint her with the truth. "There must be some sort of an inn here. Perhaps you would be willing to accompany me there and partake of a meal. Since I did not breakfast this morning, I must admit I am famished."

She consented, and since the day was so fair, they walked the short distance to the inn. Barbara was surprisingly silent. Well, that would make telling her all the easier.

There was no opportunity for private conversation until after they had been served. Hunsdon was attacking a neat's tongue when she suddenly broke her silence. The stumbling words poured from her, permitting no interruption.

"Mr. Fitzhugh—I—I am most sensible of the honor you do me—that is, it is a most awkward thing to have to tell you, and it is a great pity that we did not have opportunity to converse before—but I most particularly needed to tell you"—here she took a deep breath—"Mama said that she would not favor your suit."

He was frozen with shock. His countenance must have revealed his incredulity, but Barbara did not see it. Her gaze was lowered to her plate.

"I—it is nothing against you yourself, of course. It is simply that she feels she would be failing in her duty to my late father if she allowed me to marry a commoner. I—I find you to be a most agreeable gentleman myself," she added sincerely, raising her eyes to his at last. "In fact, I have never met a gentleman so easy to converse with before."

She must have misinterpreted his ribbon purchase, his confused brain finally decided.

"Mama said that you would naturally be interested in allying yourself with a De Neresford. I must confess that I thought that she was wrong, but I did mean to speak to you in any case," continued Barbara, lowering her gaze once more. "I meant to speak to you before . . . it was most kind of you to wish to . . . that is, I was deeply touched—I have never had a valentine before, you see—" Here she blushed again, even more vividly. "Of course, I would not have wished to raise your hopes unnecessarily. I am sorry. I hope that we may still continue as friends?"

What was he to say? "Actually, I am Lord Hunsdon, the one your mother wishes you to wed, but I am not at all interested in marrying you." It might be kinder in the end to say so now. Confound that mother! Expecting that a long family tree would make any single gentleman leap at the chance of wedding this impoverished, eccentric child of a girl! He had certainly erred in imagining Barbara to be the mentally deficient member of her family.

The little chin was lifted up bravely and those candid blue eyes were watching him. "Please?" she added hopefully. Her lower lip trembled.

He opened his mouth and shut it again. "Why, yes, I suppose we may." What a weakling he was. Still, it seemed worth it at the moment to see that radiant smile spread across her countenance. The chit was oddly taking when in a happy mood.

"I wish you were Lord Hunsdon," she announced abruptly. "I would much rather marry you than him."

Perhaps it was just as well that he hadn't told her the truth. Perhaps he might be married and gone from the neighborhood before she discovered it, he thought, temporarily abandoning his idea of helping her.

Though nuncheon with Barbara had caused him to feel that control of his life was slipping from his grasp and that he might have reason to fear for his sanity, happily dinner with Mariabella and her family accomplished the opposite. Again his universe seemed well-ordered, he was once more the master of his own fate, and what a pleasant fate it was, he thought, glancing at his lovely intended.

With Anne's help, he had contrived to make a love knot of the red ribbon. He had placed it in a little enameled box and presented it to Mariabella upon his arrival. She must know he might easily have provided her with rubies and diamonds, but he had chosen to give her a simple, more heartfelt token of his affections instead. Since she also had grown up with wealth, the homemade token must delight her all the more.

It would have pleased him if upon opening the box, she had exclaimed over it and let him know how deeply it had touched her, but she had merely thanked him politely before laying it upon a side table. Of course, her family was about and, as Anne had said, she was not impulsive. Apparently she was not demonstrative either. It was a virtue in a countess-to-be.

His mother had warned him that he could not do worse than to marry some ill-bred sort of girl who wore her heart upon her sleeve. The countess had then remembered an incident of a newly married viscount and viscountess who had spent a good part of an assembly seated *beside* each other upon a sofa. What was worse, they had actually held hands for quite some time. Naturally, everyone was embarrassed for them and invitations to the couple dropped as a consequence. His mother had fixed him with a penetrating eye and remarked that she knew her son too well to suppose he would betray himself by acting in such a manner. Horrified, he had responded appropriately. Now, as he thought about it, he had to wonder a little. Certainly circumspection was called for in public, but did that mean that one had to appear absolutely indifferent to one's love? Of course, that was not being fair to Mariabella. He should not blame her for being mistress of her own emotions. He could not expect less of her. He would hardly wish her to declare her liking for him in the same transparent fashion that Barbara did. He felt an odd twinge of disloyalty for thinking about Barbara. Still, it served to remind him that he had meant to ask Mariabella what could be done for the child. Perhaps tonight would be an opportune time. As Barbara's friend, it was a matter with which she naturally must have concerned herself. She must have some ideas. He smiled at his intended warmly. She returned his smile pleasantly.

Mariabella's mother had a positive genius for contriving situations in which they might find themselves alone together. He had to be most grateful to her for the opportunities, short as they were. Mariabella had sung for them all after dinner, and he was impressed

by her talent. It was true that her well-trained voice
had not conveyed great feeling, but he hoped that she
had directed the one love ballad to him. Now that
they were alone, she was toying on the pianoforte in
a desultory fashion. Perhaps she felt as shy as he suddenly did himself.

"Mariabella."

"Yes?"

He wished she would stop playing and turn around
to face him instead. "I have something to ask you."

His wish was granted. She rose and fixed those sin-
gularly beautiful eyes upon him.

"It's about your neighbor, Barbara. I happened
to meet her today and her mother was sending her
to the village on a donkey, if you can imagine it, for
some ribbon that she already knew that the store
didn't have."

"Oh." Did he imagine it or did she recoil slightly?
She seated herself upon the piano stool once more
with an abruptness that suggested falling.

"Yes. I was in my curricle, so I gave her a ride. It
was clear that she would never have managed to arrive
there on her own."

She had turned back to the piano again and was
playing with rather more force than before. "You are
too kind."

"Oh, there was no difficulty. I had nothing else to
do. But it made me realize what an uncomfortable
sort of life she must have."

"Quite so."

She was not entering into this discussion with the
quick sympathy he had imagined. Still, he persevered.
"I thought that . . . as her friend . . . you must have
often pitied her and that perhaps you might have some
idea what could be done for her."

There was a pause as she suspended her playing.
"What . . . could . . . be . . . *done* . . . for . . . *her*?"

"Yes." Was something the matter? There was the

violent crash of a chord, which quickly evolved into a rondo. It was apparent that Mariabella was a marvelous player. And now there was a great deal more feeling than had been present in her earlier performance.

She said nothing more and he felt obliged to elaborate. "I have no good idea myself—but surely somehow we might be able to put her in the way of meeting eligible gentlemen."

She abandoned the rondo and closed the cover with a snap before rising. "If that is what you wish, I am certain you will think of something. Now, if you will excuse me, I have a touch of the headache."

She fled the room precipitately, leaving him staring after her. Her mother was most apologetic when she entered the room. Mariabella was subject to these sudden headaches, which often were severe. He must not regard it if she had seemed rude. She had received some upsetting news today. She would be herself by the time of the ball on Thursday.

He accepted her apologies without demur, and did not reproach her for her carelessness. Obviously Mrs. Fostwick had allowed the children into the parlor, for as he crossed through it on his way out, he could see that the love knot lay crumpled in a corner of the room. One of the children must have been playing with it. He hoped that Mariabella would not be too wounded when she discovered it.

As disappointing as the evening was, it boasted one virtue. It had permitted him a narrow escape from the visit of Lady De Neresford to Blakemore House. She had called upon Roger and Anne that afternoon, after Hunsdon had already departed for the Fostwicks. As Roger recounted the story the next morning, Hunsdon held his breath, lest his deception had become apparent.

"Odious woman." Roger crouched down, and as a fluttering of wings arose, squeezed the trigger. A pheasant fell to the ground. "Hi, you—another gun."

His obedient loader took his fowling piece while handing him a freshly charged one. "Luckily I wasn't there—just Anne and two of the ladies. Lady De Neresford inquired about our guests most minutely. Seemed disappointed that you weren't there. Matchmaking for that unmarriageable daughter of hers, no doubt."

"I wouldn't say she was unmarriageable. Rather sweet girl. A little young, perhaps," protested Hunsdon.

Roger looked at him unbelievingly for a moment before a shout and a fluttering of wings attracted his attention. He fired again. "Blast! Well, Barbara must not have told her mother about meeting you, and I can imagine why. Lady De Neresford mentioned some connection who knew you, but depend upon if, if she had an introduction, she'd be fairly haunting Blakemore House."

The mother must not have referred to Mr. Fitzhugh. It was fortunate for him. He could never explain how he had fallen into this entanglement.

Roger was oblivious to his anxiety. "How was the beautiful Miss Fostwick? When are we to wish you happy?"

"I do not know." In spite of himself, he had to frown. Her behavior had been odd. "She developed a headache while we were talking after dinner and had to leave the room."

Roger let out a guffaw. "You were wasting your time by talking—that's not what a young lady wants . . . eh, Brandville?"

To Hunsdon's surprise, he found that his friend had drawn up silently beside them and had been listening to their conversation. "I cannot pretend to know what Miss Fostwick wants," Brandville said quietly. He turned with abruptness and handed his gun to a surprised loader. "These country sports pall on one so quickly. I think I will rejoin the ladies." He gave them a quick nod and set off in the direction of the house.

Hunsdon stared after his friend's retreating back in

surprise. "I say! What caused that? He's been in the most cursed mood lately."

Roger frowned. "Perhaps he shouldn't have come. Perhaps I should have ignored Anne and not invited him. Poor devil!" There was something unreadable in Roger's expression. A shout came from beyond them. "We'd best walk on to the next covey."

Hunsdon would have liked to call upon Mariabella that afternoon in order to inquire about her health, but Mrs. Fostwick had told him pointedly that her headaches often lasted for an entire day and night. It was not that he was not fond of Roger and Anne, but he was finding the rest of the company rather tiresome. He did not think he could stand to hear Mr. Eldridge recount his prowess of the morning once more. The latter had missed ten times as many birds as he had taken, yet he seemed to think his shooting remarkably fine. It was bad enough to have to listen to this, but when he and some of the other gentlemen began boasting of their past exploits also, Hunsdon thought he might very well go mad. Brandville sat listening in gloomy silence.

He excused himself and searched out his host, who had closeted himself in his office with his account books.

"Do you mind if I borrow Aghadoe?"

Roger regarded him sympathetically. "Not at all, my dear fellow—so long as you avoid another tumble. Can't bear it, eh? Neither could I."

Hunsdon had to smile. "Thank you, then. I shouldn't be out more than an hour."

"One piece of advice for you." Roger's expression was grave. "Once you are married—the fair sex are wonderful, of course—but I strongly suggest that you never listen to your wife, or at least that you refuse to allow her to involve you in any way with her schemes."

Hunsdon could not imagine what Roger was talking about, so he merely nodded puzzledly before excusing himself.

He felt a great sense of release being free of the house and its occupants. There did seem to be some great bores among their number. If what Roger had said was true, and Anne was responsible, he had to wonder why in heaven's name she had invited them.

The temperature had been dropping all day and the clouds were gathering ominously. He paused for a moment to button the very top of his coat. It looked as if at last they might have their long-overdue snow. He clucked to the horse, and leaving the road he set out again, unconsciously turning the animal in the direction of Sherbrook.

He was not riding pell-mell as before, and by approaching slowly, he was able to see the small figure in the stubble field long before he reached her. She was standing stock-still, facing away from him, her gun raised. There was barking and a bird shot up from the ground. In another moment or two she had fired, and the bird dropped from the air. He thought it best to announce his presence.

"Halloo!"

She turned, saw him, and waved, but proceeded to cross the field to claim her bird. Rob Roy might be an expert at flushing game, but he apparently was not adequate as a retriever.

Something cold and wet landed on his nose. The snow was beginning.

Barbara was wearing the same peculiar garments for shooting as before, but this time he hardly noticed them. Instead, what struck him was the remarkable brilliance of her eyes, and how becoming she looked with her cheeks flushed by the cold and the exercise. She held up her kill for him to see. He took it from her outstretched hand.

"A partridge—shot through the head," he added in some surprise.

She looked equally surprised. "Of course. Where else should I hit it? There is nothing I dislike more than having to pick shot out of my dinner."

"Your marksmanship is excellent." It was remarkable to him. He had never before known a female who hunted.

"Oh, but it was an easy shot. I had him from the side, you see, and it couldn't have been much more than sixty yards away." She patted her fowling piece affectionately. "And of course, credit must go to my Purdey. Father bought it for my birthday just before he died."

Despite their pecuniary difficulties, the late baron had obviously not found it proper to retrench as far as the purchase of sporting goods was concerned.

Her panting dog had thrown himself at her feet. "What! I suppose you think that you deserve recognition too then, Rob Roy?" She shook her head and smiled up at Hunsdon. "You see, there is no credit left for me. Any idiot might have made the shot."

She looked rather lovely like that, when her eyes shone with humor. That mischievous smile was an expression unique to her. He handed her the bird back and dismounted.

"I spent my morning with gentlemen who had scores of better shots than that, yet they only succeeded in wounding the game or missing the shot altogether most of the time."

"Shame on them. Of course, they could not be Leicestershire-bred." She added seriously, "I myself could not afford to waste so much shot."

The snow, which had begun with a few gentle flakes, was now falling thick and fast. She glanced at the sky. "I had better go home now. It looks as if we may have a storm."

They were several miles from the great house. She

obviously had to walk a distance to find any game.
"Do you have a mount?" he asked.

She shook her head with a laugh. "I make better
progress on foot. That braying donkey would only
frighten the birds away."

She would have made her farewells and departed,
but he could not repress his concern.

"It is a long distance to walk, and the cold and snow
are increasing."

"Yes, all the more reason for me to start now. I
hope you will excuse me," she said with a little
impatience.

"I am certain that Lady De Neresford will worry
about you out in the midst of this storm by yourself."

She shook her head. "Mama is well accustomed to
my ramblings."

"At the very least, you will take a chill, and at
worst—well, I do not like to imagine it. If you do not
mind sharing a horse, Aghadoe and I will be only too
happy to convey you home."

"I am never ill, but thank you, it is most kind of
you."

"I shall worry about you if I do not see you safely
home," he added frankly. "If you do not care to ride,
we will walk you back."

"It is kind, but most unnecessary—"

"I insist." There was a certain commanding tone
that he used only rarely. Barbara seemed to understand he would brook no further argument, for now
she smiled at him.

"Well, if I am to have an escort, we may as well
ride. I am afraid that you are right and that this storm
may be a serious one." She laid her game bag on the
ground and rested her gun carefully on top of it.

He locked his fingers and held them out to her.
With no pretense at false modesty, she put her foot
upon them and vaulted with ease onto the saddle. Out
of a sense of delicacy, he had kept his eyes downward,

but he could not help noticing how trim her ankle was, even covered by the scuffed boots. He handed her the game bag and the fowling piece. Her eyes clouded for a moment.

"Rob Roy."

"What?"

"I am afraid that if the snow becomes deep quickly, he may be trapped. Would you object if I held him upon my lap?"

"Not if you think you can manage him," he replied somewhat incredulously. He reached down, then handed the furry little animal to her. Rob Roy seemed to have no objection to this treatment, for he settled into her lap quietly.

Hunsdon mounted just behind her. Aghadoe took a few steps forward and Barbara slid sideways.

"I am sorry that it is not a sidesaddle," he said.

"If only my arms were less full, I might hold the pommel and it would not matter at all."

"Here, if I take the reins in my right hand, I may easily hold you with my left arm." He tucked the crop under his left arm and put it around Barbara. My word! How had he ever mistaken her for a boy . . . or a child? She was distinctly and utterly feminine. Even through the greatcoat he could feel her soft and generous curves.

Despite the freezing temperature, he could feel himself growing warm. She smelled of a not-unattractive mixture of lavender water and gunpowder. His heart was pounding in his ears and his breath was coming shorter. He could not have spoken if his life had depended on it. He could never remember a female having this overpowering effect upon him before.

"I think we had better bear to the right." Barbara's voice was husky, but perhaps it was just from forcing herself to be heard over the wind and snow. "I am afraid it is becoming so thick that we will be better off if we keep to the road."

She was undoubtedly right. The snow was making it hard to see. He clutched her more tightly to him with an unconscious protectiveness and turned Aghadoe in the direction in which he hoped lay the road.

The next fifteen minutes seemed to take hours. As the landscape began to be covered with white, his sense of direction vanished. His eyes were beginning to burn from the wind and the cold, but he kept them stubbornly open. More than once he was glad to have Barbara with him as she led them around a ditch, now almost hidden by the snow, or corrected their direction with a word or two. He was not certain that he and Aghadoe would have reached the road on their own.

Fortunately, the horse, although it stumbled a few times over some hidden obstacles, did not seem to be suffering unduly from its double load. It presented one less problem for Hunsdon to worry about. When at last they neared the road, he breathed a sigh of relief. The going would be easier now. Without warning, Barbara's body suddenly sagged against his. He realized that she had been holding herself rigidly upright with tension. Apparently she instantly realized the impropriety of it, for now she straightened herself again. "I beg your pardon."

"Think nothing of it." He could hardly tell her that he had enjoyed it.

Their progress to Sherbrook was now much easier and more rapid. When they reached the house he dismounted then took her various burdens from her and lifted her down. He held her in his arms a moment or two longer than necessary. Her eyes were wide and very blue and her lips were parted slightly. He felt magnetically drawn to her. An insistent, mad desire to sample those lips seized him. He had lowered his face part-way toward hers when he realized what he was doing. The shock of it made him release her, perhaps more forcefully than necessary. What kind of a cad was he?

"Th-thank you."

"You are welcome." His voice was hoarse, but that could be explained by the cold.

"Won't you come in and warm yourself?"

It was an appealing thought, but it ran contrary to all his better instincts, which were urging him to fly. "No, thank you. I must go."

Was there some part of her that understood it? In any event, she did not urge him. "Well, thank you again."

He watched her disappear into the house, then turned the horse and headed back for Blakemore. The ride was miserable and bitter cold without Barbara there to warm him, but even with the snow, travel on the road itself was not difficult. Aghadoe, perhaps inspired by the thought of the warm stable waiting for him, seemed to have no trouble finding his way. Still, Hunsdon had plenty of time with which to reproach himself. Why had he gone to Sherbrook at all? It would have been far better to endure the boredom of the company at Blakemore House than to thrust himself into such a dangerous position. He had been near to taking advantage of a trusting, innocent child of a girl—a girl, moreover, who had already been cursed by more than her share of misfortune. What a scab he was! She still didn't even know his true identity.

Just as bothersome was the thought of what kind of husband he would make. He was practically engaged, after all. And if he was so easily tempted before his marriage, was there any certainty that he would not betray Mariabella after it? What was the matter with him, anyway? Mariabella, who was far more beautiful, had much more polished manners, and whom he loved so deeply, had never awakened these kinds of feelings in him. He could only suppose that his affection for her was of too lofty a sort.

In any case the incident, minor though it might be, had led him to a decision. He would give up all this Valentine's nonsense and ask Mariabella for her hand at the ball tomorrow night.

With this resolution made, it might have seemed that all his problems were solved, but further trials awaited him. The snowfall had occasioned some concern, but Roger prophesied confidently that it would end before morning. There should be no obstacle to prevent the company's attending the ball. Everyone seemed in a jovial mood at dinner, with the exception of Brandville, who was more than usually morose. Even Miss Eldridge's most pointed attempts to draw him out met with but little success. He was gloomy to the point of being almost rude, and Hunsdon observed it in surprise. It was unlike Brandville to indulge himself with a fit of the sullens when he was someone's guest. He excused himself shortly after the ladies had left, so there was no opportunity for Hunsdon to inquire as to the cause of his somber spirits. It would have to wait until the morrow.

Upon waking the next morning, Hunsdon's first thought was that by tonight he should be an engaged man. It was not as blissful a notion as he could wish, but perhaps that was only natural. He rose from his bed and crossed to the mahogany chest of drawers where he had left a certain velvet box. He opened it to see the sapphire and diamond ring that he had selected for Mariabella. He had thought in his former romantic way that it would be better to surprise her with it and have it fitted later than to wait and let her choose one. Now he was not certain that he had made the right decision. The ribbon and lace lay neglected in the same drawer. He would not need them now. They reminded him of his outing with Barbara. In some ways, *he* had been the child.

As Roger had predicted, the snow had ceased dur-

ing the night, and though the temperature still was
cold, the sun was beginning to peep between the
clouds. There should be no obstacle to their joining
the Fostwicks tonight. With unusual restraint, Roger
did *not* add that Mariabella would doubtless be panting with eagerness to see Hunsdon.

It was too cold for a walk, or a ride, or a drive in
an open carriage, so Hunsdon was forced to remain
in the house with everyone else. He refused a game
of chess with his host as well as cards with others of
the gentlemen, preferring to occupy himself with a
book instead. He consoled himself with the thought
that the weather prevented his being tempted to call
upon Barbara today. He was free of that one danger,
at least.

He was therefore unprepared for disaster when it
occurred. One of the ladies of the party had perched
herself on a window seat, and now she remarked the
approach of a carriage.

"But it is so very old-fashioned and quaint-looking—
and those must be farm horses pulling it. Whoever
could it be? Oh, I remember now, Anne, did you not
have a caller yesterday who—"

Hunsdon did not catch the rest of her words. Could
it be that Lady De Neresford had decided to try her
luck once more? His first impulse was to flee and
escape discovery. He rose, then hesitated for a moment, irresolute. Of course, it would only serve that
old harridan right if she learned about his deception.
Everyone would know of his engagement shortly. Perhaps it would teach her not to cherish such unreal
expectations or to encourage her daughter in false
hopes. Perhaps it was better to finish it now. Brandville materialized at his elbow. "So this must be the
local quiz we've heard so much of—it may be that she
will enliven this most"—he yawned—"*boring* day."

When the visitors were announced, Hunsdon realized he had made a grave error. He had not antici-

pated that Lady De Neresford would bring Barbara along with her. It would be unforgivable for her to find out the truth in the midst of this company. The shock would be too severe. He moved toward the drawing-room door, but it was too late.

Lady De Neresford presented a picture in a red velvet spencer, trimmed with ermine, over a white muslin dress which was puffed and flounced and embroidered wherever possible. It was an ensemble designed to create a sensation, and it did, though unfortunately not a favorable one. She looked far overdressed for the occasion, and the impression was worse when one noticed her daughter. Barbara was wearing a worn and rather drab pelisse of brown kerseymere over an outmoded gown of white cotton, printed with pink and blue. It fit her badly, became her ill, and clearly was an old gown of her mother's that had been insufficiently altered to fit. She looked uncomfortable and awkward under the cheap straw bonnet that she wore. There was no mistaking the sneering looks and amused titters that passed between some members of the company. Barbara's head drooped dispiritedly.

Anne was making the introductions, as apparently only she and one or two of the ladies had been about to receive Lady De Neresford yesterday. The thought of the present danger recurred to Hunsdon. How should he keep the truth from coming out?

Lady De Neresford had taken a swift look about the room, and her eyes had lit upon Lord Brandville. Hardly acknowledging everyone else to whom she was being introduced, she gravitated toward their corner of the room. Clearly, like her daughter, she had mistaken Brandville for the "London swell." An idea began to form in Hunsdon's mind. He hoped that she was not paying strict attention to names.

At last Anne had reached the group with whom he was standing. "And Lady De Neresford, this is Lord

Hunsdon and Lord Brandville—" Good, Brandville
was already bowing. Hunsdon sprang forward to take
Lady De Neresford by the hand, "And *I* am already
acquainted with Lady De Neresford and her most
charming daughter." Yes, it was working. Lady De
Neresford's eyes were still fixed upon Brandville. If
he could just contrive to keep them separated for the
rest of the visit, she might continue to believe that
Brandville was himself.

As it so happened, he need not have worried.
Brandville apparently had decided that this sort of
amusement was not to his taste, or else he wished to
escape the persistent attentions of Miss Eldridge, for
he made his excuses and escaped. The thought of joining Brandville was tempting, but Barbara's eyes met
his with an unstated appeal in them and he knew he
could not desert her.

As they were seated, Hunsdon found a chair in their
part of the room. Politeness would keep them from
referring to "Mr. Fitzhugh" by name when he was
present. Hopefully, now that she had met "him,"
Lady De Neresford would have the courtesy to refrain
from mentioning Lord Hunsdon's name also.

As much as he wished it, he could not offer Barbara
any protection. The ladies of the party, bored with
indoor life, had clustered about the new arrivals as
interesting curiosities. He tried to listen with one ear
to their conversation, but the task was made difficult
by Mr. Eldridge, who had drawn up his chair next to
Hunsdon's and was boring him with his theories on
shooting.

Barbara's deficiencies were all too obvious, and the
ladies lost no time in discovering them. "No governess! Really, how very . . . how *very* odd. . . ."

"I often wished that I didn't have a governess,"
piped up Miss Eldridge rather enviously, but the others quickly silenced her.

"But do you mean that you cannot speak any other

languages at all? Nor play an instrument? You do not
even paint watercolors?" The questions were directed
rapidly, with increasing shock. There might be sympathy from some of the ladies, but Hunsdon could detect
underlying satisfaction from others. Barbara had lifted
her chin in unconscious defiance, but she was growing
pale and her monosyllabic replies were almost inaudible. Hunsdon looked around desperately for Anne to
rescue Barbara, but she was fully occupied with Lady
De Neresford.

"There are those, of course, who say that the sight
should be small and flat, but I say what's the use of
having a sight at all in that case? Do you not agree
with me, your lordship? Don't you think it's useless
to have a small, flat sight on your gun?"

He had not been attending, and had only caught
the second of the questions. Not to reply would be
rude in the extreme. "I myself prefer the sight to be
flat because the usual tendency is to shoot low rather
than high. With such a sight, the gun is less liable to
shoot low."

Another man might have been offended, but Eldridge was impervious. "But what of the stock, your
lordship? Do you not find a straight stock preferable
to a bent one?"

"Do you mean that you have never been to London? Not even once? Wherever do you buy gowns,
then?" The pity of some of the younger ladies was
obviously sincere, but it did not make Barbara's situation any more comfortable. There were mutterings in
an undertone and a giggle was clearly discernible.

"Your lordship? Do you not agree?"

He hadn't even heard the question. He murmured
an affirmative, which gave Eldridge the opportunity to
turn to the gentleman sitting next to him and proclaim
loudly. "You see, Hodges, his lordship agrees with
me!"

"Ask him why he uses a gun with a bent stock,

then," retorted the other sourly, but Hunsdon was too distracted to hear it or to notice the reproachful look in Eldridge's eyes. It was terribly frustrating to be so near to Barbara and yet to have no way to defend her. He curtly muttered some excuse and rose, strolling in the direction of her chair. The circle of ladies was such a tight one that he could not penetrate it. There was no chance even to address a friendly remark to Barbara. Blast that mother! Couldn't she see what was happening?

He found a place upon a window seat, which at least guaranteed him solitude and a good view of the company. Barbara's head was drooping again and she looked defeated, while the circle about her had grown increasingly animated and, to his eyes, vicious. He watched in helpless fury. It seemed an age until Lady De Neresford finally recalled herself and they took their leave. Barbara did not even look at him, but he could see that her eyes were suspiciously bright. Blast these ill-bred cats!

After the De Neresfords' departure the conversation abruptly rose in volume until it reached a babble. The visitors were scarcely out the door when the talk began, and for the first time the gentlemen were allowed to participate.

"My dears, no governess—can you imagine? And I must say that it shows—"

"And yet she is a baroness . . . they say—"

Hunsdon had stood silent as long as he could. "The De Neresfords are one of the oldest families in England."

The company looked at him askance for a moment, then decided that he wanted convincing. "But isn't she the oddest creature you have ever seen? That dress and that bonnet—well, my maid wears better. And her manners—so peculiar!"

He replied stiffly, "If her clothing is unfashionable it is hardly her own fault. And the only aspects *I* find unusual about her are her sincerity and the *unusual* sweetness of her disposition."

This reply had the effect of silencing many, but one young lady, nettled, decided to adopt a sportive tone. "Oh, I see what it is. Your lordship nourishes a secret *tendre* for young Lady De Neresford. Tell me, what is it about her that appealed to you most? Her air of sophistication? Or perhaps she won you over with the elegance of her conversation?"

Barbara could talk well enough when she was given a chance, he thought. His rage was such that an unforgivably rude response rose to his lips and he was just able to bite it back in time. He was a guest here, after all, and so were these persons. Instead, he bowed stiffly. "Excuse me, I have a letter to write."

"To his own true love, no doubt," murmured the jesting young lady, but he pretended he did not hear her, nor the laughter of the others as he strode from the room.

He returned to his own chamber, called for his valet, and began stripping off his coat in order to change into riding dress. There was a knock upon the door, and Roger entered. He observed his guest anxiously.

"I say, old fellow, you're not thinking of going for a ride, surely?"

"I must go see Barbara and apologize."

"*You* did nothing wrong."

"I don't care for that. She must be feeling so . . . so—"

"But my dear fellow, it is time to dress for the ball tonight. I daresay Mariabella is the most understanding girl on earth—but she just will not understand your absence."

Roger's words checked Hunsdon. He glanced at his pocket watch. It was well after four. Roger was right. He didn't have time. It occurred to him abruptly that this was the night he meant to ask Mariabella for her hand.

Roger gave him a commiserating pat on the back. "If you still feel so strongly about it tomorrow, you may go call upon her then. Can't think why Anne invited this group of mushrooms, anyway."

Yes, he could go talk to Barbara tomorrow. And while he apologized to her for the cruelty of the guests, he could tell her that he had deceived her from the beginning as to his identity and he could also mention that he was now engaged to Mariabella. It was a bitter thought. His own deception prevented him from being able to offer Barbara any comfort. He tried to think more optimistically. Perhaps once Mariabella became Lady Hunsdon they might be able to see a way to help Barbara. Once Mariabella realized all the resources that were at their command . . . In any event, he had no other ideas at the moment. Somberly, he began to dress for the ball.

Mariabella was looking particularly lovely tonight in a round dress of white satin, finished with a double fall of blond lace at the hem, and a single fall about the neck, headed by a rouleau of white satin. The short puffed sleeves were composed of a mixture of satin and lace, while the dress was finished by wide white gros De Naples sash, tied in a bow behind. She looked striking all in white, but to him there seemed to be something wrong with the picture she presented. He could not quite think of what it was. He was frowning as his name was announced, and as he looked up, he saw that she had turned almost as white as her dress. He looked around to note what might have upset her, but he saw nothing except Brandville, who had ridden in the carriage with him and who appeared more grim than ever.

Hunsdon walked over to Mariabella and took her by the hand. "My dear! Did I upset you with my scowling looks? I was merely thinking to myself. How lovely you are tonight."

She murmured something inaudible, but her eyes were fixed beyond him and he saw that Brandville had followed him.

"Have you met Lord Brandville? He is one of my greatest friends."

"We have met before." Brandville's tone was cold and Hunsdon objected to it. Anyone might succumb to a fit of the dismals now and then, but it was sheer ill-breeding to remain in the sulks for so long.

"I hope that you will save me the first dance tonight"—her mother had already promised it to him—"and perhaps two others?" It would give them the opportunity to slip away together so that he might ask her for her hand.

She murmured an affirmative, seeming more like herself, though she was still dreadfully pale. He turned back to Brandville, but saw to his surprise that his friend was gone.

Every minute seemed an eternity this evening. He could do nothing but smile and make polite conversation and drink champagne. It was his favorite wine and it seemed a good omen that the Fostwicks should serve it tonight. It seemed hours before the musicians began and he finally led Mariabella out to the floor. She danced as gracefully as ever, but she hardly spoke at all. Perhaps she was preoccupied. He was himself. Again and again his mind turned to Barbara and how miserable she must be, all alone as she was. Perhaps it was just as well that the Fostwicks had not invited her. Mrs. Fostwick had confided that Barbara did not possess a ball gown.

"And I would be happy to give her one of Mariabella's old ones—though they are not of a size—but, of course, both she and her mother are too proud to accept it. It is such a pity."

It seemed odd that she did not have even one ball gown. Of course, Mariabella's gown would probably look no better on Barbara than her mother's did, since Mariabella was so much taller. She met him at eye level, while Barbara's head only reached his shoulder.

He needed to turn his attention back to his partner. He asked how she was this evening and she made an appropriate response. He asked if the snow had discommoded them and she made an appropriate response. He remarked that they had quite a company tonight and she made an appropriate response. She was still pale. Perhaps she was not quite well, even though she said that she was fine. It seemed to him that her attention was elsewhere. Once he caught her eyes upon Brandville, standing glowering in a corner.

"Brandville is usually a much more pleasant fellow," he offered. "I do not know what has put him in such a cursed mood lately." He was struck with a sudden idea. "Perhaps if you dance with him, it may help to lift him out of the dismals. Come with me."

"Oh, no. My card is already filled," she was protesting, but as the music was ending, he dragged her unwillingly over to Brandville's corner.

"As you are the two friends dearest to me in the world, I should like you both to know each other better. Brandville, wouldn't you care to dance?"

To his credit, his friend did not protest, although he cast Hunsdon a black look. He took Mariabella's arm wordlessly and led her to the floor. Hunsdon sipped from his glass of champagne and watched them in growing dissatisfaction. Although they performed all the measures correctly, they avoided each other's gaze and hardly exchanged a word. When the dance was over, they parted with alacrity and unmistakable relief. Had they quarreled sometime in the past? It certainly looked it. Well, they must come to a better understanding. His wife and his best friend should be on speaking terms, at least.

He would have to talk to them about it, but tonight was certainly not the night. He had the next dance with Mariabella himself.

As the dance progressed, he saw that it was a perfect opportunity. They were in the farthest corner of the room. It was unlikely that anyone would notice them slipping away from the rest of the company. With a whisper, and a pressure on her hand, he led her from the ballroom into a small side parlor. He seated her on a gilt-and-satin sofa, and began.

"Mariabella, you must know how much I admire and respect you." Blast! It wasn't coming out quite right. Still, he persevered.

"Because of the unfortunate circumstances, I was not able to speak to you before you left London. I came here with the sole intent of renewing our acquaintance." That had been his intent. He felt as if he knew her even less well than before, though.

"I wish . . . I think that no one would be better suited to be the future Countess of Wittenham than you." It sounded cold, even to his ears. He knew he should be murmuring compliments and words of love, but none occurred readily to him. Well, there was no point in delaying, then. "I would like to ask for your hand—"

He was not able to complete the sentence. Mariabella burst into tears. Never having seen her cry before, he was startled and utterly at a loss. As she dug in her reticule for her handkerchief, he could make out some disjointed phrases such as "very sensible of the honor," "most sorry to cause pain," and somewhere in the middle of them he heard "would not suit" and realized to his astonishment that she was refusing him.

In the entire length and breadth of his imaginings, this eventuality was not one that had ever occurred him. All unprepared, he was at a loss as to what to do next and so for one blank minute, he merely stared dumbly at her as she inarticulately tried to express her regrets between sobs.

Eventually, however, his breeding came to his rescue and he urged her to dry her eyes, apologizing handsomely for having caused *her* such distress. "Indeed, if I had had an inkling of your sentiments I should never have—"

He was not able to finish, as she burst afresh into loud wails, exclaiming between sobs that he was "too kind," "too magnanimous," "too noble." It was clear that they had not known each other well.

He tried again to calm her, but all his words seemed only to upset her the more. At last, fearing that they might be discovered together, and despairing of his own ability to soothe her, he left the parlor after assuring himself that there was no more that he could do. As he entered the ballroom he encountered Brandville, whose own mood seemed more bleak than ever.

"I noticed that both you and Miss Fostwick had disappeared. I take it I am to wish you happy?"

Hunsdon's control over his own emotions was minimal. "She refused me," he said briefly. "Excuse me." He brushed past his friend, in his own preoccupation failing to notice Brandville's ludicrous expression of surprise.

The ball was going on just as before. Fortunately, Brandville seemed to have been the only one to remark his absence. There were no curious looks and no titters. He knew that to put a good face upon matters he should dance, but he hardly felt like it. A footman paused beside him with champagne, and Hunsdon gratefully accepted a glass. He had downed it just as another footman appeared with a tray. He repeated this sequence of events in rapid succession, hardly noticing what he did. All his thoughts were on Mariabella. Could he have been so thoroughly mistaken about her?

A hand on his sleeve recalled his attention. "Pardon me, but have you seen Mariabella?" asked Mrs. Fostwick, a trace of anxiety in her voice.

He scanned the ballroom. There was no Mariabella. He looked at his pocket watch. He had left her just five minutes before. "I will go and look for her," he offered.

Mrs. Fostwick made no protest. "If you would be so kind . . ."

It was odd how hot the ballroom was becoming. Perhaps he should suggest to Mrs. Fostwick that they open some of the windows. Of course, he had to find Mariabella first, then he could tell Mrs. Fostwick about the windows. Mariabella was probably in the same parlor, still crying her eyes out. He bumped into a dancing couple, excused himself politely, and went on.

The door to the side parlor stood open. As he neared it, he could hear a man's voice speaking. That was odd. It should be Mariabella talking, if anyone were. As he reached the doorway he could make out the words.

"—cannot stand it any longer. Before I leave this room tonight, you must tell me the truth. Why did you refuse Hunsdon?"

Someone was prying into his private affairs, he thought angrily. Mariabella was still crying.

"You *must* tell me. I had sworn to go away and never trouble you again once you had accepted him. But this! I must know the meaning of it. My darling, tell me. I love you with all my heart. I wish for what is best for you. Shall I leave you? Just tell me that I should not hope and I will go without a murmur."

"Oh, no! Justin, I love you too!"

As they were seated beside each other on the sofa, their eyes on each other's faces, they did not notice Hunsdon's arrival. He stood in the doorway and stared as Mariabella cast herself into Brandville's arms and the two exchanged a lengthy kiss. His confused mind could not take it in. Mariabella was the first one to look up and notice him. She let out a little shriek. "Oh!"

Brandville looked up in surprise. "Charles!"

He tried to say something, but his tongue had become most unruly. His best friend and the woman he loved had betrayed him. He dropped his glass, which shattered loudly on the parquet floor, then turned to rush off down the corridor.

He heard Brandville call his name again, but he could not face them, nor could he face everyone else. A footman was headed for the ballroom with a tray. Hunsdon stopped him and lifted another glass as well as the bottle from it.

Roger found him in the library some fifteen minutes later. "Ah, there you are. We've been worried about you—or Anne has, rather."

Hunsdon said nothing, but poured himself another glass.

Roger cleared his throat nervously. "I understand that you had some upsetting news tonight."

Hunsdon gave a bitter laugh and took another swallow.

Roger took a seat. "I don't know that it will make you feel any better, but Mariabella's and Brandville's attachment is of long standing. Once you appeared, her family preferred your suit, of course—who wouldn't? Anne took pity on him and invited him to Blakemore in order to introduce him to the heiress, Miss Eldridge—the father's a cit, of course, but it's a whopping great fortune. Couldn't even rouse a flicker of interest in him. I suppose the thing was meant to be, as it were."

"Great lot of comfort you are. Saying a female'd only want me for my fortune. Letting me look a proper idiot, too."

"The right female would not want you for your fortune or your position. . . ." He hesitated.

"Well, go on," said Hunsdon belligerently.

"Are you so certain that you truly wished to marry Mariabella? You've hardly seen her since you've been in Leicestershire, after all. You've seen far more of—"

Hunsdon rose from his seat, enraged. "By gad, so you think it, too! Am I such a poor prospect that you think I've no choice but to marry a rag-mannered, half-grown child of a girl?"

Roger remained seated. "She's not such a child, after all," he said calmly. "Seems to me that you were the one who said that she wasn't unmarriageable."

"Well, but . . ." He could think of no suitable retort.

"Anne was the one who put the idea in my head. Said you came rushing to her defense when those cats showed their claws. Said you didn't take your eyes from her the entire time she was at Blakemore."

"Well . . ."

"I'm not saying you're in love with the girl, mind. It's just that you've given more signs of it than of being in love with Mariabella. Anne was fair worried about you. Said she hated to see you marry without affection."

Hunsdon had sunk onto the massive library desk and was shaking his head puzzledly. "But I hardly know her."

Roger cleared his throat. "It took just one look for Anne and me to . . . Of course, everyone is different. Just wanted you to see that perhaps you haven't lost so much as you think."

It was Roger who had put him into a carriage and promised to make Hunsdon's excuses to the Fostwicks. When Hunsdon awoke in the morning with an aching head, he realized that the details of the trip back to Blakemore were lost from his memory. The rest of the evening, though, remained startlingly clear. So much of Mariabella's peculiar behavior was understandable now. She had been dazzled by his fortune and his title when they had met in London, and undoubtedly had been encouraged by her family. Reflection and further acquaintance with him had served to show her that she should not wed for those sorts of considerations. If circumstances had not intervened, if she had not had time to consider the matter, she might very well have married him. He shuddered at the thought. Married to Mariabella! Why, they had no interests in common whatever, and though of course she was very beautiful, she had to be one of the most boring women he had ever known. All that perfection of dress and manners and self-command was very well in its own way, but it would have palled on him quickly, he realized. He had been as dazzled by her appearance as she had been by his circumstances. Why had he ever imagined that he could be happy with her?

Despite the ache in it, his brain seemed to be operating particularly efficiently this morning. Roger's words of last night made perfect sense to him now. Of course he was in love with Barbara. It had taken Mariabella's refusal for him to own it. He supposed that there was some sort of pride that would not let him admit that he had been wrong in his choice of a mate. Thank God that Mariabella had the sense to see it.

Everything was quite simple now. He had the solution to Barbara's problem and his own. She would be thrilled by the ring he had selected. Suddenly, even given the pain in his head, the world seemed a brighter, rosier place. He rang for his valet and rose from the bed, whistling a happy tune.

"Morning dress, Johnson. I wish to pay a formal call today."

He was even able to smile at a nervous Brandville

when he encountered him at breakfast, and surprised the latter by congratulating him sincerely when Brandville informed him of his engagement. He thought he managed to conceal his own feelings of relief rather well.

If Hunsdon did not quite present the picture of elegance, the transformation in his appearance was dramatic enough that Barbara's surprise was evident upon seeing him. Her eyes widened, she let out an exclamation and would have made some remark but he forestalled her. Taking her by the arm, he steered her into the drawing room, closing the doors behind them.

"I must speak to you alone." Her presence was having its usual unnerving effect upon him. He could feel an unexplained warmth stealing over him.

"I would hardly know you today," said Barbara, a half smile of wonderment on her lips, as she sank into a chair. She was wearing the same green-sprigged muslin gown he had seen before. He would buy her dozens of gowns once they were married.

"I have something most important to tell you," he said with a smile.

"You're being very mysterious."

"No." He shook his head and took a chair opposite her. He drew in a deep breath and took her hand in his. "Barbara, I want to marry you." It had all the conviction his declaration last night had lacked.

She obviously reciprocated his feelings. Her eyes were shining and her lips parted breathlessly. A frown creased her forehead. "But Mama—"

"You must let me finish. Your mother will present no obstacle—in fact, she will approve of this match. You no longer will have to worry about her or finances or anything else. I will take care of everything." He drew in another deep breath. "You see, I am actually Lord Hunsdon."

She stared at him in disbelief for a moment before

speaking. "But—but you can't be," she finally managed to stammer. "I saw Lord Hunsdon myself."

"That is Lord Brandville, a good friend of mine. I did not wish for you to have to discover the truth in the midst of the company, so I kept Anne from finishing the introductions. I thought that way you might continue to take him for me," he said, with some justified pride at his own ingeniousness.

Barbara withdrew her hand from his. She did not appear as delighted as he had hoped. "In the midst of the company, and such delightful company, too. I am surprised you did not want to tell them of your little joke on me. I am sure that they would have enjoyed it."

Blast! She was misinterpreting what he had to say. "I am sorry. I meant to come and apologize to you for the behavior of those spiteful tabbies, but we had an engagement at the Fostwicks last night."

She had turned quite pale and there was a queer look about her eyes. "An engagement. You mean that you had an engagement. You are Mariabella's 'London swell,' aren't you?"

"Well, yes." Things did look a little bad in that light.

"And you came up to scratch last night—or so Alfred says. He also says that she turned you down in favor of this Brandville—"

"Well . . . yes."

"And so you thought that since she refused you, you might as well offer for this poor, uneducated little creature. How noble of you, your lordship. How magnanimous! So I will never have to worry about money again, will I? You are so very kind. Your conscience may rest easy. You have all the virtue of having sacrificed yourself for a worthy cause, but you will not have to pay the price." She choked on the sentence, and he thought he might have an opportunity to put in a word, but she rose and continued on, even more wrathfully. "I am sorry to have to be the second fe-male in as many days to refuse you, but I have no need of, nor desire for your charity. I would not marry you if you were the last man on earth." With these words she turned on her heel and stalked from the room—rather magnificently, he thought.

Roger found him giving his valet directions for packing later that afternoon. "Hunsdon, I must speak with you."

He dismissed his man with a nod and sat down heavily upon the bed. Roger drew up a chair close to him.

"Anne tells me you are leaving us."

He nodded hopelessly.

"I did not inform her where you went today. I take it all did not go well with Barbara?"

"She refused me."

Roger looked surprised. "That's odd. From what Anne said, she appeared to be besotted with you. Said yesterday she was stealing little glances at you when you weren't looking."

He sighed. "It seems that Anne was mistaken."

"Tell me about it."

Hunsdon had kept the secret to himself for too long. The rough sympathy in Roger's voice invited confes-sion. "I could have sworn that she was ready to marry me, when I first asked her," he said unhappily, "but perhaps I should start at the beginning."

It wasn't until he was three-quarters of the way through with his story that Hunsdon realized that there was something wrong. Roger had turned his face away from him and odd sniggering noises occasionally escaped him. Hunsdon began to watch him more closely, and it seemed to him that Roger's shoulders shook once or twice. His suspicions were confirmed when he finished his pathetic tale and Roger could no longer contain himself, but broke into a loud guffaw.

"Confound me if I've ever heard of a more mismanaged affair," he exclaimed between chuckles, wiping his eyes with a handkerchief.

Hunsdon was not amused. Roger patted him on the shoulder, still not quite able to contain his mirth. "I'm sorry, lad. Tell me, though, did you offer her any apology for your deception?"

"No."

"Did you tell her that you had realized that you didn't wish to marry Mariabella?"

"No."

"Did you at least tell the girl that you loved *her*?"

Hunsdon did not even reply. Roger, having regained command of himself, patted his shoulder again sympathetically. "It's your upbringing, I expect. You've always had every obstacle removed for you, so that you don't know what to do when you encounter—well, enough of that. You came to Leicestershire to woo Mariabella, didn't you?"

Hunsdon nodded.

"Well, you must do the same for Barbara. She has a right to it, doesn't she?"

"But she said that she wouldn't marry me if I were the last man in the world."

"I take that as a good sign," said Roger wisely. "She feels strongly about you, there's no doubt of it. You humiliated her. Now it's up to you to win her affections back. Stay here another few weeks and give it a try, anyway. There's no sense in throwing away your happiness—or hers."

He sat and thought for several minutes after Roger had left. There was a great deal in what he said. Perhaps there was hope, after all. And St. Valentine's Day was still two weeks away. Barbara had said she'd never had a valentine before. She had seemed to think highly of his foolish, romantic gestures. He crossed over to the chest of drawers, opened it, and stared at the neglected parcels of ribbons and lace. He ex-

tracted one before calling his valet and ordering him
to unpack. Then he went downstairs to seek his
hostess.

"Anne," he said forlornly, "could you show me
once again just how to tie a love knot?"

It was almost St. Valentine's Day, and as far as he
was concerned, there was no reason to be optimistic.
He had sent posies from the Blakemores' greenhouse,
chocolates from London, love knots, issues of the
Sporting Magazine, and earnestly collected and pain-
stakingly copied specimens of poetry. It was true that
each of his daily offerings had been accepted, but still
Barbara refused to see him. Hunsdon would have sent
her jewels and gowns, but Roger thought it would
suggest to the proud girl that he was attempting to
purchase her affections.

Roger thought it encouraging that she no longer
returned his notes unopened, but Hunsdon merely
sighed, "I daresay that her mother won't let her. At
this rate, we should be married when we're both in
our seventies."

"Don't be so discouraged. Anne has a scheme that
may well answer."

"I thought you were the one who said we should
avoid becoming mixed up in her schemes."

Roger ignored him. "She means to invite the De
Neresfords to a dinner on St. Valentine's Day. Barbara can hardly avoid seeing you then."

Hunsdon refused to be optimistic. "Why should she
come? After their last reception here, I daresay she
would want to avoid it."

"The Eldridges and most of the others are already
gone, so she will not have to worry about them. Besides, I am certain that mother of hers will insist upon
her coming." He smiled at Hunsdon's gloomy countenance. "Faint heart never won fair lady, as they say."

*   *   *

Given Roger's assurances, he supposed he should not have been too surprised by the De Neresfords' acceptance. The party would be a small one, with only ten of them there. He should have a chance to be alone with Barbara. It was odd how much the thought brightened him as dinnertime drew near. He had sent nothing to her today, preferring to give her his valentine in person. An awkward construction of satin, ribbon, and lace, it had taken him a good part of the night to finish. He had never felt so inadequate as when he was cutting and pasting and arranging everything upon it, but surprisingly, his gentle hostess had refused to lend him any aid.

"It will mean a great deal to her that you took the trouble to make it yourself, no matter what it looks like."

He hoped that she was right, for it appeared a pathetic specimen to him. Barbara would be justified in laughing in his face when she saw it.

He had botched his cravat a half-dozen times before his valet took pity on him and tied it for him. It made him feel like a schoolboy. The valentine was a bit of a problem since it would become crushed in his coat, so he went downstairs a few minutes early to hide it in a drawer in one of the side parlors.

As the other guests joined him, he made disjointed small talk and hoped that they could not see his heart pounding in his throat.

When the De Neresfords were announced, his heart stopped for a moment before resuming its erratic beating once more. Barbara looked subdued but beautiful in a simple dress of white jaconet with one deep flounce at the hem and a simple tucker of lace at the neck. It clearly had been made for her, unlike every other garment in which he had seen her, and as he gazed at her he met her mother's satisfied eyes upon him. Clearly, despite the little contretemps, and encouraged by his offerings, *she* was still bent upon impressing the "London swell."

Dinner seemed to take an eternity. Roger and Anne had made certain that he should escort Barbara in to dinner, but despite being seated beside her, he found it difficult to engage her in conversation. Her replies to his polite queries were monosyllabic, just short of rude. He could not discuss private matters with everyone else about them, and his heart was pounding so fiercely that he was having difficulty speaking anyway. His hand trembled as he helped her to a slice of the fricandeau of veal, but she did not appear to notice. For some odd reason the air was thicker than usual, and he was having difficulty breathing.

It seemed an interminable time until the final course had been served and dinner was at last over. The ladies were excused. He did not know how long he could bear to sit with the gentlemen. He threw Roger several despairing glances, and after a single glass of wine, the latter kindly recommended that they rejoin the ladies. Perhaps half an hour of conversation followed before one of the ladies was persuaded to entertain them on the harp. Now was his opportunity. In the ensuing rearrangement of the party, he moved to Barbara's side and took her by the hand.

"I must speak to you alone. *Please*! I have something to give you."

He could sense her unwillingness, but looking up he saw her mother's eyes upon them, a commanding expression in them. He had never thought to be so grateful to Lady De Neresford. Barbara went with him, albeit reluctantly.

He led her to the side parlor. Now that his moment had come he felt almost ludicrous. He was beside himself with joy and terror.

"There is so much that I wish to tell you—"

"Lord Hunsdon, you cannot persuade—" she began, refusing to meet his eyes.

"No, please! Please let me speak for a moment. You have every right to be angry with me. I behaved abominably—and I shall regret it for the rest of my life. I cannot even hope that you will forgive me. . . ."

She said nothing.

He took a deep breath. "What I wish you to know is that I was deceived in my affection for Mariabella. I thought I loved her, but I did not even know what love was. It took her refusal for me to realize that the one I truly loved and wished to be with was you. I love you with my whole heart, Barbara, and my affections will not alter. If it takes years for me to prove the sincerity of my affection, then so be it. You are the only woman for me and I will do whatever it takes to convince you of it." He had not planned the words and they took him by surprise, but he realized that he had never meant anything more earnestly.

She still did not speak. Were his words wasted? He opened the drawer and extracted the valentine. "I made this for you."

It was a pitiful thing, really. The lace had fallen loose from one side and the heart he had cut from the satin was far from artistic. He had pasted bows of ribbon upon it, but they were coming untied. He had written simply "I love you"—not very eloquent, he had to admit. He waited for her to burst into laughter. For several moments she said and did nothing. His heart was in his throat. She might very well tell him never to trouble her again.

Finally she looked up at him, and her eyes were bright. "You made this?"

"Yes."

"It is beautiful. My first valentine."

He could only gape at her.

"Oh, Lord Hunsdon—" Her voice throbbed with emotion. It seemed a good sign.

"Please call me Charles," he begged.

"Oh, Charles, I—I don't know what to say—"

"Say that you will marry me." He didn't even know where the bold words came from.

"But our circumstances are so unequal—"

"Hang the circumstances." He crushed her in his arms, and what a dizzying, satisfying feeling it was. He kissed her recklessly and felt her match his own eagerness. She was soft, ripe, and yielding, and he thought he might easily drown in her. At length, he realized that if he didn't stop this process soon, they might offend the sensibilities of the guests in the other room. Accordingly he released her, searching in his pocket for the diamond and sapphire ring, and then thrusting it onto her finger. It fit perfectly. In his whole carefully controlled life he had never known such a thing to happen.

"We were meant for each other," he said, a touch of awe in his voice.

"Yes," she replied, pinkening with a new and not-unbecoming diffidence.

How beautiful she was—not just the common, ordinary sort of beauty, either, but with a loveliness uniquely her own. He felt that he could happily sit with her hand in his and simply gaze at her the rest of the evening. He did not even notice that his artwork, which she continued to hold, had been badly crushed during their embrace. She smiled tremulously at him and his heart swelled with happiness. Well, perhaps just one more kiss would not be hurt anything. It was Valentine's Day, after all. . . .

After protracted and exceedingly reluctant farewells later that night, it was Barbara alone who had to bear her mother's raptures during the carriage ride home.

"What a marvelous match, my dear. I am sure that before I hit upon this scheme, I had despaired of doing half so well for you. Of course, even I could not be certain that everything would happen so smoothly. However, I knew in the end that it must be—as I told you, I knew that Lord Hunsdon simply could not resist the chance to marry a De Neresford! After all, 1312! Hardly a family in the kingdom can match it. Oh, yes, I knew he would be all eagerness as soon as he learned that you . . ."

Her daughter, leaning back upon the faded cushions in the roomy old coach, smiled faintly, but in actuality she was not attending. She gave a glad little sigh, a dreamy expression upon her glowing face as her ringed left hand lovingly caressed and smoothed the crumpled lace-and-satin-covered valentine that she held in her lap.

Dear Delight

by Sheila Walsh

A FEW FLAKES of snow were falling and the sky looked heavy with the promise of more to come as Charlotte Wynford walked briskly across the lawns of Lambourn Manor and took the path through the bushes to the side door. In the passage leading via the muniments room to the main hall she removed the shawl draped around the shoulders of her pelisse and shook it vigorously.

"You give that to me, Miss Charlotte," said Agnes, coming briskly to whisk the shawl away from her. "Heaven knows why you should want to go traipsing down to the cottages in this weather. February's a treacherous month, what with all that's gone before. Catch your death, I shouldn't wonder."

Charlotte smiled and allowed the maidservant to help her take off her pelisse and bonnet. "Nonsense. A little healthy exercise never did anyone any harm, and I promised poor Mrs. Allan that I would take her some of Cook's special beef tea for that sickly child of hers. Things haven't been easy for Tom Allan since the end of the war. My sister is in the drawing room, I suppose?"

"Aye. And in a proper fidget with you nowhere to be found and the weather looking fit to play havoc with the celebrations. And those girls so excited, you wouldn't believe. You'd best get up there right away and calm things down before her grace has one of her headaches. I took the tea tray in not five minutes since."

Charlotte smiled as she made her way upstairs. Agnes had been with the Lambourn family all her life, and was given to speaking her mind without fear or favor.

The Duchess of Lambourn looked up from the delicate process of tea-making to greet her younger sister, her agitation very evident in her voice. "Ah, there you are, Lottie. No need to ask where you've been. I can't think why you should choose to go ministering to the village children on a day when you are needed here."

"Such a fuss, Annis," she said good-humoredly. "I haven't been away above half an hour, and you know perfectly well that everything is in hand."

"Even so. Oh, never mind, you are here now." Her grace set the kettle down. "Do come to the fire at once. You look half frozen."

It was one of life's absurdities that the petite duchess had been married for more than eighteen years and had seven children, for at first glance she looked little more than a girl herself. Her guinea-gold hair owed nothing to artifice, and the look of sweet helplessness in her wide cerulean-blue eyes that had captured the Duke's heart when she was barely out could even now be guaranteed to bring gentlemen rushing to her aid.

Charlotte, younger by eight years, was taller and slimmer than Annis. There was a superficial likeness, but in Charlotte the vivid coloring was muted to a soft ashen fairness, her eyes to a smoky blue-gray that most often, as now, held a lively twinkle.

Friends frequently bemoaned the fact that she had refused more than one prestigious offer of marriage, and it was, in their opinion, a shocking waste for her to be dwindling her life away, waiting on the various members of her family, when she ought to have been raising one of her own.

To all such criticisms Charlotte returned the amused observation that she enjoyed her life prodigiously. Her father had left her a comfortable little manor house in Hampshire and had settled a reasonable amount of money on her, which enabled her to dress, if not in the first stare, at least with a certain elegance, thanks to her fashionable cousin Kate, who had introduced her to Yvette, one of London's most sought-after dressmakers.

What she did not tell them, what no one knew, was that there had been a brief interlude many years ago when her youthful heart had been seduced. True, no words of love had been spoken, no promises given, but she had been so sure that her sentiments were returned; too sure, perhaps, for instead she had been left heartbroken, with only her pride to sustain her. There and then she had resolved that no man would ever have the power to hurt her again. And in ten years that resolve had never faltered.

But she had not grown bitter. Instead, her natural resilience was such that she had long since pronounced herself cheerfully resigned to a life of single blessedness. Several times a year she tore herself away from Hampshire, dividing her time between Annis and her children, whom she adored, and her brother's family in Hereford. And for at least a part of each Season she visited her fashionable cousin Kate to replenish her wardrobe at Yvette's and enjoy a brief foray into society with all its absurdities.

She always visited Lambourn in February to celebrate the birthday of her twin nieces, whose godmother she was—and who, with impeccably romantic timing on their mother's part, had entered the world on St. Valentine's Day. "Such an excellent portent, don't you think?" Annis had said at the time. And as they grew from childhood to young womanhood, nature certainly seemed to have endowed them with every blessing.

The girls would make their official come-out during the London Season, of course, but Annis had decided to invite all their closest friends to a St. Valentine's Night ball to celebrate their birthday. Those traveling from a considerable distance were to stay for several days, and were due any time now, but many more would come out from Bath and the neighboring countryside on the evening of the ball.

"I still find it incredible to believe that the girls will be seventeen tomorrow." Charlotte accepted a teacup from her sister, and settled herself comfortably in a corner of the sofa nearest the fire.

"Oh, Lottie, don't!" Annis wailed. "It is wonderful, of course, and I am very proud of my dear daughters, but sitting here alone, it came to me quite suddenly that I am getting old!"

"What nonsense." Charlotte's eyes twinkled. "You know perfectly well that you consistently defy the years—and as for beauty, the twins will certainly have their work cut out to outshine you."

"Dear Lottie, you always were prone to exaggerate." The tiny frown lines vanished from between the duchess's lovely blue eyes, though a faint shadow still remained. "You don't suppose the snow will persist? After all the trouble we have gone to for tomorrow night's ball, it would be too awful if everyone was snowbound."

To hear Annis speak, Charlotte thought, one might suppose she had personally worked her fingers to the bone to ensure the comfort, entertainment, and well-being of her guests. In point of fact, a vague suggestion here, a hint there, had been the sum total of her grace's endeavors. The rest had been accomplished by Charlotte herself, with the willing cooperation of her twin nieces.

As if conjured by thought, there was a rustling

sound beyond the drawing room door. With a rush and flutter of skirts they swept in—Lady Fanny Denham and Lady Katherine Denham, as alike as two peas, and already bidding to be as fair and beautiful as their mother.

"Mama! There is a most elegant carriage coming up the drive!"

"Followed by a groom leading two horses!"

"Oh, dear . . . so soon? I had not expected anyone for at least another hour." The duchess rose with effortless grace. "I must go and change, such a fright I must look." As she never looked anything but enchanting, this pronouncement was greeted with hoots of derision, which she ignored. "Fanny, be a dear and ring for the tray to be removed at once, and ask Cook to prepare fresh tea. And Kate, see if you can find your father. I daresay he will be in the gun room. Dear Lottie—you will have to do the honours until he can be found."

In a moment Charlotte was left alone. How like Annis, she reflected. Not a thought as to whether I am presentable. But a quick glance in the mirror above the mantelshelf showed her hair to be neatly coiled, with just a few curls escaping. She exchanged a wry smile with her reflection, smoothed down the blue-chintz skirt of her second-best day gown, demurely cut with a muslin ruff at the high neck and long, tight sleeves—and went to greet the first arrivals.

The great hall was full of bustle, with Milton, the butler, already overseeing the footmen as they struggled under the weight of several large portmanteaus, while the duke's two large black retrievers sniffed around the growing pile of luggage and got under everyone's feet.

"It is Lord Frederic, Miss Charlotte," Milton murmured, as she called the dogs to heel. "His lordship is accompanied by a friend. I have sent William to inform Mrs. Buddle to prepare extra rooms."

From outside came loud exhortations to "have a care with those bandboxes, damn it! Trumble, don't let that fool lay hands on m'dressing case!" Moments later a corpulent exquisite well past the first flush of youth appeared, enveloped in a coat with at least six capes and fastened with a double row of enormous mother-of-pearl buttons, beneath which Charlotte glimpsed buff pantaloons and gleaming top boots with white turndown tops. Beneath the brim of his fashionable beaver hat, his hair gleamed with Macasser oil. This pink of the *ton* beamed upon seeing Charlotte and made her a leg.

"Freddie! What in the world are you doing here? You might have let us know you were coming."

The duke's younger brother, Lord Freddie Denham, was unabashed. "Well, you know how it is. Devilish dull at this time of year. Popped over to Paris for a spell, came back, visited Mother, pottered around London again—looked up a few cronies. Then, finding m'self at a loose end, I thought why not a week or so in Surrey, in the bosom of the family? Knew Edward wouldn't mind—spot of hunting, pot a few rabbits . . ."

"Freddie, honestly. We have upwards of twenty house guests expected any minute."

His smile widened. "A party. What luck!"

"For your nieces' birthday," she explained patiently. "Their seventeenth birthday. I did write to remind you, but as I received not a word by answer, I assumed you were from home."

"Seventeen, are they? Beats me where the time goes. Annis was seventeen when Edward married her—only seems like yesterday. Well, well. So—I'm in the nick of time, it seems, what? And the manor's big enough—plenty of room for two extra. Did I mention I'd taken the liberty of bringing a friend? Hadn't seen him for years until I ran across him in Paris a while back with the duke—and blow me if we didn't meet again in White's last week."

He stood aside to usher his companion forward. As the tall figure straightened and emerged from the shadow of the porch, Charlotte felt the blood draining from her face—from her whole body, in fact.

"Charlotte, allow me to present Colonel Luke Valentine. This is my brother's sister-in-law, Charlotte Wynford, Luke."

He had been a major when she . . . when they . . . But she must not think back. The desire to swoon receded as pride once again came to her aid.

"Colonel Valentine." Her politely extended hand scarcely trembled as his much larger one closed around it, and her voice was firm, though every nerve in her body was aware of him. "You are welcome."

"Am I?" And she knew that the deep-voiced query had nothing to do with Freddie's unwarranted invitation. The long years of campaigning had etched harsh lines in the long, aquiline face and there were gray threads in the springing black hair, but his bold black eyes were as probing as ever. "I think, perhaps, I should not stay."

"Nonsense," Freddie said. "Of course you must stay."

"Indeed you must," she echoed lightly. "A fine thing it would be if we turned you from the door with the weather growing more inclement by the minute."

A faint, almost angry gleam lit the deep-set eyes, and was gone almost instantly. "I have known worse."

At that moment the younger children arrived, led by ten-year-old Oliver, who threw himself upon his favorite uncle, plying him with questions until Charlotte said sharply, "Noll, do let your uncle be! You are old enough to know better, and are setting a shocking example to the little ones."

The boy flushed and drew back, but Freddie only chuckled and said, "Such a strapping young fellow. I scarce recognized you, m'lad. But cut along now, and we'll see what I have for you later, what?"

And then the duke was in the hall, his jovial presence restoring normality as he clapped his brother on the back, viewed the pile of luggage, and suggested with brotherly candor, "On a repairing lease, are we?"

This was greeted with a wry grin, though the question was smoothly turned off as Lord Freddie introduced Colonel Valentine, whom the duke greeted most heartily.

"Lottie will sort everything out, won't you, my dear? Don't know what we'd do without Lottie."

Oh, yes, she thought, filled with unaccustomed indignation. Lottie will sort everything out—except her own tumultuous feelings. Perhaps her only cause for thankfulness was that no one, not even Annis, knew of any connection between herself and the colonel. And in the constant bustle of new arrivals, there was no time to indulge in the luxury of hysterics.

The twins were as delighted as the rest of the family to see their uncle, and were full of curiosity about his companion.

"Isn't he the most devastatingly attractive man you ever saw, dear Aunt Lottie?" exclaimed Fanny, with all the romantic fervor, Charlotte thought bitterly, of a silly, impressionable girl, the kind of girl she had once been. "Not handsome, precisely—in fact, his face can look almost satanic in repose—but such an air of authority about him, and when he smiles . . ." She sighed.

"And only fancy his name being Valentine!" Her sister giggled, and the two girls exchanged glances brimming with mischief. "Almost as though he had been sent . . ."

"You are both being very silly," Charlotte said sharply.

"Well, you must admit it is uncanny, his arriving so close to the feast of St. Valentine. He is much too old for us, of course, but—"

"Not another word, or I shall be really cross." Charlotte turned away as a blush stained her cheek.

By dinner time, all the guests had arrived. Charlotte paid particular attention to her dress that first evening, as if she would prove to herself, as well as to Luke, that she hadn't a care in the world. The guests were assembled in the long gallery, and she stopped to exchange a smile and a word with each group—Lord and Lady Grayshott with their daughter, Mary, who was Annis's particular friend, and Charles Mayne, Mary's husband, as well as the Egertons. And in all the crush, she somehow managed to avoid Luke Valentine, who was in a corner with Freddie and a couple she did not know.

She was more than usually pleased to relax finally with Sir Pelham Ballard and his sister, Emily, who were among her dearest friends: dear Pelham, who proposed to her at least once a year, and accepted her refusal with good grace, his pleasant, fresh features creased into a wry smile as he assured her that he should not give up hope.

"You're looking remarkably fine this evening, Lottie. That purply blue color suits you—matches your eyes," he said of the exceedingly stylish lavender-crepe gown, made for her by Yvette on her last visit to London.

Emily Ballard chuckled. "Purply blue, indeed! Poor Lottie. Believe me, I have spent years teaching him how to turn a compliment, but to no avail."

"Lottie knows what I mean, don't you, m'dear?"

"Yes, of course I do." She laughed and looked up, full into Luke's brooding eyes.

Had she but known it, the colonel's emotions were every bit as confused as her own. Never would he have allowed himself to be persuaded to come to Lambourn Manor if he had known she was to be present. But now that he was here, there were a million unanswered questions seething in his brain, of which one question surfaced way above the rest.

Why had she not married?

His thoughts winged back to that spring of 1809, when he had come home, sick at heart, devastated by the death of his beloved Sir John Moore at Corunna—Sir John, who had brought them safely through a 300-mile retreat carried out in appalling conditions, and had held off the French until the wind-bound transports arrived. Smarting with humiliation, Luke, together with the remnants of the gallant commander's force, had finally retreated under cover of darkness to the waiting ships—his abiding memory, as the wind freshened with the dawn and the sails filled, the sight of a party of the 9th Foot with the chaplain, making their way slowly along the ramparts, carrying Sir John's body.

By the time he reached home, he had not been fit company for any civilized gathering.

There had been, of course, the usual means of forgetting. And when the bottle and the gambling tables palled, there were ripe beauties, bored wives, and those less respectable, but delightfully available Paphians, all drawn by the fascination of a soldier whose regimentals were more than a little battle-scarred, and whose eyes held a wary hurt look. They were only too ready to help him forget his megrims. He would have been less than human had he not succumbed.

And then fate had set the young Charlotte in his path—a refreshingly unspoiled girl in her first Season, and it was she, with her unfeigned admiration and passionate belief in him as a soldier, who had captured his heart, and given him back his self-respect. What others saw as mere innocent hero worship, he knew for something more.

She was quite different from anyone he had known—his dear delight, he had called her—so young in some ways, but endearingly wise beyond her years, and although no words of love had passed between them, the feeling that they were meant for each other was implicit in the pleasure they found in one another's company. So much so that he had relinquished his long-held belief that a serving soldier had no business taking a wife. Quite unknown to her, he had approached her father, only to be told that under no circumstances would Lord Wynford entertain the idea of his young daughter marrying into the army. Luke had been given short shrift. And lest he should retain any hope of a change of heart, his lordship further informed him that Charlotte had already received an excellent offer of marriage, and the betrothal would be announced on her eighteenth birthday.

Luke was angry and bewildered, for Charlotte had made no mention of any suitor, and he could not believe she would so deceive him. His anger hardened into a determination to hear of it from her own lips, but before the opportunity presented itself, fate intervened. The army was about to take the offensive once more, and he received orders to sail at once for Lisbon with Wellesley.

So, with his immediate future decided for him, and, believing hers to be equally assured, he had given up all thoughts of declaring his love, and instead wrote her a brief note wishing her happy.

"Colonel Valentine." It was the duchess, and with her a dazzling brunette whose gown of silver gauze left little to the imagination. He dragged his thoughts back from the past. "I believe you are already acquainted with Lady Alice Verity."

Lady Alice smiled archly at him, dark lashes fluttering over brilliant green eyes to curve her cheeks as she protested that the colonel could scarcely be expected to remember her, so long ago as it had been.

"On the contrary," he said gallantly, restraining his natural cynicism. "It was in Lisbon. You were a very new young bride. As I recall, your husband was some kind of diplomatic envoy?"

"You *do* remember. How kind." Her voice had an attractive husky quality. "My poor Arthur." She sighed. "He took a fever, some three years ago—when we were in Brighton, of all places. Prinny's own physician attended him, but to no avail."

Luke murmured his commiserations, and wondered what degree of intimacy had existed between the Prince Regent and Lady Alice to warrant such attentions on the part of Prinny's doctor.

"Forgive me if I leave you for a moment," Annis said. "I have just seen poor Mrs. Gibbons all on her own. I am surprised Lottie has not noticed. She is usually so observant. . . ." And she drifted away.

"I don't know how Annis would manage on these occasions without dear Charlotte," Lady Alice said sweetly. "Though I have often wondered if Annis's vagueness is not a convenient pose. Oh dear, does that sound terribly old-cattish?"

Luke raised a quizzical eyebrow. "How can I possibly answer such a question without giving offense?" And as her laugh gurgled again, "Does Miss Wynford live permanently with her sister?"

Lady Alice turned, her eyes very wide as they observed Charlotte in her stylish lavender gown. "I believe not. She has a small establishment somewhere in the country, where she lives with her old nurse, but Charlotte spends much of her time with various members of her family."

"But she never married?" He despised himself for asking the question.

"No, indeed. Such a pity." The words dripped, honey-sweet. "She is not ill-looking, after all, and her disposition is such that she must have made someone a charming wife. Sir Pelham has been her devoted slave for years, of course, but perhaps she cherished hopes of a better offer. However, Annis has confided to me her expectation that this celebration may create the very atmosphere to bring Charlotte and Sir Pelham together at last."

Across the room, Charlotte's cheeks burned. From the way they were looking at her she could only suppose that Luke was discussing her with *that woman*. How dare he!

"My dear," murmured Emily. "If you are not careful, poor Lady Alice will frizzle where she stands."

Charlotte bit her lip. "Was I that obvious? I can't think why Annis invites her. She has a poisonous tongue, and a way of retaining her insufferable air of sweetness and light whilst setting everyone else at odds." Very conscious that both Emily and Pelham were staring at her, she half laughed and said, "How is that for cutting up a character?"

"Well, I own I cannot quite like her," Emily said, "though I can't for the life of me say why. She has never been anything but charming to me."

"Exactly."

"Oh, come now," Pelham remonstrated, a little pink in the face. "How can you possibly dislike anyone for being charming?"

Charlotte laughed. "Dear Pel. You put us to shame. But then, you are too amiable to see anything but good in anyone."

Dinner passed off without incident. The guests were for the most part known to one another, which made for a pleasant air of informality, which continued unabated when the gentlemen rejoined the ladies later in the drawing room to take tea.

"Do you go back to Paris and your position with Wellinton, Colonel Valentine?" asked Annis during a lull in the conversation.

"No, ma'am. I expect to remain in England for the foreseeable future."

Lord Freddie chuckled. "Close, ain't he? I daresay he won't like me blowin' the gab, but I can't see why he needs hide his light. Fact is, Luke is about to become a man of even greater consequence—aide-de-camp to the Duke of York, no less."

The colonel's expression was unreadable as a chorus of congratulation filled the room. At his side, Lady Alice eyed him a little coyly.

"My dear colonel," she said, "this is wonderful news. I am sure, if I had anything half so exciting to impart, I could not have kept it to myself."

"Perhaps not, ma'am. But then, I find nothing exciting in the prospect of becoming a glorified parade-ground soldier."

"You're a man who thrives on the thrills of the battlefield, I daresay," the duke commented with a chuckle. "Well, I don't blame you for that. I hope we can provide a few thrills for you while you're here. It ain't the same, I know, but we'll be out with the hunt in the morning if the snow don't ruin m'plans."

"Enough, Edward," Annis protested. "If you wish to talk sport, you must do so later in the library. For now, Emily is about to give us a song, and Charlotte will accompany her."

Charlotte would as soon not have drawn attention to herself, but as there was a chorus of approval from those who had previously enjoyed the sweetness of Miss Ballard's voice, she was obliged to comply. Several times she glanced up to find Luke watching her with a disturbing intensity, and it was only with the greatest effort of concentration that she refrained from striking a wrong note.

A pleasant hour was passed thus in entertainment, after which, the more intrepid members of the party made up two tables of whist, and of the rest, several ladies, weary from their travels, retired for the night, while their menfolk repaired to the library to blow a cloud and discuss the apparent upturn in the economy, which might see an end to the recession that had ru-

ined so many of their friends in the years since the
war.

It was quite late when Charlotte herself retired. The
house was quiet, except for the faint hum of conversation beyond the library door, but as she crossed the
great hall toward the stairs, a figure emerged from the
shadows to block her way.

Her heart leapt and then steadied. "Must you give
me such a fright?" she protested with an attempt at
lightness.

"It seemed the only way to be certain of finding
you alone, since you have shown a marked determination to avoid me all evening," Luke said.

"That is nonsense. I have been much occupied in
attending to the needs of our guests."

"Of which I am one, though, I assure you, I would
not have come had I known you would be here. However, we need not come to cuffs over that when we
have more important issues to resolve."

There was an inexorable note in his voice. Charlotte
said swiftly, "You are mistaken, sir. I have nothing to
say to you. The past is past. We were two different
people then—let us not raise their ghosts to haunt us
now."

She turned to leave, but as she reached for the ban-
ister rail, he grasped her wrist, forcing her to look up
at him. In the dim light, his face was full of shadows.
"As you wish, but I must know one thing," he said
with low-voiced urgency. "Why did you not marry?"

The question at first surprised her, then made her
angry. "That is none of your business."

"Perhaps not. But indulge me, nevertheless."

"Why should I? If you suppose for one moment
that my single state is in any way due to your shabby
treatment of me—"

"Why should I suppose any such thing when, to the
best of my knowledge, you were well on the way to
being married before I left?"

If Charlotte had been surprised before, she was now openly astonished. "But that is not true. Who can possibly have given you such an idea?"

"Your father," he said curtly. "When I applied to him for leave to propose to you."

For an instant the world spun. Had he not still held her wrist, she must have fallen. "You saw Papa?"

"And was informed in no uncertain terms that you were already as good as betrothed. Are you now telling me it was not so?"

"Well, of course it was not! I . . ." Her father had said not one word of this, and young though she was at the time, she could scarce believe he would have kept Luke's offer from her. But why should Luke make up such a story? She endeavored to think back. "I believe there was some talk of Lord Braybury offering for me, but it was only talk. He was all of forty years old and I could never have entertained . . . !" All the anguish, the bitter heartbreak of Luke's sudden disappearance, with only a polite little note to remember him by, came flooding back as if the time between had not existed. "Oh, how could you have believed that I would promise myself elsewhere, when it must have been quite obvious to you that I—" She caught herself up short.

This would never do. She was behaving like the greenest of green girls. "Oh, well, it is all history now," she concluded with cool finality. "As for your intentions, I cannot believe them to have been entirely serious, since you apparently accepted your congé without ever troubling to discover the extent of my feelings."

Luke released her arm as though it suddenly burned his fingers. "If that is your conclusion, then perhaps what happened was for the best, for I can find in you little trace of the girl I once thought I knew."

Charlotte turned abruptly away so that he should not see how much his words had hurt her. She was halfway up the stairs when his voice came to her. "I have no wish to embarrass you further. I shall leave first thing in the morning."

And her muffled reply, thick with tears, came floating back. "There is no need for you to go on my account, but you must do as you please."

"It will be for the best." Luke awaited her reply, but none came. "Damnation!" he said softly.

Lady Alice, who had approached in catlike silence, was in time to hear their final exchange. Well, well, she thought, and emerged to say with charming diffidence, "My dear Colonel, I wonder if I might impose upon your good nature to escort me to my room? This is such a rambling house, I feel quite nervous about tackling the corridors alone—and I have been quite unable to find a servant to accompany me."

Charlotte was up very early the next morning. A night spent tossing and turning, trying to make sense of what Luke had said, had left her with a head that throbbed unbearably. More than anything at this moment, she longed for the peace and tranquility of her cottage. Instead she would be obliged to pander to the whims of Annis's guests, while at the same time striving to keep her nieces from overtiring themselves before the evening's festivities.

On drawing back the curtain, she saw that the expected snow had still not materialized, but the half light heralding the dawn revealed a heavy hoar frost almost as thick as snow. It sparkled jewel-bright as it clung to every bush and tree. Perhaps a little fresh air would clear the worst of her headache.

In a very short time, dressed in a pair of sturdy half boots, and her warmest pelisse and bonnet, with her gloved hands tucked into a sable muff, she was letting herself out of the side door. The ground was crisp underfoot, and she walked carefully, having no desire to add a sprained ankle to her other tribulations.

She had gone over and over what Luke had said until she no longer knew what to think. In five minutes Luke had cracked the veneer of maturity so carefully assumed over the years, and she was seventeen again, with all the pain and bewilderment and heartbreak of rejection. If he was telling the truth—and for all her anger and bewilderment, she had no reason to doubt that he was—then the father whom she had loved and trusted had cheated her. But much as this realization hurt, it was less painful than the knowledge that Luke had not deemed her worth fighting for.

The snap of a twig brought her thoughts back to the present. Charlotte looked around, expecting to see one of the garden boys come to throw gravel on the paths. Instead she saw Luke, striding out like an avenging angel, the skirts of his long driving coat flapping around his legs, his hands thrust deep into his pockets. At the same moment he saw her and came to an abrupt halt. Beneath the brim of his hat, his dark face wore a scowl as daunting as any angel of doom. Her heart was beating very fast, but she gave him back look for look.

"I had not expected to meet anyone from the house at this hour," he said abruptly.

"Nor I," she returned. "I am accustomed to rising early when I'm at home."

"Are you indeed? And where is home?"

"In Hampshire. I am very comfortably housed on the outskirts of a small village."

"You live there alone?"

"I have a companion." The answer seemed to afford him little satisfaction. As his lips tightened, Charlotte lifted her head defiantly. "We are very happy together, I assure you, though I would not have you dismiss me as some dab of a country cousin. In fact, I lead a very full and varied social life." And to forestall further probing questions, "You are not still set on leaving this morning?"

"I am on my way now to the stables to tell my man, John Jackson, to have the horses ready. As soon as the duke is about, I shall make my excuses."

"Which, however plausible, must inevitably seem contrived. I wish you will change your mind. This is such an important day for the twins, and for my sister, it would be such a pity if anything were to mar it. And Annis will take it amiss, I know she will, if you were to leave so abruptly. Surely you do not find my presence so repugnant that you cannot bear to be in the same house with me above a few hours?"

Luke frowned and said abruptly, "If I have given you that impression, then I apologize. Nothing could be further from the case, I promise you. If anything, it was a desire to spare you embarrassment . . ."

For a moment Charlotte felt the world spin a little on its axis. But he was simply striving to be polite. "Oh, if that is all!" She managed a light, amused laugh, and saw his frown deepen, but persevered. "Luke, why should I be embarrassed? It all happened such a long time ago. No one here, not even my sister, is aware of any previous association between us. And as I have no wish to make public my girlish infatuation, there is no reason why they should ever know. I thank you for your concern, but it is quite unnecessary."

"Is it?" Luke, momentarily piqued, watched her face. It was nipped by the cold and vitally alive, but much less revealing than the face of the younger Charlotte.

"Yes, it is," she said firmly. "After all, if you remain, you will be out with the hunt for a good part of today, and by this evening, with so many people about, there is no reason to suppose that we need even find ourselves in one another's company."

"Would that be so very painful to you?"

"Certainly not. Don't put words into my mouth." She bit her lip on the sharp retort, and continued more calmly, "Luke, I am simply trying to be practical—to spare feelings all round. Tomorrow, after the ball, you may, if you wish, leave as soon as you please without arousing comment."

"Just like that? No raking over of old coals?" Luke persisted, his eyes intent upon her face, which seemed suddenly rather pale and pinched.

"Good heavens, no. What possible purpose would that serve?" The sun was coming up like a orange ball, turning the silver frost to gold. Its beauty brought a pricking of tears to her eyes, or so she told herself, but she blinked them resolutely away. "There is nothing to be gained by opening old wounds."

"Sometimes wounds heal better when they are exposed to light and air."

"Not mine. Time healed mine a long time ago," she asserted steadily. "Though I see no reason why we should not be friends. And now, I intend to return to the house before I freeze to death, and you must do as you please."

He was silent for so long that she wondered if she had dented his pride. Then, to her surprise—perhaps, if she were totally honest, a little to her chagrin—he said equably, "Friends it is, then. And, yes, I will stay."

The twins were up and about early, too excited to stay in bed a moment longer than was necessary. They had seen their aunt from the window walking with Colonel Valentine, and accosted her in the small saloon, agog to know all.

"My dears, there is nothing to know," she said, pleasantly but firmly. "We both decided to take a walk, and our paths coincided."

"You are blushing! Kate, is she not blushing?"

"Indeed she is, Fanny." They took her hands and twirled her around the room. "Dear Aunt Lottie, we saw *all* from our window. How daring of you! And so romantic. An assignation in the garden before dawn . . ."

"Girls!" Her laughter held more than a twinge of embarrassment. "Do let me go before I grow dizzy. I wish you will get it out of your heads that there is any kind of . . . of . . ."

"Yes, Aunt?" Fanny chuckled. "Any kind of what, pray?"

"Nothing. This is foolishness beyond belief. Do stop, or I shall scarce be able to look the colonel in the face."

At this, their mirth spilled over. "But you have already done so this very morning," Kate insisted. "And you do know the old saying: 'The very first person of the opposite gender that you meet on St. Valentine's Day . . .' "

" '. . . will be your heart's desire.' " Fanny concluded triumphantly. "And today, dearest of aunts, is . . ."

"Enough!" They had come a little too near the bone for Charlotte. Her voice grew sharp. "The joke has gone far enough. I appreciate how excited you must feel, but I beg you to have a thought for others. High spirits at this hour can be exceedingly tiresome, let me tell you, when one has guests to attend to, and a million things to do."

They looked at her in astonishment, and then at each other. It was Fanny who spoke for both of them. "Aunt Lottie, we are so sorry. We didn't mean . . . we wouldn't hurt you for the world."

How nearly she had betrayed herself. She forced a smile. "I know, my dears. I'm sorry, too. It is your birthday, and I shouldn't have snapped at you. Come along now, and see what I have for you."

As they left the saloon, they almost fell over Lady Alice, who was so close to the door that she was obliged to step back, looking momentarily discomfited. Charlotte suspected that she had been listening at the door, but dismissed the notion at once as being less than charitable.

Lady Alice was dressed in an elegant morning gown of pale green crepe over which she wore a pretty fringed shawl, and her pale blond hair had been artlessly arranged into a high knot with little cascades of curls framing her face. Charlotte, made very much aware of her own plain round gown, was prey to the unworthy suspicion that she must have been up for hours to achieve such a degree of casual elegance.

"Good morning." Lady Alice smiled, at her most charming. "I hope I am not intruding . . ."

"Not in the least. I am always up and about early, and this morning the girls were much too excited to stay in bed."

"I am sure it is not to be wondered at. Dear Fanny, Kate—let me be one of the first to congratulate you. Ah, to be seventeen again, Miss Wynford." She sighed and patted her shining curls. "I remember so well how it felt—to have all one's life before one . . ."

The inference being that I cannot remember that far back, and am past praying for, Charlotte thought indignantly, holding on to her temper by a whisker. "Quite so. But memories frequently conspire to play one false." She heard the twins stifling their mirth and knew this kind of verbal dueling would not do. "If you would care to take breakfast now, Lady Alice," she said in a more conciliatory tone, "the girls were on their way to the morning room and will gladly bear you company."

"Yes, of course," Fanny said dutifully.

"How kind."

"Not at all. You will probably find yourselves greatly outnumbered as many of the gentlemen who are to hunt will already be there, but I'm sure you are well enough acquainted with them not to be shy."

This earned her a sharp glance, to which Charlotte returned a pleasant smile. Reassured, Lady Alice preened. "It is true that I feel myself among friends here. In fact, one of the reasons I am about so early is that several of the gentlemen have begged me to be present to see them ride off."

"That is what we mean to do also," Kate said with more than usual enthusiasm.

Lady Alice smiled politely and then, looking beyond Kate, suddenly became more animated. "Ah, Colonel."

Charlotte turned to see Luke approaching. He greeted each of them with the same courteous formality and wished the twins many happy returns, while they looked in vain for some degree of partiality in his manner toward their aunt.

"I told you last night that I should be up in time to see off the hunt, did I not?" Lady Alice was laughing up at him, making a teasing little moue. "And you were so unkind as to doubt me. Do you go in to breakfast? Perhaps you will be so good as to give me your arm."

"Well, honestly," declared Fanny indignantly as they went off together. "Did you ever see anything so . . . so . . . ?"

"Hush, child," said Charlotte. "The colonel and Lady Alice are old friends. Your mama told me so."

"Yes, but . . ." Kate, like her sister, saw it as a deliberate slight to their aunt.

"But nothing." Charlotte was firm. "You had better go along and get your breakfast, too, if you are to be ready in time to see the hunt off."

Later, out on the wide sweep of the drive, there was much activity as the party assembled and mulled wine was passed around amidst a lot of talk and laughter.

Miss Taylor, the governess, had the young children at a safe distance on the lawns were they could watch without getting underfoot, but young Oliver, drawn by the yelping of the hounds, had escaped and was in among them, tumbling and laughing, until his father, passing with Colonel Valentine, shooed him away, saying he was getting the horses far too excited.

"I wish I could come with you," Oliver said wistfully. "Bess can jump fences like a good 'un."

"Quite," said his father. "But hunting's a different matter, Noll. We don't want Bess to get hurt by some of those great hunters, do we?"

"I s'ppose not." But Oliver wasn't ready to concede without making his point. "I bet if you were to see Bess and me jumping, Colonel, you'd be amazed!"

Luke smiled. "I daresay I would, young 'un. Perhaps we'll have time to go for a ride together before I leave."

"I say!"

"That will do, Oliver. Cut along, now, there's a good chap," said the duke.

Oliver took his dismissal good-naturedly and, deprived of one pleasure, was soon to be observed luring one of the gardener's boys from his work in order to help him make a slide along the side of the driveway.

"Watch me, Aunt Lottie!" he cried as Charlotte approached with the girls. "I bet I can slide all that way without falling once," and proceeded to prove it.

"Oh, well done!" exclaimed Charlotte, whose favorite he was.

"Show off," Kate added dismissively.

"A lad of some spirit." Luke chuckled.

"Don't we know it," his father groaned. "We live in dread of what he'll be up to next."

Sir Giles Bingham, Lambourn's nearest neighbour, had already arrived, and he was not alone.

"Why, only fancy!" exclaimed Fanny, the glow in her cheeks not entirely due to the bite in the air. "If it isn't James and Edgar!"

"Extraordinary," agreed Charlotte dryly, seeing at once why the twins had been so eager to brave the cold. "I had supposed them to be away at college."

"Well, of course, they should be," Kate said artlessly. "Only, Agnes had it from her bosom friend, Elsie, who is the Binghams' under-cook, that they had been rusticated for two whole weeks for some trifling misdemeanor involving a gambling hell."

"Do you not think Edgar is looking particularly fine, Aunt Lottie?" Fanny sighed. "If anyone were to give me a Valentine token, I do wish it might be Edgar!"

"Do you suppose Mama would agree to their coming to the ball?" Kate asked. "They are among our oldest friends, after all. I'm sure she would ask them if you suggested it to her, dear Aunt."

"Even if she did ask them, Sir Giles and Lady Bingham may consider it inappropriate in view of their current disgrace."

"Oh, I'm sure Lady Bingham could not be so unkind as to deprive us of their company."

The two young men saw them at once, and leaving their horses in the charge of a groom, came across, doffing their hats politely.

"Ma'am." Edgar blushed, a little awed by Charlotte's presence, but James was more forthcoming. "Fanny, Kate, this is your great day, is it not? Pray accept our heartiest congratulations. You'll be surprised to see us, no doubt."

"It's a long story. You won't want to be bored with it now," Edgar insisted hastily, his words addressed to Fanny.

He could always tell the two girls apart, even when, as now, they were identically clad in blue velvet pelisses edged with white fur—and the most becoming bonnets. Fanny's eyes were of a deeper blue than Kate's, and they seemed to take on an extra sparkle whenever she looked at him—like now.

In spite of Edgar's marked interest in Fanny, Charlotte could not fail to be aware of the way his admiring glance kept straying to a small group among which Lady Alice held court, dramatically swathed in a hooded cloak of wine-colored velvet. Her husky laugh floated occasionally on the air, and although Charlotte could not blame the boy for admiring her, she wished her far away.

"Forgive me, ma'am," Edgar said at last, "but is that not Colonel Valentine? I saw him last year when he visited London with the Duke of Wellington for the great celebrations. A friend told me all about his exploits."

Charlotte, relieved by the note of awe in his voice, realized she had misread the object of his interest, and feeling very much in charity with him, she heard herself asking, "Would you like to meet the colonel?"

"Oh, wouldn't I just! But I really c-couldn't presume . . ."

"Nonsense," she said. "Colonel Valentine, could you spare a minute?"

He looked up as she called his name, hesitated, then strode across with a certain impatience, his dark face taut, a trifle forbidding.

"May I present Mr. James Bingham and Mr. Edgar Bingham, who are Sir Giles Bingham's sons."

"Sir." They both shook hands, Edgar being the more eager of the two. "It is the m-most tremendous honor to m-meet you, Colonel. I have read m-many accounts of your bravery at Waterloo. That was a f-famous victory." The stammer that had afflicted him as a child still came back to plague him when he was nervous.

Charlotte watched Luke's reaction anxiously, hoping that he would not become impatient and put the boy down. But, after a keen glance at Edgar, the colonel said almost cordially, "It was certainly a memorable battle."

"Edgar wants to be a soldier," said Kate playfully, and received a glare from her sister.

Edgar blushed, very much aware of the colonel regarding him thoughtfully. "It has always been my ambition, and F-Father says I may—w-when I come down f-from college."

"Very wise. Complete your education, by all means. It can only benefit you in the long run. The army needs men of intelligence. We have too many who think it no more than good sport."

Edgar positively glowed with pleasure.

"Was ever anything so young?" Luke murmured as the two young men excused themselves and moved aside to talk to Fanny and Kate.

Charlotte smiled. "You were very kind to him. Thank you."

He turned his piercing gaze on her. "My dear," he said, "I am not a monster."

"Of course not, but I remember how you used to dislike that kind of hero worship, and you can be very"—she bit her lip—"intimidating."

Luke frowned. "Surely not? I was never so with you."

For an instant, a wave of memory threatened to engulf them both—he, catching in the face uplifted to him, with its purity of profile, a fleeting glimpse of the seventeen-year-old girl who had captured his heart with her endearing vulnerable innocence—and she, remembering a soldier, tired and disillusioned, who had called her his "dear delight" and had appeared to find solace in her company.

Luke's voice, though scarcely above a whisper, betrayed a painful urgency. "For God's sake, Charlotte—don't! Don't look like that."

And she drew back from the abyss and smiled a little blindly at him. To her relief, the hunt was beginning to form up at last, the hounds eager to be off. Luke stood a moment as if rooted to the spot, then, hearing his name called, touched his whip to his hat and strode off to where his groom was grappling with a restive hunter. Edgar and James, not wishing to be behindhand, said a hasty adieu, and followed.

"Such a splendid sight, don't you think, Miss Wynford?" Lady Alice crooned, her eyes alight with a kind of animal pleasure, as the gentlemen rode off to shouts of "Halloo" and the baying of the hounds. "I declare, the drama of it all fires up the blood like nothing else."

"So I am told, though I must confess that I have never much cared for blood sports."

"But then, it would not do for us all to be alike, and you are so ideally suited to gentler pursuits, are you not?"

There was more than a hint of pity in the gushing observation, as Lady Alice gathered her cloak around her and swept indoors.

"Well, honestly!" exclaimed Fanny.

But Charlotte hardly felt the slight. She was still shaken by the intensity of emotion that had flared momentarily between herself and Luke. It was foolish, irrational, to attach any importance to what was no more than the briefest of exchanges. But the incident continued to preoccupy her, so that when she presently visited her sister, nestling into her pillows and sipping her chocolate, Annis was moved to say sharply, "Lottie? Is anything wrong?"

She sighed and turned away from the window. "No, of course not."

"Are you quite sure? You look a trifle *distrait*. I remember thinking so when you first came into the room. I do *pray* you did not take any harm visiting that sick child yesterday."

The note of despair in her sister's voice brought a faint smile. "No, really, my dear. There is nothing contagious about little Molly Allan's weak chest. I merely have a slight headache, which will be gone in no time at all."

"Well, I do hope so. The girls are so excited, they will be of little use to anyone, and I simply cannot cope with Lady Grayshott and Mrs. Egerton on my own. I had no idea they were at daggers drawn! It is really most provoking, not to say embarrassing, just when one wishes everything to be quite perfect."

*   *   *

By evening, Charlotte had somehow contrived to bring both ladies to a tolerable understanding, and everything augured well; the preparations were complete, the ballroom filled with flowers and greenery beneath gleaming chandeliers, and the orchestra had arrived from Bath, and was already to be heard tuning up.

They were to sit down thirty-two to dinner, the numbers being swelled by several near neighbors, including Lord and Lady Bingham, who had been prevailed upon to allow Edgar and James to accompany them.

Fanny and Kate were twin visions in white spider gauze, embroidered with tiny silver flowers that sparkled with every movement of the delicate material as they fluttered from one guest to another, their eyes a brilliant blue, their golden curls threaded with silver ribbons.

Miss Taylor, who had come to help them with their finery, sighed, confessing to Charlotte, "It doesn't seem five minutes since the girls were Oliver's age and playing with their dolls. Now their talk is all of love knots and Valentine tokens—and they spend hours peering into the mirror, applying Denmark lotion to nonexistent spots."

Charlotte laughed. "I know. One tends to forget the importance such imaginary imperfections can assume at seventeen. But the degree of sophistication is highly superficial, and is apt to crumble on the instant if Oliver should challenge them to a game of spillikins."

Charlotte did not voice her reservations about Fanny, although the way she and Edgar had looked at one another that morning at the meet had not escaped her notice. It was to be hoped that his presence at the ball would not fill her niece with any fanciful ideas. Love at seventeen could be as painful as it was sweet, as she could vouchsafe, though, she hastened to assure

herself, their cases were quite different. And Edgar
would soon be back at college.

As for Annis, she was torn between pride and distress as the two girls, having presented themselves for
parental approval, began to mingle among the guests.
"Oh, Edward! They are so lovely . . . but seventeen!
I am getting old!"

"Gammon, m'dear! The girls are well enough, but
they'll never hold a candle to their mama," the duke
declared gruffly, his eyes warming as he beheld his
wife looking enchantingly ethereal in mauve silk, her
hair softly dressed to frame her face and adorned with
a diadem of amethysts and diamonds.

Annis grew pink with pleasure, though she insisted,
half laughing, that Edward was prejudiced. It was left
to Charlotte to convince her.

"My dear Annis," she teased good-naturedly, "if
you will not believe your husband, than I must tell
you Pel was remarking to me not five minutes since
that you looked more like the twins' sister than their
mama."

"Dear Pel," Annis said, sighing. But she was
pleased.

Luke, standing nearby, had overheard the exchange. To his own way of thinking, he regarded
Charlotte as the more striking of the two sisters; she
had never been conventionally beautiful, but the
youthful inner radiance that had once captured his
heart had been translated by the years into something
more lasting than mere prettiness: she had acquired a
bloom—an indefinable sense of style and sureness that
made one look, and look again.

He was no authority on women's dress, but it
seemed that tonight this was more than ever apparent,
for she had eschewed mere prettiness in favor of a
simply cut open robe in a soft green embroidered with
gold, worn over a slip of ivory satin. It had a brief
bodice and tiny sleeves, and her hair was skillfully

dressed into a high knot secured with a gold-tipped opera comb, and her side curls had been brushed until they shone.

"My word," murmured Lady Alice, drifting close to him in a cloud of azure-blue gauze. "Poor Charlotte is looking very fine tonight."

He frowned. "Why *poor* Charlotte? Miss Wynford does not seem in need of anyone's pity."

"Of course not." Lady Alice laughed lightly. "I'm sure I did not mean to imply any such thing. Charlotte is an excellent creature. My heart was simply going out to her, knowing how hard she has worked to ensure the success of this occasion." She cast a roguish look up at him through fluttering lashes. "Not quite to our taste, perhaps. I fear the dancing may tend towards the more exuberant country dances—'Sir Roger de Coverley' and the like—in deference to the birthday girls. So energetic! But Annis assures me that we are to be allowed at least one quadrille and a waltz or two."

She watched Sir Pelham Ballard enter the ballroom and greet Charlotte with affection. "There, now—is that not a pretty sight?" she said with a sigh. "Annis is convinced that Sir Pelham will propose this evening."

Affected as she appeared to be, she nevertheless did not fail to notice the colonel's preoccupation. Something would have to be done.

By ten o'clock all the guests for the ball had been received, and the duke led Fanny out for the opening country dance, while Lord Freddie claimed it as his privilege to partner Kate. Soon the happiest of atmospheres prevailed, as the guests mingled and entered into the spirit of the occasion.

Charlotte, determined to enjoy the evening, had been danced off her feet from the start, for she was known to everyone, and was clearly popular. Luke had resolved to avoid her, but the more he watched her being swung round with easy familiarity in the arms of other men, conversing with ease, laughing up at them in a way he found not at all to his liking, the more jealously he longed to be in their place. And the more she seemed deliberately to avoid him, the more it became an object to thwart her. Finally, at the end of yet another country dance, he made his way to her side. Her partner bowed and melted away, and they were momentarily alone.

"Why, Colonel Valentine, where have you been hiding yourself? I thought Edward must have spirited you away to the card room." She was talking much too fast, laughing up at him, her breathlessness not entirely due to the exertions of the dance.

"No. I have been here. Perhaps you have simply been too much occupied to notice me."

"Oh, dear. You may be right. But is this not the greatest fun? I declare, I have scarce been off my feet all night!

"You look and sound exactly like . . ." he had been about to say "someone I used to know," but stopped himself just in time . . . "like one of your nieces."

"And you, my dear Luke, are a flatterer. Lud, I would not be seventeen again for all the tea in China." Charlotte stopped short, embarrassment flooding her face with color as she realized, too late, how easily her words might be misinterpreted. She searched his face, but found its expression inscrutable.

In fact, he was shaken to the core by the sudden revelation that he still wanted her as much—no, more, much more—than he had all those years ago. She was more beautiful, more desirable in every way. This time he must not let her escape him. The orchestra was tuning up for a waltz, and he saw Sir Pelham making his way purposefully toward them.

"This waltz is mine, I believe," he said with an assurance that took Charlotte's breath away.

She saw Pel's disappointment and managed a belated protest. "I'm sorry, Colonel," she began, "but I am already promised. Perhaps a little later . . ."

"Afraid?" he challenged, his fingers iron-hard as they gripped her arm.

"Certainly not." Oh, Lord! Pel was already looking puzzled. "This is very silly," she murmured, striving for composure.

Luke turned to Sir Pelham. "You won't mind, will you, Ballard? I have waited a long time."

It seemed a strange way of putting his request, but Sir Pelham, ever amiable, accepted the remark at face value. "Oh, quite. Very popular, is Charlotte . . . mustn't be selfish, I suppose . . ."

And so Luke accomplished his aim smoothly, without a shot fired in anger, as it were, and as the first lilting notes began, Charlotte found herself being swept away in his arms, held with a familiarity that would have been thought wicked eight years ago—was wicked even now in the sensations it evoked, as with every fiber of her being she longed to smooth away the harsh lines around his mouth, to trace with her finger the mobile, sensual mouth, to feel it against her own, warm, demanding . . . Dear God, she must not let her imagination run on.

She tried, but it proved impossible with his hand warmly possessive through the silk of her gown, drawing her ever closer, his breath moving against her hair.

"You must not hold me so. People will notice," she said in some confusion.

Luke laughed softly and drew back a little. "Oh, Charlotte, my dear delight, you haven't changed a bit—not deep down. I don't care if people notice. Would they notice, I wonder, if I were to kiss the pulse beating so wildly in your neck?" She gasped inaudibly as her eyes met his. "Oh, my love, can't you see that this meeting was meant? Your nieces have not been slow to remind everyone that this is the night for lovers."

"Luke, stop! I can't think—you aren't being fair."

"True. I am just a rough soldier, used to getting my way. But you are fair enough for both of us, my dear delight. Oh, come, we have wasted so much time. Why waste more?"

My dear delight, he had called her—twice! He had not forgotten. The pulsating music filled her senses, mingling with her own fast-beating heart until she knew not which was which. This could not be happening. She was a sensible woman of mature years, long past the foolishness of youth. And yet . . .

"You weren't really contemplating marrying that bumbling fellow, Ballard, were you?"

"I am very fond of Pel. He is the kindest of creatures." She was driven to defend her dear friend.

"Undoubtedly. And I am seldom kind," he murmured against her hair. "But is he capable of loving you as I would love you?"

The question took her breath away, set her heart racing with absurd hope. The music must end at any moment, and if she were sensible, she would wish the end to come quickly. But it was hard to be sensible when his very presence made her feel like a girl again. "Luke! You mustn't . . . how can you expect me to take such an impossible question seriously after all this time?"

"What has time to do with it? We are still the same people deep down. Give me five minutes alone with you somewhere quiet, and I will prove it to you. How about showing me round that magnificent conservatory when everyone is occupied at supper?"

"I cannot . . . oh, this is foolishness beyond belief!" But even as she spoke, her heart was already ruling her mind. Then the music came to an end.

"The conservatory at midnight," Luke repeated softly as he released her, bowed politely, and escorted her from the floor.

From that moment on, the minutes seemed to drag interminably.

"Are you all right, m'dear?" inquired Sir Pelham as she almost missed her timing in the quadrille. "It ain't like you to be air-dreaming."

"Are you all right, Aunt Lottie?" Fanny asked, when during supper Charlotte twice failed to answer a question. "You do look a trifle flushed."

"Oh, what nonsense! It is a trifle hot in here. Do you not find it so?" I must pull myself together, Charlotte thought, resisting the urge to look yet again at the pretty ormolu clock on the dining-room mantelshelf, which must surely have stopped, and feeling like a schoolroom miss who had taken leave of her senses.

Yet when the fingers of the clock finally came together on twelve, and its tinkling chimes rang out above the buzz of conversation, she almost jumped out of her skin. She glanced around to see if anyone had noticed, but Pel was listening with patient good nature to some long tarradiddle of Mrs. Egerton's, and everyone else was similarly engrossed in conversation. Of Luke she could see no sign. As though she had no control over her limbs, she smiled and rose, excusing herself with a somewhat incoherent remark about seeing that all was in order.

It was quiet in the conservatory after the noise of the dining room, only the gentle splash of water breaking the silence. Charlotte stood just inside the door, allowing her eyes to adjust to the darkness. The atmosphere was somewhat humid, and she longed for a draft of cool fresh air to calm the delicious confusion that filled her. I am too old for such sweet madness, she told herself with deliberate self-mockery. If I had a grain of sense, I would leave now, as silently as I came. . . .

And then a movement over by the central fountain caught her attention, and she moved forward on a surge of elation, knowing her way so well that she needed no light. A giant frond reached out to brush her lightly as she approached the fountain, and at the same moment, the moon sailed from behind a cloud to illuminate two figures, intimately entwined. There was no mistaking Luke's imposing height, or the floating draperies of his companion. Nor was there the least doubt about their purpose in seeking the privacy of the conservatory.

How could you, Luke? Oh, how could you? The accusation reiterated itself over and over in a corner of Charlotte's mind as she stood there, twice betrayed. She must have uttered a strangled cry, for the two drew apart with the suddenness of guilt, and in those seconds before the moon slid once more behind the clouds and she turned to stumble away, there was all the time in the world to see Luke's discomfited face, to hear his muttered "Damnation!"

Charlotte had no idea how she got through the remainder of the evening. It was as though someone else took over—laughed and danced, taking great care never to let Luke come near her. And when, toward the end of the ball, Sir Pelham proposed yet again, she heard herself saying with every appearance of happiness, "Yes, oh, yes, dear Pel. You have been so patient with me. I would be honored to marry you."

Amid all the congratulations that followed, the kissing and the back-slapping and the toasts drunk in their honor, a tiny corner of her mind was acutely aware of Lady Alice looking like the cat who had stolen the cream, of Luke's face, livid beneath its tan, as her glance momentarily encountered his blazing eyes and shied away, and his "Oh, you little fool!" so quiet that only she heard it.

When the last of the night's guests had departed, Charlotte made quite certain that she was never in any danger of being alone with Luke. And when the duke finally carried Sir Pelham off to the library with the remaining gentlemen to drink his health yet again, she accompanied the twins to their rooms. Fanny was in a dream, her mind still filled, Charlotte suspected, with thoughts of Edgar, but Kate, in an ebullient mood, was full of her aunt's betrothal.

"Of course, we are glad for you, dear Aunt Lottie. And it was splendid that you should choose this special night to make your declaration. Sir Pelham is very agreeable, and will make a jolly sort of uncle for us." She could not, however, quite hide the hint of regret in her voice. "Though we had rather hoped for a more *romantic* outcome, had we not, Fanny?"

"M'm?" Fanny roused herself. "Oh, quite. Very romantic."

"Fanny, do stop thinking of Edgar, and pay attention."

"Girls," Charlotte intervened as lightly as she could manage, for the last thing she wanted was to discuss her rather precipitate betrothal. "You have had a wonderful birthday ball, and I had not meant to steal your thunder."

"You didn't," Fanny exclaimed. "It was only . . ."

"Not now, dear. It is much too late, and we are all tired."

Kate opened her mouth to speak, looked at her aunt, and with a maturity that had hitherto eluded her, closed it again, contenting herself with an extra loving hug.

Luke undressed, but found sleep hard to come by. Freddie had insisted on toasting Ballard in the library after the ball, and he was given no opportunity to absent himself. As a result, he had drunk liberally of the duke's brandy, which, far from making him forget, had left him remarkably clear-headed.

Now, pulling on his dressing robe, he paced the floor, castigating himself over what had happened. No use blaming Alice Verity because too much wine had made her so indiscreet as to pursue him to the conservatory. He should have been more careful. And he could hardly blame Charlotte for thinking the worst when she found Alice with her arms entwined around his neck.

For what had happened, the blame was his, and his alone.

How his fellow officers would laugh, could they but see him now, for his reputation with the ladies was second only to his military prowess. What had begun as a bid to banish all memory of his dear delight became a kind of game. Lucky Luke, the regiment, almost to a man, had dubbed him. In Lisbon, Salamanca, Madrid, Paris—he was invariably the one with the prettiest woman hanging upon his arm. It was all quite harmless, a release from the rigors of the campaign, and when the army moved on, he left behind him not a trail of broken hearts, but fond sighs and happy memories. And in the process, he thought he had forgotten.

Now, meeting Charlotte again, and finding her so little altered—older, of course, and more assured, but still curiously untouched—had come as a shock. Something that he had thought dead had stirred in him in spite of her insistence that one could not turn back the clock. If anything, that very insistence had proved a challenge—and he never could resist a challenge. But now, when it really mattered, he had handled the whole affair with a clumsiness that touched upon his pride almost as much as it cut him to the heart.

He flung himself down in an armchair beside the dying fire to wait the morning. He had already informed the duke of his intention to leave Lambourn Manor. Freddie had tried to talk him out of it, but he could not wait to be gone, to put the whole wretched affair behind him. If Charlotte had not acted so precipitately, he might have been able to convince her of his love—for only when it was too late did he fully realize the overwhelming nature of his feelings.

Even now, the idea of her wasting herself on that amiable ass, Ballard, who would bore her within a week, filled him with rage. She was too fine, too intelligent, for such a fate, and the blame was his.

He awoke, cramped from sleeping in the chair, to find daylight streaming in at the window, and a manservant bringing in hot water for his shave.

"What time is it?"

"Gone nine, Colonel."

"Damnation!" He was out of the chair and reaching for his clothes.

"I'm sorry if you was kept waitin', Colonel sir, only what with young Lord Oliver gettin' up to one of his pranks on account of the snow, there's been such goin's on as you wouldn't credit!"

The servant showed every intention of being garrulous. Luke was about to silence him in his best parade-ground manner when Charlotte's name came up.

". . . and Miss Charlotte in such a taking . . . the little lad bein' her perticler favorite . . ."

"Stop, man. No, forget the shave. Just tell me calmly from the beginning."

Luke, used to dressing swiftly and without fuss, listened as the manservant explained how the young lad, seeing the snow, had escaped the vigilant eye of Miss Taylor, the governess, to go racing outside without so much as waiting for his breakfast.

"She was properly put out, o' course, but knowin' as boys will be boys, she didn't worry till he'd been gone a fair while. Then she went a'lookin' for 'im. One of the gardener's boys said as he'd seen him harin' off across the lawns towards the lake, with the two dogs in hot pursuit, an' that started all the fuss—well, proper treacherous, that lake can be, if it ain't frozen 'ard, like, though 'is little lordship knew that well enough . . ."

Luke pulled on his top boots and coat and hurried downstairs. He found the front door wide open, and heard the sound of voices beyond. A good four inches of snow had fallen, and a few flakes were still drifting down on the ever-widening group of people, including the duke and Charlotte, who had had gathered on the drive, all intent upon talking at once. He watched Charlotte, wrapped in a warm cloak and close-fitting bonnet edged with sable, turn, her eyes widening with fleeting surprise which swiftly turned to pleading as they met his.

The duke, too, turned at his approach. "Ah, Colonel. The very man to advise us. My young scapegrace of a son has put us all in a pucker . . ."

"Yes, I have heard, your grace," Luke said, cutting short the duke's attempt to explain. "I am at your disposal. Would you care to tell me what is being done?"

The duke said that he was organizing a search, made up of small groups, to cover a wide area, particularly around the lake. "Noll is a very adventurous child. Yesterday it was slides on the drive. Today, I fear the lake may prove to be a greater lure, for all that he has been warned often enough about keeping well clear of the lake until it has been pronounced safe for skating, so I cannot think he would be so foolish . . ."

The confidence of the words was belied by a note of uncertainty in the duke's voice.

"I'm sure you are right," Luke said calmly. "However, if you would permit me to put what little experience I have gained at your disposal . . ."

"My dear Colonel, any advice you can offer will be most gratefully accepted. Anything which might lead to the safe return of my son . . ." Here the duke's voice wavered again. "Annis is still asleep, thank God."

"Then let us strive to ensure that all cause for anxiety is at an end by the time she wakes," said Luke, making his voice deliberately brisk. "Perhaps someone could be sent to the stables for my servant, John Jackson? Tell him what has happened and he'll know the kind of things we need—some sturdy planks of wood, a length or two of rope, blankets. It may well save precious time to have them in readiness."

While the duke gave his orders, Charlotte came across to say in a low voice, "Thank you, Luke. You cannot know what this means to Edward . . . and to me. Noll is such a fearless little boy. He sometimes forgets . . ." Luke was staring out toward the lake, but hearing the tremor in her voice, he turned to look down at her. She met the look squarely. "I am only too aware that you must be eager to shake the dust of Lambourn from your feet . . ."

"Stuff and nonsense," he said abruptly. And then, more kindly, "Try not to worry, my dear. Small boys are amazingly danger-proof, you know. I daresay he is even now absorbed in some ploy, quite unaware of the hue and cry he has created."

"I do hope so." She wondered if he was aware of having used that small endearment. Probably not. And this was not the moment to dwell on such trifling considerations.

A stocky man clad in stout breeches and a leather jerkin was striding toward them, followed by a small gaggle of estate workers bearing an assortment of equipment, which was shared between two groups, one led by the duke and one by Luke.

"Excellent," Luke said. "When we reach the lake, I suggest that your grace takes the left bank and we will take the right. That way we can make a systematic search." He smiled reassuringly. "And try not to worry, sir—your son is probably absorbed in some game and has quite forgotten all sense of time."

"Yes, of course." The duke's voice was overhearty. "That's young Oliver—never does anything by halves, y'know. Charlotte, you had much better go back in-doors now. You'll take your death, waiting round out here."

"Indeed, I shall do no such thing, Edward. I mean to go with Colonel Valentine." She saw that he seemed on the verge of arguing, and continued swiftly, "I am warmly clad and wearing my pattens. If you find Noll he'll be fine, but he barely knows Colonel Valentine, and if he should be hurt or frightened— oh, I'm sure he won't be, but even so, he may need the reassuring presence of someone he loves."

"I suppose you're right, m'dear. But I don't want your safety on m'conscience as well as . . ." His voice trailed away.

"Oh, Edward, do get along and don't talk such fustian. I am well able to take care of myself."

"And I shall make doubly sure that Miss Wynford comes to no harm," said Luke, a faint gleam in his eyes.

The lake seemed deserted as they approached, a huge white ampitheater surrounded by snow-capped trees and wrapped in its own awesome desolate beauty. But, as far as it was possible to see, there were no cracks in the smooth surface where a small boy might have come to grief.

The two parties separated, and soon the voices of the duke's party faded. Charlotte could feel panic mounting in her as their cries brought no response. Oliver couldn't have vanished into thin air. Perhaps he hadn't come to the lake at all.

And then, out of nowhere, there came a series of excited yelps, and a large black body came hurtling out of the undergrowth and flung itself at Charlotte.

"Hector." She knelt, heedless of the snow, and calmed the excited animal. "Easy, now." He began to whimper and tug at her cloak. Charlotte looked up at Luke in mingled hope and fear. She scrambled to her feet. "Come on, boy—show us where Oliver is."

They found the child lying at full stretch, half on the ice, his feet hooked around a tree root on the bank, his fingers tenaciously wrapped around the paws of the second dog, who had obviously strayed onto the ice at a weak point and fallen in. Charlotte's heart lurched, for at first glance Oliver seemed barely conscious. But when he heard voices, he roused to croak through chattering teeth, "I have Ajax . . . s-safe, Aunt L-Lottie . . . but I can't lift him . . ."

One of the estate men rushed forward, but was stopped by Luke's curt, "*Don't*! If we try to move the boy, the ice will give and he could go under." He summoned his man, who in turn called for some rope and bound two of the planks of wood together. A further length of rope was looped loosely around Oliver's body before a third plank was carefully slid beneath him.

"Just a precaution. I doubt we'll get the child to loose his hold on the dog, though it could well be dead by now," Luke explained to Charlotte in a low voice. "So we'll need to move them both together."

John Jackson laid the extra planks alongside Oliver from the bank to the hole in the ice, and at a sign from Luke, he lay at full stretch, with a couple of stout workmen holding onto his legs, ready to take the dog's weight as Luke carefully moved Oliver back from the brink, and eased his icy fingers from the dog's paws.

"Blankets, quickly!" demanded Charlotte, spreading a doubled one out to receive her nephew, who was as cold as death.

"One moment." Luke knelt to remove Oliver's stiff, wet garments. "The blankets will have little effect if you leave these on. He'll do better without them."

She tucked Oliver's poor frozen hands into her sable muff, and wrapped the blankets around him, piling extra ones on top. Someone had been sent to tell the duke, and by the time he arrived Charlotte was kneeling on the snow with Oliver in her arms, well cocooned, though his teeth still chattered uncontrollably. "Is Ajax s-saved t-too, Aunt Lottie?"

"Yes, darling. He is here beside you." She glanced across to where someone had wrapped Ajax in a blanket. She had no way of knowing whether the dog was alive or dead as Hector prowled around him, whining softly, and at this moment, sad though it was, she couldn't really care.

The duke, down on his knees beside her, had eyes only for his son. "Is he . . . ?"

"He's safe, Edward," Charlotte said, as calmly as she was able, for her own teeth were beginning to chatter now that the first shock was over and there was time to think what might have happened.

"Here." Luke thrust a flask unceremoniously beneath her nose. "Take a good swig of this, Charlotte— and I think, perhaps, a few drops trickled into the youngster's mouth, don't you, sir?" He glanced briefly at the duke, who was gathering his son into his arms. "To counteract the cold?"

The duke appeared not to hear.

"Edward?" Charlotte's voice rasped a little against the fiery brandy.

"What, m'dear? Oh, yes, yes, whatever you say, Colonel . . ."

"And it might be as well to send someone now for the doctor," Luke added gently. "The sooner he sees young Oliver, the better."

"Of course." The duke brushed the sleeve of his coat across his eyes, then cleared his throat to address his senior stable lad. "Rob, be so good as to go for Dr. Glaister, if you please. Tell him . . . tell him it's a matter of some urgency."

"Yes, your grace."

"Would you like me to carry Oliver, sir?" Luke offered.

"No, no, Colonel. Appreciate your concern and all that, but—" He climbed to his feet in ungainly fashion, his son clutched to him. "You've played your part, a part indeed for which I can never adequately repay you."

"Oh, let us have no talk of that," Luke said

abruptly. "Just get young Oliver home and into his bed. He'll soon perk up, you'll see."

The duke strode away, followed by a keeper carrying the inert body of the dog, with Hector sniffing and whining at his heels, and the rest of the party bringing up the rear. Soon only Luke and Charlotte remained.

"Come. You can't stay here," Luke said, watching her standing with her cloak wrapped tightly around her, watching her brother-in-law disappearing into the trees. "At this rate, you'll take a chill, too—and how will they all manage without you?" When this appeared to have little effect, he spoke more sharply. "Charlotte. Come along. Your sister will certainly have need of you."

She came to with a shudder. "Yes, of course . . . I . . . Oh, Luke!" He gathered her into his arms and held her, rocking her gently. She struggled to lift her head. "Will he really be all right?"

It would have been so easy to utter platitudes, but Charlotte deserved better of him. "I really cannot say, my dear. We have no way of knowing how long he'd been there."

"Poor baby. He looked so—so small and lost—so b-blue with cold."

"Don't! Oh, my dearest girl!" Luke couldn't bear the anguish in her eyes. He bent to kiss her cold lips, and she did not resist as their mouths met and clung, seeking warmth and comfort from one another, until gradually the initial purpose was forgotten and their mouths took on an urgency and possession of their own. Oliver, the extreme cold—everything was forgotten but their need for one another.

"No, no. This is madness," she whispered, breaking free at last. "It must be the shock—the brandy."

"It's nothing of the kind, and well you know it."

"No, you are wrong. How can you even suggest

that I would contemplate . . . that we might . . . ? It is impossible. I am not free. I must go now—at once."

"It is no more impossible than the notion that you consider yourself bound by a ridiculous announcement made in the heat of the moment. If you had only allowed me a few minutes to explain." He attempted to pull her close again, but she evaded his grasp and began to walk, stumbling a little because her feet were frozen.

"It isn't ridiculous. It was a decision I should have taken ages ago. I am very fond of Pel, and I know that he will do everything in his power to make me happy."

"We've been through all that," he said harshly, suiting his impatient stride to hers, taking her arm to steady her step. "But, for all that you think me fickle, you shall hear me out."

Flakes of snow were drifting down, landing on her eyelids like frozen tears as she raised her head briefly to meet his glance. She blinked and brushed them away, then lowered her head so that he should not see the real tears that hovered as they walked on.

"I cannot stop you. But it will make no difference."

"What you saw last night—what you thought you saw—was no more than a cruel trick of fate, though without maligning the character of the lady concerned, it is impossible for me to go into detail. Despise me if you will, but at least believe that I would never knowingly have subjected you to such humiliation."

Charlotte knew this to be true. It must have been all too easy for someone like Lady Alice, seeing herself and Luke together, to put two and two together and come up with four. And she had made no secret of the fact that she considered Luke to be her catch. But the damage was done.

"I don't blame you, Luke," she managed in a stifled voice. "I understand exactly how it must have happened, but perhaps it is all for the best."

He opened his mouth to refute such a piece of nonsense, but the strategist in him decided that this was neither the time nor the place.

Dr. Glaister arrived shortly after they returned to the house to find Edward pacing the hall, waiting for him. It took but a moment to glean the facts before proceeding to the nursery wing. Annis had already been roused by Edward, and was with her son, bearing up well, but very much in need of Charlotte's support, so that all other considerations must be laid aside.

Nurse had ordered the fire to be built up so that the room was already growing warm, and had drawn a screen between the bed and the door to avoid the risk of drafts. Several hot bricks wrapped in flannel had been brought and placed around Oliver, who was lying beneath a pile of blankets, still looking alarmingly white against the pillows, and shivering violently from time to time.

"You've done well, Nurse," the doctor congratulated the stout elderly woman who had raised all the Denham children with a mixture of firmness and love.

"Thank you, sir. But credit where credit's due— that Colonel Valentine gave me a tip or two. Very sensible gentleman, if I may say so."

"Well, now," the doctor said quietly, looking grave as he completed his examination and drew them behind the screen, out of Oliver's hearing. "I've no need to tell your grace that the little fellow is in poor shape just now—"

Annis uttered a muffled cry and clung to Charlotte.

"However," he added hastily, "it's early days. Lord Oliver is a sturdy little boy, and if we can get his blood temperature back up, and his lungs are not adversely affected, we should soon see a decided improvement."

"And if he should suffer an inflammation of the lungs?" Annis whispered.

"We will do all we can to contain it, your grace."
Dr. Glaister smiled reassuringly. "I have administered
a mild paregoric, and will return later in the day to
see how his young lordship does, but if you are in the
least anxiety, send for me at once." He turned to
leave. "As for your friend, Colonel Valentine, I'd say
you owe him a debt of gratitude. His prompt action
may well have saved your son's life."

Annis was a little easier in her mind after Dr. Glaister's visit, but she could not be persuaded to leave
Oliver's side.

"Charlotte, will you say all that is proper for me to
our guests? They will understand, I know, and you
are far better at arranging for their comfort than I
ever was."

The news had gone before her, however. Lady
Grayshott was already instructing her maid to pack.

"There is no need, Maud," Charlotte insisted.
"Annis said to be sure to tell you that you are very
welcome to stay as long as you wish."

"I'm sure we are, my dear." Her ladyship smiled.
"And it is just like Annis to say so. You may assure
her that we have had a perfectly splendid time, but
you cannot deny that guests, however welcome, are
very much *de trop* at such an anxious time. I believe
the Egertons are of the same mind."

"But you cannot—the weather . . ." Charlotte was
torn between the natural instincts of hospitality and
relief.

"My husband informs me that the weather is im-
proving by the minute. That fall of snow has led to
the onset of a thaw, and now the sun is out, he has
every confidence that we shall have no trouble on the
road."

"Well, if you are sure . . . ?"

"Quite sure, my dear Charlotte. I only hope that
poor Oliver's escapade may not have taken the shine

off Fanny and Kate's celebrations, to say nothing of your betrothal."

Charlotte had hardly given Pel a thought since her return to the house. Now guilt made her blush, which must have given quite the wrong impression.

"Pel won't know yet about Oliver," she said to cover her confusion. "He is not an early riser, but I must find Emily and tell her what has happened. And the girls will doubtless sleep late."

In the hall she found Luke in conversation with Edward. They both turned as she descended the last few stairs, and it grieved her to see the pain in Edward's eyes, though he greeted her in his usual kindly way.

"Ah, there you are, m'dear. I've had a word with Glaister. Young Oliver not so good, I take it?"

Charlotte tried to be positive. "Well, you know how wary doctors are of committing themselves to an opinion, and of course Dr. Glaister chose his words with care in front of Annis, but there was no disguising his concern." She glanced at Luke, and added gently, "We may be in for a worrying few days. But don't despair. Oliver is strong, and I am confident that he will recover."

"Yes. Yes, of course, m'dear."

"And you may well have Luke to thank . . ." The name slipped out, but Edward was too abstracted to notice the small familiarity. "The doctor was convinced that his prompt action may well have saved Oliver's life."

"So Glaister told me, too. I've been trying to express m'thanks to the colonel, but . . ."

"There is no need." Luke was brusque. "There are few emergencies I have not been called upon to deal with over the years. I merely followed my instincts."

"Even so . . ." Edward persisted, but Charlotte laid a hand on his arm.

"I think Annis might like you to go up, just to reassure her."

"Oh, quite. Yes, indeed. Excuse me, Colonel . . . m'dear . . ." He hurried away up the stairs.

"Poor Edward." Charlotte sighed. "He feels so useless at times like this."

Luke watched her face. "It strikes me, they'd both be in a poor way without you."

"Oh, heavens, no! I am not here all that often, and there are plenty of people—Nurse is a tower of strength, and Miss Taylor and the staff are very supportive."

"Very fine. But I am not blind."

Lady Alice came drifting down the stairs in a morning gown of amber crepe, her hair in charming disarray. "Such goings on! I have just seen Lady Grayshott and she tells me they are leaving! In fact, most of your guests would seem to be leaving."

"I do hope not," Charlotte said. "Annis will, of course, be preoccupied, but she asked me to assure everyone that they are very welcome to remain."

"Even so, I cannot think it a good idea. Her son's condition must cast a blight over us all. How is Oliver, by the way?"

It was so obviously an afterthought that it took every ounce of Charlotte's good breeding to reply with even a modicum of politeness.

"Well, there you are." Lady Alice turned to Luke, and if the events of the previous evening embarrassed her, it did not show. "I am right, am I not, Colonel?"

"If you mean that our consideration for the duke and her grace at this time must make any other course untenable, then I agree."

"Yes, of course that is what I meant," she retorted, a flush staining her cheeks. "I certainly shall not stay. In fact, I was about to order my carriage to be ready for noon. Perhaps," she added in softer tones, casting him a limpid glance, "you would be so kind as to lend me your company on the journey back to London?"

Charlotte held her breath. It could be nothing to

her, of course, if Luke chose to accompany Lady
Alice. He was a free agent.

"I'm sorry," she heard him say abruptly. "But being
somewhat involved, I have a mind to stay around until
Oliver's condition improves."

Fury flared momentarily in Lady Alice's eyes, to be
swiftly disguised. "As you will," she said lightly, and
turned on her heel.

Left alone with Luke, Charlotte was achingly conscious of his presence. "Thank you," she said at last.

"For what?"

She could hardly say *for not going with Lady Alice.*
"For caring about Oliver, I suppose—and for not
wishing to rush away."

"Oh, I am not going anywhere until a lot of things
have been sorted out," he said softly. "Oliver is only
one of them."

"Luke, please—not again. Not now."

He heard the panic in her voice. He longed to hold
her, to crush her in his arms and soothe away all her
fears. But he only said, "No. Not now. Go along and
do what you have to do."

Fanny and Kate awoke to find Charlotte drawing
back their curtains to let in the daylight.

"Heavens!" Kate screwed up her eyes and buried
her head under the sheet in mock horror. "Aunt Lottie, pray close the curtains! The sunlight will set my
head spinning again!"

"I told you not to drink so much champagne,"
Fanny muttered without attempting to open her eyes.
"Have we slept shockingly late, Aunt Lottie?" And
then, as full realization hit her, she shot up in bed.
"Oh, no. Edgar promised to ride over this morning
. . . they go back to college very soon. What time is
it?"

"A little after ten."

"Oh, that's all right, then. I have until noon."

Fanny settled back with a sigh. "Wasn't it the most wonderful ball?"

"Wonderful," Charlotte agreed.

Something in her aunt's voice made Fanny look at her more closely. Aunt Lottie didn't look at all like someone who had just become engaged. And because the two girls almost always thought alike, Kate caught her mood.

"Is something wrong?" they demanded in chorus.

She told them, as simply and undramatically as she could. "I'm sorry that it should happen so soon after your lovely day . . ."

"Oh, bother our day!" Fanny was already out of bed. "What does that matter? Oh, poor Noll!"

"And poor Mama," said Kate, following suit. "She will be distraught. We must go to her at once!"

"Well, not just now, my dears. She is sitting with Oliver. But I know it would please her, and be a support to your papa, if you would perhaps help me with the guests. Most have decided to leave, and I think it would be rather nice if you were there to bid them safe journey—in place of your mama—and thank them for coming." And it will keep you occupied, Charlotte added silently.

"Yes, of course. Where is Florence? Ah, there you are." Their maid stepped from the shadows. "Florence, be so good as to lay out our morning gowns—the blue, I think . . ."

Charlotte left them, knowing that they would be keen to prove their newfound maturity.

By midday only Lord Freddie, and Luke, and Pel and Emily remained. The latter begged to be allowed to stay if they should not be in the way.

"It don't seem proper to walk out on you," Pel confessed. "Not much of a hand at makin' m'self useful, and you won't want to be talking of bridals just now, I know, but—well, I can at least offer moral support."

"That is very sweet of you," Charlotte said, and meant it.

"And Emily's a dab hand in a sickroom. Nursed our mama for years."

When Edgar rode over, Charlotte insisted that Fanny should take a walk with him on the grounds. The snow had all but melted and the fresh air would do her good. Edgar gallantly offered to escort Kate also, but she only grinned.

"And watch you two ogling one another? No, thank you, Edgar! I shall sit with Mama."

Annis had been persuaded to let Charlotte take over from her in the sickroom, while she went to rest. Nurse, having the greatest confidence in Charlotte, was also persuaded to lie down for a while.

It was warm in the small room, the air fetid, and it was very quiet except for Oliver's breathing, which was beginning to rasp. Several times she got up out of her chair to bend over him. His eyes were open, and she laid a hand on his brow, which now, far from being cold, was burning.

"Would you like a drink, Noll? Cook has made some of her special barley water just for you."

He managed a few sips and then pushed the glass away, complaining that his chest hurt. If Dr. Glaister had not promised to return, she must have sent for him there and then. Instead, she wrung a cloth out in cool water to wipe Oliver's face and hands.

"How is he?"

She had not heard Luke come in. "Feverish," she whispered, inexpressibly glad to have him near. "I was about to sponge him down."

"I'll help you. Has he a clean nightshirt?" he asked, and together they made Oliver more comfortable.

"Does Ajax have hurts in his chest?"

Charlotte glanced at Luke, remembering that sad bundle that had been carried away to be buried. "No, sweetheart," she said softly. "Ajax has no hurts."

"Good." Oliver began to cough, and as she forbade him to say more, her eyes met Luke's. He lifted an eyebrow, but said nothing until they were out of earshot.

"As I feared, the little chap's in for a rough time."

"But he will recover? He must!"

"I'm sure he will. Has Glaister been again?"

"No, but we are expecting him anytime now."

"Well, if he isn't here in the next hour, I think he should be sent for—just to be on the safe side."

"Oh, Luke!" She turned to lean her head against his chest, and his arms came around her. He made no attempt to do more than hold her, but she drew new strength and hope from him.

"Is everything all right?" Emily whispered from the door, and they stepped apart.

For two days Oliver's life hung in the balance. Annis, unable to bear the sight of her son so ill, was banished from the sickroom except for brief visits, lest her distress might communicate itself to the child. The bulk of the nursing devolved upon Charlotte and Emily, for although Nurse was adamant that she must do her part, she was getting too old to take the full responsibility.

"You are doing too much," Luke accused Charlotte, when she came down to dinner on the second evening. "You have black circles under your eyes, and I'll swear you have lost weight."

"In two days? What nonsense!" she replied, her heart leaping with the knowledge that he had noticed. "We are all playing our part. The girls are helping to keep Annis's hopes high, and Pel, too, is kindness itself to her, for which I am most grateful since Edward is not at his best in such a situation."

It was true. The duke felt helpless, and worked off his own frustration by prowling the manor, or striding out across the estate with his brother and Luke to shoot rooks, and although they all came together for dinner, the conversation was often forced.

By the third afternoon everyone was feeling the strain. Charlotte returned from her daily walk in the garden to find Nurse fast asleep in the chair by the fire. She felt a momentary irritation that Emily had left her alone, but perhaps there had been a reason, and all seemed quiet. And then she realized that it was too quiet—no wheezing, not a hint of the cough that had racked Noll's poor frame for the past two days. Only silence.

Half afraid, she crossed to the bed.

"Aunt Lottie, I'm thirsty."

It was a peevish, accusing little thread of a voice, but she had never heard a more beautiful sound. As she lifted him to help him drink, she noted that his skin felt no more than normally warm, and his eyes were clear.

"Oh, Noll! Dear, wonderful Noll!"

Charlotte ran in a most unseemly manner down the corridors, dispensing the good news to Annis and the girls, to Emily, who met her on the way, full of apologies for leaving the sickroom—and downstairs, where Milton received the news with one of his rare smiles.

"I believe his grace is in the library, Miss Charlotte," he informed her, and strode before her to fling open the door.

At first sight she could see no sign of Edward, but Luke, who had been perusing a magazine, rose at her entrance.

"Edward?" she faltered.

"He's just gone down to the gun room. Is it . . . ?"

"Luke! Oh, Luke!" she cried, bursting into tears—and ran across to fling herself into his arms.

"Oliver?" he queried, his heart sinking as he felt the rapid beating of her heart.

She raised her head, laughing through her tears. "He's going to be all right."

"God be praised," he said quietly.

"Amen to that," echoed Pel, rising more slowly from the chair that had hidden him from her gaze. He looked from one to the other—and when she would have spoken, stopped her. "It's all right, m'dear. I may be a bit of a buffoon, but I'm not quite blind. You're only confirming what I already knew, and didn't want to admit to m'self."

"You're not a buffoon, Pel. You're a lovely man and a dear friend. It's just . . ."

"That I'm not the right man for you." His face was creased, as though he might cry, but he straightened his shoulders in a determined way. "I believe I've always known that, too."

"I'm sorry," Luke said. "This all goes back a very long way . . ."

"Don't doubt it, m'dear fellow. Deuced tedious things—explanations. Best we take it that the other night never happened and no harm done. Too much champagne, what?"

Then Edward burst into the room, having heard the good news from Milton, and thereafter a spirit of rejoicing ran through the house. And although Oliver still had a long way to go, and there were many explanations to be made, dinner that evening had an air of celebration about it.

"We told you, didn't we, dear Aunt Lottie?" Fanny said, thoroughly approving of the bloom of love that her aunt could not disguise, in spite of her laughing disclaimer.

"And what exactly did you tell her?" Luke demanded with mock severity.

Kate giggled. "About Saint Valentine's Day. And how the first person of the opposite gender you meet that day will be your one true love."

"I see." Luke's eyes twinkled as he watched the color creep into Charlotte's cheeks.

"And there was your name as well—it seemed

meant. Of course, we didn't know you had loved and lost one another all those years ago." Fanny sighed. "That really is romantic."

Annis, remarkably recovered, now that her anxiety was at an end, was full of astonishment that her sister had carried such a secret all those years. "And I always thought you an open book!"

Much later, when they were alone, Luke held Charlotte very close, as though he would never let her go. And his first kiss as her betrothed, for which she had waited so long, was all and more than she had dreamed of—his mouth questing, caressing, demanding—and when they both drew breath, leaving her wanting more. "Happy?"

"Delirious," she said tremulously. "So much has happened in so short a time, I dread waking up to find it was all a dream."

"Then I must do my best to convince you otherwise, my dear delight," he murmured, pressing a kiss into the palm of her hand that made her catch her breath. "So much time lost."

"And so much more to come"—she chuckled softly—"my own dear Valentine."

February Falsehoods

by Sandra Heath

"SO THERE YOU have it, Marianne. I wish you to seriously reconsider the Forrester match, which you so foolishly discarded two years ago." Mr. Cromwell stood by the drawing-room window with his back toward his youngest daughter. He gazed steadfastly out at the winter-morning scene in the Mayfair street, as if he found it completely absorbing. The truth was that he wasn't in the least interested in the goings-on of Berkeley Street, but rather that he was intensely uncomfortable about having to broach such a difficult subject with his reluctant offspring. The Forrester match was very advantageous indeed, and Marianne could count herself exceeding fortunate that negotiations had been resumed. Maybe Brandon Forrester wasn't a titled prize like Sir Piers Sutherland, but at least he was steadfast and dependable, and Mr. Cromwell was determined that this time everything could be satisfactorily finalized.

Marianne sat by the fire behind him, her large hazel eyes reproachful as she glanced at her father for a moment before returning her attention to the valentine card on her lap. It was an almost foolishly romantic lace-edged confection of cherubs, love knots, and pierced hearts, and she had made it herself.

Mr. Cromwell turned reluctantly from the window, a little exasperated by her silence and by the accusation he knew he would see in her eyes. He was a little given to stoutness, and his gray hair had receded,

leaving a gleaming bald pate that would have been at
the mercy of the winter chill had he not protected it
with a tasseled cap. Over his shirt and breeches he
wore a damson brocade dressing gown tied at the
waist with cord, and there was a warm knitted shawl
over his shoulders. Firelight flickered cheerfully over
the room, but outside there was a thin layer of snow
on the ground.

He looked at his last remaining daughter, and then
exhaled slowly as he tried to maintain his patience,
always a difficult feat when faced with her intransi-
gence regarding marriage. She had been mulish in the
extreme since the debacle of her broken betrothal to
Sutherland, but the time had come for the past to be
set aside, and the future attended to. She was twenty-
six now, and in his opinion overdue to become a wife.
Her dear departed mother had been married at seventeen, and the mother of four daughters by the time
she'd reached Marianne's age. Three of those daughters had long since been taken off his hands, but Marianne . . . Oh, Marianne.

He sighed, studying her as she sat on the crimson
silk chair. Maybe she wasn't a beauty, but she was
certainly very striking. The only one of his daughters
to take after her mother, with the same cloud of russet
curls and the same huge hazel eyes. It was a pity that
she had freckles and that her mouth was a little wide,
but she had an excellent figure, and when she smiled
she was quite enchanting. How demure she looked in
her cream merino gown, but how plaguey stubborn
was the set of her chin. Well, my girl, you're going to
have a fight on your hands this time, he thought. He
wanted the Forrester match, which would unite two
prominent Cheshire families, and when he chose he
could be as mulish as she.

"Have you nothing to say, Marianne?" he inquired.
"Brandon Forrester is a very fine catch, and you may
regard yourself as very privileged indeed that he is

still prepared to accept you. Deuce take it, girl, the terms are excellent, and it's not as if you dislike the fellow, for he's one of your oldest friends!"

"I know, Father." That was the trouble. Brandon was too old a friend.

"Is that all you can think of in reply?"

"I will consider the match again, Father." Marianne toyed with the valentine card, running her fingertips over the frothy lace she had stitched so laboriously all around the edge.

"You said that far too lightly, my girl. Don't think you can dillydally and that it will all go away. I won't have it this time. I know that you suffered greatly at Sutherland's hands, but—"

"Please don't mention him," she interrupted quickly.

"But he has to be mentioned, my dear," her father said more gently. "What happened was most regretful, but—"

"Regretful?" She got up swiftly from the chair, the valentine card falling to the floor. "Father, I loved Piers with all my heart and I wore his betrothal ring, but then I found out that he was conducting a liaison with the most notorious and abandoned courtesan in London! I hardly think that that can be termed merely regretful!"

He drew a long breath, and then nodded. "Well, perhaps I chose an unfortunate word, but the fact remains that you and Sutherland are no longer betrothed, and haven't been for over a year. Damn it, he's across the Atlantic in America, and seems likely to remain there, so I fail to see why you are digging your heels in over any other marriage. You're twenty-six years old, and if you don't take care, you'll become an old maid. You cast Brandon aside in Sutherland's favor before, and it was a grave error of judgment. Don't compound the error now by refusing the match a second time."

"Father, I have said that I will consider the match,

and that is what I will do. It's what you wish me to say, isn't it?"

"What I wish you to say is that you accept." His glance went to the valentine card, and for the first time he realized what it was. Striding across the room, he bent to retrieve it. "What's this? A valentine?"

"Yes, Father."

He studied the beautifully painted front, and then opened it to read aloud the verse she'd composed inside.

> *"Please say you'll be my valentine,*
> *Take my heart, and I'll take thine.*
> *I'll love you forever, my sweetheart divine,*
> *And so I beg you, be my valentine."*

Marianne waited in silence, knowing that he was bound to leap to the wrong conclusion. She was correct.

His eyes flew to her face. "Is there something you've been keeping from me, miss? Some fellow you've been neglecting to mention?"

"No, Father, there isn't anyone."

"Then why this?" He waved the valentine.

"I didn't make it for myself. It's for Chloe."

"Chloe? The Pendeven wench?"

"She is the only Chloe we know, Father, and she also happens to be my closest friend," Marianne pointed out quietly.

"She wears far too much rouge," he muttered, pushing the card back into her hands.

"Rouge is very fashionable at the moment, as you well know. And although I know you regard Chloe as a little frivolous and empty-headed, I assure you that she is neither. I happen to like her very much, and I've thoroughly enjoyed her society since she arrived in town six months ago."

He cleared his throat. "So you've gone to endless

trouble so that she can give a pretty folderol to her latest admirer?"

"If you put it like that, yes."

"Who is it this time? I've lost count of the suitors who've crowded to her door since she arrived."

"She can't help it if she's all that is beautiful and fascinating."

"I suppose not, and the size of her father's fortune helps a great deal," he observed dryly.

"I cannot deny it." Chloe's father, Mr. Pendeven of Severn Park in the Forest of Dean, was immensely wealthy, and his only daughter stood to inherit everything.

Mr. Cromwell glanced at the card again. "So who is it for?" he asked again.

"I really don't know," Marianne confessed.

"I'll warrant the fellow is unsuitable. An adventurer, probably, intent only upon her fortune."

"Don't be cynical."

He smiled. "Perhaps I am. Chloe is a nice enough young woman, and I don't dislike her as much as I pretend. It's just that I see her being besieged with offers at the age of only twenty, and here you are, still being awkward about the only offer you've had in over a year."

"Thank you, Father, you've done my self-regard immense good," she replied.

"Oh, let's not continue in this vein, for it will provoke an argument. So the valentine card is for Chloe's latest swain, whose identity is a mystery."

"Yes."

"You must have spent hours making it."

"I didn't mind, for she really is my dearest friend, and anyway, I thoroughly enjoyed making it."

His brows drew together as he glanced at the card again. "Actually, it looks a little familiar."

"Really?" She felt dull color begin to stir into her cheeks. Yes, it *was* familiar, for it was the same design and verse she'd done two years ago when first she'd fallen in love with Piers.

"You really are very talented with paint and brush, my dear, and you don't get it from me, that's for sure. Your mother was a clever artist."

"Yes, she was." Marianne looked at the pretty watercolor of a Cheshire landscape hanging above the mantelpiece.

"Forgive me for being hasty a moment ago, but when I realized it was a valentine—"

"That's quite all right, Father. I promise that I haven't been keeping anything from you, and that there isn't a secret admirer who has been climbing up to my window." The words slipped out before she realized they were on the tip of her tongue, and the color in her cheeks became suddenly fiery. In the past, when Piers had been laying determined siege to her in order to win her away from the match with Brandon, there had been several occasions when he'd climbed up the walnut tree to her balcony in the dark of night. His advances had never gone beyond the bounds of propriety, but they had been so gallant and romantic that it would have been impossible for her not to have fallen desperately in love with him.

Mr. Cromwell didn't notice the telltale color in her cheeks. "I will leave you now, my dear, for I've said what I came to say."

"I promise that I will think carefully about marrying Brandon, Father."

"See that you do, my dear, for I pin great hope upon it. If things had gone well between you and Sutherland, I would have been delighted for you, but they didn't, and now you must put him from your thoughts once and for all."

"I know."

He went to the door. "By the way, I will be going out shortly. I have certain financial matters to attend to."

"I will be out as well. Chloe sent a message about an hour ago, requesting me to call upon her as soon as possible as she has something of immense importance to discuss with me."

"No doubt she wishes your opinion upon which gown to wear," he replied drolly.

"Possibly, but I fancy it is more likely to be the matter of the recipient of this card."

"No doubt. I trust you will be taking the carriage to Curzon Street?"

"It is much quicker and simpler to use Lansdowne Passage."

He sighed. "I would prefer it if you took the carriage. Footpads have been known to lurk in the passage."

She went to the window and looked across the snowy street toward the entrance of the subterranean tunnel which led for about one hundred and fifty yards between the grounds of Lansdowne House and Devonshire House, two of Mayfair's greatest mansions. The narrow mouth of the passage was set in the high boundary wall of the Lansdowne House garden, and a flight of steps led down into the shadowy way which offered easy access to Curzon Street and the western side of Mayfair.

Mr. Cromwell repeated his request. "The carriage would be more sensible, Marianne."

"But it's so tedious going all that way around. Besides, will you not require the carriage yourself?"

"I, er . . ." He cleared his throat. "I hadn't thought of that. I will summon a hackney carriage."

"There isn't any need. I will take my maid and hurry through the passage. It isn't far, and footpads don't usually go there during the day."

He thought for a moment, and then nodded. "Oh, very well. The last thing I want now is another disagreement with you. Just be very careful, and promise me that if you see anyone in the tunnel when you enter, you will come back to the house immediately."

"I promise."

"*À bientôt,* my dear."

"*À bientôt,* Father."

When he had gone, she looked out of the window again. He was right to want her to accept Brandon, whose faithful interest in her had not wavered, in spite of her passionate desertion to Piers. Poor Brandon, he was as foolish to want her as she had been to want Piers. Brandon was everything any woman could wish for, charming, amiable, wealthy, and understanding, but he was nothing at all if that woman was in love with the likes of Sir Piers Sutherland.

An ironical smile came to her lips, for where Piers was concerned, she had been the greatest of gulls. From the moment she had looked into his warm gray eyes, she had been lost beyond redemption, and when he had whispered her first name, he had robbed her of all caution. He was tall, golden-haired, and heart-stoppingly handsome, but behind all his charm he was a cruel womanizer who had thought nothing of betraying her with Elizabeth Lavery, a shameless demimondaine with a list of admirers that included a large portion of the aristocracy.

Finding out about his liaison with Elizabeth had been the most painful and humiliating moment of Marianne's life, for she had been foolish enough to love and trust him completely. She had ended their betrothal, but she had never stopped loving him. It was a love she now kept well hidden, however, for even thinking about him made her eyes sting with tears. They were stinging now, and if she did not keep herself firmly composed, she would give in and start to cry. There were nights when she wept into her pillow for what she had lost, because she knew she would never love again the way she'd loved then. With Piers there had been sweet abandonment, heady desire, and a stirring excitement from just being next to him. His touch had electrified her, and his kisses had melted her soul. After a love like that, everything else became pale, and could only be second best. Did poor Brandon deserve that?

She thought about him for a moment. They had known each other since childhood, for their families' estates adjoined each other in Cheshire, and as they'd grown up, a match between them had seemed the most obvious thing. Except that she had begun to regard him as a brother, and one simply did not marry one's brother. She had allowed herself to be swept along, and Brandon had quite obviously wanted to marry her, but then, just as the betrothal was about to take place, Piers had entered her life.

She had broken Brandon's heart, and for that she felt endlessly guilty, especially as he had forgiven her and made every effort to maintain their friendship. Whenever he was in London he called upon her, and if she was in Cheshire, then he frequently rode over to see her. She had thought that by now he would have accepted that they should simply remain close friends, but it seemed that he still carried a torch for her. And now Father was determined to conclude the business that had been interrupted two years before. Was she wrong to draw back from marrying Brandon? Maybe they would be perfect together. The Forresters, Father, and Brandon himself evidently thought so, and maybe she was the only one who was out of step.

Turning from the window, she gave a sigh. The match would have to be thought about very carefully indeed, but for the moment she had to call upon Chloe. She glanced down at the card, smiling at the plump cherubs and pierced hearts. She had labored over it, just as she had labored over its predecessor two years ago. She had given the first card to Piers on Saint Valentine's Day, 1815. By the same day the following year, she had discovered his unfaithfulness. In a few more weeks it would be Saint Valentine's Day again. Should she celebrate it this time by finally accepting Brandon?

Holding the card close, she hurried from the room to change.

Mr. Cromwell had yet to depart when she and her maid emerged into the snow shortly afterward. Marianne wore a fur-trimmed crimson velvet cloak over a white fustian gown, and beneath her hood her russet curls were pinned up into a Grecian knot. There were ankle boots on her feet, and her hands were deep in a warm fur muff. The valentine card reposed in a large reticule looped over her arm.

She and the maid trod with great care past the Cromwell town carriage waiting at the curb, and then went over the slippery street toward Lansdowne Passage. There was ice on the cobbles beneath the snow, making everything very treacherous indeed, and when they reached the steps leading down into the tunnel, they took extra care not to lose their footing. At the bottom of the steps, they paused to look along the passage to the other entrance in Curzon Street. There was no one else there, and so they began to walk along it, still taking care because there was more ice in places. Beneath the flagstones they could hear trickling water, for the River Tyburn passed under the tunnel.

When they were halfway along, a man suddenly entered the tunnel from the opposite direction. Marianne's steps faltered in alarm, but then she realized that it was a gentleman. He was dressed fashionably, in an ankle-length greatcoat and tall hat, and there was a cane swinging casually in his gloved hand. Spurs jingled from the heels of his Hessian boots as he walked, and the sound carried clearly along the passage to the two women as they continued toward him.

The closer they drew, the more Marianne thought there was something familiar about him. She was convinced that she knew him, but it wasn't until they were only a few yards apart that she realized with a dreadful jolt that it was none other than Piers.

Her breath caught and she stopped, staring at him as if at a ghost. She had thought him thousands of miles away in America, not here in London. Seeing him again so suddenly took her completely by surprise, and robbed her of the wit to do anything except stand and stare at him.

Beside her, the maid had halted as well, glancing nervously from her to Piers, and then back again. The girl had only been with Marianne for a few weeks, and so knew nothing of Sir Piers Sutherland or his significance in her mistress's past.

At last Piers recognized Marianne, and the cane became still in his hand as he too halted. His remembered gray eyes swept briefly over her, and then met her unsettled gaze, before he removed his tall hat and inclined his head.

"It's been a long time, Marianne," he murmured.

The sound of his voice cut through her like a knife, and looking into his eyes was like looking into lost happiness. How handsome he still was, and how golden his hair, even in the shadows of the passage.

Her silence seemed to amuse him. "Are you snubbing me, Marianne? Or does your muteness merely signify your inability to choose which blistering response to employ?"

At last she found her tongue. "I didn't know you were in England," she said, knowing that her voice was trembling.

"I came back a week ago."

"I trust you mean to leave again soon."

He raised an eyebrow, still amused. "I'm cut to the quick by the warmth of your welcome."

"You surely did not expect me to smile sweetly and

tell you I'm delighted to see you again?" Except that I *am* delighted to see you, because I'm still fool enough to love you. . . .

The cane swung idly to and fro in his hand. "Well, I had hoped we could at least be civil now."

"The past cannot be lightly forgotten."

"So it seems."

She held his gaze. "Did you truly think I would forgive and forget?"

"I had hoped you would."

"Then I fear I must disappoint you, sir, for I am not that noble." Oh, liar, liar! You want him still; you want him with all your silly heart.

"I don't ask you to be noble, merely civil."

"I cannot be that, either."

"I'm sorry to hear it." He studied her. "I'm told that you have still not married, and I confess to being surprised. I thought that you and Forrester would have tied the knot by now."

"Not yet."

"So you're still considering him? I wondered if your unmarried state signified—"

"A bleeding heart on your account? I'm sorry to disappoint you, sir," she interrupted.

"You've become sharp-tongued, Marianne."

"Only with you, sir, and for that you have yourself to blame."

"Do I?"

"You know it, Piers. You deceived me with that . . . that . . ."

"Woman of ill repute?" he supplied dryly.

"Yes."

"It was a sin I more than paid for."

"*Paid* for?" she cried, amazed at his hypocrisy. How dared he pretend to have suffered in any way, when *she* was the one who'd been made a fool of and humiliated. All he had endured was a succession of nights in the arms of his infamous demirep! His arrogance now was insufferable.

Unable to bear it a moment longer, she made to hurry on past him, but she forgot the ice, and in her anger was unwary. Her boot slid from beneath her, and her ankle twisted agonizingly. With a cry of pain she began to fall, but with great presence of mind he caught her around the waist.

The pain was so great that for a moment she almost passed out. Her face was drained of color, and it was all she could do to cling weakly to him.

"It's all right. I have you," he said, holding her firmly.

She closed her eyes as another agonizing stab rushed hotly through her.

He glanced down at her pallor, and immediately swept her up into his arms, his cane falling unheeded to the flagstones. "I'll carry you home," he said, beginning to walk toward the steps leading up to Berkeley Street.

"No . . . !" She tried to pull away.

"Don't be foolish, Marianne. You can't possibly walk on an ankle you've just twisted badly. You may not want me to help you, but I'm afraid you're just going to have to put up with it."

She fought back tears of pain and frustration, but had no option but to link her arms around his neck, and allow him to carry her home.

The maid picked up his cane from the floor, and then hurried after them. As they reached the top of the steps she went ahead of them, rousing the household to action. By the time Piers had carried Marianne into the entrance hall, a running footman had already been dispatched to bring the doctor.

Mr. Cromwell was waiting anxiously inside, and he stared in astonishment when he saw who was carrying his injured daughter into the house. "You?"

"Yes, sir. Me, sir," Piers replied, laying Marianne

down carefully on the sofa before the hall fire, and then straightening to look at her father. "Do not concern yourself unduly, sir, for I assure you that I am as intent upon leaving again as you are to see me go." Bowing, he turned on his heel and strode from the house, snatching up his cane from a table as he went.

Marianne managed to hold back the tears until the door had closed behind him, but then she hid her face in her hands, her shoulders trembling as she began to sob. All the heartache and wretchedness of the past was with her again, as was the full force of her love. For a long and unhappy year she had striven to come to terms with what had happened, but now she was back at the beginning again, as if his betrayal had taken place only yesterday.

As dusk fell that afternoon, it began to snow lightly again, and from her candlelit bedroom at the rear of the house, Marianne could see the flakes drifting slowly past the balcony and through the bare branches of the walnut tree against the wall.

She was propped up in her four-poster bed, with her hair brushed loose about the shoulders of her ribboned nightgown. She had a huge mound of pillows, between which soothing muslin bags of lavender had been slipped, and she had just been persuaded by her maid to drink another infusion of valerian and honey. The doctor had earlier prescribed a compress of comfrey root for her ankle, and had warned her that it would be at least a week before she would be able to walk comfortably again.

Her father had sat with her for most of the afternoon, but had gone downstairs now because a friend had called upon him. Her maid was tidying the dressing table.

A fire flickered in the hearth, sending dancing shadows over the blue-and-white-striped walls, and the golden ormulu clock on the mantelpiece chimed sweetly.

Marianne stared out at the gathering darkness. The sunset had been magnificent, a glory of crimson and gold in a frozen sky. A true February sunset. But the snow clouds had crept in from the east, seeming almost to have been stealthy in their approach, as if they wished to catch London unprepared.

Marianne's lips twisted wryly. Being caught unprepared had been her speciality today. Oh, plague take Piers for having returned, for it made consideration of the match with Brandon all that much more difficult. And plague take her own foolishness, not only for still being vulnerable to Piers, but also for being so clumsy as to slip on the ice and wrench her ankle like this.

The maid went to draw the curtains at the French doors that gave onto the balcony, and as she did so she gave a startled gasp. "Miss Marianne! Someone is climbing up the tree!" she cried.

Marianne's lips parted and her eyes widened. Only one person had ever climbed that tree. Surely it couldn't be . . . ? As she looked, a shadowy figure clambered over the edge of the balcony. She saw in a moment that it was Piers.

The maid gave a squeak of alarm, and turned to hurry from the room, but he had come inside before she reached the door, and his gray eyes went swiftly and warningly to Marianne. "Arouse the whole house if you wish, but I will swear I came by invitation."

She put out a hand to halt the maid. "Wait!"

"But Miss Marianne!"

"He means it, and I have my reputation to consider." Marianne looked at him. "How dare you come here like this, sirrah! How *dare* you!"

"I dare because things must be clarified between us," he replied, tossing his top hat and gloves down upon the dressing table, and then removing his heavy Polish greatcoat. Beneath it he wore an indigo coat and cream kerseymere trousers. His gilt spurs jingled slightly as he moved, and the tassels at the front of his Hessian boots swung from side to side. There was a sapphire pin in the folds of his neckcloth, and it flashed in the candlelight as he faced her. "Marianne, I don't want to be at odds with you, and I apologize for climbing up to your bedroom like this, but I thought it was probably the only way I'd manage to speak to you. Would you have received me had I called at the front door?"

"No."

"Then my audacity was justified."

"Justified? Piers, you may think things need clarifying between us, but as far as I'm concerned they are already crystal clear. I don't want to have anything more to do with you. You hurt me far too much for that."

He came to the foot of the bed. "I know, and I am truly sorry."

"Are you? I doubt that very much."

"I *am* sorry, Marianne, whether you choose to believe it or not, and all I want now is to be sure that any future encounters we may have will not be as vitriolic and disagreeable as that which took place today in Lansdowne Passage. I said then that I hoped we could be civil to each other, and that is still my wish. I don't think it is a great deal to ask, especially as we are bound to meet socially."

"Provided I accept invitations, or indeed choose to go out at all."

He searched her face. "Do you hate me so much that you would prefer to imprison yourself indoors rather than risk seeing me?"

She didn't reply. Hate him? Oh, if only he knew the sorry truth!

He breathed out slowly. "I really am sorry for my past actions, Marianne, but what was done was done, and now we have to go on. Can't we at least show ourselves capable of conducting ourselves with decorum from now on?"

"I will be polite if we meet, sir, but I would prefer it if we both did everything in our power to avoid each other." I'm going to deny you the chance to hurt me any more than absolutely necessary.

"As you wish." He turned away from her, and as he did his glance went to something on the dressing table. It was the valentine card, which had been put out in readiness to give to Chloe, who had sent word that she would call later to see how Marianne was.

Marianne's gaze followed his, and her heart sank in dismay. Would he recognize the design? Please, don't let him . . .

Picking the card up, he studied it for a moment and then looked at her. "Is this for Forrester?" he asked.

"No. Actually I've made it for a friend of mine to give to her sweetheart." Marianne's cheeks were aflame.

The faintest of smiles played fleetingly upon his lips as he replaced the card. "I'm relieved to hear it, for it wouldn't do for Forrester to be as honored as I was."

"He would deserve it more."

"I think not."

She met his gaze squarely. "What a shabby valentine you were, putting your ring upon my finger, and then taking yourself off to Elizabeth Lavery's bountiful charms."

"It wasn't as simple as that."

"As far as I'm concerned, it was every bit as simple as that."

"Marianne, I—"

He broke off, for the maid, who was still by the door, gave a sudden gasp. "Miss Marianne, your father is coming!"

Marianne's heart sank with dismay, and she looked imploringly at Piers. "Please go!"

For the space of a heartbeat he gazed into her eyes, but then he turned to snatch up his things and step out onto the balcony. The maid ran to close the French doors behind him, and drew the curtains just as Mr. Cromwell tapped at the bedroom door and came in.

Later that evening a carriage drew up at the curb in Berkeley Street, and Miss Chloe Pendeven alighted. She wore a fuchsia-pink pelisse and matching gown, and there were ostrich plumes springing from her pretty gray silk hat. Her hair was the color of honey, she had a flawless complexion unmarred by a single freckle, and her eyes were wide and blue. Since her arrival from her father's immense estate in the Forest of Dean, she had become justifiably acknowledged as one of London's most beautiful young women. Her admirers among the gentlemen were legion, as were her friends among the ladies, but Marianne was her closest confidante, and the two had become inseparable over the past six months.

She was shown directly up to the bedroom, and Marianne gave a glad smile as she entered.

"Chloe! Oh, it's good to see you."

Chloe hurried to the bedside and took her hands. "Poor you. How are you feeling?" she asked, sitting down on the blue-and-white coverlet and looking concernedly into Marianne's eyes.

"I'm furious with myself for not taking more care," Marianne replied. She had decided not to say anything about Piers, not because she didn't trust Chloe, but rather because she was afraid she'd give herself away if she spoke about him. She gave a bright smile. "Now then, what was it you summoned me for so urgently earlier today?"

Chloe released her hands, and then sat more comfortably. "Actually there are two things, but first of all I must know how on earth you came to grief today.

I know that you twisted your ankle, but that is all I know."

"I was on my way to see you as planned, and I slipped on the ice in Lansdowne Passage."

Chloe searched her face suspiciously. "And that is all?"

"Yes. Why?"

"Because I know when you are keeping something from me. Something happened in Lansdowne Passage, didn't it?"

"No."

"Fibber. Tell me, for if you don't, I will only keep on and on until you do."

Marianne lowered her eyes. "I'd rather not talk about it."

"You're upset, and I want to help if I can."

"You can't help. No one can." The temptation to confide suddenly swept over Marianne. "You know that I was once betrothed to Sir Piers Sutherland?"

"Yes."

"Well, I thought he was still in America, but he's here in London, and I bumped into him in Lansdowne Passage. We . . . had words, and I was so angry that I quite forgot the ice and slipped."

There was a rather odd expression on Chloe's face. "Your tone would seem to suggest that you haven't forgiven him for what happened."

"Forgiven him? Certainly not. He actually had the gall to imply that *he* had suffered on account of it."

"Perhaps he did. Perhaps he regrets it all now."

"That's what he says, but it's all very well to be apologetic after the event. He said sweet words to me, and then bedded the most expensive doxy in London."

Chloe was taken aback by such frankness. "Marianne!"

"Well, it's true. He did bed her. That Lavery creature is a *belle de nuit,* and he was pleased to add himself to her legendary list of lovers. No one requested him to do it, no one forced him or threatened

him, he chose to climb into her amazingly accommo-
dating bed. Suffer? Him? No, he didn't endure anything at all, but I was made unutterably wretched and
unhappy, and I will never *ever* forgive him."

Chloe was startled by her vehemence. "I . . . I had
no idea you still felt so strongly about it."

"Oh, it's just the fact that I've seen him again.
Twice in one day." As she said this last, Marianne
could have bitten off her tongue, for the visit to her
bedroom was most definitely not for further transmission.

But it was too late. "Twice in one day?" Chloe
repeated.

Marianne pressed her lips together, angry with herself all over again.

Chloe looked intently at her. "You may as well tell
me, for I will only be like the proverbial dog with the
proverbial bone."

Marianne drew a long breath. "Earlier this evening,
he climbed up the walnut tree to this room."

Chloe blinked. "He what?"

"I'm not repeating it."

"He actually climbed up to your balcony?"

"Yes, but not in the finest romantic tradition, I assure you. He merely wished to ensure that in future
I would be civil to him. And he wished to say that he
was sorry for the past."

"That is surely something, isn't it? Well, isn't it?"

"Oh, Chloe, I'm sure that he only wishes to be
certain of avoiding an uncomfortable scene in some
fashionable drawing room. No doubt he doesn't wish
the world to recall the cause of our parting."

"You aren't very reasonable where he is concerned,
are you?"

"No, and it isn't surprising, given his actions, past
and present."

Chloe was silent for a moment. "Marianne, are you
quite sure it is over between you? I mean—"

"It's most definitely over," Marianne interrupted

quickly. "He feels nothing for me, and I despise him. That is the end of it. Besides, I'm now considering another match."

Chloe was astonished. "Another match? You sly boots, why haven't you mentioned this before?"

"Because I only knew about it today myself. It isn't another match, exactly, but rather an old one revitalized. It's with Brandon Forrester."

"I see." Chloe lowered her gaze for a moment.

"Father is quite determined that I will accept this time."

"And will you?"

"I've promised to think about it. Oh, enough of me, let's talk about you instead. What were those two things you wished to discuss?"

"There is only one thing."

Marianne was surprised. "But you said there were two."

"Did I? I can't imagine why." Chloe shifted a little uncomfortably.

"Chloe, is something wrong?"

"Er, no. Actually, as far as *I* am concerned, everything is wonderful. Well, nearly wonderful."

"How can something be nearly wonderful?" Marianne asked, smiling.

"When one is head over heels in love, but one's father is set against a match."

Marianne stared at her. "Tell me about it."

"I've met a gentleman who means everything to me, and I'm more in love than I ever dreamed possible. You know him socially, and I fear you won't approve any more than father does."

"Why? Who is he?"

"Jerry Frobisher."

Marianne's eyes widened. "*The* Jerry Frobisher?"

"I'm afraid so."

Marianne was dismayed, for Sir Jeremy Frobisher's high spirits were always getting him into one fix or another, and his luck at the gaming tables was nothing short of phenomenal.

Chloe looked defiantly at her. "I know what you're thinking, but you're wrong. And so is Father."

"Chloe, Jerry Frobisher's name is a positive byword in society."

"It *was* a byword. Marianne, he's a reformed character now, and all he wants is to make me happy."

"Leopards do not change their spots."

"They do, Marianne. In fact, a surprising number of them do," Chloe added a little mysteriously.

"What do you mean by that?"

"Oh, nothing." Chloe looked at her again. "We are deeply in love, Marianne, and he means it when he says he has changed his ways, but as soon as I mentioned him to Father, there was a dreadful fuss."

"I can imagine."

"Jerry isn't after me for my inheritance, Marianne, for he has ample fortune of his own, and he has won far more at the gaming tables than he has ever lost."

"That much is true," Marianne conceded.

"Anyway, the outcome is that Father is now taking me home to Severn Park, in order to separate me from Jerry."

"Oh, Chloe . . ."

"I'm so low about it all, Marianne, for in the space of only a week or so my whole world has been turned upside down."

"Yes. So who is the sly boots now, mm?" Marianne leaned over to put a comforting hand on her friend's. "How did you meet him?"

"At a ball at Devonshire House about three weeks ago. We danced a waltz, and that was that." Chloe smiled ruefully. "I've never danced such a wonderful waltz before."

"And now you're sunk?"

"Shipwrecked completely."

"To the point of wishing to give him the most adoring valentine imaginable?" Marianne pointed to the card on the dressing table.

Chloe got up quickly and went to examine it. "Oh, Marianne, it's quite perfect! And the verse is just right. You're so clever, much more clever than I will ever be. It's almost as if you were me."

Marianne looked away, for if the card and its sentiments were the result of her own foolish love two years before, then of course it was perfect for Chloe's situation now. But maybe Chloe's love for Jerry Frobisher wasn't foolish, maybe he had turned over a new leaf and was all that Chloe believed him to be.

"Chloe, are you quite sure Jerry has mended his ways?"

"Oh, beyond all shadow of doubt."

Marianne smiled. "Then I wish you every happiness, and if I can help in any way, you have only to ask."

"I wish you could help, for my father likes you immensely, and actually pays attention to what you have to say."

"I'm flattered to know it, but I doubt if he pays that much attention."

Chloe stared at her, as if some brilliant notion had suddenly occurred to her.

Marianne was uneasy. "What is it, Chloe?"

"I think I have an idea which may solve everything."

"What idea?"

"I can't say anything yet, not until I've spoken to Father. If I hurry home now, I'll catch him before he goes out to dine at his club. I'll call upon you again in the morning. Oh, and I'll bring Jerry with me, so that you can judge for yourself what he is like now."

"Chloe—"

But Chloe had already gathered her fuchsia skirts and hurried from the room, the valentine card clutched tightly to her breast.

Marianne stared after her, wondering what on earth this sudden idea could be.

There was sunshine the next morning, and the snow sparkled beneath a clear blue sky. Marianne's ankle was still painful and swollen, but she refused to languish in bed, and so sat by the fire instead. Her maid had pinned her hair up on top of her head, with soft curls framing her face, and she wore a peach dimity gown with a warm cashmere shawl over her arms.

Her father was not at home when Chloe arrived, and as promised, brought Jerry Frobisher with her. They were shown directly up to Marianne's room, but Jerry lingered uneasily in the doorway, unsure of the reception he might receive.

He was of medium height and athletic build, with dark hair and brown eyes, and he was very good-looking, although not in the same arresting mold as Piers. His fashionable coat was sky-blue, and his tight-fitting trousers gray, and there was a pearl pin on the knot of his starched muslin cravat.

Chloe hastened toward Marianne in a flurry of lime-green bombazine. "How are you this morning?"

"My ankle is still complaining quite considerably, but the rest of me is very well," Marianne replied with a smile, her glance moving toward the doorway. "Good morning, Sir Jeremy."

"Good morning, Miss Cromwell."

Chloe turned to hold her hand out to him. "Come, Jerry, for Marianne is our ally in this."

Marianne's heart sank a little. Their ally in what, exactly? Please don't let Chloe have dreamed up something that would lead to a scrape.

Holding his hand, Chloe returned her attention to Marianne. "Have you decided about the Forrester match?" she asked suddenly.

Marianne was a little taken aback at such an unexpected and direct question. "No, not yet."

"Then I think my little plan will give you an excellent opportunity to consider it all at leisure."

"Oh?"

"You will recall that I said yesterday I'd had an idea which might solve everything?"

"Yes, I remember," Marianne replied cautiously.

"I had to speak to Father first, of course, for I knew he would be opposed to it, but after a great deal of sobbing, wheedling, and pleading on my part, he eventually gave in and agreed. Marianne, when Father and I return to Severn Park, you must accompany us, and what is more, Jerry and another gentleman will join us there."

Marianne stared at her. "Your father agreed to that?"

"Yes. You see, we will be there for Saint Valentine's Day, and I reminded him that he and Mother were married on that day, and that they were only able to do so after a great deal of opposition from Mother's family, who thought him far too much older than she was. I said that it was unfair of him to condemn Jerry out of hand, without first having taken the time to get to know him, and I said that you were in favor of Jerry."

"You did? But Chloe, I don't really know Sir Jeremy." Marianne looked apologetically at him. "Forgive me, sir, but it's true. We've met socially, but I can hardly say that I know you, can I?"

"Er, no. Not really," he agreed, glancing at Chloe.

Chloe had no intention of allowing such minor details to stand in the way of her grand plan. "Marianne, it was your comment which gave me the idea in the first place. You said that if there was anything you could do to help, then you had only to be asked. I'm asking now."

"Yes, but—"

"If you are there at Severn Park with us, you will be able to work upon my father."

"Work upon him? Chloe, you credit me with far more influence than I actually possess."

"Father thinks you very sensible and reliable, Marianne, and that is what counts. All I wish you to do is praise Jerry whenever the opportunity arises."

"You make me sound like a jack-in-the-box. Whenever Sir Jeremy is mentioned, out I pop with my eulogy at the ready. Your father isn't going to be convinced in the least."

"He will be, because you will mean what you say," Chloe declared.

"But I've already explained that I don't know Sir Jeremy," Marianne repeated patiently.

"All you need to know is that he is a new man, that he loves me, and that we should be allowed to marry with my father's consent."

There was no mistaking Chloe's desperation to have her way in this, and so Marianne looked appraisingly at Sir Jeremy. "*Are* you a reformed character, sir?" she asked.

He shifted his feet awkwardly. "Yes, I am, Miss Cromwell, for I love Chloe more than I ever dreamed it was possible to love. My bad old ways are behind me now, and all I want is to be able to make her my bride. It is important to her that she has her father's blessing, and so I am prepared to do anything she wishes in order to bring that about."

"Would it not be simpler to elope?" Marianne inquired bluntly, deciding to test him.

Chloe was dismayed. "Marianne!"

Marianne ignored her, but kept her gaze firmly upon Sir Jeremy. "Well, sir? Why don't you persuade Chloe to run away to Gretna Green with you?"

"Because she wishes to have her father's blessing," he replied. "Her happiness is what counts, Miss Cromwell, and so an elopement of any kind is quite out of the question."

Marianne continued to hold his gaze, trying to assess him. His replies were more than gallant and satisfactory, and in spite of her doubts about his character, she could not help liking the candor in his eyes. Yes, Sir Jeremy Frobisher was a new man. She smiled then. "You have my support in your suit, sir."

Chloe gave a squeak of delight, and bent to hug Marianne as tightly as she could. "I knew you'd approve of him, Marianne!" she cried.

Marianne hugged her in return. "I'm sorry to have asked about an elopement, but I thought I would learn a lot about Sir Jeremy from his response."

Chloe positively glowed as she straightened and went to take Jerry's hand again.

Marianne thought of something. "Who is the gentleman who is to come too?" she asked. "Do I know him?"

"Maxwell Odrington," Chloe replied.

"Maxwell Codrington," Jerry answered at exactly the same time.

Chloe gave him a look. "It's Odrington, Jerry," she pointed out.

"Eh? Oh, yes. I'm afraid I'm always getting it wrong."

Marianne glanced curiously from one to the other, for there was something distinctly odd in their manner. But what could be odd about it? Maxwell Odrington was her second cousin, and she had always liked him. They had been paired off in the past to make up numbers, especially at dinner parties, and they were on very amicable terms. She looked at Jerry. "Are you and Maxwell well acquainted, Sir Jeremy?"

"Oh, yes. We go back years."

She wondered how it could be that he still made a mistake about the name of someone he'd known for years, but she said nothing more.

Chloe swiftly moved on to the traveling arrangements. "We will leave in a week's time, Marianne, and Jerry and Maxwell will follow within a day or so.

We should all be there just before Saint Valentine's
Day. I understand that Maxwell has affairs to attend
to which prevent him leaving with us. Your ankle will
be better by then, won't it?"

"I sincerely hope so," Marianne replied with feeling.

"Good. I mean to make it quite impossible for Father to reasonably withhold his consent for me to
marry Jerry. Everything must go smoothly, without so
much as the tiniest ripple to spoil it. I want Father to
find the whole visit an exceeding gracious and civilized
affair."

Marianne smiled. "Which it will be, since we are
all gracious and civilized beings," she said.

Chloe bit her lip ruefully. "You know what I mean.
I want it all to be special, and so you and Maxwell
must get on well throughout your stay."

"Maxwell and I always get on well," Marianne
pointed out, but then a thought occurred to her. "Actually, I was under the impression that Maxwell was
in Scotland at the moment."

Jerry shook his head. "Oh, no, for I was with him
at his lodgings in Conduit Street only yesterday."

Chloe cleared her throat. "Brook Street. His lodgings are in Brook Street," she said.

"Er, isn't that what I said? Yes, of course they are
in Brook Street."

Marianne was perplexed, for there was definitely
something strange in their conduct. But why on earth
would that be? The most obvious explanation was simply that Jerry was still nervous about being on trial,
so to speak. Yes, it had to be something like that,
for why else would he stumble over facts which quite
patently must be well known to him?

Chloe was at pains to smooth the moment over.
"Oh, Jerry, your memory is quite atrocious at times.
I vow you might one day forget to turn up at the
church."

He smiled. "That is something I will never forget

to do," he murmured, putting his hand briefly to her cheek.

Chloe's fingers closed fleetingly over his, and then she turned as there was a tap at the door. Marianne's maid came in with another infusion of valerian and honey for her mistress.

Chloe decided it was time she and Jerry took their leave. "We'll go now, Marianne, for I don't wish to tire you out and delay your recovery. That wouldn't do at all! I'll call again tomorrow, you may be sure of that."

"It was good to see you, Chloe. And you, Sir Jeremy." Marianne smiled at him.

He stepped forward to take her hand and raise it to his lips. "Chloe and I will be eternally grateful to you, Miss Cromwell."

"And to Maxwell," she pointed out.

"Eh? Oh, yes, and to Maxwell, of course."

Chloe took his arm and steered him toward the door. "Until tomorrow, Marianne."

"Until then."

They withdrew, and the maid advanced with the valerian and honey. Marianne pulled a face at it.

Outside, as their carriage drew away, Chloe and Jerry exchanged secretive smiles. Chloe looked well pleased with herself, and ignored her maid, who tried to appear invisible in a corner seat. "It's going excellently, is it not?" she said.

"It would appear to be."

"No thanks to your memory, sir."

"I promise to do better from now on."

"I trust so, or you may prove our undoing."

He reached across to take her hands. "You may count upon me to carry it off handsomely, my darling," he murmured, pulling her gently toward him.

She came willingly, and their lips met in a long, sweet kiss.

An unwilling observer, the maid felt her cheeks grow warm, and she turned her attention determinedly upon the street. She wondered what Mr. Pendeven would have said had he seen his daughter's conduct at this moment.

On the afternoon before the planned departure for Severn Park and the distant Forest of Dean, Marianne decided it would be sensible to exercise her ankle, to be certain that it was strong again. A leisurely stroll around nearby Berkeley Square seemed the obvious thing, and so at three o'clock precisely, she and her maid set off north along Berkeley Street.

Marianne wore rose poplin, a tightly belted pelisse over a matching gown, and there was a filmy rose gauze scarf trailing from her cream silk jockey bonnet. She wore cream leather ankle boots, and her hands were warm in a green velvet muff.

The snow had gone now, and the February sun was almost warm. Carriages bowled elegantly past, their glossy teams stepping high, and close to the southeastern corner of the square, the calls of a young flower girl echoed over the cobbles as she sold posies of snowdrops picked fresh in the countryside that morning.

Berkeley Square was very beautiful, with fine brown brick houses, and a railed garden in the center. The garden was surrounded by plane trees, and was presided over by an equestrian statue of the king as Marcus Aurelius. The statue was not a success, for it was made of lead, and was far too heavy for the horse's legs, with the result that they bowed alarmingly at the knees, but it was placed in a small paved area where there were shrubs and a bench, and it was to this bench that Marianne and the maid repaired after completing a circuit of the square.

They sat facing Gunter's, whose famous confectionery and cream ices were much sought after in summertime, when it was the thing for gentlemen to bring the ices to their ladies, who sat in open carriages beneath the leafy plane trees. The trees were bare now, and in such weather it wasn't at all the thing to eat ices, but a constant stream of carriages arrived and departed as society sampled the other delights Gunter's created.

Marianne's thoughts were upon the forthcoming stay at Severn Park, and whether or not she had instructed her maid to pack everything she would require. She wasn't looking at anything in particular, just gazing around in general, and so it was that her wandering glance fell upon a stylish yellow cabriolet drawn up at the curb in front of a house a little to the north of Gunter's.

It was a very dashing vehicle drawn by a single black horse, and was in the care of one of the small liveried grooms known as tigers, who perched on tiny seats at the rear when their masters were at the reins. The door of the house opened, and the tiger turned swiftly, as if in expectation. Seeing the gentleman who emerged, the tiger touched his cap, and prepared to give the reins to him.

Belatedly, Marianne remembered that the house was the residence of Piers' uncle, for it was Piers himself who had come out to the waiting cabriolet. He was dressed in a dark brown coat and white cord trousers, and he paused for a moment to tease on his kid gloves and then put his hat on. As he did so, something made him look directly toward the bench, almost as if he had felt Marianne's steady gaze. He hesitated, and then shook his head at the tiger before crossing the road toward the garden.

She thought about hurriedly getting up and walking away, but that would have been childish, and so she remained reluctantly where she was.

He removed his hat as he reached the bench, and the sunlight was vivid upon his golden hair. "Good afternoon, Marianne."

"Good afternoon, sir."

His gray eyes flickered. "Still as frosty as ever?"

"Civility was what was agreed upon. No more and no less."

"Ah, yes, so it was," he murmured with a sigh. "I trust that it is in order to politely inquire after your ankle?"

"It is in order, sir, but I would prefer it in future if you addressed me by my surname." She was amazed at how cool and collected she sounded, for inside she was in turmoil.

"As you wish," he replied a little stiffly. "My purpose in approaching you now is simply to inform you that I will shortly be leaving London for my estates in Yorkshire, and so you will not need to fear encountering me again."

"I am leaving town myself," she answered.

"Ah, yes, no doubt you are. Marriage contracts require much attention, do they not?"

"Marriage contracts?"

"That is why you're going, isn't it?"

"Nothing has been settled yet, sir."

"But I understood from your father that it was virtually signed and sealed with Forrester."

She was surprised. "You've spoken to my father?"

"We, er, came face-to-face at our mutual club. It wasn't exactly an agreeable meeting, but endured long enough for him to inform me with some alacrity that your future with Forrester was now certain."

"My father is anticipating somewhat, sir, for I have yet to make up my mind."

"Indeed? Well, I'm sure your father's eagerness is understandable, for he always espoused Forrester's cause against mine."

"That isn't so, sir. My father merely wishes me to be happy."

"Something he was sure I would not make you."

His eyes were very gray in the sunlight, almost as if he could see into her soul.

She had to look away. "He was right, was he not?" she murmured.

A wry smile touched his lips, and he didn't respond.

Marianne rose to her feet. "I think we have been civil for long enough, don't you?" She found it unbearable to be so close to him without reaching out. She wanted to touch him, to be in his arms, to be kissed, to be coaxed into submission. . . . Treacherous feelings threatened to take over, and a telltale blush began to seep into her otherwise pale cheeks. She had to get away from him, for if he should realize how she really felt, she would be humiliated and crushed all over again.

As she began to walk away, followed by the maid, he called after her. "I wish you well should you accept Forrester, Miss Cromwell, and I trust that you will be equally as generous in your response to news of my betrothal."

She halted, and whirled about. "Your betrothal?"

"Yes."

A hot knife cut through her. "Then . . . then of course I wish you well. Do I know the lady concerned?"

"You do."

"Who is she?"

He smiled a little. "I fear there are obstacles to naming her just yet."

She looked at him. "Obstacles, sir? Surely it cannot be that you have been caught in unfaithfulness a second time? How very careless of you."

"How typical of you to leap to that particular conclusion, Marianne."

"One speaks as one finds," she replied.

"Such sourness does not become you, Marianne," he said softly. "I preferred you as you were."

"A gullible fool?"

"A sweet, loving, adorable creature, whose trust I unwisely forfeited," he corrected.

She stared at him, and then gathered her skirts to hurry from the garden toward Berkeley Street. After a moment, her maid hastened after her.

Piers watched them go. His gaze followed them until the last flutter of Marianne's gauze scarf as she vanished from his view. Then he tugged on his hat, and strode across the garden to his waiting cabriolet. He seized the reins and vaulted into the seat, flinging the horse forward almost before the tiger had had time to clamber on to his perch at the back. The yellow vehicle skimmed around the square and then turned north toward Oxford Street.

The horse flew over the cobbles, and Piers handled the ribbons like the expert he was, but his driving was almost automatic, for his thoughts were all of Marianne.

"Damn you, Marianne Cromwell," he breathed. "Damn you to perdition and back!"

London was far behind as Mr. Pendeven's traveling carriage drove west toward Gloucestershire and the Forest of Dean. A second carriage followed, conveying their luggage, maids, and a valet. The weather was still fine and sunny, and all trace of the recent snow had gone, even from the hilltops.

The carriage's three occupants had made themselves as comfortable as possible for the journey, with rugs over their knees and warmed bricks in cloth beneath their feet, for in spite of the sunshine, it was still February and still cold.

Mr. Charles Pendeven, Chloe's widowed father, had nodded off to sleep, his head lolling against the brown leather upholstery. He was a tall, rather gaunt man, with receding sandy hair and a Roman nose, and when his eyes were open, they were a watery blue. He was well wrapped against the winter, with a coat that boasted numerous shoulder capes, and a scarf that was wound several times around his neck. His hands were pushed into a fur muff of immense proportions, and even in his sleep he was conscious of the motion of the carriage gradually causing the rug over his knees to slide off, and he put a hand out from the muff to retrieve it.

Marianne and Chloe were respectively bright and modish in yellow trimmed with ermine, and crimson with plaid accessories, and were never at a loss for something to talk about. They conversed happily on subjects ranging from fashion and etiquette to scandalous whispers and even about whether or not the Prince Regent would ever be reconciled with his loathed wife, Princess Caroline of Brunswick. But it was of the marriage of the royal pair's only child, Princess Charlotte, that they were talking when Mr. Pendeven was at last aroused from his slumbering.

Chloe was sighing over the romantic good looks of the princess's new husband, Prince Leopold. "He is so handsome," she breathed. "And with those dark, dark eyes, he quite puts me at sixes and sevens when he looks at me."

Mr. Pendeven sat up quickly, thinking that she was speaking of Jerry. "Eh? What's that? Look here, Chloe, m'dear, I know I've allowed myself to be cajoled into this dashed difficult stay, but if you imagine I am going to permit you and young Frobisher to make sheep's eyes at each other, you are gravely mistaken."

Chloe colored. "Father, I wasn't talking about Jerry but about Prince Leopold."

"Oh." Mr. Pendeven gave a rather scathing grunt. "That dry prig? Can't think what the women see in him. He hasn't an ounce of humor in him, and I don't give him long in his wife's good books. She's too much of a hoyden, and will soon find him a dull fish."

"They are deeply in love," Chloe replied a little crossly.

"That's as may be, but it won't last, you mark my words. Love can be very transitory and very ill-judged," he observed, giving his daughter a meaningful look. "Which is, of course, how I view your infatuation with Frobisher."

"It isn't an infatuation, Father. Jerry and I will always love each other," Chloe declared stoutly.

"That I doubt very much, for the likes of Frobisher do not settle down to a faithful married life, and if he sets one foot wrong while he's under my roof, he'll be out on his worthless ear."

Chloe tossed Marianne a pleading look, and Marianne hastily gathered herself for her appointed task. "Mr. Pendeven, I am sure that you are mistaken about Sir Jeremy, for I have found him to be everything that is honorable and attentive toward Chloe. I am sure that he truly loves her."

Mr. Pendeven gave her a fond smile. "What a loyal friend you are, Miss Cromwell."

"I would not say it if I did not believe it, sir."

"I know, Miss Cromwell, and it is only because of your support for Sir Jeremy that I have been persuaded to give this harebrained scheme a chance."

Marianne's accusing glance crept to Chloe. *Only* because? Evidently Chloe had jumped the gun somewhat where her, Marianne's, backing was concerned.

Chloe lowered her eyes a little guiltily.

Mr. Pendeven continued. "I will give Frobisher the benefit of the doubt, but I warn you that if anything, anything at all, disturbs the peace of this visit, I will call a halt to it immediately. I am afraid that I must be totally honest and say that I am looking for an excuse to send him packing. I don't want someone of his reputation as my son-in-law, and I certainly mean to protect Chloe from him if I possibly can."

There was silence, and no one said anything more

as the carriage continued to bowl westward along the highway.

They spent the night at the ancient market town of Northleach, high on the exposed Cotswold Hills, and when Marianne immediately fell into a deep sleep, her dreams were of Piers.

It was Saint Valentine's Day, 1815, and she was waiting for him to call. She had dressed with great care, putting her hair up into a knot with a single heavy ringlet tumbling to the nape of her neck, and she wore an ice-green muslin gown embroidered with tiny white flowers. There was a bloom in her cheeks, and her eyes were alight with happiness. The valentine card she had so carefully made lay waiting on the table beside her as she looked out of the window for his carriage to drive along Berkeley Street to the house.

He came at last, pausing almost impatiently to surrender his coat, hat, and gloves to the butler, and then he was in the room, stepping swiftly over to her. Their fingertips touched, and suddenly she was in his arms, crushed close and dear as his lips sought hers. She could feel his heartbeats, and she was aware of how her whole body stirred to meet him. His lips were warm and firm, becoming more urgent as he felt her yield against him.

Rich desire overwhelmed them both, and his face was flushed as he drew back. "Would you have me anticipate our vows and take you here and now?" he breathed, his eyes dark with passion.

"I love you so much, Piers," she whispered.

"As I love you. Dear God, as I love you." He cupped her face in his hands and covered it with kisses until at last their lips were joined again.

It was several minutes before they pulled apart, and she turned to give him the valentine card. The betrothal ring on her finger caught the February sunlight through the window as she held the foolish card out to him.

"You are my valentine, Sir Piers Sutherland, and you always will be," she said softly.

Their hands brushed as he took the card, and when he had read the verse, the desire was still bright in his eyes as he looked at her again. "My sweetheart divine," he murmured, smiling at her.

"I have never been more happy in my life, Piers."

"You will be, on the day you become my bride," he promised, and then he took a small package from his pocket. "Did you think I would fail to give you a valentine gift?"

"What is it?"

"A trinket."

She opened the little present, and her breath caught as she saw the emerald-encrusted comb inside. "It's beautiful," she whispered.

He took the comb out and fixed it to the knot in her hair. "There. The perfect adornment for the most perfect of women."

"I am hardly perfect. I have dreadful freckles, my mouth is horridly wide, and—"

He stopped her words with his finger, pressing it lovingly to her lips. "To me you are perfection, Marianne Cromwell, the most perfect and precious thing in all the world, and I will be your slave forever." He bent his head to kiss her again.

The dream faded away, and Marianne lay in the strange bed in the cold light of the February dawn. She could hear stagecoaches in the yard outside, and the sound of someone singing in the kitchens directly below her room, but it was as if she were in another place, a quiet place where no one could see her misery. The dream had gone now, but she could remember it only too clearly.

For all his loving protestations, he had betrayed her, and when she had returned his betrothal ring, she had returned the emerald comb as well. But he had never returned the valentine card. No doubt he had consigned it to the fire.

It was almost sunset on the day before Saint Valentine's Eve when at last the carriage drove up the straggling main street of the town of Newnham, perched on a low rocky hill above the tidal River Severn, which was several hundred yards wide at this point, and a place of sandbanks, currents, dangerous tides, and hundreds of waterfowl. To the east, on the other side of the river, the land was flat and fertile until the foot of the Cotswolds; to the west, behind Newnham, rose the high wooded hills of the ancient royal forest.

Half a mile above the town, set in a glorious park which swept right down to the water's edge, was Severn Park, home of the Pendeven family for almost two hundred years, since the land was granted to them early in the reign of Charles I. Newnham and the Pendevens had been staunchly Royalist during the Civil War, and had been at daggers drawn with the Parliament-supporting village of Arlingham across the river.

The house was in the Dutch style, built of warm pink brick with stone dressings, and it had beautiful gables that were adorned with scrolls, whorls, and pediments. The mullioned windows were pedimented as well, with lead lattices, and the stone porch jutted out into the wide gravel area where the curving drive ended in front of the house.

Marianne alighted, and halted in breathless admiration as she gazed down through the park toward the river. It was a glorious scene, made all the more memorable by the setting sun, which sank behind the forest in a blaze of crimson and gold.

Chloe came to her side, and gave a wistful sigh as she too gazed down at the panorama stretching away below them. "Just think, in a day or so from now, perhaps even on Saint Valentine's Day itself, I will be

able to stand here with Jerry. Can you think of anything more romantic?"

"It's very beautiful indeed," Marianne agreed.

Chloe gave her a sly glance. "And just think too,
you might have been able to stand here with Sir Piers,
but now it will probably only be with Mr. Forrester
instead."

With that she turned and followed her father into
the house, leaving Marianne to stare after her in astonishment. Surely Chloe couldn't have meant to
speak so disparagingly of Brandon? Nor could she
have intended to hint that to be with Piers would have
been infinitely preferable, since she didn't know him.
Yet that was exactly the impression she had given.
And given very clearly.

After a delicious dinner of Severn salmon caught
that very morning, they adjourned to the drawing
room, where conversation again touched upon Mr.
Pendeven's opposition to his daughter's proposed
match with Jerry. He made it abundantly clear that
he would pounce upon the first excuse to bundle Jerry
out of the house, and when he had retired to his bed,
leaving Chloe and Marianne alone at last, Chloe immediately and anxiously reminded Marianne that
nothing was to be allowed to go wrong.

"Nothing will go wrong, Chloe," Marianne replied,
taking her hands sympathetically.

"I'm just so very anxious, for if Jerry is sent away . . ."
Chloe's voice broke, and she bit her lip as she tried
to quell the sob that rose in her throat.

"I will do everything I can to help, and I'm sure
Maxwell will as well," Marianne promised. She paused
then. "Chloe, when we first arrived tonight, you mentioned Brandon."

"Did I?" Chloe's eyes were wide and puzzled. "I
really don't remember."

"You mentioned Piers as well. It was as we were

standing looking at the view before coming into the house."

Chloe shrugged. "I'm sorry, Marianne, but I really don't recall saying anything. What did I say?"

"That I might have been able to look at the view with Piers, but instead would probably have to make do with Brandon instead. Something along those lines."

Chloe seemed surprised. "Did I really say that? I didn't mean to, truly I didn't. I must have spoken without thinking, I'm afraid I do that sometimes. You see . . ." She broke off, and lowered her eyes.

"What is it?"

"Well, I can't help being aware that you loved Sir Piers very much, and that you are only fond of Mr. Forrester. I'm sure that the way you once felt about Sir Piers, you would have been overjoyed to be with him looking at our view. I'm also sure that the way you feel about Mr. Forrester isn't at all like that. Am I right?"

Marianne looked away. Yes, of course she was right. . . .

Chloe squeezed her hands. "If you still love Sir Piers, in spite of everything, please think very carefully indeed before you accept Mr. Forrester."

"I don't love Piers," Marianne replied, but she knew the words sounded hollow. Taking her hands away, she left the drawing room to go to her room.

Chloe pursed her lips thoughtfully. "You're a dreadful fibber, Marianne Cromwell," she murmured. "I'm far, far better at it than you; indeed, I have a positive talent." She smiled.

Marianne slept very soundly that night, so soundly that she didn't hear the traveling carriage arrive in the small hours and draw up on the gravel below her window. The first thing she knew about it was when Chloe crept silently into her room in her nightgown and wrap, and placed a lighted candle on the table before coming to the bed and shaking her shoulder to awaken her.

"Marianne? Wake up, please," she whispered urgently.

Marianne stirred slowly. "Mm?"

"Wake up, please." Chloe shook her again.

With a start, Marianne's eyes flew open and she stared up at her friend in the candlelight. "What is it? What's wrong?"

"I think you'd better put on your wrap and come downstairs with me. And don't make a sound, for we mustn't wake Father."

Astonished, Marianne sat up in the bed. "Go downstairs? Why?"

"There is something vital we have to sort out now, before we all come face-to-face in the morning," Chloe replied mysteriously, taking Marianne's pink woolen wrap from the chair by the dying fire and handing it to her. "Please come with me, Marianne, for it's very important indeed."

Marianne slipped from the warmth of the damask-hung bed, shivering as she put on the wrap. Her hair tumbled in confusion about her shoulders, for she always scorned to wear a night bonnet, and she paused for a moment to drag a brush through it before facing Chloe again.

"I'm ready, but are you sure you won't explain anything further before we go anywhere?"

"I would, if I knew what to say." Chloe looked quite wretched. "Everything has gone wrong, Marianne, and now I'm afraid that the atmosphere here will be so awful that Father will soon send Jerry packing."

"Sir Jeremy has arrived?"

"Yes."

"Then what is wrong?"

Without replying, Chloe picked up the candlestick and led her from the room. They went down the shadowy dark oak staircase, and then across the richly paneled great hall to the drawing room, the door of which stood ajar. Candlelight swayed within, and as they approached, Marianne could hear the murmur of male voices.

Chloe entered the room first, and then stood aside for Marianne to do the same. Two gentlemen stood by the huge, ornately carved fireplace. One was Jerry. The other was Piers.

Marianne halted in startled dismay. "Piers?" His name slipped from her lips.

He straightened and faced her, executing a brief bow. "Marianne."

She stared at him. His greatcoat had been tossed casually around his shoulders, his blond hair was tousled, and his gray eyes were a little uneasy as he met her gaze.

"I didn't know, I swear it," he said. "I agreed to assist Jerry out of a difficulty, and had no idea that you would be here as well."

Jerry looked wretchedly apologetic. "It's my fault entirely, Miss Cromwell. Maxwell had to cry off at the last moment, and since Piers is my friend, I asked him to step in. I'm afraid I quite forgot what happened . . . a year ago." He shuffled his feet uncomfortably, and then took off his heavy greatcoat and dropped it on to the table. Running his fingers through his dark hair, he faced Marianne again. "Forgive me, please, Miss Cromwell, for I didn't intend to embarrass either you or Piers."

Chloe put her candlestick down, and then looked imploringly at both Marianne and Piers. "I know it's a great deal to ask, but it's so important to Jerry and me that I have to beg you to put your differences aside, just while you are here."

Piers glanced at Marianne and then looked at Chloe, shaking his head. "It's out of the question that I should stay here, Miss Pendeven."

"But you must! My father is just waiting for a reason to call the whole business off, and if he does that . . ." Chloe's voice trailed away into tears, and Jerry hurried to her, pulling her lovingly into his embrace.

Over her bowed head, he looked at the other two. "Please do this. For us. All we ask is that you tolerate each other for a short while. Chloe is desperately anxious to have her father's blessing for our marriage, and that is the whole point of this visit." He searched their faces in the candlelight. "A congenial *ambiance* is what is required over the coming days, especially on Saint Valentine's Day itself. If you will do this for us, we will be forever in your debt."

Marianne returned his look wretchedly, and then turned hesitantly to Piers. Would it be possible? For their friends?

He saw the inquiry in her eyes, and then nodded, although with how much reservation she could not tell. "I will try if you will, Marianne."

Chloe's breath caught, and she whirled about to gaze entreatingly at Marianne, who nodded. With a joyous cry, Chloe ran to fling her arms around her neck. "Thank you! Oh, thank you! And you too, Sir Piers," she added, turning to smile at him through her tears.

Jerry took Marianne's hand and raised it to his lips. "I am very grateful to you, Miss Cromwell, especially as the fault was entirely mine. Believe me, I would not have dreamed of knowingly placing either of you in this embarrassing position."

He cleared his throat, and gave a rather uneasy smile, almost as if he were guilty of a small fib. And yet that could not be so, thought Marianne, a little curious. She smiled at him. "Please do not feel obliged to apologize again, Sir Jeremy, for there is no need. I came here to help you and Chloe, and that is what I will do."

Chloe composed herself. "It is settled, then. We

proceed as if Sir Piers were Maxwell. I will have someone arouse Father's valet to inform him that our other
guests have arrived a little earlier than expected." She
clasped her hands before her, her eyes shining. "Oh,
this *must* go well! It simply must."

Jerry nodded. "I echo that sentiment. Well, we will
know at breakfast tomorrow whether or not we are to
achieve our purpose. If we carry it off then, we'll no
doubt be able to carry off the whole thing."

Marianne felt Piers' gaze upon her, and reluctantly
she looked toward him. He didn't look away.

The following day was that of Saint Valentine's Eve,
and it dawned bright and wonderfully clear. From her
bedroom window at the front of the house, Marianne
gazed down through the open park toward the river,
which sparkled in the sunlight at the foot of the hills.
To her right, yellow dogwood bloomed against the
high wall that shielded the kitchen garden from view,
and beneath the ornamental trees close to the house
there were sheets of snowdrops and early crocuses.
Farther away, huge drifts of tightly budded daffodils
would soon be in full spring glory. Dense woodland
tumbled down on either side of the park, and half a
mile away she could see Newnham on its small hill
above the grand sweep of the Severn.

She wore her cream merino gown, and her hair was
swept up into a knot on top of her head, leaving soft
curls around her face. The strain of the night showed
on her face, and she had had to resort to rouge to
give herself a little color. Chloe had already called in
briefly to see her, to be sure that what had been
agreed in the small hours still held good in the cold
light of day. Marianne felt she had been able to reassure her, and now could only pray that the reassurance
was soundly based. It wasn't going to be easy to pretend that nothing had ever happened between Piers

and her, but she would call upon every ounce of acting ability if it would help Chloe.

She drew a long breath, and turned from the window. What was it going to be like? They would both behave amiably toward each other, but all the time they would know it was a sham. Why had fate chosen to be so cruel? She had feared all along that Chloe's machinations would lead to a scrape, but it hadn't occurred to her that she herself would be the one involved. After a year of trying to get over Sir Piers Sutherland, here she was, not only staying beneath the same roof, but also pledged to be all smiles and agreeability toward him. It made her promise to her father almost impossible to keep, for how could she give sensible and balanced consideration to the match with Brandon when all she could think of was the match she had lost?

The clock on the mantelpiece struck the hour. It was time to go down. Steeling herself for the ordeal ahead, she left her room. But fate was bent upon making things as awkward as possible, for Piers reached the top of the staircase just before she did and, to her dismay, he waited so that they could go down together.

Sunlight from a nearby window shone on his golden hair, and upon the signet ring on his hand as it rested on the topmost newel post. He wore a gray-green coat and cream corduroy trousers, with Hessian boots and a gray silk neckcloth. As he looked at her, she knew that he could not have failed to observe the way her steps faltered for a moment before she reluctantly continued toward him.

He gave a faint smile and inclined his head. "Good morning, Marianne."

"Good morning."

He glanced around to see if anyone could overhear, and then continued in a low tone, "I know that our meetings so far have proved prickly, to say the least, but I sincerely hope we can forget our differences. Jerry is an old and good friend of mine, and it is clear that Miss Pendeven is very close to you, so we must unite in order to help them. I promise that I will do everything in my power to see that this visit is all they wish it to be."

He smiled into her eyes, and her foolish heart turned over, but she managed to conceal her inner disarray by responding with a small smile of her own.

His gaze wandered over her for a moment, and she instinctively put a hand up to her hair, thinking a pin was loose.

"Is . . . is something wrong?" she asked.

"No, nothing at all. I had merely forgotten how very delightful your smile is."

She colored. "We have agreed to behave amiably toward each other, sir, but you do not have to compliment me."

"My observation had nothing to do with our pact, Marianne." He looked at her. "I know that in London you requested me to address you formally as Miss Cromwell, but I'm afraid that I find that difficult. I think of you as Marianne, and I can't help addressing you as that. In our conversation we are bound to convey the fact that we have known each other for some time, and so I think it best, under the circumstances, if we use our first names. It will avoid awkwardness should I slip up."

She nodded. "Very well."

His eyes were very clear in the sunlight from the window. "Very well, Piers," he said in correction as he offered her his arm. "Shall we go down?"

She placed her hand on his sleeve, and together they descended the staircase to the hall. There was something very strange about being at his side like this. It was almost as if she were still asleep, still in the happy past, as on the day she'd given him the valentine card. She could almost believe it possible

that at any moment he would put his hand over
hers. . . .

The others were already at the breakfast table, and
Marianne detected an awkward atmosphere the moment she and Piers entered. An odd silence hung over
the sunny room, making the delicious smell of food
seem almost oppressive.

Chloe was very pretty in green gingham, with
matching ribbons fluttering from her little lace morning cap, and opposite her, Jerry was uncomfortable in
dark blue, with a gold pin in his voluminous neckcloth. Mr. Pendeven was seated at the head of the
table, a displeased expression on his face. He wore a
maroon coat, and a napkin was tucked beneath his
chin as he applied himself to a hearty breakfast of
crisp bacon, sausages, kidneys, eggs, and tomatoes.

Chloe's plate was untouched, and as she looked up
into Marianne's eyes, it was clear she was close to
tears. Jerry tried to eat, but was really only pushing
the food around the plate. Things were evidently not
going at all well with Mr. Pendeven.

Marianne smiled brightly. "Good morning," she
said cheerfully, going to the sideboard to select from
the line of silver-domed dishes.

Piers uttered a similar greeting, and as he followed
her along the sideboard, he glanced over his shoulder
at Chloe's father. "Mr. Pendeven, I understand from
Jerry that you own a shipyard in Newnham, and that
a new vessel is soon to be launched?"

Mr. Pendeven's interest was kindled. "Er, yes, indeed it is. Newnham has been a shipbuilding town for
centuries, because of the coal and iron in the forest.
A trow is to be launched tomorrow."

Marianne sat down on the chair the butler drew out
for her. "What is a trow?" she asked.

"It is what we call the vessels peculiar to the Severn," Mr. Pendeven explained. "They have to be very
sturdy to cope with the strong tides, of which the Sev-

ern boasts some of the fiercest and highest in the world. I shall be going to the yard later this morning to see that all is coming along as it should."

Marianne smiled at him. "May we come too?"

"Of course you may, my dear," he replied, bestowing a warm smile upon her in return. "Maybe you can be of assistance, for I fear I have yet to think of a suitable name for the new vessel."

"If she is to be launched tomorrow, perhaps she should be called *Saint Valentine,*" Marianne offered.

"I would, were it not that I like all my trows to be of the feminine gender."

Chloe strove to enter into the conversation. "*Sabrina* would be appropriate, for it is the Roman name for the Severn."

"There is already a *Sabrina* operating out of Lydney," Mr. Pendeven replied.

Jerry cleared his throat suddenly. "I, er, have a suggestion," he began.

Mr. Pendeven gave him a look that was eloquent of a complete lack of interest in anything he might have to say, but Jerry persevered.

"I, er, believe there are to be northern lights tonight, and that they will be seen as far south as this. Would not *Aurora* be a suitable name for the vessel?"

Mr. Pendeven's face changed. "Upon my soul, what an excellent notion," he declared. "Northern lights, eh? Yes, indeed, I think *Aurora* is the perfect name."

Chloe's face was a picture of relieved delight, and suddenly she found her appetite. Jerry looked as if he could hardly believe his tentative remark had borne such fruit.

Piers sat down next to Marianne, and under the pretense of leaning across for the saltcellar, he whispered to her, "You and I are oil upon troubled waters."

"So far," she replied, picking up the saltcellar and

giving it to him. Their fingers brushed, and she drew her hand quickly away again.

The rest of the day preceding St. Valentine's Day went well, with Jerry and Mr. Pendeven on almost amicable terms as they all went to the shipyard in Newnham to see the new trow.

Marianne found it easier than she'd expected to behave amiably toward Piers. Perhaps it was because she was sure that he would respond in kind, and therefore there was no need to be constantly on the defensive— or the offensive, as he himself might regard it.

Chloe and Jerry conducted themselves perfectly, with just the right amount of intimacy, and Mr. Pendeven, in spite of all his dire warnings, seemed to be pleased enough with the way things were going. He wasn't sharp with his prospective son-in-law, neither was he all that encouraging, but all the same the general impression seemed to be that the visit so far was a success.

That evening they all enjoyed an agreeable dinner of celery soup, followed by roast duck and then cherry pie. The meal was accompanied by fine wine, and was ended with fruit, nuts, and sweet liqueurs, so that they were all aware of a certain inner glow as they went out into the night to observe the *aurora borealis*.

The sky seemed to be on fire, with a broad band of shimmering light stretching across the sky from west to east. There were balls of brightness, and fiery sparks, as if flaming spears were being brandished by huge invisible hands. It was this impression which gave the lights one of their other names, Burning Spears, but Marianne preferred to call them the Merry Dancers, which was the name she had learned in her childhood.

After watching the magnificent display for a long time, Chloe, Jerry, and Mr. Pendeven went back into the warmth of the house, but Marianne and Piers remained outside.

Beneath her fur-lined cloak, Marianne wore a peppermint silk gown, and there was a diamond flower ornament in her elaborately dressed hair. More diamonds trembled from her ears, and the precious stones flashed and winked in the dancing light from the night sky.

Everything was silent except for the hooting of an owl somewhere in the woods to the north. The sunset had been splendid, with an open, crimson sky, and there was gossamer in the bare branches of the trees.

After a moment Piers spoke. "An auspicious omen for Saint Valentine's Day, is it not?" he said, gazing up at the display overhead.

"I trust so, for Chloe and Jerry's sake," she replied.

"And what of you? Do you have plans for Saint Valentine's Day?"

"Me? No."

He glanced at her. "Isn't Forrester about to become your valentine?"

"I haven't thought about it," she replied truthfully.

"Is it fair to keep him dangling?"

Her hazel eyes swung to meet him, for the question pricked her. "And what, pray, would you know about fairness?" she inquired.

"I have become an authority, believe me."

"I trust that that bodes well for your wife-to-be, whoever she is."

He smiled a little. "Oh, yes, I think it bodes well for her."

She turned to face him properly. "Are there still obstacles? Or can you name her now?"

"There are still obstacles."

"Do I know her?"

"Yes. Very well indeed."

"How mysterious you are. Could it possibly be that the obstacles include an inconvenient husband?"

"No, it couldn't, for I do not count wife-stealing among my sins, although no doubt you would prefer not to believe that."

"Believing what you tell me is a risky business, sir, as I've found out to my cost."

"So you persist in reminding me." He drew a long breath. "Marianne, I thought we'd agreed to conduct ourselves in a friendly manner."

"So we did, but that agreement did not include giving you the freedom to remark upon my match with Mr. Forrester."

"You are pleased to remark upon *my* forthcoming match," he pointed out reasonably.

"That was after you started it."

"How very childish."

She was stung. "If you find me childish, sirrah, I suggest you keep well away from me, apart from when our obligations require the contrary!"

"What a vixen you are, to be sure. Perhaps I am well out of it after all."

"I'm certainly well out of it," she countered, her eyes bright with anger and hurt.

"Indeed? There was a time when you were pleased enough to contemplate a future with me. In fact, there was a time when there was quite a flame between us."

"Your lamentable conduct doused that flame," she replied coldly.

"Did it? I wonder."

"And what is that supposed to mean?"

He held her gaze. "It means that you would try the patience of a saint, Marianne Cromwell, and I am most definitely not a saint. Pretend that it is over between us if you wish, but I know better. There will always be a flame, Marianne, and I intend to prove it."

Before she realized it, he had pulled her into his arms. His lips were hot and searing upon hers, and he gave her no quarter as he held her so tightly that she could not do anything but submit. He pressed her body against his, his fingers twining sensuously in her hair as he employed all his considerable skill. It was a knowing, passionate kiss, designed to storm her defenses, and in spite of herself she felt her treacherous body succumbing.

The desire she had striven to conquer now came rushing back to overwhelm her. All she had to do was surrender. To her senses. And to him. Oh, what ecstasy would await her in sweet submission. But, oh, what a betrayal it would be of her pride. . . . With a huge effort, she suddenly pulled sharply away from him.

He gave her a cool, mocking smile. "So the flame is extinguished, is it? I think not. Marry poor Forrester if you wish, but you'll always be mine, whether you like it or not."

A choked sob caught furiously in her throat, and she dealt him a stinging blow to the cheek. Then she gathered her skirts to run into the house.

Rubbing his cheek, he stayed where he was, but when he glanced up at the dancing sky again, there was the ghost of a smile on his lips.

On Saint Valentine's morning, Marianne was awakened by her maid, who had discovered a valentine gift outside the bedroom door.

"Oh, Miss Marianne! Look!" she cried, hurrying toward the bed with a posy of snowdrops and early violets.

Still sleepy, Marianne sat up in the bed, pushing her tangled hair back from her face. She stared at the posy. "Who is it from?" she asked.

"It's anonymous; it has to be if it is a true valentine," the maid replied, giving her the flowers. "Snowdrops for hope and violets for sincerity. I wonder if it could be from—?" Biting her lip, she fell abruptly silent.

Marianne held the posy to her nose and inhaled the fresh fragrance. "I doubt it very much," she said dryly. "If that particular gentleman were to give me a posy, it would most likely be of weeds. My suspicion is that the posy is from Sir Jeremy, and is actually meant for Miss Pendeven, but that in the darkness he mistook the door."

"Do you think so, miss?"

"Yes, I do." Marianne smiled at her then. "You seem in excellent spirits this morning. Do I take it that you have had a valentine gift?"

"No, miss, but the first man I saw this morning *was* the handsomest of the footmen, and he did give me a smile."

"Then I wish you well, but take care, for handsome footmen can be the very devil with unwary maids."

"I know, Miss Marianne, but I mean to lead him a merry dance."

Marianne glanced out of the window at the sunny morning sky, for the maid's words reminded her of the Merry Dancers last night. She could feel Piers' scornful lips upon hers, and hear his last words. *Marry poor Forrester if you wish, but you'll always be mine, whether you like it or not.*

"What gown will you wear this morning, Miss Marianne?" the maid asked.

"Mm? Oh, the lavender-and-white muslin, I think."

"Will you pin the posy to your hair?"

"I think not, since I am convinced it wasn't intended for me. I'll do my best to return it secretly to Sir Jeremy."

"But what if he didn't put it there?"

"He did."

Shortly afterward, Marianne was dressed and ready to go down to breakfast, which this morning would consist of traditional valentine buns. As she walked toward the staircase, she again saw Piers just ahead of her. He heard her light tread upon the polished floor, and turned. Their eyes met for a long moment, and then he went on down the staircase without waiting for her or even greeting her.

She lingered until she had heard him enter the breakfast room, but then, just as she was about to follow him down the stairs, she heard a door open and close behind her. Turning, she saw that it was Jerry.

She smiled, and held out the posy. "I think you left this at the wrong door, sir."

He came toward her, looking blankly at the posy. "I, er, don't understand, Miss Cromwell."

Her smiled faltered. "Didn't you leave this posy? For Chloe?"

"I certainly left a posy for Chloe, Miss Cromwell, but it was of red rosebuds from the hothouse."

Marianne felt a little foolish. "Oh. Forgive me, I . . . I thought that in the darkness you had mistaken my door for Chloe's."

He smiled. "I fear not, Miss Cromwell."

"But . . . who could have left it?"

"Perhaps it is from Piers?" he suggested tentatively.

"I think not," she replied shortly.

"Things have not improved between you?"

"The very opposite, but please do not be concerned, for we will still honor our promise to you and Chloe. At least . . ."

"Yes?"

"I will honor it, Sir Jeremy, but I cannot speak for Piers. I saw him a moment ago, and he cut me."

"Oh, dear."

"So, you see, it is most unlikely that he left the posy for me."

"Was he the first man you've seen this morning, Miss Cromwell?" he asked suddenly.

"Yes. Why?" She colored then. "That is one valentine tradition which is going to be proved hopelessly wrong, Sir Jeremy."

He said nothing more, but offered her his arm, and together they proceeded to the breakfast room, where the others were already enjoying the hot valentine buns.

Chloe looked delightful in dusty-pink dimity, and she had pinned several of Jerry's valentine rosebuds in her honey-colored hair. She was aglow with happiness, for the card Marianne had made for her had been very well received indeed.

Marianne sat at the table, and selected a bun from the large dish in the middle. She had greeted everyone in general as she entered, but Piers had not responded.

Now he did, however. "Good morning, Marianne," he said, catching her unwilling eye across the table.

"Good morning, Piers."

His glance flickered to the posy of snowdrops and violets, which she had placed by her plate, and he said nothing more.

Mr. Pendeven's appetite was as hearty as ever as he buttered another bun. "What plans are there for today? This morning I must stay in because the Newnham children will come for their traditional valentine pennies. Oh, and I must give guineas to the servants, of course." He ate the bun, and then licked his fingers. "Hopefully, the *Aurora* should be launched on this afternoon's tide, should you all wish to come."

Chloe's face brightened still more. "Oh, yes, please. I love seeing launches."

"Very well. We will all drive together. What will you do this morning when I am philanthropically occupied?"

Chloe shrugged. "I really don't know."

Piers glanced up. "If you don't mind, I'd appreciate the chance to ride. Perhaps we could go down to the riverbank?"

Chloe clapped her hands. "Yes! We can go to the summerhouse. I know, we'll take a light luncheon there. The servants will take it down, and we will simply enjoy it when we've ridden sufficiently. I know it isn't exactly picnic weather, but the summerhouse faces south." Without further ado, she got up from her chair and hurried out to issue instructions.

Mr. Pendeven smiled fondly as he sat back in his chair. "There are occasions when she so reminds me of my dear Elizabeth. Especially today," he murmured.

Elizabeth. The name reminded Marianne of a certain *belle de nuit*. She glanced briefly toward Piers, and found his gaze already upon her. Quickly she returned her attention to her breakfast.

Unaware of the undercurrents, Mr. Pendeven mused about the past. "She was quite the most beautiful creature I have even known, my sweet Elizabeth. I proposed to her on Saint Valentine's Day. Ah, one can always recall magical days, can one not? And for me, it was that particular Saint Valentine's Day."

Marianne could bear it no longer. Putting her hand up to her hair and deliberately dislodging several pins, she gave a cry of quick dismay. "Oh, dear, my hair . . . Forgive me, sirs, but I simply have to return to my room."

As with Chloe a few moments before, the three men had no time to rise politely from their seats as she hurried from the room.

There were tears in her eyes as she hastened up the staircase, and when she reached her chamber, she flung herself on the bed and surrendered to the sobs that racked her.

Mr. Pendeven was distributing the valentine pennies to the children as Marianne, Piers, Chloe, and Jerry went riding later that morning. The sun was still shining, and the horses' hooves drummed pleasantly on the grass as the four riders made their way down toward the river.

Marianne rode a pretty cream mare. She wore a

kingfisher-blue riding habit, with a black beaver hat from which trailed a long white gauze scarf. Chloe was in lilac, with a plumed gray hat, and she rode a strawberry roan. The two gentlemen were in the pine-green riding coats which were almost *de rigueur* in fashionable circles, and their mounts were large, restive thoroughbreds which fought the bit all the time and thus gave them both good cause to show off their equestrian skills.

Behind them the dark green of the forest rose against the skyline, and before them lay the Severn. The tide was low now, and the sandbanks were dotted with wild fowl. Across the river, the tower of Arlingham church rose above the fertile meadows, and its bells were pealing.

Chloe gave a delighted laugh, and urged her mount forward. "A wedding! It must be a wedding!" she cried.

Marianne smiled at her excitement, and then reined in for a moment to glance back at Severn Park, so serene on the hillside behind. How beautiful it was here. A matchless place.

Her gaze wandered over the forest and then descended slowly toward the fields that lay to the south. The first lambs gamboled in the sun. To the north, Newnham looked almost Mediterranean upon its hill, and the river was so still that the little town was reflected on the surface.

A stream made its way down the hillside along the border of the woods, and it was lined with pussy willow and hazel catkins. Brimstone butterflies fluttered by the branches, and in the woods the birdsong seemed to echo almost shrilly.

The summerhouse was built on a level area of the riverbank that was above the surrounding land, and was therefore safe from all but the very highest of the spring tides. It was a small wooden building, designed to resemble a Greek temple, and it faced downstream, where the estuary widened as it swept around another curve toward the sea. The tide, when it came, would be so swift that it was visible, and at this time of the year especially it would form a wave known as a bore. From low water to high water did not take long, and the level of the river rose sharply as the Severn flowed back upon itself. When the tide was fully in, the water became stationary, and then began to flow downstream again. The speed and noise of the incoming tide frequently alarmed the cattle in the meadows, so that they fled away from the riverbank to escape the rushing water. Marianne knew of all this, but she had no idea that before the day was out the Severn bore was going to change her life forever.

They all reined in by the summerhouse, and as Jerry lifted Chloe down, she pointed to little circles of toadstools in the grass. "Look! Fairy rings! Be careful no one treads on them, or we will all be enchanted."

Piers dismounted, and came to assist Marianne. He held his arms up, and she slid lightly down from the saddle. He gripped her for a moment, his fingers tight upon her waist.

"Marianne, I left the posy, and it was no mistake," he said softly, and then he released her. Turning, he quickly took the reins of both horses, and led them away to be tethered to a bush with the others.

She stared after him, but there was no chance to say anything more because Chloe came to take her hand and hurry her toward the summerhouse.

Without thinking, Marianne stepped through one of the fairy rings.

Chloe pretended to be dismayed. "Oh, no! You're enchanted now, Marianne. The fairies have you in their power." Then she giggled and ushered Marianne into the summerhouse, where a commendable feast had been laid out earlier by the servants from the house.

The view down the estuary was astonishing, and it

was hard to remember that this was February, for the horizon shimmered in the sunshine. Chloe and Jerry were so rapt in each other that they didn't notice the awkwardness between their two companions. Piers lounged back on the summerhouse seat, a thoughtful look in his gray eyes as he stared at the estuary. Marianne sat nearby, her eyes downcast as she thought about the posy. Why had he left it? Why bother with a valentine when they had parted so bitterly the night before? He was soon to be betrothed to his mysterious lady, and so whatever his motives now, they could not be honorable. It was just another example of his shabbiness. And yet *still* she loved him with all her heart. . . .

After an hour, which Chloe and Jerry found delightful, and the others simply endured, they all remounted and rode back up through the park toward the house. Soon it would be time to change for the drive to Newnham and the launch of the *Aurora*. The tide was about to change, and the new trow would be launched at high water.

The thought of being confined in a carriage with Piers and the others was suddenly not very appealing to Marianne, and on top of that she realized that she'd left her riding crop in the summerhouse. It was a valuable present given to her by her father, and had a beautifully engraved silver handle. She had almost reached the house, but nothing would do but that she return to the summerhouse.

Chloe was dismayed. "But there isn't time, Marianne, not if we are to go with Father to Newnham."

"I . . . I don't think I will go now, Chloe. I have a headache, and when I've retrieved my riding crop, I'll go to my room to lie down for a while. Please extend my regrets to your father, won't you?"

Without waiting for a reply, Marianne turned her horse around, and urged it back down toward the river.

When she reached the summerhouse she quickly dismounted, meaning merely to collect the riding crop and then return to the house, but as she left the horse to go to the little building, she again walked through the fairy ring.

Stopping, she crouched down to touch the tiny toad-stools. Enchanted? Was she? Yes, and had been these two years or more, ever since she'd met Sir Piers Sutherland. He'd beguiled her, cast fairy glamour into her eyes, and she'd been under his spell ever since. He was right. Even if she married Brandon, she would still belong to her first love.

Straightening, she went into the summerhouse, where the remnants of the luncheon party were still littered on the table. Piers' wineglass stood where he had left it, and almost unconsciously she put her fingertip on the rim, running it slowly around, knowing that she must touch where his lips had been.

She closed her eyes then. She was lost beyond redemption in this passion. She had tried in vain to cast him out of her heart, but still he was there. It would be wrong to marry Brandon. Totally wrong. She would never be able to forget Piers, and Brandon deserved better than that. Her father would be disappointed, but she knew what she must do. The Forrester match had to be rejected a second and final time.

The riding crop lay upon the bench, but as she bent to pick it up, a new sound filled the air, a rushing, bubbling, hissing sound totally alien to the quiet that had just preceded.

She went to the entrance, staring downstream toward the noise. She could see a frothing line of white stretching across the river. It was the bore. The cows in the meadows took fright as it passed, kicking up their heels as they fled from the bank, and flocks of waterfowl rose with a clamor as the incoming tide swept swiftly over the shining sand.

Marianne watched as the foaming wave raced noisily upstream toward her. She wasn't in danger, and
knew she could remain where she was as the bore
flashed and gurgled against the rocks right by her.
Too late she remembered that she hadn't tethered her
horse, and even as she turned to snatch at its reins,
the animal threw up its head in alarm and galloped
back up the park toward the haven of its stables.

Marianne gazed after it in dismay. Now she would
have to walk back to the house. For the moment,
however, there was the spectacle of the tide to watch.
It was exhilarating to be so close to the churning,
boiling water. The bore itself had already passed upstream, and now the swelling tide surged along behind
it. Driftwood bobbed and spun, and the birds wheeled
excitedly. There was a new freshness in the air, an
almost invigorating tang from the open sea.

She was fascinated, and suddenly felt as if the
wretchedness of the past had been swept away and a
new future had come to her. It was a foolish feeling,
but so strong that she could not ignore it. What did
it augur?

She was so absorbed that she gave no thought to the
alarm that would be raised when her riderless horse
returned to the stables.

Mr. Pendeven's carriage was at the door in readiness for the short drive to Newnham, and everyone
had just emerged from the house when they heard the
galloping hooves.

Piers turned toward the sound, and his eyes sharp-
ened uneasily as he recognized the cream mare.
"That's Marianne's horse," he breathed.

Chloe gave a gasp of dismay. "Oh, no . . ."

Without another word, Piers ran to the stables,
where he shouted to a groom to bring him a mount
immediately. He waited only long enough for the man
to put a bridle on the bay thoroughbred that was

brought out, and then vaulted onto its bare back and kicked his heels to fling the startled horse out of the yard and down the park toward the summerhouse far below.

Behind him the others stood by the carriage. They had by now perceived Marianne standing unharmed on the bank, but they made no attempt to call any reassurance to Piers as he dashed to her rescue.

Chloe gave a sleek, satisfied smile. "This could not have gone better had I planned it," she murmured, shading her eyes against the sun as she watched Piers.

Jerry and her father exchanged long-suffering glances, and then her father sighed. "Chloe, my dear, it must be about the only thing you *haven't* planned recently. I've never known so much engineering and fibbing."

"In a good cause," she pointed out in a slightly injured tone.

"I trust so."

She was arch then. "Look at the way he's rushing to save her," she said, pointing toward Piers. "Need I say more? Of course it's in a good cause."

Marianne was now seated in the summerhouse, watching the river as it rushed noisily inland. She didn't hear Piers' horse approaching, and the first she knew of his presence was when she heard him calling her.

"Marianne! Marianne, can you hear me?"

Startled, she left the summerhouse and saw him as he reined the horse in and then looked anxiously around for her. His face was taut and worried as he controlled his nervous, capering mount.

"Piers?" She hurried toward him.

Relief lightened his brow, and he slipped from the horse. "Thank God! When your horse returned . . ."

Her face fell guiltily. "I . . . I didn't think. The tide came in and frightened the horse while I was watching the river. Forgive me."

"I'll forgive anything, provided you are all right," he replied quietly.

She looked up into his eyes. "I'm quite all right, Piers. I'm sorry to have alarmed you."

"This bank may be safe enough, but at the same time it is a very hazardous place. One false step, and . . ." He didn't finish, but looked toward the surging river. His glance flickered briefly back to her. "It wouldn't do for some mishap to befall you on the eve of your betrothal to Forrester, would it?"

"There isn't going to be a betrothal," she replied.

He turned to face her. "There isn't?"

"No. It would be a terrible mistake. I know that Brandon thinks he loves me, but I'm sure it isn't the sort of love which should be between a man and his wife. We have known each other for so long that it is sibling love we feel. I know that I do, and in my heart I think Brandon does as well."

Piers was silent for a moment. "Are you sure about this? I mean, you were on the point of marrying him when I first met you, and he stayed around throughout our betrothal. Now he's still here, and on the point of marrying you again."

"He's my dearest friend, after Chloe."

"Marianne, I'm glad you're not marrying him."

She looked at him. "What of your own match? Why won't you tell me who she is?"

"Well, perhaps I may do now, for a serious obstacle has just been removed."

"Has it?"

He gave the wryest of smiles. "Marianne, why do you imagine I left that posy at your door this morning?"

"I . . . I don't know."

"Have you no notion at all?" He drew a long breath, and looked at the river. "No doubt you credited me with further shabby motives?"

She went a little pink. "I didn't know what to think."

"Which can only mean that you didn't regard it as an honorable or even loving gesture."

"Loving? Piers, when we parted last night, things were very acrimonious between us."

"Were they? It seems to me that the flame was enduring very sweetly," he said softly.

The pink intensified in her cheeks. "Perhaps dinner had been a little too convivial."

"Oh, yes. It would have to be something like that, would it not?" he murmured almost mockingly. "Come now, Marianne, why do you not simply admit that whatever else lies between us, the attraction has never died."

Her eyes flew to his face. "Please don't, Piers—"

"What will you do? Begin your walk back to the house? Marianne, I will simply walk with you, and continue with this discomfiting conversation. When I kissed you last night, you responded. Am I right?"

Mortified, she lowered her eyes.

"Silence can be so eloquent," he observed, and then added, "and past actions can be equally as eloquent of emotions that overwhelm everything else. Marianne, ever since I have known you, I have been envious of Brandon Forrester. No, perhaps envious isn't the correct word. Jealous is more appropriate."

She stared at him. "I cannot believe that."

"It is true. He has always been close to you, always in your heart. He was there before me, there while I was betrothed to you, and, damn it, he's there now as well."

"But I've explained, he is like—"

"A brother. I know. Deuce take it, Marianne, he isn't your brother, he's a man who desires you and wants you to be his wife! He's always wanted you. Just as I have always wanted you."

She drew back a little. "You had me, sir. Your ring was on my finger, but you betrayed me with London's most fashionable courtesan."

"I didn't."

Her lips parted, and she searched his face disbelievingly. "Isn't this a little late for protestations of innocence?"

"Perhaps it is, but until now I have always feared that Forrester would be the ultimate winner, and I allowed my male pride to get in the way. Besides, I'm not entirely innocent. I was jealous of Forrester's place in your life, consumed with jealousy, in fact. I saw you with him one day, in the garden of your house in London. Your heads were together intimately, and I was convinced he'd succeeded in stealing you back."

"Nothing could be further from the truth. I loved you, and only you."

"Jealousy makes fools of us, Marianne. It certainly made a fool of me, and has continued to do so right up until this very moment. What I'm about to tell you should have been told in full the moment I knew what really happened. I could have told you in Lansdowne Passage, and at any time since then, but somehow I couldn't." He drew a long breath. "Elizabeth Lavery had been pursuing me for some time, and caught me at a moment when my wretchedness over Forrester was at its height. I was ripe for the plucking, and I also happened to be somewhat in my cups, having consoled myself with a decanter of cognac. I wanted her to seduce me, just as I thought you were being seduced by Forrester, but when it came to the point, all I could think of was you, and how much I loved you. It ended with me falling asleep in a chair, but when I awoke the next morning, my head fuddled with the effects of the cognac, I found myself in her bed, and I was led to believe that I'd more than proved myself."

Marianne stared at him. He hadn't been false to her?

He went on. "Do you remember Freddie Jameson?"

"Yes."

"He was at Elizabeth's house that night, as were several other acquaintances. At his instigation, they deemed it an amusing prank to carry me from the chair downstairs to Elizabeth's bed upstairs, and then they all pretended I'd conducted myself with commendable passion. I had to believe them. I only discovered the truth when I bumped into Freddie again, in New York of all places. His confession resulted in him being confined to his bed for some time, as I certainly wasn't pleased with what he'd had to say. Marianne, you are the woman in my life, the woman I wish to marry. You'll never know how glad I was when I arrived here and found you beneath the same roof. I'd decided in Berkeley Square that day that I had to fight for you if I could, but there seemed such a gulf of mistrust and hostility between us that I really didn't know how to go about winning you back again. I love you, Marianne, and I think now that you still love me. Now that you know I didn't betray you with Elizabeth, and now that I know once and for all that Forrester isn't your real love, can't we begin again?"

An incredible joy was already flooding through her, and tears of gladness shone in her eyes. "I've never stopped loving you, Piers. I wanted to, but I simply couldn't."

His arm was around her waist, and her body yielded to him as he pulled her close. She raised her parted lips to meet his.

Mr. Pendeven, Jerry, and Chloe had abandoned all thought of the *Aurora,* and had adjourned to the drawing room, where Chloe was very improperly observing the proceedings on the riverbank through her father's telescope. As the two distant figures came together in a passionate embrace, she gave a cry of triumph.

"Success at last! All my plotting and scheming has come to fruition!"

Mr. Pendeven gave a heartfelt sigh of relief. "Does that mean that Jerry and I can stop fibbing now?"

"Yes. Oh, yes." Chloe was so pleased with herself that she ran to Jerry to hug him. "I *knew* they still loved each other, and only needed help!"

Jerry returned the hug. "You're a clever girl," he said.

She drew back. "There were times when I thought it would all fail. When Piers came back to England and asked you about Marianne, I thought all I had to do was bring them together, but she made it quite clear that she hadn't forgiven or forgotten anything. That put me out, I can tell you, but when she went on to say she was actually considering marrying Brandon Forrester after all, I was hard put to keep going. However, I think I can flatter myself that I carried it all off to perfection."

"You vain creature," her father said. "You fibbed well, I grant you, but you received a great deal of judicious assistance from your nearest and dearest. Jerry and I were drummed into line whether we liked it or not."

Chloe was a little repentant. "Did you mind very much?"

"Well, it isn't exactly pleasing to have to play the cruel father, and I'm sure Jerry didn't relish his role, either." But Mr. Pendeven's eyes were twinkling. "Still, if all's well that ends well, no doubt it was worth it."

Jerry grinned. "I've discovered one thing in all this, and that is that I make a very poor conspirator. Time and time again I seemed to flounder. Right in the beginning I got Maxwell's name wrong, and yet I was supposed to know him well!"

Chloe gave him a cross look. "Yes, and you gave him the wrong address as well. I thought Marianne was going to query it all, but she didn't. Jerry Frobisher, there were times when I despaired of you."

"I know."

She smiled then. "But you are very noble and gallant, and I still adore you."

"I don't know that I still adore you, you scheming minx," he replied. "I am utterly dismayed at the ease with which all those falsehoods slipped from your tongue."

"But it was all in a very good cause, and I promise faithfully never to fib to you, my dearest," Chloe protested.

He glanced at her father. "Dare I believe her, sir?"

"At your peril, sir," Mr. Pendeven replied, giving him a wink she did not see. The two men had never been at odds, but had liked each other from the outset. Their so-called differences had been Chloe's invention, plucked from thin air for the benefit of the star-crossed lovers who had now been brought together on the riverbank.

Chloe pouted. "I think you are both being quite horrid to me," she declared.

"Well, because of you, this February has been a very wearying month so far," her father replied, shaking his head regretfully, again giving Jerry a wink.

This time, however, Chloe intercepted it. "You beasts!" she cried, but had to smile.

Mr. Pendeven went to a small table upon which stood a decanter of sherry and some glasses. "I know that this should be champagne, but it will have to do. We must toast the triumph of Chloe's machinations." He poured three glasses, and they each took one.

"What shall we say?" Jerry asked.

Chloe thought for a moment. "To Saint Valentine's Day?" she suggested.

Her father shook his head. "No, I think we should salute our efforts this month. To February falsehoods."

The glasses chinked. "To February falsehoods," they all said together.

On the riverbank, Marianne and Piers were locked in each other's arms, oblivious to the river and the cries of the excited seabirds overhead, and oblivious also to the fact that they had been pawns in Chloe's quick-witted game of human chess. They were conscious only of each other and the love that had been thwarted for so long.

Piers' face was flushed with desire as he drew back from Marianne. "I hardly dare believe that this is happening."

"I feel the same," she whispered, her eyes still shimmering with happy tears.

"Do you remember this day two years ago?"

"Of course."

He took something from his pocket. "Your card is a little battered now, but I always have it with me just as I also still have the emerald comb."

She took the card. It had been folded several times, and the lace was flattened and limp, but the colors were still bright, and the verse inside as clear as ever as she read it.

> *"Please say you'll be my valentine,*
> *Take my heart, and I'll take thine.*
> *I'll love you forever, my sweetheart divine,*
> *And so I beg you, be my valentine."*

He put his hand tenderly to her cheek. "Are you my valentine now, Marianne?"

"I always have been."

"And will you be my wife?"

She nodded, the tears wet on her cheeks. "Nothing would make me happier," she whispered, her voice barely audible above the rushing of the river.

His thumb moved lovingly against her skin. "We've

wasted so much time, my darling. I can't bear the thought of waiting too much longer, but if we rush, there will be chitter-chatter."

"Let them chitter-chatter, for I want to be rushed," she replied, closing her eyes with a sigh as he kissed her again.

There's an epidemic with 27 million victims. And no visible symptoms.

It's an epidemic of people who can't read.

Believe it or not, 27 million Americans are functionally illiterate, about one adult in five.

The solution to this problem is you... when you join the fight against illiteracy. So call the Coalition for Literacy at toll-free **1-800-228-8813** and volunteer.

Volunteer Against Illiteracy. The only degree you need is a degree of caring.